BURY
THE
LIVING

Also by Jodi McIsaac

The Thin Veil Series

Through the Door

Into the Fire

Among the Unseen

Beyond the Pale: A Thin Veil Novella

A Cure for Madness

for Mike

Abbreviations and Terms

Free State—The term for semiautonomous Ireland from 1922 to 1937, before a full republic was declared. Does not include the six counties of Northern Ireland.

IRA—Irish Republican Army

Irregulars—derogatory term for supporters of an Irish republic during the Civil War

NDU—North Dublin Union

PIRA—Provisional Irish Republican Army (active in Northern Ireland 1969–2005)

Provos—slang for Provisional Irish Republican Army

RUC—Royal Ulster Constabulary, the British-controlled police force in Northern Ireland from 1922 to 2001

UDA—Ulster Defense Association, a Protestant paramilitary organization in Northern Ireland

Chapter One

Belfast, 1990

When she was fifteen years old, a simple knock on the door changed Nora O'Reilly's life—again. The knock was hard and impatient, like the people in her neighborhood. Nora ignored it. Maybe, just this once, her mother would rouse herself off the sofa. But no. Her mother hadn't answered the door since the day Nora's father had done so and been thanked for his trouble with a bullet through the eye. Nora's small red footprints had tracked across the beige linoleum. The Saint Brigid's cross that had hung over the doorway for as long as Nora could remember had failed in its promise to protect them.

Ten years had passed, and now the linoleum was more gray than beige. Nora slipped to the front window and peered out. It was the middle of the afternoon; she'd only just arrived home from school. There'd been no warning of a raid—no banging of dustbin lids on the sidewalks to announce that the peelers had dared venture into Andersonstown. Two men she didn't recognize stood on her doorstep. They must have been looking for Eamon.

Nora opened the door a crack. The first man jammed his black boot into the opening. *Ballix.* Adrenaline flooded her body. She shoved the door against his foot, berating her stupidity. What had she been thinking? What if these men were Prods, come to finish off the rest of them?

"Relax, kid. We just want to talk." The man forced the door open farther. "You Nora O'Reilly?"

"Depends on who's asking. Who're you?" He had bottlebrush hair and wore a brown leather bomber jacket. He looked old enough to be her father, only her father had been wiry, and this man looked like a rugby fullback. His companion had a thin, sharp face and kept looking over his shoulder.

"Doesn't matter. We've been told to fetch you."

"Fetch me where?" Nora tried to push the door closed again, her mind lurching. Whoever these men were, she wasn't going anywhere with them.

"The commanding officer of West Battalion has a few questions about your extracurricular activities. C'mon now. Let's go without a fight."

Nora's fear turned to dread. "Like hell I'm going with youse." She stamped on his foot, but he responded by putting his shoulder to the door and sending it flying. Nora staggered backward, colliding with the coatrack.

Shite, shite, shite. She scrabbled to her feet. She'd almost rather be caught by the Brits. The Provisional IRA didn't tolerate petty crime in their area, and they certainly didn't believe in such luxuries as courts and trials.

"Ma! Ma!" she screamed. Her mother would know these men; Nora's father had been a PIRA member from the beginning.

Her mother came padding into the hall, still in her dressing gown, weaving slightly, a glass of whiskey clutched in her hand. "Paddy Sullivan, what is the meaning of this?"

"Sorry, Mrs. O'Reilly, but O'Connor wants to see her. Seems she's been selling drugs up at the school."

Think, Nora, think. She grappled for an explanation, a plausible denial, anything that would get her out of this. But panic clogged her brain, and all she could think was *I'm fucked.*

She didn't know her mother could move so fast. Suddenly they were nose to nose. "Oh, aye? Is that true?" Mrs. O'Reilly demanded.

"No, it's a load of shite!" Nora protested.

"You watch your language. Jesus, Mary, and Joseph, what am I going to do with you? What would your poor father say?" Her mother shook her head, then turned back to the PIRA men. "Whatever she's done, we'll take care of it here, so we will. Youse all head out, now."

"Sorry, Mrs. O'Reilly, but we've got our orders." Paddy nodded to his companion, who brushed past Nora and her mother and pounded up the stairs toward the bedrooms.

"Oi! Houl on! Youse said you just wanted to talk!" Nora shouted after him. Mrs. O'Reilly looked like she was about to follow, but Paddy laid a hand on her arm.

"Just let him do his job," he said.

"Ma, I've done nothing wrong! I swear it!" A faint sheen broke out on her forehead, and the blood drained from her fair skin.

The sound of drawers being emptied and furniture being over-turned traveled down the stairs. Mrs. O'Reilly sank down into a kitchen chair and took a large gulp of whiskey. She set the glass down with a clunk and put her head in her hands.

"Ach, Nora, I've tried my best with you, sure I have. Where is Eamon?"

"He went out with the lads," Nora mumbled. She glanced toward the door.

"Don't you be thinking of doing a runner," Paddy warned. He wrapped his meaty hand around Nora's upper arm.

"I'm not! But youse wait until Eamon gets home. He'll sort youse out, all right."

"She's quite the lip on her, hasn't she?" Paddy said to the slumped form of her mother.

Loud footsteps on the stairs made them all look up. Paddy's friend tossed him a clear plastic jar of tiny white pills.

"Oh, aye, what's this, then?" Paddy asked.

"It's not mine! I don't know where you got it," Nora said.

"I got it from your room," the other man said with a sneer. "Unless you're telling us your ma or your brother put it there?"

"Don't be an eejit," Nora spat.

"Nora! Are you trying to get yourself killed?" Mrs. O'Reilly said, locking her watery gaze on her daughter. "Do you think I don't have enough trouble as it is? Answer the man! Is this yours? What's in that bottle?"

"I don't know. I said they're not mine. Headache pills, prob'ly."

"Oh, aye?" Paddy said, his grin widening. "With wee happy faces stamped on them? Looks like a fine stash o' Molly to me."

"It's not," Nora said. She stared at the floor, letting her lank red hair fall forward to hide her face.

"Right, we'll be off, then," said Paddy. "We'll bring her back after."

"Where are youse taking her?" Mrs. O'Reilly asked.

"Can't say. She'll not be hurt. But O'Connor wants to talk to her himself, so he does."

"Then tell him he should come here!" Nora said. They ignored her.

Mrs. O'Reilly groaned. "Maybe he can talk some sense into her. But sure and you'll be bringing her back here as soon as he's asked his questions."

"Aye," Paddy said. "Don't you worry. No one'll be hurting Jimmy's daughter."

"Ma! You're not letting them take me?" Nora's brown eyes widened with panic. "They'll knee me, so they will!" She'd seen it once, a man with both kneecaps shot through. She could still hear his screams, see the blood running down his legs. But then again, he'd been lucky not to get a bullet in the head, like her father.

"You and I both know they'll not give us a choice, now, don't we? Go on with the lads, and answer their questions," her mother answered, pulling herself unsteadily to her feet. "Mind you be polite. Maybe you'll listen to Mick O'Connor more than you do your own mother."

With a nod to Mrs. O'Reilly, Paddy and his friend each took hold of one of Nora's scrawny arms and dragged her out the front door toward a waiting van.

"Someone help! I'm being kidnapped!" Nora yelled, craning her head frantically in search of a savior. Neighbors peeked out from behind curtains, and two boys stopped their game of football down the street to stare. No one came forward.

"Shut yer gub!" Paddy said, giving her a rough shove into the van. "I told yer ma we wouldn't hurt you for your da's sake, but if you make it hard for us, all bets are off."

"Eamon!" she yelled, clinging to the door, hoping her brother was somewhere nearby. He'd stand up to the Provos. He'd protect her. "Eamon!"

Paddy gave her another shove, then climbed in behind her and slammed the door shut. The other man jumped into the passenger seat. Nora fell hard into the back of the van, which started moving almost at once.

"Christ, Nora," said Paddy. "Yer just like yer da. He had more spirit than brains, too."

"Don't go talkin' about my da. I'm not ascared of youse. Youse don't know shite. He'd kill youse for this!"

The driver laughed. "Whaddya pick up, Pad, a live grenade? Best bag her. She's not to know where we're going."

"No!" Nora scrabbled to the back of the van. She glanced hopefully at the door, but if she threw herself out of the van, she'd more likely kill herself than escape. Besides, the Provos would find her. They were gods in this part of town.

"If you don't struggle, I'll just put it on loose-like, so you can still breathe fine. But rip it off and I'll tie your hands, y'hear?"

Nora stared back at the man with as much loathing as she could muster. "I'm one of youse," she said. "Why are youse doing this?"

Paddy's face softened. "Your da was a good man, and a good fighter," he said. "And I know your ma's had a hard time of it. But it's our job to keep order here."

Then he pulled a heavy black bag out from under his jacket and tugged it over Nora's head. Behind this rough veil her face crumpled, and heavy, silent tears began to run down her neck.

They drove for at least twenty minutes, though Nora couldn't be sure of the time. The blindness and fear of suffocation had sent her into fresh waves of panic. Finally, the van stopped and a door slammed.

"Where are we?" she asked as Paddy hauled her to her feet.

"Don't matter," came the brusque reply. "Watch your head."

She let him guide her out of the van. She listened for any clues as to where they might be, but there was only the sound of distant cars. It was cold and damp, and she hadn't brought her jacket. She stumbled along beside Paddy, who jerked her to a sudden stop. A sharp rap on metal, the sound of a door opening, and then Paddy shoved her inside.

"Can you take the bag off now?" she asked, not daring to lift it off herself.

"Not yet." Paddy steered her into a chair. "Sit down." She felt for the chair beneath her and lowered herself into it.

"This her?" came a new voice.

"Aye."

"Take the hood off, for fuck's sake. Christ."

Paddy yanked the hood away, tearing out a handful of hair in the process. Nora blinked rapidly and sucked in a lungful of air. They were in a warehouse of sorts, no bigger than a large garage. Men armed with

Armalite rifles stood at each of the two doors. Nora's hair was matted and sweaty against her forehead. She pushed it off her face, then got to her feet and glared at the men directly in front of her.

"Sit down," said the new man sharply. He had thick black hair and a long face. Half his ear was missing. He didn't look much older than Eamon.

She stood her ground for a few more seconds, just to prove she could, then sank stiffly back into the chair.

"You'll be Mick O'Connor, then?" she asked.

"Aye. And you'll be Jimmy O'Reilly's wee brat."

"Fuck you. I'm no one's wee brat."

He quirked a dark eyebrow and shook the pill jar they'd found in her room. "Tell me about these."

"They're not mine."

"Then what was it doing in your room? Were you keeping it for a friend? Your brother, maybe?"

"My brother doesn't go near that stuff," she said.

"So we've heard. He'd make a good Volunteer," O'Connor said.

"He wants nothing to do with youse. Leave him out of it."

O'Connor shook the jar again. "Then tell me the truth. You're young, Nora. I know you're not the only one involved. I can't say that I even blame you." He squatted down so they were at eye level. "This war's been hard on us all. Father dead, mother on the dole. No one would fault you for wanting a little extra money. Maybe buy a nice dress . . . save up for a car . . . Making a few quid on the side sounds pretty good to all of us."

Nora clenched her jaw. She pressed her hands under her legs to keep them from shaking.

"But you see, Nora," O'Connor continued, "if these were just for you, well, then I'd say it's none of my business. But word has it you're selling these to your schoolmates. And that's creating a problem for us. D'you know why?"

Still, Nora said nothing. O'Connor leaned in closer. She could smell his breath, stale tea and vinegar. He reached up and patted her cheek. "I said, d'you know why?"

She shook her head.

"I'm not the bad guy, Nora. I'm just trying to keep our lads out of trouble. Because if we're going to win this war, I need every able-bodied young man I can muster. D'you follow?"

"Aye." What else was she supposed to say?

O'Connor stood up and crossed his arms. "Good. I'm glad we're in agreement. Now I'll ask you one more time. Tell me about these pills."

The chair beneath Nora seemed to be sinking. If she told them the truth, she didn't know what they would do to her. But if she insisted they weren't hers, suspicion would fall on Eamon. Why hadn't she hidden the pills better? Who had ratted her out? Her eyes flickered to the guards at the door. She didn't even know where she was. There was no chance of escape. Finally, she spoke.

"It's just E."

"Speak up."

"Ecstasy. It's what's in the pill bottle."

"And what exactly are you doing with Ecstasy?"

"I was just . . . sharing it. With my friends."

"Oh, aye? What if I brought someone in here who said you sold it to them?"

"I . . . It was stupid, I know. It's like youse said, I just wanted the extra money. I thought it might . . . help."

"Help what?"

"Help us . . . start over."

The look on Mick's face told her this had been the wrong thing to say. "Right. You're going off to England to find work, is that it?" Mick paced in front, running a hand through his hair. "I'm sick of it. Everyone saying how much they love Ireland but leaving the first chance they get. Is that what you were planning?"

"I don't know; I hadn't really thought it through yet. It wouldn't be forever—"

"Were you selling these drugs in the school, Nora?"

"Aye, but—"

"And where did you get them?"

"I can't." Nora shook her head. She tried to steady her voice. Failed. "If I . . . if I tell you, he'll kill me."

Mick squatted down in front of her again. "If there's one thing I hate, it's people who turn their own countrymen into drug addicts. But you know what I hate worse?"

Her voice came out in a squeak. "No."

"Men who get children to do their dirty work."

She wanted to say she wasn't a child but stopped herself. "I promise I won't do it again."

Mick stood up, leering down at her. "Nora, Nora, Nora. You're one of us. Your family's *always* been one of us. This isn't about you—you're just a kid who got caught up in something you shouldn't have. But we have to stop it. Tell us who gave you the drugs."

"Are you going to kill him?"

"That's none of your concern."

"Just talk to him . . . I know he'll stop. He doesn't mean any harm . . ."

"Give me a name!" Mick's hand jerked toward her, but he stopped it in midair. She flinched away, and a memory flashed through her mind: the sound of a gunshot, her father lying faceup on the linoleum, blood seeping from his head.

No. That was the Brits. These are your people.

"I promised her ma we'd not hurt her, Mick," Paddy warned.

"Did you now? Then she'd better give me what I want. Come on, Nora. It's like you said: we're all on the same team."

"Robbie Grady," she whispered.

"Robbie Grady?" Paddy exclaimed. "Isn't he the one you suspected of being a grasser, Mick?"

"Aye."

"He's not an informer," Nora cried out. "He's just the same as us—wantin' to get out of here."

"He'd be of better use fighting the English instead of trying to poison our lads," Mick said. He gave a nod to the man standing at the back door. "Take Tim and Seamus. Bring Grady here."

"Oh, Jesus," Nora said, "Please, just let him be. Don't kill him. I swear it, I'll talk to him . . . We'll both leave it alone."

O'Connor ignored her. "Take her back home," he said to Paddy. "And see if young Eamon is around. Tell him it's time to pick up his father's torch."

"Don't talk to my brother!" Nora yelled as the hood was forced back over her head. "He's got nothing to do with this."

"We just want a friendly chat, nothing to mess your head about," Mick said. He lifted up the hood so she could see his face. "But if we catch you again, I might not be so nice. Y'hear?" His voice was calm, but his eyes glinted with the threat.

Nora nodded, her lips pressed together. She wouldn't show she was afraid. She was as tough as any of them'uns.

"Good girl." He winked at her, then lowered the hood.

She sat in silence on the drive home. Maybe that wasn't even where they were headed. What if Mick had given Paddy orders to shoot her and dump her body in the Lagan? She suppressed a whimper. Paddy sat beside her, breathing loudly and grunting whenever he shifted position. Finally, he lifted the hood off her head.

"We're here," he said. The familiar length of her street stretched out in front of them through the van window.

"You're not going to kill me," she said. If she said it out loud, maybe it would be more likely to be true.

Paddy raised an eyebrow. "Nah. But I don't know what Mick'll do with yer man Grady. Or with you if he finds out you haven't learned your lesson." He slid the door open. "Stay here, I'll not be a minute," he said to the driver.

"Nora!"

Nora peered around Paddy, who was climbing out of the van. Eamon was running toward her, his thick red curls lit up by the streetlights. "Are you all right?" he said, reaching out a hand to help her. "Did they hurt you?"

"Eamon," Paddy said with a nod.

"I'm okay," Nora said.

Eamon rounded on Paddy. "What's this about?"

"Steady on, lad," Paddy said. "Let's all go inside."

"You'll not be coming into my house after treating my sister like that," Eamon said, standing firmly on the footpath.

"Oh, I will. Mick O'Connor wants me to have a word with you," Paddy answered.

"Is that Nora?" Mrs. O'Reilly called from the door. "Is she all right?"

"I'm grand, Ma," Nora called. Lights went on in the houses next door. "It's all right, Eamon, he can come in," she said, keeping her head down and stalking into the house. She allowed her mother to lead her to the kitchen table and inspect her face for injuries. Nora turned away. Her mother smelled like a distillery.

Eamon faced Paddy, who had followed them into the house. "You think you're a big man, lifting teenage girls, do you?"

"Simmer down, Eamon. She's all right. Mick could'a done worse. She herself said she's been selling drugs up at the school."

"That's a lie, so it is," Eamon said, getting closer.

"It's true," Nora said. "I'm sorry, Eamon."

He gaped at her, his mouth parted as though in the middle of a word. After a long, horrible pause, he said, "We'll talk about this later."

He jerked his head toward Paddy. "You said you wanted a word. Get on with it, then."

"Aye. Mick wants to know when you'll be joining up. Says it's time you followed in your father's footsteps."

"Is that what Mick wants? Me to follow in old Jimmy's footsteps? Does his offer include a bullet in the head?"

"It was the Prods who shot him, not us. You well know that."

Mrs. O'Reilly's face went slack, and she stifled a sob. Nora wrapped her hands around her mother's. "Shhh, Ma, don't worry. Eamon's no fool." Then she turned to Paddy. "Can't youse see we've been through enough? Now fuck off and leave us alone."

"Watch your language, Nora. I can handle this," Eamon said without looking at her. "You've done enough to 'help' today."

His words punched her in the gut. She looked down at her hands, intertwined with her mother's, so no one would see her cheeks burn. She'd rather face Mick O'Connor again than hear the disappointment in her brother's voice.

"We could use a smart lad like you, Eamon," Paddy said.

"Aye, I'm smart enough to stay out of it. I won't do it. I've a family to take care of."

"And what about your Irish family?"

Eamon leaned in. "Listen, I want the Brits out as much as you do. You think I'm not serving my country just because I don't pick up a gun? I'm one of the few lads on this street with a job. And I'm trying to keep this family together. If more of us would do the same, then maybe we'd all be in a better place."

Paddy shook his head. "You think we'll ever get ahead with the Brits in charge? These lads you speak of don't have jobs because the fuckin' Brits keep all the jobs for their Proddy pals while they shove us God-fearing folk onto shoddy estates like this one. There's only one thing the Brits understand: *force*. They've done it in the South and we'll do it here in the North. If you think we'll be in 'a better place' before then, you're away in the head."

"Aye. Well, it's time for you to go, Paddy. And leave my sister alone, y'hear? She's my responsibility now."

"You mind that," Paddy said, giving Nora one last significant look before he slipped back out into the night.

No one said a word until the van had driven off. It was Nora who broke the silence.

"Eamon . . . ," she started. She felt wretched—worse even than she'd felt in the warehouse.

"Not tonight," he said. "Go on up to bed. We'll talk about it in the morning."

Wordlessly, Nora released her mother's hands and walked up the stairs to her ruined bedroom.

Chapter Two

A rough knock on the bedroom door woke Nora the next morning. She groaned and turned over. A lecture was coming, and she wanted none of it.

"Up you get," Eamon said as he came into the room. "I've brought you a cuppa."

"Go away," Nora moaned.

"Not likely. C'mon. Sit up. It's time we had ourselves a wee chat."

She rolled over and squinted at him with one eye. He was indeed holding a cup of tea, as well as a plate of chocolate biscuits. She hauled herself up to a sitting position. "Biscuits for breakfast?"

"Aye. Thought you might need it after yesterday."

She bit into one, then washed it down with a gulp of tea. "You're not ragin'?"

"I was," Eamon said, taking his own biscuit. "Last night. But I was more ascared than anything, y'know? If something had happened to you . . ."

"I was fine," she protested. "I can handle them shites."

Eamon's expression darkened. "They're desperate men, Nora, and more dangerous than you think. Now tell me, what's this about you selling drugs? Are you popping them, too?"

Nora plucked at the thin bedspread. "I'm not. It was just a wee lark to see if I could make some extra money. You work too hard. And Ma not at all," she added bitterly.

"Ach, you know Ma's not been the same since Da was killed. She's not strong like you, Nora. But what were you thinking?"

"Robbie told me it would just be a couple of times, that I'd make enough for us to move to Manchester, or to Dublin with Aunt Margaret."

"Robbie Grady? That useless tout? Is your head cut? All he wanted was to make you his mule. Soon enough, you'd have found yourself owing him. I thought you were smarter than that."

"I didn't think . . . ," Nora said, her eyes filling with tears.

"Aye. You didn't. Are you so desperate to get out of here that you'd risk going to juvie, or worse, pissing off the Provos?"

"I knew it was dangerous; I'm not stupid. But I thought it would be some quick cash, no harm done. They're going to buy drugs from someone, might as well be me."

"That's one of the daftest things I've ever heard," Eamon said, his voice rising. He jumped up from the bed and paced the small room. "We don't need the money that bad. I've a job, remember? And I've got enough to worry about without you causing trouble."

"Now you sound just like Ma," Nora spat back.

"Ach, you'll do my head in, so you will. You know Ma needs us to be strong for her. Do you want to end up like her, at the bottom of a bottle or a jar of pills every night?"

"No, o'course not. I told you I wasn't takin' any of them."

"You gotta give me your word you'll leave it, Nora. I'm serious. Them lads in the Provos, they're not much for second chances."

"That's what Mick said."

"Oh, aye? Well, you'd better pay attention."

Nora didn't respond. Eamon stopped pacing and sat down beside her on the bed. "Listen," he said. "I've been saving as much as I can. I figure in a year I'll have enough to move us to Dublin. We can get away from all this."

"D'you think Ma will leave?"

"Aye, if we do."

"I wish we could leave today," Nora said, fidgeting with the bedcovers. "Does that make me a traitor?"

"No. It means you have some sense in your head."

She leaned against his shoulder. "How come you don't want to fight, Eamon? Is it because of Da?"

"Partly. I dunno. I hate the Brits, I do. You should see how some of the lads at the factory talk to me, just because I'm Catholic. But we've been fighting this war for eight hundred bloody years. What's done is done. We can't change the past. We'll have a free and united Ireland someday, I'm sure of it. But if we tear each other apart, what's the point of it all?"

"Don't let Mick O'Connor catch you speaking like that."

He shrugged. "What can they do to me? They can't force me to sign up, so they can't. As long as we keep out of trouble, they'll have no reason to trouble us."

"Do you really want to leave?"

"Aye. Belfast is my home. But it's not normal, livin' like this. Wouldn't you like to go shopping or to the cinema without being afeared you'll be blown up? Go down the pub without looking over your shoulder for RUC thugs?"

"Aye, I would. That's why I did it."

"We'll figure out another way. I can take on more shifts at the factory. College can wait. But you stay out of it, y'hear?"

Nora nodded. Eamon reached into his pocket and pulled out a closed fist. "I've something for you," he said. He opened his hand and poured a cluster of polished wooden beads the color of coffee into her palm.

"Rosary beads? But I already—"

"You're still using those crap plastic ones we got as kids. These ones are better. Thought you might take them more seriously."

Nora flushed but accepted them. She rolled the smooth beads between her fingers and inspected the tiny Jesus dangling from the end. "I will. I swear it."

After Eamon left for work, Nora crept into the hallway and peeked into her mother's room. She was still asleep, an empty bottle of booze on the nightstand. Nora closed the door quietly and returned to her own room. Paddy's friend had emptied her drawers onto the floor and turned over her nightstand, all of which she'd set to rights before going to bed. But he hadn't been terribly thorough. It was only out of sheer laziness on her part that the wee bottle of pills in her nightstand hadn't been hidden with the rest.

She grabbed hold of the bed frame and dragged it into the middle of her room. Then she snatched up a butter knife from her dresser and pried up one of the floorboards. Old, shoddy houses like this one had loads of hiding places. She felt around for the string she'd tied to one of the slats between floors. Even if someone pulled up the board, they'd be hard-pressed to notice the string unless they knew where to find it. Tied to the end of the string was a cloth bag the size of a loaf of bread. She set it on the floor and opened it up. Inside were a dozen wee packets of white powder. It was all still there.

This was what Robbie Grady had really wanted her to sell. He'd unloaded the stash on her to get a little distance from the game, but he'd

Jodi McIsaac

referred her to all of his former clients. Of course, Grady had threatened her with disembowelment and all sorts of horrible things if she turned on him. But the rewards had seemed to outweigh the risks. Her half of the profits from selling this lot would have amounted to £600.

But who had grassed on her? The only deal she'd made so far was with Peadar Hobson. It couldn't have been Peadar—everyone knew he was always high or plastered, just like his whole family. If he had grassed on her, his supply would dry up.

She wrapped the bags back up, made sure the string was secure, and hammered down the floorboard with the blunt end of the knife. Then she pushed her bed back against the wall and sat down on it, drawing her knees up to her chest. She hadn't told Eamon about giving away Robbie Grady. She hadn't told him how scared she still was. Robbie'd be coming after her now, for sure. Unless the Provos got to him first.

She shook her head and went downstairs to make another cup of tea. After a few minutes, her mother stirred upstairs.

"Be a luv and go fetch some bread from Donagh, will ye?" her mother asked as she came into the kitchen, pulling her dressing gown closed.

Nora hesitated. What if Robbie was just around the corner, waiting to plug her? "I'm not dressed, Ma," she protested.

"Then get dressed. Come on, now. And mind you don't get anything with sultanas."

Nora trudged back upstairs and pulled on jeans and a jumper. Donagh came round every Saturday morning, selling buns and loaves out of the back of his van. Nora's favorites were the wee hot cross buns, but her Ma hated sultanas with a passion, so they never bought them.

She stumbled as she made her way out of the house and approached the van. "Morning, Donagh, what's the craic?" she said.

"Can't complain, Nora. How's yer mum?"

"She's grand, so she is. Sent me to get a couple loaves. The usual."

"Aye. Here y'are." He handed her a couple of bags, and she gave him a note. When he handed back her change, he glanced around before leaning in and saying, "Mind yourself, now. The lads were active last night."

"Oh, aye?" She tried to hide the quaver in her voice and made a deal of stuffing the change into her pocket.

"Found Robbie Grady's body by Saint Dom's, just outside the gate. What are they thinking, dumping a body by a school? Thank God it's the weekend."

Nora stared at the bread in her hands, sure Donagh could hear her heart thrashing around in her rib cage. "Ta," she squeaked out before turning on her heel.

"Right, then. Give your mother and Eamon my best," Donagh called after her.

Nora ran back down the road, the loaves swinging in her hands. She darted into the house and pushed the door closed, then double-checked the locks. Her mother was rattling around in the kitchen, but Nora didn't move. She just leaned against the door, breathing heavily. Robbie Grady was dead.

That could'a been me. But the Provos wouldn't have shot her, not for a first offense, not given who her da had been. Would they? Robbie'd been given loads of warnings, so she'd heard. And now she'd not have to worry about him coming after her. She felt repulsed . . . and relieved.

On Monday morning Nora walked to school with a couple of friends. She tried to nod and laugh in all the right places as they nattered on, but her mind was fixated on the bags of cocaine stuffed deep into her rucksack. She'd decided there was no point in dumping it, not when she could still make a fair sale of it. Then her family wouldn't have to wait to leave town. She'd sent a message to Ernie Farrell, saying she'd sell him the lot at half price. He'd been Robbie Grady's only competition in this part of town. There was no way he would say no. Then it would be out of her hands.

At the lunch break she waited in the stacks at the library, just as she'd promised to do in her message. The Irish-history section, which was always empty. She read the titles with interest while she waited. Her school, like many others, preferred to focus on European and world history. Irish history was too controversial, too close to home. But Eamon's love for it had rubbed off. He was always throwing obscure bits of history into their conversations or telling her about great battles and chieftains who'd lived hundreds of years ago. She'd soaked it all in—a sparkling vision of Ireland that was a sharp contrast to her own bleak reality.

Nora waited the entire lunch hour, but Ernie never came. Had he even been to school that day? She hadn't seen him. Maybe he was sick. Maybe he'd chickened out after hearing about Robbie.

She left the library and headed back to class. She was late enough that the hallways were empty. Then she heard heavy footsteps behind her. She glanced back and stopped dead in her tracks. Paddy Sullivan was standing in the hallway, grinning at her.

"Hiya, Nora," he said.

"What the hell are you doing here?"

"Ach, don't be like that, Nora. We've some more questions for you." He jerked his head toward the front door.

"I've answered your questions," she said, clutching her rucksack close to her stomach. "Youse said you'd leave me alone."

"Things change. C'mon. Let's go."

"I've got to get to class. I'm late."

"We're on the way to see your brother. Don't you want to come?"

Nausea swept through her. He was bluffing, sure he was. *But what if he means it?* "I told youse to leave Eamon out of this! What do youse want him for?"

"Ernie never showed up to your little meeting, did he?"

Nora felt faint. "I just . . . wanted to talk to him."

"Uh-huh. Seems you didn't take our warnings seriously. Now come on. We don't want to make a scene here in the school, do we?"

Nora felt as though her legs were embedded in the ground. All she could do was stare at Paddy, unable to move, while the world spun around her. She had to ditch the bag, somewhere, somehow.

"I . . . I just have to . . . I have to use the bogs first," she stammered.

"I'm sure you can hold it," he said. His hand clamped on to her arm, and he marched her out of the side door, where a car was waiting. She shifted her rucksack to one hand and prepared to drop it in the bushes, but he grabbed it.

"For a petty criminal, you're pretty daft, Nora."

"Wait, please, you don't understand—"

"You've got balls, I'll give you that. Thought you'd just pick up where Robbie left off?"

"No! I was just trying to get rid of it, I swear." Nora tried to wrestle herself from Paddy's grip, panic building in her like a smoking volcano. "Don't take me to Mick. You can have the coke—it's worth a lot of money."

"Mick's interested in something far more useful to him than coke," Paddy answered as he stuffed her into the back of the car. He got in the front seat, then turned around. "I think he'll be wanting to make a deal."

Nora drew back against the upholstered seat, horror spreading across her face. "He'll not . . . be wanting . . ."

Paddy grinned again. "To pimp you out? Is that what you're afraid of? You're an attractive girl, Nora, but Mick's not like that. He's a decent lad."

"Then what?"

"You'll find out."

A few minutes later, they pulled up outside a pub Nora'd never seen before. It looked run-down, but then most Belfast pubs were rather sketchy. She was just glad they hadn't put the bag back over her head this time. She still hoped she could buy them off with the coke and a lot of bravado.

Paddy nodded to the bartender and headed toward the wooden stairs at the back of the pub. The bartender called out to him to wait, and the two of them had a hushed conversation. The other man kept glancing in her direction. Finally, he seemed satisfied, and Paddy took her by the elbow again and led her upstairs. He knocked twice on a closed door at the end of the hall. Mick O'Connor opened it.

"Listen, I've a good explanation for this, and you'd better listen to me!" Nora said, stomping into the small bedroom and jabbing her finger at Mick's chest.

"Oh, aye?" Mick said, the corners of his lips twitching. Nora ignored this.

"Yes, and it's the truth! Robbie left me with all these goods, and I just wanted to be rid of them. Why flush them down the bogs when they could be put to a good cause? I was going to sell them to get them off my hands, then give the money to youse."

"You were, were you?" Mick asked, this time grinning broadly.

"I was. But youse ruined my plans, so you can take the goods and sell 'em yourself." She snatched the rucksack from Paddy, grabbed the bags of powder from it, and tossed them down on the bed.

There was someone on it, bound and gagged.

Eamon.

Mick barked a loud laugh at the look on her face. "Well, this has been much more amusing than I'd reckoned."

"Eamon!" Nora ran to her brother and reached for his bonds, but Paddy grabbed her arm and held her back. Eamon's golden-brown eyes were wide with fear . . . and fury. Nora wrenched herself out of Paddy's grip, leaving stinging nail marks on her pale skin. "Let him go!" she said, her own fear forgotten. She charged at Mick, her fists flailing. Paddy came after her, but a well-aimed kick to the groin sent him sprawling on the ground.

"That's enough!" Mick said, grabbing Nora by the hair and holding her at arm's length. "Calm the fuck down." He shoved her onto the bed beside her brother.

"Please," she begged. "Leave him alone. He had nothing to do with this."

Mick bent in closer, his face only an inch from hers. "I've got more important things to do, Nora. You're gettin' annoying, so you are. But I like your spirit. So here's what we're going to do. We gave you a warning, and you ignored it. So now you owe us. I'll allow you to work off your debt, so to speak."

"How?" Nora asked. Now that it appeared she and Eamon weren't going to be immediately shot, she was beginning to recover some of her confidence. Or the appearance of it, at any rate.

"Delivering messages. Helping us transport supplies."

"Running arms, you mean."

He shrugged. "Maybe. Not likely the Brits will suspect a pretty young thing like you."

"Leave her alone!" Eamon had managed to work free of his gag, and his sudden outburst made both Nora and Mick start.

Mick recovered himself quickly. "I thought you might have something to say about this. Untie him," he said to Paddy. While Paddy set to work on Eamon's wrists and ankles, Mick drew a handgun out of the desk drawer and pointed it at Nora's head. "Just so youse don't do anything stupid."

Nora slowly turned her head and looked at her brother. "I'm so sorry," she whispered. "I just wanted to help . . ."

"Shut up, Nora." With his hands held out in front of him, Eamon slowly got off the bed so he was facing Mick. "I know what this is about."

"Do you now?"

"You want me to join youse."

"I want you to *want* to join us. You've the makings of a great Volunteer, Eamon. Just like your da."

"Fine. I'll do it."

"Eamon, no!" Nora cried from the bed.

"I said shut up," he shot back, and Nora cringed into the pillows. "Just leave my sister out of this. She's not to be involved. *At all.*"

Mick lowered the gun and held out his hand. After casting a glance at Nora, Eamon clenched his jaw and shook Mick's hand, then let it go as if it had burned him. Without looking at her, he said, "Come on, Nora." She slid off the bed, head down, tears dripping off her chin.

Chapter Three

Almost a year passed without incident. Nora kept her promise to Eamon and took religion more seriously. She went to Mass several times a week with her mother, and Eamon joined them as often as he could. When her mother was too drunk to leave the house, Nora went alone. She found a strange comfort in the ritual of it all—the prayers, the kneeling and the rising. Whatever was happening in her own life, the church remained unchanged. Her prayers became more fervent and sincere.

Then the phone rang.

It was close to midnight, but there was no sign of Eamon. She rarely saw him anymore. He kept to his room or sat quietly with their mother in the sitting room, staring blankly at the television. Once she'd made the mistake of asking him when he thought they could leave. His only response had been to shake his head sadly and leave the room. She hadn't asked again.

The Troubles continued to rage around her. The Ulster Volunteer Force and Ulster Defense Association continued their campaigns of terror against the Catholics while the police force looked the other way. The Provos responded accordingly. She tried not to think of what Eamon had seen—or done—to cause that vacant look in his eyes. Tried not to panic every time the phone rang or there was a knock on the door. She turned off the television whenever there was news of a bombing, not wanting to know if Eamon had been involved. Then she would turn it back on, unable to resist.

Mrs. O'Reilly had gone to bed with her bottle hours ago, and Nora was up finishing a paper due the next morning. When the phone rang, her pen skidded across the paper, leaving an ugly black scar. She stared at the receiver hanging on the wall, then forced herself out of her chair.

"Hello?" she said, her voice barely above a whisper.

"Nora, it's Paddy Sullivan." She relaxed. Paddy came over loads now that he and Eamon were working together. He kept trying to be her friend, to make jokes and ask about her school, as though he hadn't kidnapped her the year before. She ignored him as much as she could. It wasn't unusual for him to ring their place, looking for Eamon.

"Eamon's not here."

"I know. He's at the Mater. You need to come."

She stopped breathing. "The hospital? What's happened to him?"

"Just get your ma and get over here." He hung up.

She stood staring at the phone in her hands for a long moment, unable to block out thoughts of revenge beatings and assassinations, of blown-out knees and bullets in foreheads. Her hand flew automatically to the rosary nestled in her pocket and convulsed around the beads. Then she slammed down the receiver and sprinted up the stairs.

"Ma! Ma!" She burst into her mother's room, but she was already asleep—or passed out, judging by the smell. Nora shook her a few times, but her mother only grunted and rolled over. "Ma, get up, it's Eamon. He's in hospital!" The only response she got was a deep sigh.

Too anxious to wait, Nora ran back down the stairs and rang for a taxi. She found money in her mother's purse and went outside to wait. The street was empty, and the lamp closest to their house was flickering. Normally she'd not dare to be alone on the street at this time of night, but all her fear was directed toward Eamon.

"Come on . . . ," she whispered, stamping her feet to keep warm. If she could just get to him, he'd be all right, whatever had happened. The seconds seemed as long as hours as she stared fixedly down the road. Finally the taxi's lights turned the corner, and she waved to hail him. "The Mater," she said as soon as she got in the backseat. The driver gave her a dark look but didn't say anything. Nora was starting to think they'd get there in record time when the taxi slowed down.

"Security check ahead," he said. A roadblock had been set up in the middle of the street, and the flashing lights of the Royal Ulster Constabulary ordered them to a stop. The driver rolled down his window as a police officer approached.

"My brother's in hospital, please let us through!" Nora yelled from the backseat. The officer beamed his flashlight in her face and then turned to look at the driver.

"Is that where you're headed?"

"Aye."

"Which hospital?"

"The Mater."

"Both of youse get out. Open the boot, please."

"What? No, we have to keep going!" Nora cried out.

"Mind you do what they say," the driver warned. Fuming, Nora got out of the car and stood with her arms crossed while the officers went through the car in minute detail. Then she held out her arms like a crucifix while a female officer patted her down. It was all she could do to stand still and not sprint off into the darkness.

After several excruciating minutes, the officer who'd stopped them said, "It's clean."

"If my brother died while youse were treatin' us like criminals, you'll pay for it," Nora snarled.

The taxi driver stepped between Nora and the officers and ushered her back to the car. "Are you trying to get us both arrested?" he said. "Now get in and keep your gub shut."

A few minutes later, they pulled up to the hospital. The driver waved away her money. "Get in there now and see to your brother."

Paddy was waiting for her in the entrance. He wasn't smirking this time. He shook his head.

"I'm sorry. He's gone."

The floor wavered beneath her, like pavement in a heat wave.

"No."

It was impossible. Paddy was lying. Eamon was her brother; he was the only one who truly loved her. He couldn't—*wouldn't*—be dead.

"I'm sorry, Nora. We tried to save him . . ."

"No, you're having me on. Where is he? I want to see him."

A nurse looked up from the reception desk. Paddy put his arm around Nora, but she jerked away. "Don't touch me."

"I'll take you to him. Where's your ma?"

"Plastered, o'course." A rage burned in Nora unlike anything she'd ever felt before. She followed Paddy down the hall, still telling herself it was all a terrible mistake. They were just trying to trick her, scare her. Eamon would be all right.

Her family's priest was leaving the room just as Paddy stopped outside it.

"Father Donovan!" Nora said. "It's not true, is it?" Surely the priest wouldn't be messing with her.

Father Donovan's brown eyes were full of pity. "I'm sorry, Nora. It is." He placed a heavy hand on her shoulder. She shrugged it off and took a step back. "He made his confession," the priest said, as though that would comfort her. "His soul rests with the Lord now."

"But . . ."

"Where is his mother?" Father Donovan asked Paddy over Nora's head.

"She's at home. We'll send someone round for her."

"I have to see some other patients, but I'll come back," Father Donovan said.

"Ta, Father," Paddy said, steering Nora toward the door.

"Wait," the priest called. "Are you sure she should see . . . ?"

"I'm *going* to see my brother," Nora said, her teeth clenched. But the priest's words worried her. Why shouldn't she see him? What had happened to him?

"She can handle it," Paddy said. "Come on, now. Just prepare yourself. He's looking rough."

Nora stepped into the room. There were other people gathered around the bed, but she took no notice of them. Her eyes were fixed on the still figure that lay in front of her. She wavered on the spot, but shook off Paddy's arm when he tried to steady her.

It was Eamon, but she hardly recognized him beyond the shock of red hair against the white pillow. His face had been beaten so badly it was a mass of purple and deep red gashes. His nose was crushed, and his jaw jutted out at an unnatural angle.

For a long moment, all she could do was stare, conscious of the sudden silence that had fallen on the room. She tore her eyes away from his ruined face and watched his chest under the white hospital sheet, certain that if she could only see it rise and fall, ever so slightly, everything would be okay. They wouldn't wait until they had the money this time; they would leave Belfast the minute he was released from hospital. They would do whatever it took to survive outside this godforsaken country.

But his chest remained still.

Someone reached over and lifted the sheet over Eamon's head, hiding his face from her view. It was Mick O'Connor.

"How?" Nora asked, her voice foreign to her own ears. "Who did this?"

"UDA," Mick said. Ulster Defense Association. "Picked him up on his way home from the factory. Dumped him outside the pub where we were meeting. He was still alive when we brought him here, but he didn't last long. Father Donovan's just done giving him the last rites."

"They . . . beat him to death?"

"Aye."

"And he was unarmed?"

"Aye."

"But *why?*"

"Why else? He was a Catholic," Mick spat. "The UDA and the rest of the Prods want nothing more than to kill us or send us running. That's what Eamon was fighting for, Nora. An Ireland where you can be safe. Don't forget that."

"Mick, I don't think this is the time . . . ," Paddy started, but Nora was only half-listening. Her eyes were fixed on the stillness of the figure beneath the sheet, her thoughts consumed by one dreadful realization.

This is my fault.

She pushed past Paddy, heading out of the room. The bright lights of the hospital corridor mocked her. She walked, not caring where she was going, just needing to get away from the suffocating guilt in Eamon's hospital room.

A chapel loomed at the end of the hall. She stormed up the center aisle and threw herself on the railing in front of the altar. She squeezed the wooden rail with her hands, as though it would keep her from dissolving completely. She tried to pray but couldn't remember the words.

"Nora?"

Her head whipped around at her name. Father Donovan stood in the doorway. He came and knelt beside her.

"I'm very sorry about your brother," he said.

She couldn't answer. Her nostrils flared with the effort of breathing.

"He was a very good lad," Father Donovan continued. "One of the best of us."

"I need . . . ," Nora croaked. "Confession." But it didn't matter, not really. Nothing could absolve her now.

"Confession? Ach, Nora, this wasn't your fault. It's natural to feel that way when someone you love has passed away, but you mustn't blame yourself."

"He only joined up because of me," Nora forced out. The weight of Father Donovan's hand settled on her shoulder.

"His was a noble fight, my dear. You should not regret that."

"But he's dead." The statue of Jesus on the cross behind the altar seemed to glare at her. Judging her. "He's dead."

"You didn't kill him, Nora. But you *can* continue his fight."

She tore her eyes away from the crucified Christ to look at the priest.

"What do you mean?"

"We need young people like you to fight for Ireland."

And end up dead, like Eamon?

"I'm afraid," she whispered.

The priest's hand tightened on her shoulder. "God will be with you."

Something stirred in Nora's gut. What else was she to do? Avenging her brother's death would give her purpose. And if she met with the same fate . . . well, it would be no more than what she deserved.

She stood, still gripping the railing. "Sign me up."

Chapter Four

Fourteen years later
Darfur, Sudan

"November Oscar, it's go time!" The voice crackled over the walkie-talkie hanging from Nora's hip, calling out her code name.

"Aye, I'll be right there!" Nora shouted, taking one last glance at the clipboard in her hands. She shoved it into a khaki bag on the folding table in front of her and then swung the bag over her head.

She cracked open the flaps of the tent—a few strips of canvas and a sheet of corrugated tin propped up by a wood pole—that served as the Catholic Relief Services office in this part of the internally-displaced-persons camp. She fished her sunglasses out of her bag and tugged a ball cap over her hair, which was tied back in a loose braid that hung down her back.

The children in the camp loved to touch her hair, and sometimes—on the rare occasions when she wasn't running between emergency and disaster—she'd sit outside a family's lean-to and let the little girls take turns braiding and unbraiding the red waves. A few of the kids ran after her now as she walked toward the two lorries that had just pulled up on the western border of the camp.

"Miss Nora! Miss Nora!" They grabbed her hands and clothes. Nora stopped and squatted down to face them. They giggled and tugged on her braid, a few of the shier ones hiding behind their friends.

"Aren't youse supposed to be in school?" she said, addressing the older kids, who had a bit of English. They nodded sheepishly. "Off youse go, then," she told them, smiling to show she wasn't angry. The older ones spoke to the rest, and together they turned and ran back toward the half wall of stones that served as the school. She waved at their departing grins as she got back to her feet. How she ached for these kids. The ongoing war in Sudan had already created tens of thousands of orphans, and each day the camp was flooded with more tiny survivors, sometimes with parents or aunts and uncles, but too often they were alone. Her hand flicked to her pocket, where a cluster of worn wooden beads lay coiled. She would say an extra prayer for these children tonight.

She'd been doing relief work for the better part of the past four years, and yet she'd never seen anything like Darfur. Of course, she'd said that about every disaster zone. How many had it been, now? Haiti, Afghanistan, Zimbabwe, Columbia . . . There was always a humanitarian emergency somewhere in the world. Always someone who needed help. She stifled a yawn as she trudged toward the lorries—she'd been up until 4:00 a.m. at their base in the town, filing a report and a request for more supplies. Her computer had only crashed twice during the process, which was better than usual.

"What have we got?" she called out to her boss, Jan, who was directing two supply trucks through the gate and toward a large shipping container. "Please tell me there are more medical supplies in there. And coffee."

He grinned at her. Jan was the field coordinator for this camp, in charge of keeping things running as smoothly as possible under the tragic and ever-changing circumstances. The Sudanese staff was assembling by the lorries, ready to off-load the supplies into the container.

"We will have to see," he said in his Norwegian accent. "But they tell me there are some more jerry cans, food supplies, along with some High Energy Biscuits and Plumpy'Nut for the kids."

"Thank God," Nora said. Most of the children arriving at the camp were severely malnourished.

Jan examined the bill of goods handed to him by the driver. "Ah, a diplomatic container," he said with a grin. Nora grinned back. Diplomatic containers couldn't be searched by local authorities, which meant it was usually stocked with alcohol and coffee for the expat staff. Then Jan frowned. "But only a week's worth of basic food supplies. I was hoping for enough for a month."

"Better than nothing?"

"Always the optimist. How does it go with the latrines?"

"I just talked to Francis about that. Some are starting to fill up, so he's going to cover them over and dig more tomorrow. And Christopher said the new water pump in section D is up and running."

"Good, good. Now tell me this: While you were being so productive, did you manage to get any sleep?" Jan peered at her face closely, and she glanced away. He knew her too well.

"Aye, after a while. I just had to finish those reports. Oh, and I put in another requisition for school supplies. The teacher said the kids are writing in the dirt, and there's only a handful of books to go around."

"Mmm-hmm. And sleep?" Jan pressed.

"A couple of hours," Nora admitted.

Jan shook his head. "For someone with as much experience as you have, you push yourself too hard. It's a good thing you're leaving for R&R tomorrow. I'm worried about you burning out."

"I won't burn out. I know what I'm doing."

"Any more dreams?"

Nora blushed. She'd made the mistake of telling Jan about the series of interconnected dreams that had been stealing the peace from what little sleep she managed. In each dream, the face of a man appeared to her. It was not a face she recognized, but it was the same man each time. Though the dreams were vague and incoherent, they were imbued with a sense of urgency that awoke her in a cold sweat. They'd been happening more frequently lately. Jan thought it was a sign the stress was getting to her.

"I'm grand," she said. "Nothing a couple of weeks on the beach won't cure."

"You still plan to go to Mombasa?" he asked. "When was the last time you were home?"

Nora shrugged. "Not long enough. My ma's funeral, I suppose."

She was saved from saying more by the opening of the first lorry. Nora joined the others, grabbing crates and sacks of rice and stacking them inside the container, where they'd be sorted later. Given the toxic security situation in the area, it was important to get them into a secure location as quickly as possible. She tried to push the dreams out of her mind as she threw herself into the work. There was always more work.

Nora took Jan's advice and went to bed early that night, back in the relative safety of the compound in Nyala, several miles away. From the small window in her room she could see the broken glass and barbed wire rimming the wall outside the building. She prayed for those gathered together back at the camp. Hopefully their numbers would ensure they got safely through the night. Then they could start trying to reconstruct their lives. Wasn't that what she was trying to do?

Her thumb caressed the smooth wooden beads of the rosary as she whispered another Our Father. She closed her eyes again and continued the same prayer she'd whispered every night for too many years, for too many people. The prayer for the dead. Then she surrendered to sleep.

In her dream, land spread out in front of her, lush and green and full of life, a sharp contrast to the wasted desert outside the compound. Clusters of large, broad-leafed trees swayed in a soft wind, and foot-high limestone fences wound their way over the emerald hills like a network of veins. As she walked, the warmth of the sun on her skin was comforting, not scorching. She was barefoot, and the grass tickled her feet. She was tempted to lie down in it, to revel in its fresh smell and feel before she had to wake again, but something stopped her. A man was sitting on the fence about a hundred feet away. It was him, the one she'd been dreaming about; she could tell even from this distance. She ran toward him, her feet thudding into the grass, desperate to see him clearly before he disappeared, before he faded away as he'd done so many times before.

Her hopes rose as she drew closer and his figure remained solid. She could see his features much more clearly this time: a long, straight nose, a high brow, full lips. His eyes were closed. His skin was clear and unwrinkled and his body straight and strong. But his hair was perfectly gray, almost silver. He wore it short and swept to the side in an old-fashioned style. His clothing was old-fashioned, too, a three-piece suit and a black trilby clutched in his hands. He appeared to be sleeping. She stood and watched him for a moment, so close she could touch him, trying to fix his features in her memory before he disappeared. But he didn't disappear this time. And so she reached out a hand toward him, hesitating just before brushing the top of his shoulder with her fingers.

His eyes opened.

They were as blue as the water that lapped at the Giant's Causeway, where her father had taken her and Eamon as children and told them stories of ancient heroes. Paired with his strange gray hair, those eyes made the man in front of her look like the ocean itself, turbulent and strong. His eyes bore into her, and she had no words. She wanted to touch him, to understand him, to know why he kept appearing to her. A tremble passed through her body like a wave.

"I need your help," he said. Her breath quickened. This was the first time he'd spoken to her. "Go to the church at Kildare and ask for Brigid," he continued. "She'll explain everything and lead you to me. *You must come.*"

Nora struggled to hang on to his words. "Why? What's wrong?"

"The church at Kildare. Brigid. I don't have time to explain."

"But . . . where are you? *Who* are you? Are you in trouble?"

At this, he tore his gaze away from her and stared out at the rolling hills. "Please, there is not much time. You must come and help me." His voice sounded distant, ethereal.

"But . . . help you with what? I don't understand." The man didn't answer—he only got up from the fence and strode away from her. She tried to follow, but her legs would not move. "Wait!" she called after him. "Who are you?" There was no answer. He faded into the hillside, and she was left alone.

She opened her eyes in the darkness, then rolled over and switched on the lamp beside her cot. She was breathing fast, and her cheeks felt hot. "It was just a dream . . . ," she muttered, willing her heartbeat to slow down. Still, she couldn't forget the desperate look in the man's eyes.

She opened her laptop, looking for a distraction. Maybe she'd get another requisition form in the pipeline before she left for Kenya. She'd be more likely to actually relax on her break if she knew the camp would be adequately stocked when she returned.

Jan's question about going home niggled at the back of her mind. It *had* been a long time. But what was there to go home to? Her family was dead. And her other family—the Provos—well, she had left Belfast for a reason. No good would come out of going back. She pulled up the homepage of the *Belfast Telegraph* and scanned the headlines. Same old bickering between politicians, same old . . . wait.

She read the headline again.

PIRA Member Mick O'Connor Killed in Pub Brawl.

She scanned the article, her heart pounding. Mick had been released from prison early as part of the Good Friday Agreement, but she'd made no effort to get in touch, not even to tell him she'd left Belfast.

She'd felt bad about it at the time. In those lost, wild years after Eamon's death, Mick had become both father and brother to her. He'd tamed her rage and channeled it into something productive: breaking the grip of the British on their country. She'd loved him, or at least she'd thought she did. But everything had changed after he was caught and sent to prison. Nora had finally dared to dream of a life away from it all. Away from the constant fear, from the devouring hatred. Away from the ghost of her brother. Away from her own guilt.

And now Mick was dead.

She read the article again. The memorial service was in three days. Maybe Mombasa could wait.

Chapter Five

Nora sat with her back to Eamon's gravestone, staring up at a towering stone cross decorated with intricate scrollwork. Belfast's Milltown Cemetery was empty, and it was nearing dusk.

She pressed the heels of her palms into her forehead. Why had she returned? Going to Mick's funeral had been a bad idea. Too many memories. Too many reminders of everything that had been lost. They'd shared so much, the two of them, both blazing with hatred and the driving need for revenge. The fact that Mick had died so ignobly   in a pub brawl, of all things—would have been laughable if it weren't so sad. He'd have hated to go out that way.

Her eyes found an inscription on a nearby plaque that read, "To Ireland's Glorious Dead."

"That's shite, so it is," she whispered to Eamon's grave. "I'd rather Ireland be enslaved and you be alive." She felt guilty for saying that. Most of Ireland was free now, but that had only been achieved out of the blood of its sons and daughters. Would she really prefer for the entire island to be back under the thumb of the British Empire, for her people to be dispossessed and landless and starving to death by the hundreds of thousands?

All the same, she wished she could take Eamon's place. If only there were more like him: softhearted, intelligent, and peaceful. Eamon would have been able to tell her what to do.

She wiped at her eyes and rearranged the lilies she had brought in a silver vase, leaning them more securely against the stone. "I wonder what you would think of these strange dreams I've been having." She tried to imagine what he would say. He'd think they were interesting, to be sure. He'd press her for details and then discuss all the possible meanings with her. He wouldn't laugh at her. He'd probably say God was trying to speak to her.

Maybe he was, but if so, she didn't have a clue what he was trying to tell her. She could still picture the gray-haired man's face clearly, and she could hear the sound of his voice as he begged her to come help him. He had told her to go to Kildare. To Brigid. But would he be in Kildare? Besides, hundreds of Irish women were called Brigid—how was she to know which one to look for? None of it made any sense.

Which is why you should just forget it, she told herself.

Dreams had no meaning in real life. She picked up some dirt from the ground and let it run through her fingers. *Dust to dust, ashes to ashes. This is all we are.*

A breeze blew behind her as she left the cemetery. Years ago, she'd sold the family home and bought a tiny flat near the center of the city. She rented it out most of the time, but it was between tenants at the moment. She let herself in, turned on the telly, and cracked open a beer. She sank into one of the two chairs in the living area and sighed. Bare-bones furnishing and a single suitcase of clothes—this was what she had to show for thirty years on the planet.

She changed the channel to the news and immediately regretted it. Pictures of a ruined police station flashed across the screen. The stern-faced newscaster appeared beside the carnage and announced, "Today's bombing killed two police officers, Sergeants Elizabeth Law and Stephen Mitchell. No one has yet claimed responsibility for the attack, but it brings into question the ongoing talks regarding a possible cease-fire."

She ran to the toilet and threw up.

"Ballix!" She fumbled around for a cloth beside the sink and wiped her mouth. Then she stared up at her reflection in the mirror. Her eyes were bloodshot and her cheeks flushed. "Can't I get away from you?" she whispered.

She brushed her teeth, then phoned for a cab.

The doorman looked up at her in surprise as she stomped past him, her one suitcase in hand. "Hiya, Nora. Where you off to, then? You've only just arrived back."

"Anywhere but here," she said, pushing open the glass door and heading out to the street, where her cab was waiting. "Central Station, please," she said as the driver put her suitcase in the back.

At the station, she bought a one-way ticket to Dublin. It wasn't as far away as she would have liked, but it was far enough. For now. Besides, her aunt was there, and she needed to see a friendly face.

When she arrived, she checked into the first hotel she found and collapsed onto the bed. She was both relieved and depressed that absolutely no one knew where to find her.

She had the dream again that night for the first time since leaving Darfur. They were standing in a barren courtyard this time, surrounded by high stone walls. The ground at their feet was stained red.

Her pulse quickened as he grabbed her hands and pulled her close. "Nora," he said, his eyes flickering. "You must not delay. You must come at once. Please, I beg you."

"I still don't understand why . . . or how," Nora said, unable—unwilling—to look away. "Where are you? *Who* are you?"

But there was a roar of gunfire, and they both fell to the ground.

Nora sat upright in bed, awoken by her own scream. She listened, but the night was silent around her. Five a.m. Determined to shake off the dream, she took a shower, then grabbed her coat and umbrella and headed out onto the streets of Dublin.

Kildare was only an hour away. She'd come this far, all the way from Sudan . . .

She shook her head. *It was just a dream.*

But was it? The very night the stranger had told her to go to Kildare, she'd found out about Mick's death, which had drawn her back to Ireland for the first time in several years . . .

Don't be daft.

She went to a café and waited until it was a reasonable hour, then pulled out her cell phone and rang her aunt Margaret.

"Hiya, Auntie Margaret, it's Nora."

"Nora, love, how are ye? *Where* are ye, I should be askin'?"

"I'm in Dublin, actually. Mind if I pop round for a visit?"

"Do you even have to ask? Come on over; I've got the kettle on. Do you need me to collect you?"

"I'm grand, ta. I'll take the bus. See you soon."

Twenty minutes later Nora was enveloped in the warm embrace of her father's younger sister. Margaret's salt-and-pepper hair was pinned up in a loose bun, and her dark eyes sparkled as she held Nora at arm's length to inspect her.

"You're as skinny as ever, child. You look like a Biafran!"

Nora flushed. "We don't really use that term anymore, Auntie."

Margaret raised a dark eyebrow. "No? Well, whatever you want to call it, you need feeding. Have a seat while I fetch us some scones and tea."

Nora relaxed into the sofa. Black-and-white photographs stood on the mantle over the fireplace. Jesus smiled benignly at her from a frame on the wall. Years had passed since Nora's last visit, but her aunt's sitting room hadn't changed since she was a kid.

When Margaret was twenty, she had met and married a man from Dublin. Nora and Eamon had visited her a few times as kids, but the relationship was strained by Margaret's disapproval of her brother's politics. After Nora's da had been killed, the visits to Margaret had stopped altogether. But even though they weren't close, Nora had always been interested in this stately woman, who always wore her hair up and made the best scones Nora had ever tasted.

"Where's Uncle Peter?" Nora asked when her aunt came back into the room. She gratefully accepted a cup of tea and a scone.

"He's down to the races today," Margaret said. "I'll not be expecting him back 'til after tea. So what brings you to Dublin? Last I heard you were in some war zone in Africa."

"Sudan. I'm on 'rest and relaxation.' It's mandatory every few months for humanitarian workers. Helps us keep our sanity." She attempted a smile but ended up grimacing into her teacup.

"Ach, aye, I can imagine. Have you been up home, then?"

"Just for a couple of days. A friend of mine died, so I went home for the funeral. But there was another bombing, and . . ." She hesitated, not sure how to explain her abrupt flight from Belfast. "I don't know. I just felt like getting out."

Margaret nodded soberly. "I understand. I felt that way when I was younger than you, so I did. I don't know why any sane person would want to stay."

"Love of their country, I suppose?" Nora said with a wry smile.

"Ach, well, there are other ways to love your country than blowing people up. Our family has a long history of warring with our countrymen, ever since O'Reillys were kings of Breifne. Some thought it was treason for me to leave the way I did, like I was turning my back on generations of O'Reillys. Anyway, you didn't come here to talk politics, I'm sure."

"Actually, I'm interested. Ma never talked much about Da's side of the family. I barely remember my grandparents and don't know much about them."

Margaret cocked an eyebrow. "You sure you want to open that can of worms? I have to say I wasn't surprised when your da signed up, nor young Eamon. Rebellion is in the O'Reilly blood, so it is. Maybe your ma didn't tell you the stories because she didn't want you following in their footsteps."

"What stories?"

"The O'Reillys have been Volunteers for a long time, to be sure. The 1916 Rising, the Tan War, the Civil War . . . You name it, we were there. And we paid for it in blood. We'll need another pot of tea for this. I'll put the kettle back on."

Margaret bustled back into the kitchen. Nora stood and stretched, then crossed to the bookshelf. She'd never looked closely at it before, but her fingers trailed the spines of the books as if they were searching for something. She stopped on an old leather-bound photo album on the bottom shelf. A small burst of dust erupted when she drew it off the shelf.

"What's that you've found, now?" Margaret said, coming back into the room with a fresh pot of tea.

"I saw it on your bookshelf," Nora said, embarrassed she'd been caught snooping. "Mind if I have a look?"

Margaret peered at the book in her hands. "Ach, I haven't looked at that one in years. I inherited it from one of my aunts. It's been a long time since I've seen some of these faces." A wistful look flickered across her face.

Nora sat down beside Margaret and opened up the photo album. Black-and-white faces stared up at her as she leaned in closer. "Are these all O'Reillys?" she asked.

"Some of them, aye. This here is my aunt Sheila. She married a Moynihan."

"What is she wearing?" The photo was of a young blond woman dressed in a stiff dark jacket with shining metal buttons and a brimmed cap. A leather strap crossed her chest, and she wore a brooch in the shape of a rifle.

"She was Cumann na mBan, the women's branch of the Republican movement. This was during the Tan War, you see."

Nora squinted closer at the picture. Every Irish child knew about the Tan War, the bloody War of Independence against Britain that followed the failed 1916 Rising. It was called the Tan War after the Black and Tans, a particularly barbaric auxiliary group recruited in England to help the British-run police force in Ireland. The entire country had descended into guerrilla warfare, and the fighting had only stopped after a treaty was signed with Britain. Rather, the fighting against the British had stopped, and the fighting between the Irish had begun. The Anglo-Irish Treaty had given Ireland Free State status—meaning it was still part of the dominion of Great Britain, but with its own government. For some, this was enough. Others would settle for nothing short of a completely independent Irish republic. Nora suspected which side the O'Reillys had been on in the Civil War that followed the signing of the treaty.

"What was her role in the war?" she asked, pointing at the picture.

"Oh, she never said. Not to me, anyway, or my parents. Most Cumann na mBan were dispatch carriers who helped move arms, care for the wounded, things like that. But some fought right alongside the men. After the Civil War, Sheila got married, had five children, and, as far as I know, never breathed a word of her wartime activities to anyone. But I reckon she had a story or two to tell."

Nora turned the page. Two young men stood side by side in a black-and-white photograph, their faces smiling and their arms around each other. They were standing outside a whitewashed cottage. Both were wearing suspenders, white shirts, and caps, and each had a cigarette dangling from his fingers. "That's your grandfather," Margaret said, pointing to the man on the left. "My da. And that's his younger brother, Roger. This must have been taken before Roger went to Dublin."

"Why did he go to Dublin?"

"Well, you have to remember it was all one country back then, so it wasn't unusual to move around for work. But Roger was a soldier through and through. Da never talked much about him, except to say he was a prison guard for a time. He died quite young. Here, the date's on the back. April 4, 1923. It's a shame and a pity." Aunt Margaret crossed herself absentmindedly.

She kept turning pages, stopping to point out relatives and tell Nora what little she knew of their lives.

"Wait," Nora said suddenly, driven by some impulse she couldn't name. "Go back a page."

Margaret obliged, and Nora's teacup rattled on its saucer.

It was the man from her dream.

His eyes stared out at her from the page, and she heard his voice in her head. *Come find me, Nora.* It was unmistakably him—his nose, his cheekbones, even his prematurely gray hair. Nora stared back, her heart in her throat. Was this really happening? Had he led her here, to this photograph in her aunt's living room? She shivered despite the warm cup of tea in her hands.

"Are you all right, dear?" Margaret asked, looking between Nora and the photo.

"Who is this?" Nora whispered, unable to tear her eyes away. "Who is this man?"

"I have no idea," Margaret said. "A friend of my father's, I assume. Let's see if there's anything written on the back." She gently prized the photograph from the corner tabs holding it to the page. Scrawled on the back in faint writing, it read: *Thomas Heaney, IRA. Killed in action, 1923.*

Chapter Six

Margaret forced another cup of tea on Nora and closed the photo album, laying it on the coffee table.

"Can I keep this?" Nora asked, still holding the photo of Thomas Heaney. She'd searched through the rest of the album for other pictures of him, but this seemed to be the only one.

"I suppose there's no harm in it, but are you going to tell me what this is about? You look like you've seen a ghost."

Maybe I have. "Are you sure you don't know anything else about this man?"

"I told you, I have no idea, save for what it says on the back. But it seems to me that *you* know something about him."

"I don't," Nora admitted. "It's just . . . I saw him in a dream. Several dreams, actually. He looked exactly like this. I'm sure it was him." The longer she stared at the picture, the more certain she felt. He had the same look of longing in his eyes, as if he were far away . . . or wished to be.

Margaret crossed herself and muttered, "Mary, save us." She took the photo from Nora and examined it, then handed it back. "'Tis never a good sign to dream of the dead. But perhaps you've seen his photo before and have just forgotten."

Nora shook her head vehemently. "No, I've not seen him before. Only I've been dreaming about him for months now. He's even spoken to me."

Margaret's gray eyebrows arched. "Oh, aye? And what did your man have to say?"

Haltingly, Nora told her aunt about how the dreams had increased in clarity until the man—Thomas Heaney—had finally spoken to her and told her to find him in Kildare. "I wasn't even supposed to come back to Ireland—I had planned to go to Kenya for my break. But the same night he told me to go to Kildare, I found out my friend had been killed. So I came home instead."

Margaret watched her warily but said nothing.

"Then in last night's dream, we were in a stone courtyard, surrounded by high stone walls. There was blood on the ground. There was the sound of guns being fired, and then I woke up."

"Well, I don't pretend to know what it means," Margaret said slowly. "But there's a fine museum down at Kilmainham Gaol. That's where many of the political prisoners were kept during the Tan War and the Civil War. They might be able to tell you more about this Thomas Heaney, if he was IRA."

Nora reread the inscription on the back of Thomas Heaney's photo. *Killed in action, 1923.* "Do you think he was killed at Kilmainham? Is that why I had that dream?"

"I've no way of knowing, do I? But it's a possibility, I suppose. The Free State executed dozens of IRA Volunteers. O'course, the IRA killed their fair share of Irishmen, too." She shook her head and glanced up at Jesus on the wall. "A dark, dark stain on our history, if you ask me. And it's still going on in the six counties, so it is."

"It seems pretty far-fetched that I would dream of someone who's been dead for decades," Nora said, changing the subject. "Maybe you're

right; maybe I saw this photo in Da's things when I sold the house."
But would she have remembered his features so perfectly from a single
glimpse at a photo? Something told her the explanation wasn't anything
so simple.

"Why don't you go down to the jail and see if they'll let you have
a look at the records? You can find out if he was a prisoner there,"
Margaret suggested.

"Maybe . . ." Nora considered this. "But the records might not even
be there. You don't happen to have a computer, do you?"

"Me?" Margaret laughed. "I'm too old for that."

"Auntie Margaret, you're not even sixty," Nora said reprovingly.
"But it doesn't matter. I can go to the library later on."

"This has gotten you quite tied up, hasn't it?" Margaret's eyebrows
were knit together.

Nora blushed and got to her feet. "No . . . I'm just interested, that's
all. It feels strange to know so little about one's own history. Maybe the
dreams were just a sign that I should learn about this man. He could
be related to us somehow."

"And maybe they mean absolutely nothing at all," her aunt coun-
tered. "Why would the Lord put such things into your head?" Nora had
been wondering the same thing. Margaret patted her cheek. "I'll say a
prayer for you. But don't let it upset you too much. You've had a lot to
deal with lately; it's no surprise your mind is spinning."

"I won't. I should get going, though. Thanks for the tea. And the
scone was delicious."

"Ach, not at all, dear. Come and visit anytime. How long are you
on this break?"

"It's supposed to be a couple of weeks. But I might go back early."

"Well, you're welcome to stay here; I hope you know that."

"I do," Nora said with a smile. She kissed her aunt's cheek. "But
I'm better off alone just now. I'll let you know if I find anything more
about this Thomas."

"You do that."

Nora walked a couple of blocks to the bus stop but then decided to keep walking the rest of the way to the city center. It was an unusually fine summer day—and such weather begged to be enjoyed, particularly in Ireland. Besides, she needed time to think. She kept pulling the picture out of her purse to look at it. She turned it over and over in her mind as she walked, replaying everything she could remember from the dreams, as well as what she knew about the Civil War.

An hour later, she found her way to the public library and logged on to a computer. Her search for "Thomas Heaney IRA" turned up nothing. She scrolled through pages of results, but nothing seemed to match the man and date from the photo. Perhaps her aunt was right, and she'd do best to visit the Kilmainham Gaol museum. She plucked a brochure for the museum out of a stand near the entrance of the library and studied it for a moment. The sun shone on the sidewalk outside the glass doors. Tourists and locals flooded the streets. The economy was thriving, and for the first time in Ireland's history more people were moving to the country than were leaving it. *It really is a beautiful country. I should see more of it.*

She was so close to Kildare . . .

Don't be ridiculous.

She read the Kilmainham brochure again. Maybe the courtyard from her dream had no real-world equivalent. On the other hand, there was a chance the museum would have photos of some of the prisoners. It wouldn't hurt to check.

She boarded a bus and a few minutes later disembarked at the gates of the jail, a harsh, ugly stone structure framed by tall, leafy trees on an unassuming street. A crowd of American tourists was just getting off a large green tour bus. She stood at the back of the group as they filed in through the front entrance. Barred windows winked down at her as she shivered in a sudden chill breeze. Carved into the stone above the open doorway were five twisting dragons with wide, rolling eyes, their necks held in place by heavy chains. She was reminded of a Chinese fairy tale she'd once read. A painter created stunning depictions of dragons for a new temple, but he refused to draw the eyes because doing so would bring the dragons to life. The emperor ordered him to draw the eyes, awakening the dragons and causing untold destruction. She could almost picture these scaled figures breaking their stone chains and taking flight over Dublin.

"Intimidating, aren't they?" A young man wearing a red Office of Public Works shirt nodded up at the snakes.

"What do they mean?" Nora asked.

"It's simple enough. Murder, rape, theft, treason, and piracy—the five serious felonies back when the jail was built."

"Cheery," Nora muttered as the line inched forward. She paid her admission fee just inside the door. "I'm looking for a particular courtyard," she told the woman at the desk. "All right if I just have a look around?"

The woman shook her head. "Access is by guided tour only, though you're free to visit the museum for as long as you'd like."

"Right," Nora said. She pulled Thomas's photo out of her purse, already feeling ridiculous. "And I'm wondering if this man was ever a prisoner here . . ."

"You'd have to make an appointment with Archives," the clerk said, already accepting a credit card from the next person in line. "Talk to one of the museum staff."

Nora frowned, disappointed, then took her receipt and caught up with the American tourists. She followed them through a narrow corridor lined with books for sale, then into a large square room filled with displays and exhibits. But before she had a chance to look around, the next tour was announced and she hurried to join the group.

The young guide smiled at the guests and beckoned them closer. "Welcome to Kilmainham Gaol," she said in a bright, clear voice that belonged on a stage and not in a prison. "My name is Liz, and I'll be your guide today. If you'll follow me out these doors, our first stop will be the chapel, where we'll watch a short video."

Nora tagged along with the group, half-listening to the tour guide and craning her neck for anything that might remind her of Thomas or her dreams. They watched a short film about the history of the jail and some of its more prominent prisoners, but Thomas wasn't among them. Then they toured the old section of the prison, three floors of claustrophobic corridors, cramped cells, and peeling paint. As they rounded a corner, Nora noticed something written in large block letters on the wall above a barred window: "Beware of the risen people that have harried and held, ye who have bullied and bribed."

Nora shivered, frozen in place for a moment, then hurried to catch up with the group. She listened as Liz told them about the dark, desperate years of the Great Famine, when people would purposefully commit crimes in front of the authorities. They knew they were guaranteed at least one meal a day in prison, which was better than starving to death on the outside.

How bad must it have been, to want to come to this place?

Next they were onto the East Wing, which Nora recognized from the film *In the Name of the Father*. The soaring ceiling gave it an open, airy feeling that reminded her of a cathedral. It was shaped like a horseshoe, with cell doors all around the outer edge on three levels. An iron staircase descended from the third floor down to the main level, where they stood. Liz explained that this layout had allowed the wardens to see every single cell at once. Nora craned her neck with the rest of the tourists, scanning the three floors to see if this was true. Then her eyes fell back on the iron staircase, and her hands flew to her mouth.

Dozens of women were descending the staircase, but not willingly. Soldiers dragged them by their hair, slamming their heads against the iron rails as they pulled them down. One of them landed at Nora's feet, and she stepped back, nearly colliding with the man standing behind her. The woman on the floor looked up at Nora, blood running into her eyes. Her lips were clenched together. As Nora watched, the woman rose and charged at the staircase, only to be tackled and wrestled to the ground.

Nora spun around wildly to see if anyone else was observing the same thing. Perhaps it was a special effect, some part of the tour. But no one else seemed to notice the women piling up at their feet. They were all either listening to Liz or blandly surveying their surroundings. When she looked back at the staircase, the women were gone.

Nora closed her eyes tightly. Her breath was ragged and shallow, and she struggled to control it. *What the hell was that?* The group was dispersing to look inside some of the cells, but the tour guide came toward Nora. "Are you okay?" she asked quietly.

"I . . . I . . ." Nora stammered. "I just thought I saw some women on the staircase, that's all. Must have been a trick of the light."

Liz looked at her thoughtfully. "This place has a long and tragic history. You're not the first visitor to get a glimpse of the past. I don't often say this in my tours, but I believe some of the inhabitants of Kilmainham have never left."

Nora smiled awkwardly. "I think . . . I'm just tired," she said, pulling her arms close to her chest. The bright sunlight shone through the large skylights in the ceiling, but it did nothing to dispel the chill she felt deep inside. She cast a nervous glance back at the staircase, then meandered over to one of the open cells. Carved into the doorframe were the words, "The Manse." Who had carved that, and why? She stepped inside. It looked as if it had been recently whitewashed. A small window was set into the far wall, a good distance above her head. It let in a tiny ray of sunlight. Nora stood in the beam of light, willing it to warm her.

"Creepy place, isn't it?" asked a middle-aged woman who had entered the same cell.

"Oh, aye," Nora answered.

"Are you a local?" the woman asked in an American accent, a delighted look on her face.

"No. I'm from Belfast."

"Oh, I see," the woman said, looking concerned. "Do you know anyone who's been bombed?"

"What?"

"They told us we shouldn't go to Belfast because of the bombs. Have you been bombed?"

"No," Nora said, turning away.

"Well, that's good," the woman answered. She continued gazing around. "I wonder who was kept in this cell."

"Annie Humphreys," Nora answered without thinking. How did she know that? And yet it was true; she was sure of it.

"Oh, you've done the tour before!"

Nora turned around slowly. Her eyes skimmed over the woman's excited face and kept turning, taking in the four walls of the cell. "No," she said softly. "I haven't." What was going on? First the women on the stairs, then this. Was her mind even her own anymore? She pushed past the woman back into the open atrium, where she found Liz.

"Do you recognize this man?" she asked, showing her the photograph of Thomas Heaney. "I'm wondering if he was a prisoner here."

Liz examined the picture closely and then turned it over to read the inscription. She handed it back, shaking her head. "I don't recognize him, no. But there were hundreds of political prisoners here in the early nineteen hundreds. Was he a relative of yours?"

"I don't think so."

"Well, once the tour is over you can ask the museum staff; they might be able to help you." Turning away, Liz called out to the rest of the group, "If you'll follow me, we've one more stop on our tour." Nora followed her through a narrow doorway and down a claustrophobic corridor, her fingers trailing the stone walls. Liz opened a door and motioned for Nora and the others to step outside.

This is it. She knew it with the same unshakable surety with which she'd known so many impossible things lately. It was the courtyard she'd visited last night in her dream.

She stepped into the center of a stone yard, surrounded on all sides by thick, windowless walls rising at least thirty feet high. She spun in a slow circle as the tourists milled around her. The highest branches of a single tree waved just above the wall, a taunting reminder of the world outside this cold monolith. A small cross, only a foot tall, stood at one end. She held her breath and waited, looking for some vision or sign that would guide her next steps. But there was only the sound of Liz's voice as she explained the significance of the yard. Once used for hard labor, it was the site of the 1916 executions that had fanned the flames of the War of Independence.

Is this where Thomas Heaney was killed? She walked slowly around the yard, touching the stone walls, listening for a voice from the grave. "Thomas?" she whispered.

Nothing. She was the last to leave when Liz directed them back into the museum. Disappointment settled in her stomach. She took one last glance back at the empty courtyard before the door closed behind her.

The museum was fascinating, two floors of informational plaques and glass-covered displays containing everything from old prison locks to playing cards to heartfelt letters prisoners had written before their execution. But there was no indication Thomas Heaney had ever been here. As she wandered through the brightly lit room with other tourists, the tension in her gut lessened slightly.

She bent over to examine a collection of small autograph books. The sign beside the glass cabinet said the prisoners would sign each other's autograph books as a way of commemorating their time behind bars. Nora peered in closely, examining the books lying open under the glass and reading the poems and slogans that filled the pages.

"How are you feeling now?" Liz asked from behind her. "Any more visions?"

Nora swiveled around. "No." She hesitated before saying, "But I did have the impression that I knew whose cell I was standing in earlier. A woman named Annie Humphreys. I don't know why—the name just came to me."

Liz raised her eyebrows. "Annie Humphreys? She was here during the Civil War. Have you read about her?"

Nora shook her head. "I've never heard of her before. It was just a feeling."

"How interesting," Liz said, her dark eyes fixed on Nora. "I believe that some people are more sensitive to the spiritual realm, if you don't mind me saying so. Maybe some of those who have passed on are trying to speak to you."

Oh, sweet Jesus, I hope not. The dreams were maddening enough. Did this mean she was to start having visions of the dead in the daytime, too? "I should get going."

She stumbled past the rest of the displays and squeezed through a group of German tourists who were clogging up the entryway. Once outside, she walked briskly to the bus stop.

Go to Kildare.

"Fine," she said out loud, startling the man standing next to her. Maybe going to Kildare was the only way she'd find answers. Then she could get back to her life and forget this madness.

She took the bus back to the city center, then walked to her hotel. She got as far as the front door before she turned around. A drink—she needed a drink before she did anything else. A few minutes later, she sat down at the bar of Murphy's Pub and nodded to the barman.

"What'll you have, then?"

"Jameson."

The barman poured and mixed and conversed all at once, and she watched him to avoid thinking of the women on the stairs at the jail, of Thomas Heaney's haunting voice, and of the chill in her bones she couldn't shake.

"Rough day?" he said to her once her glass was nearly empty. It hadn't taken long.

"Aye," she said, swirling the rest of the amber liquid in her glass.

"You from the North, then?"

"Aye. Belfast."

"Derry, myself," he said. "Just here for the weekend?"

"I don't know. I'm on break from my work in Darfur."

"Darfur!" he said, raising his brows. "Now there's a fucked-up place. You a relief worker?"

"Aye."

"Well, then, the next one's on the house. Saving lives—that's a whole lot better than pulling pints."

She smiled at him. "I'm sure you've saved a life or two without even knowing it."

"Ha. Mebbe. Ready for another?"

"Aye."

You're making something out of nothing, she told herself as the barman returned to his other patrons. Perhaps Jan was right and she was just burned out. But then she remembered what the tour guide had said.

Maybe some of those who have passed on are trying to speak to you.

Was Thomas Heaney trying to send her a message from the afterlife? If the saints could do miracles and there really was a life after death . . . was it so impossible? She supposed she would soon find out.

Chapter Seven

When Nora awoke the next morning, she felt strangely invigorated. It took her a second to remember why. Then she sat up and flung the covers back.

I have a mission.

She showered and dressed with the efficiency of an assembly-line worker, then pulled on her favorite leather jacket. She ran across the road to grab a bun and cup of tea from the baker's opposite her hotel. The sun was shining between clusters of cloud in the freshness of the morning as she walked from the baker's to the train station, past shining office towers and ancient cathedrals. The River Liffey was glittering in the sunlight, a ribbon of silver through an ever-changing city.

Now that she'd made the decision to go, she didn't know why she'd been so hesitant. Finally, this was something she could do. There were so many things she could not control in her life, but at least she could do this, as far-fetched as it seemed. The dreams, the strange experiences at Kilmainham—they all had to mean something. She'd go to Kildare, find a woman named Brigid, and see if there was some kind of message waiting for her. If there was one, then she'd have to figure out what to do about it. And if there wasn't, she would tell Thomas Heaney to leave her the hell alone the next time she dreamed about him.

She bought her ticket from a machine outside the station and soon boarded the train. The brick and concrete turned into blurs of green as they sped toward the southwest. Less than an hour later, the automated voice broke into her thoughts with the announcement that they were approaching Kildare Station.

Nora stepped onto the platform, then watched the train continue on its way with a cocktail of foreboding and anticipation. She'd felt this way every time she'd entered a new country, a new disaster, a new opportunity for her to prove herself. *Right. Don't just stand there. Let's get to work.*

Her first destination was the tourism office, which she found on a map she'd snagged at the station. It was only a couple of blocks away. As she walked toward it, a large cathedral loomed on the right, just down the street. Behind it was a tall round tower that soared even higher than the cathedral spires. She checked the map. Saint Brigid's Cathedral. Thomas had told her to talk to Brigid. Had he meant she should go to the cathedral? To pray to the saint? Or was there an actual woman here named Brigid who might have the information she was seeking?

Saint Brigid of Kildare was one of Ireland's patron saints. Nora's ma had even hung a Saint Brigid's cross above their doorway in Belfast. She'd loved Brigid above all the saints. Nora had never thought to ask why.

She found the tourism office with little difficulty. A tall, thin man was just flipping over the "Open" sign. He smiled when he saw Nora approaching. "Good morning to you!" he called.

"Good morning."

"Are you a visitor to our fine town, then?" the man asked, ushering Nora inside. The tourism office was tiny, not much more than a desk and a few shelves of maps and tourist kitsch.

"I am. My first visit," Nora said. "I'm doing a bit of . . . research, and I was wondering if you might help me."

"Of course! We get a lot of amateur historians in here. Kildare has a long, proud history. If you're wanting to take one of our walking tours, my nephew Oisín—"

"Actually, I'm trying to find out more about this man." She showed him the picture of Thomas. "Someone told me he might have a connection to this town."

"Hmm, well, I can't say I recognize him," he said. After flipping over the photo, he peered down at it through his bifocals. "Thomas Heaney, so it says. A relative of yours?"

"I don't think so. I was told to look for a woman named Brigid. Do you know of anyone by that name?"

He laughed. "Besides our precious saint, you mean! I know of a couple Brigids, but I don't think they'll know who this young man is, if that's what you're thinking. What kind of research are you doing?"

"Um . . . Civil War."

He shook his head and frowned. "A sad time for Ireland, that was. There are a few local history groups that might be able to help you better." He shuffled around behind the desk and pulled out a printed list. "Here are their names and contact information. They meet on various nights of the week. But if you ring one of these numbers, they might be able to help you out. How long are you here for?"

"Good question," Nora answered. "Until I find what I'm looking for, I suppose."

"Do you have a hotel already?"

"No, but I've got one back in Dublin."

"Well, here's a list of some of our recommended accommodations." He handed Nora another handmade brochure. "And here's some information about the cathedral, the tower, and the holy well."

"Is the cathedral open now?" Nora asked.

"Yes, it should be. Just cross the street, and you'll see the entrance gates straight ahead."

"Ta."

Nora stuffed the papers into her purse and stepped back out into the sun. Was Thomas Heaney buried in the church graveyard? The thought made her shiver. If he was truly dead, how could he speak to her?

A stone fence, as tall as Nora, was built around the cathedral, but the iron gate in front was open. A silver car was parked on the gravel patch outside the church door, above which was carved a skull and crossbones. Odd. Nora gave it a sidelong glance, then veered left into the graveyard.

She tried to make out the names on the stones. It was near impossible on most of them, and those that she could read were not the final resting markers for Thomas Heaney. She sat down on a smooth, low, rectangular stone wall that, according to the plaque, marked the site of Saint Brigid's Fire Temple. Candles, flowers, and prayer cards had been placed against the back wall.

Without warning, a flame erupted in the dead center, shooting at least six feet into the sky. Nora scrambled back off the wall and held up an arm to block the heat. When she lowered it, hooded figures stood around the flames, chanting. And then the entire scene was simply gone, just like the women on the stairs at Kilmainham. No ash, no scorch marks, no sign of anything out of the ordinary. A vase of silk flowers seemed to wink at her as they swayed softly in the breeze.

"Sweet Jesus," Nora whispered, backing away from the site and almost tripping over a fallen headstone in her haste. She ran to the church doors and heaved them open.

"Hello? Is anyone here?" she called, her voice echoing in the cavernous space. Just inside the entrance was a series of standing display cases and several large stone sarcophagi. A thin woman popped her head around the corner.

"Can I help you?"

"Do you work here?"

"I'm one of the volunteers, yes. My name's Suzanne. How can I help you?"

Nora thrust the picture of Thomas into her hands. It was time for complete honesty, come what may. "Right, Suzanne, I know this is going to sound crazy. I'm not off my head, I swear it. But I've had several dreams about this man. He told me to come to Kildare so I could talk to a woman called Brigid. And then I found this photo of him. See, it says here he died in 1923. And I keep seeing visions of the past, knowing things I shouldn't know. So I've come here, just like he asked." She stopped, unable to believe she'd confessed all of that out loud to a complete stranger.

The woman glanced at the photo for a moment, then handed it back. "Are you looking for prayer?"

"No! I'm trying to find out how a man who's been dead for almost a century is getting into my head."

It was clear from Suzanne's expression that she thought Nora was mentally unstable. "Have you checked at the heritage center? They might be able to—"

"Yes, and they sent me here. I'm not making this up! Someone must know—"

"Is there a problem?" Another woman emerged from a door at the side of the church. She was short and on the plump side, with closely cropped coarse brown hair and an uneven fringe. She wore a long green shawl with a gold brooch.

"May I?" Suzanne said, taking the photo from Nora. She passed it to her colleague. "She's trying to find out about this man. He's called Thomas Heaney. Do you recognize him, Mary?"

Mary's mouth opened, then closed, then opened again. "Yes, I do," she said slowly, her eyes drinking in the photograph. Finally, she stared up at Nora. "*You're* the one looking for him?" Her voice held a hint of incredulity.

"Aye," Nora said warily. Was this woman having her on? Or was she really about to find some answers?

Mary pressed her hand over her heart. "It's a fine day. Why don't we take a walk outside? Thank you, Suzanne, I'll help this young lady from here."

Nora followed Mary past another stone coffin and a display of Kildare in the fifth century, back into the churchyard.

"Well," Mary began once they were well away from the front door. "I'm not exactly sure how to proceed, but I'll do my best. You see, we've been waiting for you."

"You've been waiting for me?" Nora repeated, dumbfounded. "Why?"

"Are you a religious person, Nora?"

"Yes, o'course." They were behind the cathedral now, wandering among the tombstones. The round tower loomed overhead.

"That's good to hear. So many young people have left the church these days. If they only knew how it sustained us in days gone by. But I digress. I belong to an order called the Brigidine Sisters."

"A Catholic order? But isn't the cathedral Church of Ireland?"

"It is now, but that hasn't always been the case. The church you see now was built in the thirteenth century, but it rests on the site of the church Saint Brigid herself had built in the fifth century. Before that, it was a site of worship to the pagan goddess Brigid. So I count it a privilege to volunteer at the cathedral as part of my devotion to the saint."

"Makes sense." They had walked to the base of the round tower, which was surrounded by gravestones.

"But it may surprise you that a few months ago, several of us experienced the same vision while praying at Saint Brigid's Well. Have you been there?" Nora shook her head. "It's down on Tully Road. It was here that Brigid herself appeared to us. She told us a young woman would

63

come looking for a man with gray hair called Thomas Heaney. And that she wished to bestow upon this young woman a very special gift." Mary's face shone with excitement as she leaned toward Nora.

Nora stopped walking. "Are you saying Saint Brigid appeared to you and told you I would be coming? *I* didn't even know I would be coming until this morning."

"That's exactly what I'm saying. And it wasn't just me. My Sisters all had the same vision. Many of us work or volunteer in some capacity at the cathedral. She must have wanted to ensure one of us was there to greet you when you finally came looking. I'm just so glad I overheard your conversation with Suzanne. She's not a Brigidine Sister, you see."

Nora chewed the inside of her lip. She was Catholic, sure, but the idea of saints actually appearing to people wasn't something she'd considered before. It had certainly never happened to anyone she knew. The logical side of her rebelled. "And you all had the same vision?"

"I know how it sounds," Mary said. "But you yourself said you've seen visions of the past, have you not? And dreamed of a man who is long dead?"

"Yes, but . . ."

"It's hard to fathom, I won't deny it. If Brigid hadn't told me herself, if I hadn't seen her with my own eyes, I'd not believe it."

"Right, so, you said she wanted to give me a gift. What is it? And who's this Thomas Heaney? You'll forgive me for not understanding what this is all about."

"Think with your heart, not with your head," Mary said. "When you had this dream of Thomas, how did you feel?"

Longing. But she couldn't say that out loud. She hardly wanted to admit it to herself. "Like I wanted to help him. More than anything. He begged me."

"And these visions? Do you believe they were real?"

What if she did? Would it mean she was going mad? "I don't know. They felt real."

"Then they were. It doesn't matter if it was just inside your head, or if you were seeing something that was really there. What matters is that Brigid was trying to speak with you."

"Yes, but why?"

"I don't know why she chose you. Or how exactly you're supposed to help this young man. Or why she even wants you to help him. But she has made it *possible*."

"*How?* He's been dead for eighty years."

"For this, we must go back to the church."

Nora bit her tongue and followed Mary into the cathedral. Suzanne popped her head around the corner as they entered. "Everything all right?" she asked.

"Grand, thank you," Mary answered. "We're just going to have a peek at the records downstairs." She led Nora down a narrow stone staircase into the basement of the church. They passed walls lined with bookshelves and stacks of boxes labeled in minute handwriting. Then they entered another small room, which was empty save for a dark fireplace set into the wall. Mary turned so quickly Nora almost ran into her. "You must swear to never reveal this to anyone."

"Reveal what?" Nora was beginning to think this was some elaborate hoax . . . or a cult. She eyed the door nervously.

"What I'm about to show you is one of the greatest kept secrets of the church. Brigid, in her wisdom, has chosen to share it with you. You'll be the first outside our society to have this knowledge."

Nora narrowed her eyes. "What kind of society is this?"

Mary gave an apologetic shrug. "The complicated kind. To the outside world, we are the Brigidine Sisters, an order committed to service and harmony in the spirit of Saint Brigid. We were nearly destroyed during the Dissolution of the Monasteries. We survived, underground, until we revealed ourselves in the eighteen hundreds. All of that is true, but we've also kept this sacred knowledge secret and protected for centuries. And if you do not do the same . . ." She let her threat hang in the empty air, but Nora was not so easily cowed.

"Right, I'm beginning to think this is all a joke. Someone's acting the maggot with me, so they are. Forget it." She turned to leave.

"Wait!" Mary called. "I'm sorry. It's just . . . It's precious to us. We've guarded it for so many years."

"What it is, then?"

Mary counted the stones around the fireplace. Then she pressed hard against one with the heel of her hand. On the other side, a stone popped out about an inch. Mary pulled at it until it loosened, then reached inside the hole. When she withdrew her hand, it held a small red box with gilt edging. Nora stepped closer. "What is it?" she asked.

"'Tis the only true relic of our precious Saint Brigid," Mary said, holding the box as though it might trickle through her fingers if she looked away for a moment. "A church in Portugal claims to have the blessed saint's skull, and they've sent fragments to Killester and Kilcurry, but we Sisters know that *this* is the only true relic."

"Why don't you display it? Why keep it secret?"

"Because it has power," Mary said, still speaking in a hushed, reverent tone. She gently opened the decorated lid and handed it to Nora. "Do not touch it. Not yet."

Nora looked into the box. It was, as she had expected, a bone. Only an inch long, it was polished white and smooth, nestled on a ruby-red cushion.

"It was from her finger," Mary explained.

"Is *this* the gift? What am I supposed to do with it?" Nora asked, closing the lid.

"No, my child, that is not the gift. But the power of Brigid's relic will bestow on you the gift she wishes you to have: the ability to travel through time."

Chapter Eight

"Is there something wrong with you?" Nora said angrily. "All I asked was for you to help me identify this man, and now you're messing me around with talk of time travel? I'm not an eejit."

Mary closed her eyes. "I feared you might react this way. What sane person wouldn't? But then I thought perhaps Brigid had appeared to you as well."

"No. It wasn't Brigid who told me to come here; it was Thomas, whoever the hell he is. I can guarantee you no saint has ever communicated with me, no matter how faithful I've been."

"I can't make you believe. But everything I've told you is true, no matter how it sounds. Just . . . try doing what she asks. If it doesn't work, you can leave. But we're all here for a reason, Nora. This was mine: to pass on this message to you. Don't you want to find out what your reason is?"

Nora held Mary's gaze for a heartbeat, then looked down at the relic in her hand. What *was* her reason for being in this world? For a while she'd thought it was to avenge her brother and help free Northern Ireland. And then she'd believed it was to relieve the suffering of others. But could there be something else?

"Fine, I'll humor you. How does it work, then?" she asked.

"I don't know exactly how it works, only that Brigid has power beyond our understanding. Her message was simple. Take the relic, which will give you the ability to travel back in time. Then you must find one of the Brigidine Sisters. You are to tell them that Brigid sent you and you are the bane of Aengus Óg."

"The bane of Aengus Óg? What the hell does that mean?" She wanted answers, but there were only more riddles.

Mary shook her head. "I'm only the messenger. Aengus Óg was one of the Tuatha Dé Danann, the old gods of Ireland. Perhaps Brigid sends you to triumph over paganism."

"I doubt it. I'm not that holy," Nora muttered.

"She knew you would be reluctant. There aren't many people who are willing to risk themselves to help a complete stranger."

"I've spent the last several years of my life helping complete strangers," Nora pointed out.

"She also said that if you succeed in helping Thomas, you might be able to help others who are close to you."

Nora took a step back, her eyes narrowed. "What do you mean? Who?"

"I don't know. Are any of your friends or relatives in trouble? Anyone close to you who needs help?"

There's no one close to me at all.

And that sealed it. What did she have to lose? If it worked—she couldn't believe she was even considering this as a possibility—no one would miss her. No one would even know she was gone. Besides, she already had so many regrets in life. If she didn't even try, perhaps she would regret this, too. *I couldn't help Eamon. Maybe I can do something for this Thomas.*

"Brigid has chosen you," Mary continued when Nora didn't answer. "You only need to put your trust in her. She offers you a great gift."

"This is mad." Nora took a deep breath and stared at the box in her hand. "What am I supposed to do?"

"Hold the relic in your palm. Think hard about Thomas. Ask Brigid to guide you to him. And have faith."

Fingers shaking slightly, Nora picked up the bone and closed her eyes. *Christ, have mercy.* She pictured Thomas as clearly as she could—not the man frozen in the picture but the man from her dream, sitting on the stone wall, speaking with her in his soft voice, pleading for her to come find him. *I'm trying. Where are you?*

Then she felt an overwhelming dizziness. She was falling, but when she tried to open her eyes, she couldn't quite remember how. She threw out her arms to break the fall, and then there was darkness.

Nora opened her eyes. Her head was pounding, and she was lying on a cold floor. The room was dark. *Why am I here? Have I been shot? Am I in hospital?* She felt as if she had been beaten. Every muscle ached, and her skin was painfully tender.

Slowly, the events that had brought her here came back. "Mary?" she groaned. She crawled into a sitting position, her body protesting at the movement. She was still in the basement of the cathedral, but it seemed empty and dark. "Mary?" she called out a little louder, getting to her feet. Then she remembered the relic. She'd been clutching it when she fell, but it was no longer in her hands. It was impossible to see in the shadows, so she got back to her hands and knees and felt around. Why had Mary left her here alone—and in the dark, no less? Perhaps she'd gone to get help . . .

Nora felt her way to the doorway of the room and moved into the hallway lined with bookshelves. But instead of the smooth wooden shelves she remembered, she felt only cold, rough stone beneath her fingertips. Finally, she located the stairs, and the light grew brighter as she gingerly crept up them, approaching the top of the stairway. She pushed on the wooden door at the top and entered into the main sanctuary of the cathedral.

"Mary!" she called out again. Still no response. There was something different about this space, but she couldn't put her finger on it. The wooden pews looked the same, the stone tombs still stood in silent vigil, and the stained-glass windows loomed over the empty space. But one of them was broken.

The tourist information was gone, too—the cases of displays, the placards and signs on the walls, the box requesting a suggested donation to help continue the conservation work. Strange that they would take it all down at the end of each day . . .

Unless.

No.

Nora burst out of the front door of the cathedral, wincing at the pain in her joints and muscles. The silver car was no longer in the gravel driveway. The day's light was beginning to wane. The churchyard appeared the same; the round tower stood sentry as before. But then her eyes flew to the Fire Temple, where she'd seen the vision of flames surrounded by hooded figures. The smooth low wall was gone; in its place was a broken crumble of stone on only one side of the rectangle. On the other sides, there was nothing, just the odd stone and a few tufts of grass.

"What the hell?" Nora muttered. She flipped open her cell phone. No signal. She ran toward the iron gate, her whole body aching, then stopped short. The street before her, while still recognizable, was utterly transformed. Instead of black pavement beneath her feet, there was only dirt. The wagon that had been selling icons of Saint Brigid was gone. There was no Tikka Palace restaurant next to the cathedral. Instead, the white lettering in the shop window read, "MacMahon's Irish Lace." A man sitting outside the shop stopped smoking his pipe to gawk at her. He was wearing a white shirt, suspenders, and a pageboy cap.

"Do you need help, er, miss?" he asked, his wide eyes fixed on her jeans and leather jacket.

"What happened to the tourist stand here?" she asked.

"The what?"

"And this was an Indian restaurant. I walked by it this morning." Nora turned slowly in a circle as the truth hammered away at her reason.

"I don't know what you're talking about, to be sure. No Indians in this town that I know of."

She stared at him, unblinking. "Are you an actor? Is there a historic festival going on?"

"An actor!" the man cried. "Now that's a good one. I'll have to tell the lads."

"Could you tell me," she asked in a voice barely above a whisper, "what year is it?"

"The year? Are you sure you're all right?"

"Just tell me the damn year!"

He scowled at her. "You'll be from Ulster then, judging by your accent and your manners. It's the year of our Lord 1923, if you didn't know. Don't they teach you how to keep track of time up there?"

1923. It had worked. Her mind wrestled with the impossibility of it, with the chance that it could be some kind of mistake or practical joke. But if it was a joke, it was the most elaborate joke she'd ever heard of. And to what end? No, though her mind and reason rebelled against the idea, her senses—and her gut—were telling her that Mary had spoken the truth. For some unknown reason, by some unknown means, she had gone back in time over eighty years.

She quickly rifled through her purse. The tourist brochures were all there, along with the map of Kildare and—most importantly—the picture of Thomas.

"Do you know this man?" she said, thrusting the photograph in the smoking man's face.

"Jesus Christ, woman! Are you drunk?" he said, flinching away from her. She didn't move, so he took the photo and bent over it. "No, never seen him." Before Nora could stop him, he flipped the photo over and read the inscription on the back. "Well, it says right here that he's dead."

"I know. But I need to find him."

"Well, the graveyard is that way," the man said with a jerk of his thumb. "But if he was one of them Irregulars, then I say good riddance. We finally got rid of the British, only for them to start tearing the country apart."

Nora snatched her photo back, but she felt the man's gaze on her as she walked down the street. She felt dazed, as if she were back in one of her own dreams. But this was more real than any dream. A fine drizzle dampened her face. She walked slowly, cautiously, as though on a tightrope of sanity. Had she gone mad? She felt perfectly rational, with the glaring exception that she seemed to be in the wrong century. Many of the buildings were the same, only shabbier—the windows darker, the trim not as freshly painted. There were fewer trees and no cars parked along the streets. She recognized the whitewashed walls, stone upper floor, and domed windows of the tourism office . . . only it was run-down, the paint chipped and a large pipe running up the side of the building. A placard beside the front door read "Market every Thursday." She peered inside the windows, but there was no one inside, only barrels and wooden crates.

"Excuse me, miss," someone said, and she stepped aside to let a man pass. He lifted a long pole up to the nearest streetlight, and with a flick, a flame flared in the glass lantern. Nora whipped her head around—electrical wires were strung between some of the buildings, but there were nowhere near as many as there would be in a modern town. The streetlights were still lit with gas. She looked farther down the main street. Where were the cars?

If this was a hoax, it was one for the history books.

The gaslighter was starting to stare, so she continued her dazed walk down the street. A door opened ahead of her, and warm light and the sound of voices spilled out onto the sidewalk. A pub. *If there's anything I need right now, it's a drink.*

The conversation died down when she stepped inside. She lowered her head and went straight to the bar. The barman did a double take but then said, "What can I get ye?"

"A whiskey, please," she said, her eyes on the bar. She could feel the gaze of everyone in the pub but refused to turn around. The barman poured her drink slowly, then walked over and set it down in front of her.

"You new in town, then?"

"Just visiting."

"Where from?"

"America," she said. He nodded, as though that explained her strange clothing.

"America, you say. I've a cousin who emigrated there last month. What is it like?"

"Oh, it's grand," she said. "Loads of jobs. People everywhere."

"Then what brought you back here, I wonder?"

Good God, is this a pub or an interrogation room? She met his eye and said, "Family," in a tone that meant the conversation was closed.

"I see," he said. "Holler if you want another."

She sipped her whiskey and listened to the conversations around her pick up. A long mirror stretched in front of her, providing her with the opportunity to take in her environment without turning around. The pub itself seemed like any other small-town Irish pub. But the people . . . the men wore old-fashioned caps, like fedoras and bowlers and trilbies. A few sported suits with waistcoats, but most wore trousers and shirts in various states of disrepair. And several tables had been pushed together at the back to accommodate about a dozen soldiers. They wore dark green uniforms with gold buttons, complemented by polished black boots that came up almost to their knees. Several of them had rifles leaning against their chairs. Nora's stomach tightened and her mind raced. Were they British soldiers? No, this was 1923; the British had left in '21. These would be Free Staters, soldiers of the fledgling Irish government created after the signing of the Anglo-Irish Treaty. She was the only woman in the room.

What the hell am I doing here? She needed to hide, to figure out which end was up. The last thing she should have done was march clothed in twenty-first-century leather and denim into a pub full of soldiers.

She reached into her purse for her wallet. *Shite.* All she had were euros, which hadn't been created yet. The bartender swiped up her empty glass. "Another?"

"No . . . ," she said slowly, her mind spinning. "How much do I owe you?"

"Six pence'll do it."

She pulled out a euro and placed it on the counter. "I'm afraid this is all I have. But it's worth much more than six pence."

"Is it, now?" the barman said, picking it up and examining the coin. She prayed he wouldn't notice the date stamped on it. "And what exactly is it?"

"It's American. I've only just got back, you see, and haven't had time to get my money changed."

"And what am I supposed to do with American money?"

"Ah, keep it, Bill!" said a man sitting a few stools down at the bar. "We'll all end up there someday, the way this country is going."

The barman snorted. "Is that what you think, Ned? Think someone'll give a job to a worn-out coot like yerself?"

"I can still put in a good day's work when there's work to be had," Ned retorted.

"I don't see you sitting over there with them lads," the barman said, pointing his chin at the tables of soldiers.

"I'm not desperate enough to join the army. Not yet anyways," Ned said darkly.

Nora took advantage of their bantering, slipped off her stool, and left the pub. The door had just closed behind her when it opened again. Three of the soldiers who had been drinking inside followed her onto the street.

"You there!" one of them called. She kept on walking, but they quickly caught up and blocked her path.

"What's your name and business here?" the tallest of the three asked. His hair was dark and cropped short, and the eyes under the black brim of his cap were narrowed in suspicion.

"I was having a drink, just like you," Nora said, ducking her head and trying to move around them. Her heart pounded. Could she out-run them? How was it that she'd not been in this century for an hour and she was already getting into trouble?

"Likely story," he said, stepping in front of her again. "I'll ask you one more time. What's your name and business here?"

Nora looked him in the eye this time. "My name's Nora O'Reilly, and I was having a drink, as you clearly saw. Now get out of my fucking way."

One of the boys gave a low whistle. "Got a live one here, Kevin."

"Where do you live?" Kevin, who seemed to be the officer in charge, demanded.

"Boston," she said through gritted teeth.

"Where are you staying *here*?" he asked, impatience lining his words.

"Not with you, that's for sure," she snapped. "Is harassing ladies on the street after dark the way things are done here?"

The other two soldiers looked down at their feet. *God, they're young.*

"What is a 'lady' doing on the street after dark, I wonder?" Kevin asked.

"I feel perfectly safe being out here, knowing you fine men are doing such a spectacular job keeping our country safe." They seemed to be unsure of whether she was being serious or making fun of them.

"Well, I think we should escort the lady back to her lodgings, don't you agree, lads?"

The other two seemed to think this was an excellent idea, and the three of them formed a semicircle private guard around her.

"I don't need your protection," Nora said. "I can walk on my own, thank you very much."

"We insist," Kevin said, giving her a little prod in the small of her back. She slowly began to walk forward, struggling to keep an outer composure to mask her inner panic. Where could she go? She could lead them back to the church, but what good would that do? She had to get away—and avoid getting shot or arrested in the process.

They continued walking, the stomp of the men's boots breaking the silence. Ahead, another group of soldiers approached them.

"Stay with our visitor," Kevin told one of the younger men. Then he and the other guard called out to their comrades and crossed the street to greet them. The man who'd been left with Nora stood a little straighter, gripping his rifle firmly in both hands.

Nora bent down by the side of the road under the pretense of tying her shoe, using the opportunity to palm a large, jagged stone. In one fluid movement, she leapt to her feet, her arm swinging, and struck the soldier on the side of the head with the stone. He dropped, and she ran, ignoring the screaming protests of her muscles.

She didn't need to hear the shouts behind her to know the other soldiers were hard on her heels. Her trainers pounded the dirt as she spun into an alley, her hair waving behind her like a red flag. She turned again and again, trying desperately to keep track of which direction she was headed so she wouldn't loop around and run straight into them. A stray cat hissed at her from a doorway. Nora tried the door, but it was locked. Her breath was ragged as she hunched over in the dark alcove, listening for the sounds of her pursuers. Loud, angry voices erupted nearby, and she stiffened. But the racket was muted, as though it was coming from the next street over.

"We saw her come down this way. If anyone here is found harboring her . . ."

"What are you chasin' after a woman for, Kevin Miller? You and your boys have been at the pub too long; I can tell by the smell of you."

"Now, Mrs. McCurdle, I'm an officer of the National Army, not some farm boy you had at your table—"

"I'm starting to regret ever having you at my table, Kevin, if this is how you've turned out. Disturbin' decent people at this time o' night, accusin' them of harborin' fugitives!"

"Grand so, we'll let you get back to your evening, Mrs. McCurdle."

Nora listened as the soldiers' voices faded. She peered into the alley, which was still empty, save for the cat. Slowly now, listening for the fall of boots around each corner, she crept through the town. She had no idea where she was headed, only that she needed to find somewhere safe to hide—and think—for the night. If she could find the main road again, she could make her way back to the cathedral. Then she'd track down one of the Brigidine Sisters in the morning and find out what the hell was going on.

The road she found herself on was not lit by gas lamps like those in town. Hazy clouds obscured the moon, but she could still see well enough to make out the path ahead. Going back to the cathedral would mean turning around and heading back through town—and risking another encounter with the Free State Army. Perhaps it would be best to head out into the country for the night, or even to the next town over. She trudged along the road, keeping an ear and an eye out for approaching vehicles.

It was unnaturally quiet. In the refugee camps, there was always the sound of babies crying, people making their way to the latrines, new arrivals being ushered in, and tents being hastily erected. Even the staff compounds were filled with the sounds of people coming and going. And in Belfast, she was lulled to sleep by the rumble of lorries and late-night revelers. This silence was disconcerting.

A hardened rut in the dirt road caught her foot. She stumbled but couldn't regain her footing and ended up sprawled on the road. "Ach, that's just brilliant," she muttered, searching for a tissue in her purse to wipe the mud off her hands. One of the knees of her jeans had torn open, and her scraped skin stung. Her stomach cramped pain-fully—reminding her she should have ordered some food to go with that whiskey.

The shape of a couple of large buildings loomed off the road in front of her. Barns, maybe? Perhaps she could lay low there for a few hours. Sleep seemed out of the question, but she needed time to figure out which end was up, and what she was going to do come daylight.

She picked up her pace as the buildings grew closer, but then swore silently and flattened herself against the road. Guards were silhouetted on either side of an iron fence. A lookout tower rose above the build-ings. There were two armored lorries parked in the yard outside. These buildings weren't barns—they were barracks.

Shite, shite, shite. Nora rolled over into the ditch as silently as she could, praying that the sentry hadn't spotted her in the darkness. Slowly, she crawled inch by inch back the way she'd come. The water from the day's rain had gathered in the ditch, and soon her entire front was soaked through. An owl hooted overhead. Her arms burned, and her scraped knee cried out in protest. Should she stay in the ditch until morning? No. She needed to get far away from the barracks. Otherwise, she'd be hauled in for questioning before daybreak. And she was in no condition to answer any questions right now. Not unless she wanted to end up in an insane asylum—or worse.

After she was out of sight of the barracks, she crawled out of the ditch and lifted herself painfully to her feet. A road on the left led away from both the town and the barracks, so she took it, her eyes peeled for any kind of shelter—a barn, a chicken coop, even a pile of old ruins would hide her from passing eyes. Finally, a dark shape emerged on the side of the road—a thick copse of trees. She stumbled toward it. The darkness thickened as she passed under the first branches. She had gone only a few feet when she tripped again. This time, she didn't even try to get up for several minutes. Eventually, she pulled herself to sitting and leaned against the thick trunk of a tree. She found Eamon's rosary in her purse, pressed it to her lips, and started to pray.

An explosion ripped through the night, jolting her awake. Immediately her instincts—and training—kicked in. She threw herself to the ground and covered her head. Shouts and cheers followed the explosion. Something shattered through the trees and landed with a thud beside her.

She opened her eyes and peeked through her arms. Lying on the ground at her feet was the naked, bloodied body of a man.

Chapter Nine

Nora stifled her screams, her wide eyes fixed on the man splayed on the ground beside her. He moaned, and she pressed her hands against her mouth. The men on the road jeered, and someone shouted, "We'll come back when it's light to collect the bodies, lads." The roar of lorries bumping down the uneven road faded. Then silence.

"Jesus, Mary, and Joseph," Nora breathed. She was shaking too badly to stand, but she managed to crawl closer to where the red-haired man lay bleeding. The clouds had cleared, and the moon shone through the trees. She felt for a pulse—he was still alive. "Hello?" she whispered. "Can you hear me?" His only answer was a tortured moan. He did not even open his eyes.

Nora scrambled to her feet, then leaned against the nearest tree as a wave of dizziness passed over her. "Right. Get yourself together," she muttered. Moving as slowly and quietly as she could manage, she crept through the trees until she could see the road. There was a rough crater in the middle of it. Around it, glowing eerily in the moonlight, lay the destroyed remains of several men. Nora covered her mouth in horror. The men had been blown up by some sort of explosive—a land mine, by the looks of it. Body parts were strewn around haphazardly, limbs torn from torsos, entrails spilling out into the dirt, faces unrecognizable. The stench of charred flesh filled her nostrils. Nora stepped back too quickly and found herself sprawled on the ground beside a chunk of flesh that was still burning. With a stifled yell, she got to her feet and ran back to the man in the woods. The sole survivor of this massacre.

He was still breathing. She stripped off her jacket and covered his torso, laying it gently over him so as to not exacerbate his injuries. What was she supposed to do now? She couldn't leave him here to die alone in the woods. But she knew she couldn't hope to carry him—or even drag him—very far. She looked up at the sky. How long until the soldiers came back?

Go, get out of here, get back to the cathedral, she told herself. But the man at her feet moaned again, and his eyes fluttered open.

"Shh, it's okay, I'm going to help you." She placed her hand on his forehead and smoothed back his singed hair, then gathered leaves and light branches and covered the rest of his body as best she could. "You must stay quiet," she said, not sure if he could even hear her. Her own ears were still ringing from the blast. "If they come back, they might look for you. I'm going to get help."

But from where? Who could she even trust? She squeezed his hand lightly, then found her way back to the road, praying she wouldn't step on anyone. Once clear of the bodies, she ran. The sun was starting to lighten the horizon. Soon she spotted a thatched, whitewashed cottage across a field. She made for it, keeping an eye out for soldiers all the while. A figure—a young woman, judging from the shape of her—emerged from the door of the cottage, carrying a basket under one arm. Seeing Nora, she stood stock still. Nora kept running until she reached her.

"Help," Nora gasped, doubling over in front of the woman, who looked to be in her late teens or early twenties. "I need help."

"Are you hurt?" the girl asked, setting down her basket and taking Nora by the arm.

"No. There was an explosion on the road—"

"We heard it," the girl said. "What happened?"

"I can explain later," Nora said. "But a man is badly injured. He needs help. I can't carry him myself."

"You'd best come inside," the girl said, looking down the road. Nora followed her into the cottage. The interior was dark, lit by a couple of oil lamps and a fire burning in the hearth at the end of the main room. The sweet, smoky smell of peat filled the room. "Ma!" the girl yelled. "Da!"

A man and a woman came out of another room behind the fireplace. "Who is this? What are you yellin' about, Pidge?"

"She just showed up. Said that sound we heard was an explosion, and someone's been hurt."

Both of the adults eyed Nora suspiciously. "Who are you, then, and how d'you know about this?"

Nora glanced around the room, hoping something would give her an idea as to what kind of people these were. A tall pine dresser stood against the wall, its shelves filled with plates, bowls, and mugs. A settle bed with a high back stood against another wall. A wooden table with a bench and three chairs was the only other furniture in the room. A brooch lay on the dresser, beside a bowl of flour. It was the same brooch she'd seen in the photos Aunt Margaret had showed her of the Cumann na mBan. She took a chance on the truth.

"I was hiding from the soldiers in the woods. I fell asleep but was woken by the sound of an explosion. Then a man landed at my feet. He's badly wounded. When I went out onto the road . . ." She shuddered. "It looked as though several men had been killed."

"God between us and all harm!" the woman of the house exclaimed, crossing herself. Her husband and daughter did the same, and Nora followed suit.

"I came looking for help," Nora said. "I don't know how much longer he'll last." The husband and wife exchanged glances.

"I'll collect Stephen from the field and go with the cart," he said.

"Are you sure, Sean?" the woman said, her eyes pleading. "What if they find you there?"

"The soldiers left," Nora said hastily. "But they said they'd come back when it was light enough to collect the bodies." They all glanced at the window. The sun was just peeking above the fields.

"I'm allowed to drive on the roads by my own farm, am I not?" the man said hotly. "They've no reason to arrest me!"

"What if it's a trap?" his wife argued with a sharp glance at Nora.

"I swear I'm telling the truth," Nora said. "You'll see for yourself. The mine went off maybe a mile down the road. He's in the woods, about a hundred yards to the left of the explosion. I covered him with some branches and my coat." At the mention of her coat, they all gave her a once-over. She was sure she looked a fright—covered in mud, with one knee torn and bleeding and her hair a wild, tangled mess. But she didn't care. "Please, I told him I'd find help. I'll go with you."

"Don't be absurd," the woman said. "You look dead on your feet. We'll let the men go." She nodded curtly to her husband, who grabbed his cap and jacket from a hook on the wall and left without another word.

"I'll go too, Ma," the young girl said, reaching for a shawl.

"You'll do no such thing. Now go fetch a basin of water, and let's get this girl cleaned up." The younger woman looked keen to argue, but she went outside and came back with a bucket of water, which she poured into a shallow basin and warmed up with water from the kettle that hung on a hook over the fire. Nora sank into the chair she was offered, feeling dazed and exhausted.

"I'm Mrs. Kathleen Gillies," the older woman said, dipping a cloth into the basin and handing it to Nora. "This is my daughter Hannah, but everyone calls her Pidge. And you are . . . ?"

"Nora O'Reilly." She rubbed her face with the cloth the girl had offered her and rinsed it out before moving on to her arms and hands.

"And what's your business here, Nora O'Reilly? What has you running?"

Nora wondered if Mrs. Gillies was trying to bait her in order to determine her allegiance. There hadn't been enough time to think of a convincing cover story. What was she to say—that she'd come from the future to help a man she'd never met? She pretended to wash her face again while thinking of a suitable lie.

"Let her rest a minute, Ma!" Pidge exclaimed. "Cuppa, Nora?"

"Please, thank you," Nora said. Mrs. Gillies stood in front of her, hands on her generous hips. Her dark hair was pulled back into a loose bun, and she wore a simple, long-sleeved brown dress that fell to mid-calf. Her stockings and shoes were both black, and she wore a clean beige apron over her dress.

Pidge handed Nora a cup of tea, which she accepted with a grateful smile. The hot liquid brought new life to her exhausted, aching body. Pidge was a handsome girl with a wide mouth and dark curls that fell to her shoulders. She wore a plain dress much like her mother's. She looked at Nora with open curiosity.

"I'm not a criminal, if that's what you're asking," Nora said cautiously.

"But you said you were runnin'," Mrs. Gillies pointed out. She took a seat at the wooden table beside Nora and poured her own cup of tea.

"I arrived from Belfast earlier today," Nora said, knowing she'd not be able to hide her Ulster accent.

"On your own?" Mrs. Gillies asked with a raised eyebrow.

"Aye." She remembered one of the history lessons Eamon had given her over a pot of tea many years ago. Before the country was officially divided, the Protestant majority in the North had fought the prospect of a Catholic-run independent Ireland tooth and nail. After the treaty, Catholics in the six northern counties were beaten and murdered in unprecedented numbers, their bodies mutilated and left as a warning to other Catholics. So-called match and petrol men burned out and terrorized entire Catholic neighborhoods, all with the tacit bless-ing—including weapons and soldiers—of the British Crown. Pogroms, Eamon had called them. The message was clear: get out. Thousands of refugees streamed over the newly created border into the Free State, seeking refuge in a country already traumatized by a vicious war with Britain and a looming civil war of its own.

Nora's cheeks burned. This was material she could use to form her story, but she had to be careful what she gave away. She didn't know how her new hosts would react. But even so, she could never pretend to be a supporter of the British. "My family was burned out by an Orange mob in Belfast. I came down to stay with my uncle in Kildare, only I couldn't find him. His home was empty. Looked like it had been wrecked."

Mrs. Gillies and Pidge shared a look.

"These soldiers started harassing me on the street while I was look-ing for another place to stay. I ran away from them, but they chased me. I hid until I found a stand of trees to sleep in for the night. And that's when I heard the explosion."

"Our boys, harassing a young woman on the street!" Mrs. Gillies looked scandalized. "I would never have thought them capable of it!"

"They're not 'our boys,' Ma," Pidge muttered. "Not anymore."

"They are and you know it," her mother retorted. "Every one of them, born and bred in these hills."

Pidge muttered something that sounded like "traitors," but she went to stoke the fire before her mother could offer a reply.

Mrs. Gillies turned her attention back to Nora. "And you say you don't know who detonated the mine?"

"I didn't see any of the soldiers," Nora explained. "Only the bodies."

"It could have been ours, Ma, so close to the barracks," Pidge said, her forehead creased.

"Hush, girl!" her mother snapped. Her eyes roamed over Nora. "Is this how they dress in Belfast, then?"

"Oh . . . aye, these are my traveling clothes. My bags were taken by the soldiers, so they were." Nora looked self-consciously at her muddy clothing. The sooner she could blend in, the better.

Mrs. Gillies clucked her tongue. "Well, you look about the size of my Pidge. Go on now, the two of you, and see if you can't find something decent for Nora to wear."

Pidge smiled warmly. "Come on, then," she said to Nora, leading the way to a small room in the back of the cottage. "This is my room," Pidge explained. "Stephen sleeps in the loft." The room was tiny and plainly furnished, with a metal bedstead and a homemade quilt covering the mattress. A chest of drawers stood against one wall, and dresses hung from wire hangers on a hook behind the door. A crucifix had been nailed above the bed.

"I really don't want to be a bother," Nora said.

"Don't be daft!" Pidge exclaimed. "You can't be going out wearing only that." She appraised Nora's T-shirt with interest while she handed her a striped blouse and a long green skirt. "D'you have stockings?"

"Um . . . no. Just my socks, that is."

"Here's a pair of mine, then," Pidge said, digging around in the chest of drawers and pulling out a thick black pair.

"Thank you, Pidge. You've all been very kind. I'll return these things to you as soon as I can get some clothes of my own."

"It's no matter. I'll leave you to get dressed." With that, she left the room. Nora sighed and stripped off her ruined jeans and T-shirt. She shrugged the blouse over her head and pulled on the skirt. The garments were lighter than they looked, and she felt better once she was dressed. Perhaps looking the part would help her play the part. She took Pidge's hairbrush off the top of the chest and tried to work out some of the knots in her hair. She considered putting it up like Mrs. Gillies's hair, but she had no idea how to do that. Besides, for all she knew, it might be a style reserved for married women. Carrying her folded jeans and T-shirt in her arms, she went back into the main living area, where Mrs.

Gillies and Pidge were having a hushed conversation. She hesitated, not wanting to intrude.

"Ah, that's much better," Mrs. Gillies said, looking at Nora approvingly. "We'll have some breakfast while we wait for the men." She moved to the end of the table, cutting thick slabs of bread and coating them with butter. Pidge poured everyone more tea but remained silent.

Nora accepted the bread gratefully. "Ta. And thank you for helping the wounded man. I hope he's all right."

"We'll find out soon enough," Mrs. Gillies said, looking out the window. "Here they come now."

Pidge ran out of the cottage. "Da!" she yelled. "D'you find him?" Mrs. Gillies pushed up her sleeves and followed her daughter into the yard. Nora hovered uncertainly in the doorway.

"We found him, all right," Sean Gillies said. He and a young man lifted a body out of the back of a cart attached to a pair of horses. They'd wrapped the wounded man in a blanket and covered it with straw, bits of which floated to the ground as they brought him into the house. Pidge and Mrs. Gillies hurriedly cleared the table of their breakfast dishes so the men could lay him down. Mrs. Gillies unwrapped the blanket from around him and gasped.

"Oh, sweet Jesus, it's Frankie Halpin!"

"Oh, Stephen," Pidge moaned, wrapping her arms around the young man who had helped bring Frankie into the house. She saw Nora watching them and explained, "This is my brother, Stephen. Frankie's his best friend." Stephen, a tall, thin lad of about eighteen, stared down at the table, his eyes burning with anger. Without a word, he tore himself out of Pidge's arms and stormed out of the house.

"Stephen!" Mrs. Gillies called after him.

"Leave him be," Mr. Gillies warned.

"What if he goes after them? You know they're only looking for a reason to lock him up like the others!"

"He's smarter than that. Just let him blow off some steam."

"He's still alive," Nora said, feeling a faint pulse in Frankie's wrist. "But he needs a hospital. Can you take him?"

The Gillies family exchanged a long look; then Mrs. Gillies spoke. "It would be best for us to care for him here."

Nora stared her down. "He needs proper medical attention. He could die!"

"Open your eyes, Nora," Pidge said. "The government was trying to kill him. You think taking him to hospital will help? It will only make it easier for them to finish the job. I'll get the bandages, Ma."

"And the iodine," Mrs. Gillies called after her. She brought out a stack of clean cloths from the bedroom and began laying them out on the sideboard of the dresser. Nora grabbed the two pillows from Pidge's room and used them to elevate Frankie's head and feet. If she couldn't convince them to take this man to the hospital, at least she could help them. She'd been trained in emergency first aid; now was the time to use it.

"I need some soap," she said. "Let's get him washed; then we'll treat his wounds. We'll need to see if anything's broken—I don't see how he could have survived that blast in one piece."

Mrs. Gillies regarded her curiously as she tore a sheet into strips and dipped it into the boiling water on the stove. "Are you a nurse, then?"

"No, not really. I've just had some medical training."

"As have I," Mrs. Gillies said. "It came in handy during the Tan War, that's for certain."

Nora said nothing. For her, the War of Independence had been almost a hundred years ago. For this family, it had only just ended—and they lived in fear that, should the Anglo-Irish Treaty fall apart, it could start again at any moment. But as Nora picked the straw and mud out of the boy's bloodied leg, she couldn't help but marvel that their own countrymen had done this to Frankie and those other boys. This was different than the Troubles—she didn't consider the Protestant

Unionists of Northern Ireland her own countrymen. They belonged to Britain, and she belonged to Ireland. But this was Irish against Irish.

Pidge returned with a roll of bandages and a jar of some kind of ointment, then grabbed a cloth and swabbed Frankie's torso.

"What was it like, Da?" she asked. Mr. Gillies paced the room while the women worked, one eye always on the window.

"It's not for your ears, Pidge," he said.

"But was it like she said?" Pidge persisted.

He shot his daughter an exasperated look. "Aye. 'Twas like she said. The bodies were still there. The birds were already feasting."

Mrs. Gillies crossed herself with a bloodstained hand.

"Why'd you not bring them back?" Pidge demanded.

"Because the army would come looking for them. Given the state of things, they'll probably not notice one man missing. But if they were all missing, they'd be searching this farm by noon. And what would we do with the bodies, anyway?"

"Can we not bury our own dead?" Pidge's cheeks were flushed. "Did you not recognize any of them?"

"I didn't look too closely, to be honest." He dipped his chin and stared at the floor. "Even these lads' own families would be hard-pressed to identify them, the state they were in. We found young Frankie in the woods, right where our friend here said he would be." He regarded Nora thoughtfully. "That's a sorry thing for a woman to witness. Your stomach must be lined with steel."

"I've seen worse," Nora said, thinking of a village in Rwanda her team had visited after the genocide. The bodies had been dead for a week, left to rot in the unforgiving African sun. And there had been children . . . so many children, their tiny heads bashed against walls, chests split open from navel to sternum.

"In Belfast, you mean?" Mrs. Gillies said in a shocked tone.

"Aye," Nora said quickly.

"I'm sorry to hear it," Mr. Gillies said. "John Brennan's wife just took in three Belfast orphans. Arrived on the train yesterday." Nora nodded, wondering about her own family, and why they had stayed when so many others had fled. She'd have to ask Aunt Margaret about it . . . if she ever made it back to her own time.

"They arrested Frankie just last week. I thought he'd've been sent off to Mountjoy Prison by now," Mrs. Gillies said, as if trying to reason it out in her head. "Never thought they'd do something like this."

"They'll call it a 'retaliation,' I'm sure," Pidge snapped. "As if we don't have the right to fight for our own country!"

"Hush, Pidge," Mrs. Gillies said. Her eyes flicked toward Nora.

Nora took the bull by the horns. "Mrs. Gillies, you're all right. I'm as Republican as they get. You don't have to worry about me repeating anything."

"And who's to say *we're* Republicans?" Mrs. Gillies shot back.

Nora cocked an eyebrow. "You've said as much. But it doesn't matter either way. I didn't know which side this man was on when I came to get help. And I don't care about your politics, either. I'll help you here with Frankie, and then I'll be on my way." She felt along his shinbone and winced. "We'll need some sticks for splints. I'm not much for setting bones—"

"I'll do it," Mrs. Gillies said briskly. "Let's just pray he stays out cold. Sean, can you get us some straight pieces to use for splints? And the poitín, in case he comes to."

Mr. Gillies glanced out the window again, then left the cottage.

"Nora, you've done right by Frankie here, and we're grateful," Mrs. Gillies said. "I'll not have you going back into Kildare on your own, not after what you've experienced there. Did you get any sleep at all last night?"

"Not much," Nora admitted. Adrenaline had been keeping her on her feet, but it wouldn't last forever.

"Then you'll stay with us. You can have the settle bed." She nodded toward the large bench against the far wall. "You said you have family in these parts?"

"Only an uncle, but I don't know where he's gone. And thank you for your kindness, but I'm sure I can find a room in town." She needed to get back to the cathedral as soon as possible to find the Brigidine Sisters.

"Well, you're a grown woman, and I'll not be making decisions for you, but I insist you stay until you're rested and recovered from your ordeal. Sean will take you back into town later today if that's what you want, and he can help you in finding a room. As for your uncle . . . well, it seems like half the men in the country are in Mountjoy, Kilmainham, North Dublin Union, or one of the other prisons. Perhaps he's been arrested. One can be arrested for anything these days—even for the contents of one's private thoughts, so it would seem."

Frankie twitched.

"Christ have mercy, does he have to wake up now?" Mrs. Gillies muttered. "Where is Sean with the poitín?"

A minute later Mr. Gillies rushed into the room with several thick pieces of timber and a glass bottle of clear liquid, which he set on the sideboard. Frankie moaned, and his eyelids fluttered open.

"How're you feeling, Frankie?" Mr. Gillies asked, leaning in close.

Frankie looked around at them all, his eyes wide. "Where am I? What happened?"

"Shh, it's okay, you're safe. You're at our house now," Pidge said softly. He gave her a blank look.

"What? What did you say?"

"O'course. His hearing is still impaired from the blast," Nora said, remembering how it had made her own ears ring.

"Well, damn," Mr. Gillies said. He tried raising his voice. "Frankie! Can you hear me?"

Frankie stared at him for a moment, then nodded. "A bit. I can make out what you're saying."

"There was a land mine. Do you remember?" Mr. Gillies asked loudly.

"I . . . I remember being tied to the other lads. And then I was flying . . . and now I'm here," Frankie said. He closed his eyes again.

"Let him rest," Pidge said, but her father leaned in and shook Frankie gently.

"You're badly hurt, lad. We need to set some broken bones. But try your best not to cry out, will ye? We don't want the Staters to hear you. D'you understand? Now I'm going to give you something to help with the pain." He lifted the bottle to Frankie's lips. "Take some good swigs, as much as you can."

"Mr. Gillies, are you sure we shouldn't take him to hospital?" Nora asked. "I really think—"

"Thank you, Miss O'Reilly, but we know how to take care of our own," Mr. Gillies cut in. "Pidge, go fetch Stephen. He won't have gone far. And then close all the windows."

Pidge hurried to obey. Stephen mustn't have been far because the two of them came in a scant moment later, and Pidge immediately started to close the shutters.

"Hold him down, Stephen," Mr. Gillies said.

"What can I—" Nora started to ask, but Mrs. Gillies stepped in front of her and said, "We'll take it from here. You can keep the water boiling, if you don't mind."

Nora frowned but took a brick of turf from a basket on the floor and added it to the fire. Then she stared at the smoke while trying to block out the sound of Frankie's screams.

Chapter Ten

Finally Frankie passed out again and the Gillieses were able to work in silence. Nora helped however she could, by sterilizing bandages and passing jars of strong-smelling ointments. She boiled the bloody rags and fetched clean water from the pump in the yard. She felt useful again a wonderful feeling.

"Thank you, Nora," Mrs. Gillies said, accepting a towel to dry off her hands, which she'd just cleaned of blood. Nora took back the towel and handed her a cup of tea.

"You were amazing, so you were," Nora said. "So calm and efficient."

"Ah, well, it's not the first of our lads I've had to tidy up a bit." Mrs. Gillies sank into one of the chairs they'd shoved against the wall and wiped her forehead with the back of her hand.

They all sat silently. Stephen hadn't spoken a word all morning. After a moment, he and his father both stood. "Well, back to work, then," Mr. Gillies said. "We've already lost a good few hours."

"We should move him," Mrs. Gillies said. "'Twill be no good for any of us, havin' him on our table if the Free State comes knocking."

Mr. Gillies nodded grimly, casting a sideways glance at Nora.

"She's fine, Sean," Mrs. Gillies said. "She'd 'a left long ago if she was going to turn us in."

"O'course I won't," Nora said. "I swear to it."

"The wall, then," Mr. Gillies said, nodding to his son. "Easy now." Together they gathered up the sheet beneath Frankie, holding it taut so it hung like a hammock. They headed into Mr. and Mrs. Gillies's room, which was hardly larger than Pidge's. Pidge and Mrs. Gillies pushed the large chest of drawers to one side; then Mrs. Gillies bent down and lifted a latch near the floor and another one above her head. A section of the wall swung open to reveal a tiny space, just large enough to accommodate a man. Pidge stripped the quilt off her parents' bed and spread it out on the floor. With difficulty, they eased Frankie into the small space.

"We added this when we built this room after Pidge was born," Mrs. Gillies told Nora. "Used it to hide the lads during the war with the British. Now it looks like we'll be using it again."

"I'll sit with him," Pidge said. "If I hear any commotion, I'll close him in and move the chest back."

"Let's pray there won't be any commotion," Mrs. Gillies said. "But there's a farm to be run. Off you go," she said to her husband and son. Then she turned to Nora. "And you, my dear, need some sleep."

"I couldn't," Nora protested. "At least I can sit with Frankie if Pidge has other things to do."

"I insist," Mrs. Gillies said. She took Nora's elbow and steered her into Pidge's room. "You saved a man's life today. The least you can do is reward yourself with a little sleep."

She closed the door, and Nora sat down hard on the stiff mattress. The adrenaline was finally wearing off. She collapsed back onto the bed and stared at the ceiling.

There was no other way around it. This was no period festival, no practical joke, no dream or hallucination, no psychotic break. She had really traveled back in time to 1923. She'd run from the Free State Army, witnessed the massacre of several men, and saved Frankie Halpin's life.

This can't be happening, her rational mind told her. But even though she did not understand how or why Brigid's relic had done this, it was undeniable that it had.

Panic flared in her chest as the implications sunk in. Was she stuck here forever?

I have to get out of here. I have to go back to Kildare. She sat up and swung her legs off the bed. But as she stood, a rush of dizziness made the room spin, so she sat back down, her head between her hands. *Sleep first. Then Kildare.*

Sleep would not come easy. What of Thomas? He had been driven from her thoughts by the chaos of the last few hours, but now that she was alone in this quiet room, his face surfaced in her mind again. She reached for her purse to examine his picture, then realized it wasn't with her.

Had she left it in the front room in all the commotion? Another jolt of adrenaline got her off the bed. What if they went through her purse? Its contents were decidedly not from 1923. The British government had issued her driver's license, and it had her date of birth on it. There were euros stamped 2005. The bag also contained her tourist brochure for Kilmainham Gaol, her cell phone, and her picture of Thomas.

She tiptoed toward the door and opened it gently, suppressing her panic. Mrs. Gillies wasn't in the main room. No one was. She knocked gently at the other bedroom door and opened it when Pidge answered. Pidge was sitting on the bed, a pile of mending in her lap.

"All right, Nora?" she asked.

"Yes, I'm just looking for my bag—the one I had with me when I arrived. Have you seen it?"

"Oh, yes, I tucked it in the corner when they brought Frankie in, so it wouldn't get blood on it," Pidge said. She started to get to her feet, but Nora waved her down.

"You're grand. I'll find it," she said. She went back into the main room. Mrs. Gillies was standing by the door, Nora's purse in her hands.

"Is this what you're looking for?" she asked. Her expression was inscrutable. Nora met her eyes and tried to keep her face equally neutral.

"Yes, thank you," she said, taking the bag. Was it her imagination, or did the other woman hold on to it for just a fraction of a second too long?

She felt Mrs. Gillies's gaze on her as she walked back to Pidge's room, trying to keep her steps as even as possible. Even after she closed the door, she maintained her aura of calm. How many other secrets were hidden in this house?

She unclasped her bag and looked inside. Everything seemed to be there, but she couldn't tell if it had been rifled through. She tucked Eamon's rosary in her pocket. She'd toss the Kilmainham brochure in the fire the first moment she had. And her phone, the euros, and her modern ID could be buried somewhere if need be. But surely she wouldn't be here, in the past, that long. The woman at the cathedral had told her she had a job to do—to help Thomas. Surely she could go home as soon as she found him and helped him. She glanced at the photo one more time. Then, cradling the bag in her arms, she sank down into the mattress and let the sleep that had been clawing at her senses take her away.

When she awoke, her first thought was that she was back in Sudan, on her cot in the staff quarters. But there was a plaster ceiling above her . . .

Belfast. I came home for Mick's funeral. No, something else had happened after that. Slowly, her mind caught up. Dublin. Aunt Margaret. Kilmainham. *Kildare.*

She sat up, her fingers gripping the homemade quilt wrapped around her. Her body was still stiff and sore, but sleep had helped somewhat. Wide eyes surveyed the room and listened for voices. *I'm still here.* She threw back the quilt and stood up. Her purse had fallen on the floor, its contents spilling out. She picked up Thomas's picture and a pen. As best she could, she scratched out the *Killed in action, 1923* written on the back. She didn't need any more questions about why she was searching for a dead man. Then she tucked her purse under Pidge's bed. That would have to do for now.

Quietly, she eased herself into the main room. The house seemed empty. "Pidge?" she called out softly. There was no one in Mr. and Mrs. Gillies's room, but the door of the secret nook was ajar and a soft moan escaped throughout the crack. Nora crossed the room and pulled the door open a little wider. Then she knelt down by the injured man.

"How are you feeling?" she asked, unsure whether he could even hear her.

"Like I've been blown up," Frankie answered, but he managed a small smile. Nora's heart constricted. The boy looked to be about the age Eamon had been at his death.

"I'll see if I can find Mrs. Gillies. She might have something more for the pain."

"Who are you? Are you Cumann na mBan?"

"No. I'm just . . . visiting. My name's Nora."

"Nora," he repeated. "They say you're the one who found me."

"More like you found me. You nearly landed right on top of me."

He laughed, then winced. "Well, lucky for me I did." Then his eyes darkened. "Not so lucky for the other lads."

"No." Nora looked away. "I'm sorry for your loss." She held up the picture of Thomas so that Frankie could see it. "I'm looking for this man. Thomas Heaney. He's IRA. Do you know him?" A horrible thought struck her. What if she was too late? What if she'd been sent here to stop the bombing? "Was he with you yesterday?"

Frankie looked at the picture with glazed eyes. "No," he said. "I don't think I know him. But I only just signed up." He looked like he was about to say something more, but his eyes closed and his breathing steadied. Nora didn't press him. She adjusted his blankets and then closed the hidden door most of the way, leaving only a crack of light shining in on him.

She found Mrs. Gillies in the yard, filling a tub with water. "Ah, here you are! I was just about to wake you. How did you rest?"

"Grand, ta," Nora said. "What time is it?"

"Just about time for tea," Mrs. Gillies said. "I expect the men back shortly. What do you have there?" She nodded at the photograph in Nora's hand.

"I was wondering if you recognized this man," Nora said, handing it to her. As expected, Mrs. Gillies turned it over and read the name on the back.

"Thomas Heaney," she said. "No, I don't know anyone by that name. There's the Heaney family down in Stradbally, but I don't believe they have a Thomas. Might be a cousin of theirs, though. Handsome fellow. A friend of yours?"

"A . . . distant relation," Nora said. "My cousin in Belfast asked me if I would look for him while I was visiting my uncle."

"Well, I'm afraid I can't help you, but I'm sure there's someone in these parts who can. Ah, here come the men."

While Mr. Gillies and Stephen washed, Nora helped Mrs. Gillies spread a clean cloth on the table and lay out the crockery. Mrs. Gillies brought over a plate of potato cakes and a pot of stew that had been hanging from the crane over the fire, plus a basket filled with warm wedges of soda bread. Pidge came in through the front door and set down a large basket of washing. Nora joined her at the basin on the sideboard, where they washed their hands.

"Did you get any sleep?" Pidge asked with a friendly smile. She had a dimple in her cheek Nora hadn't noticed before.

"I did, yes. I checked in on Frankie. He seemed to be in quite a bit of pain, but I think he fell back to sleep. I was wondering if you might have something for him when he wakes again."

"That boy is full of poitín already," Mrs. Gillies said from behind them. "But I'll have a look at him when he awakens." She beckoned them to the table. Nora and Pidge sat on one side, across from Stephen,

98

and Mr. and Mrs. Gillies sat on the ends. They all bowed their heads, and Mr. Gillies said a prayer.

"Bless us, O Lord, and these thy gifts, which we are about to receive from thy bounty, through Christ our Lord." There was a moment of silence as they all thought of the men who had been blown apart the night before. Then Mr. Gillies said, "Amen," and they filled their plates with food.

Nora hadn't realized how hungry she was. The food was plain but surprisingly good. She'd never learned to cook, so she'd grown accustomed to eating whatever was available on the field—sometimes rice and beans, sometimes a boiled egg and fried chicken leg, sometimes noodles with spicy sauce. There were few foodies among humanitarian aid workers. Occasionally she and her colleagues would flee to the closest large city in search of a McDonald's or KFC, but these splurges usually left her stomach roiling, so she indulged infrequently.

"This is delicious," she told Mrs. Gillies between bites of stew.

"Thank you, dear. Pidge made it," Mrs. Gillies said with a proud glance at her daughter. "She'll make a fine wife someday."

Nora raised an eyebrow at this comment but said nothing. Pidge did not appear to be pleased with the compliment, but she, too, held her tongue. "It's wonderful," Nora told her.

"It's not all I'm good at," Pidge said, lifting her chin. "I can shoot straight through a can from two hundred yards."

"Oh yes, a fine skill for a respectable young woman to have," Mrs. Gillies snapped.

"I'm not a respectable young woman, Ma," Pidge said. "I'm a Republican."

"That's enough, Pidge," Mr. Gillies said.

"I don't know why you thought it was a good idea for her to learn how to shoot," Mrs. Gillies said, turning toward her husband.

"Every farmwife needs to know how to handle a rifle," he remarked calmly. "You're a fair shot yourself."

"Besides, Ma, it was Cumann na mBan who taught me most of it," Pidge said, coming to her father's defense.

"Are you both members?" Nora asked, intrigued. As a young woman she'd idolized the IRA women's auxiliary organization, but had never met someone with firsthand knowledge.

"We are, though apparently it's illegal now. As is possessing a gun, distributing anti-treaty literature, and assisting Republicans in any way," Pidge said haughtily.

"Well, we don't have it as bad as Nora did up in Belfast, I reckon," Mrs. Gillies said. "And it will all be over soon, Lord willing."

Stephen, who had wolfed down his food, pushed his chair back with a screech. "I'm going to brush the horses," he said, then left the house. Mrs. Gillies watched him go with a worried expression on her face.

"He's a quiet young man," Nora remarked. The others exchanged dark glances.

"Been that way ever since . . . well, since Nicky was killed," Pidge said. "He was our older brother. Fought in the Tan War. The Tans tortured and murdered him, then left his body on the church steps. Stephen was the one who found him."

"I'm . . . I'm so sorry," Nora said, closing her eyes against the image of Eamon in his hospital bed. "I shouldn't have said—"

"It's all right," Pidge said. "That was three years ago. But you can understand why we've no love for the Brits or those who want to get in bed with them."

"Tell us about your family, Nora," Mrs. Gillies said, her voice thick.

Nora stared down at her plate. "My father was killed when I was wee. Shot dead in our own home. Still don't know who did it, but it doesn't really matter. He was an IRA man. My mother couldn't handle it, so she took to the drink. She did her best, but it was really my brother Eamon who raised me."

"What happened to him?" Pidge asked softly.

"He was beaten to death by a Protestant gang. That's when I joined the cause."

"So you're Cumann na mBan as well!" Pidge exclaimed. "Why didn't you say so?"

"I told you I was a Republican, so I did," Nora said, trying to smile.

"Yes, but now we're sisters," Pidge said.

"Where is your poor mother, Nora?" Mr. Gillies asked.

"In the grave, along with the rest of my family," Nora said. "She drank herself to death."

"I thought you said you came here because your family was burned out of their home?" Mrs. Gillies asked with a forced-casual tone.

"My cousins," Nora quickly invented. "That's who I lived with after my mother died."

Mrs. Gillies looked embarrassed. "Of course. I'm so sorry. It must have been so hard for you to lose her that way."

"Aye," Nora admitted, cursing herself for the slipup. "Sometimes I'm still so angry with her. But other times I can't blame her. I think I feel sorry for her, the most." She blushed. She'd revealed too much of herself to these strangers. But Mrs. Gillies reached over and patted her arm.

"I know how you feel. It's a difficult thing, to wish for revenge and peace at the same time. Lord knows I of all people want a free Ireland—with no British masters. But at what price? When does it become too high? That's the question I struggle to answer."

"We're going to win this war, Ma. We're going to get the Republic we've been fighting for all these years. The one Nicky died for." Pidge's eyes were bright, and her cheeks were pink. "Isn't that right, Da?"

"It is, Pidge. But you leave the fighting to the men. There's plenty of other work for the women to do."

Pidge deflated and buttered another piece of bread.

"Why don't you show Sean and Pidge your photograph, Nora?" Mrs. Gillies said. "They might know your young man."

"What young man?" Pidge asked, watching with obvious curiosity as Nora retrieved the photo from the bookshelf where she'd set it before dinner. She passed it to Mr. Gillies.

"He's a distant relative," Nora explained. "I'm to try and find him while I'm here."

"He's IRA? Do you know what division he's stationed with?" he asked.

"No," Nora said. "That would help, I know. I believe it's somewhere near Kildare, but my cousin didn't know for sure."

"I don't recognize him, but there are so many lads in and out of these parts, and he could be stationed down in Kerry for all we know." He handed the photograph back to Nora, who surrendered it to Pidge's eager hands.

"Ooo, he's a right-looking fellow!" she exclaimed, giving Nora a wink.

"Behave yourself!" Mrs. Gillies said. "He's a relative of Nora's!"

"Yes, but he's no relative of mine!" Pidge said, laughing. "Is his hair blond? It looks shiny in this photo."

"It's gray, actually," Nora said. Then she added quickly, "According to my cousin. I've never seen him."

"Is it really?" Mrs. Gillies asked, leaning over Pidge's shoulder. "I didn't notice before. But his face looks so young."

"Betty Maguire went gray when she was only twenty-four," Pidge said. "I suppose it can happen to men as well."

"Do you recognize him?" Nora asked.

Pidge shook her head. "I wish! But no. Don't look so sad. I've a plan."

"Oh, aye?"

"Indeed." Pidge lifted her chin. "You've helped us—God knows what Stephen would have done if his best friend had been killed—so I'll help you. It will be easy. Some of us Cumann na mBan girls are going over to where one of the columns is training tomorrow. We'll do some cooking and clean up the place. They might be soldiers, but most of them haven't a clue how to keep a room tidy. You'll bring that photo and come with me. Someone there is bound to know where to find your man."

"Sounds like a fair enough plan," Mr. Gillies said as he pushed his chair back. He kissed his wife on the cheek. "I'll be in the barn."

"So what do you think?" Pidge asked Nora as they gathered up the dishes.

Nora nodded firmly. On the one hand, she wanted to go back to the cathedral to find the Brigidine Sisters and try to get some answers. On the other hand . . . she was here, so she might as well look for Thomas. "I think it's a brilliant idea. I'd love to go with you tomorrow. If you don't mind me staying the night, that is . . ."

"Of course we don't mind!" Mrs. Gillies said. "I've never turned a person away from my door, and I don't mean to start with you."

Nora spent the rest of the evening trying to make herself useful—and trying to gather information. She feigned ignorance as much as she could, and Pidge was more than happy to chatter away about the war and the ever-shifting politics. Nora tried not to sound too eager; she didn't want to give them reason to suspect her of being a Free State spy. But Pidge seemed happy to be able to talk with another woman interested in politics. As they swept out the chicken coop, Pidge went on about the late Michael Collins, the great hero of the War of Independence, who had, in her opinion, betrayed his country by agreeing to the Anglo-Irish Treaty, which made Ireland a free state, but still a dominion within the British Empire.

The worst part of the treaty, according to Pidge, was the division of the country's thirty-two counties. The southern twenty-six counties were now part of the Free State, while the northern six remained part of the United Kingdom. And thus the conflict that would define Nora's life was born.

"Just look at your own poor family, Nora," Pidge said. "That's all at Michael Collins's door—him and that Protestant bastard Craig, the so-called prime minister of Northern Ireland. Why settle for a mere free state when a full republic was within our grasp? And to think that Collins was one of the top men in the IRA. He, of all people, should have been willing to take the fight all the way, to finish it, once and for all. Now that job is up to the few of us who are left. Of course, he did a great deal for Ireland, and I was sorry when he was killed, but he chose the wrong side in the end."

"Aye," Nora said. "It was a shame, so it was. We could have won if he had stayed true to the Republican cause."

Pidge stopped sweeping and gave her a strange look. Nora dropped her eyes. *Eejit. You need to act like you don't know how this all ends.*

"We *will* win, Nora. Don't you believe that?"

"I want that, I do. But sometimes it feels as though the cards are stacked against us. Don't you find?"

Pidge took up her broom again, and Nora relaxed. "That's nothing new—they've always been stacked against us. We brought the British to their knees, and if Cosgrave and his crew insist on getting into bed with the British, then we'll bring them to their knees as well."

"D'you mind if I ask how old you are?" Nora asked.

Pidge drew herself up straight. "I'm twenty-two. Why do you ask?"

"No reason," Nora said quickly. "You just seem very . . ."

"Opinionated?" Pidge said with a smile. "That's what Da always calls me."

"I was going to say 'mature.' You're far more mature than I was at your age, so you are."

"I'll thank you to tell *that* to my parents." Pidge blushed. "They're grand, really. They just worry about me."

Nora felt a rush of affection toward the younger woman. "Something tells me you can take care of yourself just fine."

Chapter Eleven

Nora and Pidge rose early the next morning. The horizon was a haze of mauve through the soft rain. After a slice of bread and a quick cup of tea, Pidge gathered several heavy loaves of soda bread her mother had made the day before and wrapped them in tea towels, along with a half dozen blocks of butter. She brought out two bicycles from the back shed and filled their baskets with the loaves and butter, covering the food with several sheets of newspaper to shield it from the rain.

"Got your photograph?" she asked Nora.

"Aye. Where exactly are we going?"

"West," Pidge said simply. "If we get stopped, we'll say we're going to my sick aunt's in Portarlington."

"You've done this before, so you have."

"Oh, plenty of times. The Tan War kept us all busy. I've only been to this particular camp once before, though."

Nora hadn't been on a bicycle since she was a child, so she wobbled along unsteadily behind Pidge. Judging from the way she wove around potholes and stayed clear of the ruts, the younger girl was obviously a seasoned rider. After they'd been riding for almost an hour, Nora could no longer hold back a groan.

"All right?" Pidge called back.

"Grand. It's just that my arse is killing me. I'm not used to a bike, so I'm not."

Pidge stopped, and Nora gratefully slid off the seat for a moment's rest. "How'd you get around up in Belfast then? Did you have a car?" Pidge's eyes were round.

"Not my own, no," Nora admitted. "I, um, walked a lot." She had no idea what year public transportation started in Ireland.

"We're almost there. Come, let's walk for a bit. We should run into a scout soon."

"Are your brother and father involved in the fighting?" Nora asked, thinking of her own family.

"They are, though Ma tries to keep them out of it. I think she invents urgent things to do around the farm to keep them close. We've a horse with a broken leg that Da and Stephen are tending to now. Wouldn't surprise me if she broke that horse's leg herself." Her lips quirked in a sardonic smile.

"But they're not with this column—the one we're headed to now?"

"No, this group is from further north. But the Staters have taken over their area, so they've had to train elsewhere. I don't know many of these lads."

They walked in silence for several minutes, pushing their bicycles beside them. The land around them was rugged, patches of green interspersed with dark gray rock. The rain continued to drizzle softly, and Nora shivered despite the warmth of her borrowed wool coat. Pidge led them off the road and onto a small, nearly indecipherable trail. They hauled their bikes over boulders and the occasional fallen log and leapt across a narrow stream that frothed and bubbled under their feet. The farther they went, the harder it was to believe they'd find anyone out there. They seemed so far removed from civilization, as though they had entered an ancient world where giants and gods walked freely.

Nora's thoughts found their way back to Thomas. Once she found him, once they were face to face in the waking world, he'd have to answer her questions. Would he look the same in real life? Her stomach twinged at the prospect of their first real-life encounter. How would he react to seeing her? Perhaps they'd lock eyes . . . then he would rush to her, maybe grab her hands or throw his arms around her neck. "You've come at last," he'd moan. "How can I thank you?"

She rolled her eyes and gave her head a shake. This wasn't some trashy bodice-ripper novel. This was war. She had to keep her head on straight.

"Houl on," a voice barked at them. Nora's fingers clenched on the handlebars of her bike. Her eyes scanned the brush and boulders around them but saw nothing.

"It's me, Jimmy—or have you forgotten me already, you lout?" Pidge called out. A young man in a dirty beige shirt and brown cap stepped out from behind a crop of boulders. Pidge raised an eyebrow at the hurling stick clutched in his hand. "Now just what are you intending to do with that?"

Jimmy swung it around. "Just doin' my job, Pidge. How are ye?"

"Grand, thank ye," she said, smiling coquettishly. "You going to let us through? Or do we have to fight our way in?"

"Who's this?" he asked with a jut of his chin.

"This is Nora. She's Cumann na mBan up in Belfast. She's going to help me feed the lads."

"How d'you know she's not an informer?"

Nora scowled, but she let Pidge do the talking. She was well aware of how the IRA dealt with informers.

"Because she saved your man Frankie Halpin's life, for one. And she lost almost everything to the Unionists in the North. She's one of us, Jimmy. She's even staying with my family."

He peered at Nora from under the brim of his cap. *So young. They're all so young.*

"What's your name?" he asked.

"Nora O'Reilly."

"And what do—"

Pidge cut him off. "Leave it alone, Jimmy. She's with me. That should be good enough. When have you ever doubted me, hey?" She ripped a chunk of bread from a loaf in her basket and tossed it to him. "You look half-starved," she said, her voice softer.

He inhaled the scent of the bread and sighed happily. "Would be, too, if it weren't for you lot."

"How about a fag, then? As trade for the bread?"

"You drive a hard bargain, Pidge. I'm down to my last pack. But I'd give it all up for your cooking." He pulled a slightly flattened box out of his chest pocket and offered it to them.

Pidge took out a cigarette and then passed the pack to Nora. "Don't you smoke?" she asked when Nora hesitated.

"I did," Nora said. Her brother had made her swear to never start, but she'd failed him in that way as well. She'd forced herself to quit a couple of years ago. "I suppose one can't hurt." She drew out the long white cylinder and rolled it gently between her fingers before lighting it with Jimmy's proffered match.

"Mother hates it," Pidge said. "But all the girls do it. There's no harm in it, surely."

Nora didn't answer—she was too busy savoring the tingling sensation in her lungs, as though she were drawing a full breath for the first time in years. "Mmm. I've missed it. They say it'll kill you, though."

Pidge and Jimmy looked at her as though she were crazy. "Who says that?" Pidge asked.

"Doctors, mostly."

Jimmy laughed. "That's mad. Eddie Needham's brother is a doctor, and he smokes more than I do—and that's a lot. Here. Take one for the road."

Pidge and Nora each took one more. Pidge tucked hers down the front of her dress. Nora slipped hers into the pocket of her borrowed coat.

"Go on, now," Jimmy said. "Rose and Lizzie are here already. Oh, and Lynch is supposed to be coming by today, so look sharp."

"Who's Lynch?" Nora asked as they led their bikes down a steep hill.

Pidge looked astounded. "Who's Lynch? Only Liam Lynch, chief of staff of the IRA. Surely you've heard of him."

"Oh, him, yes, o'course," Nora said quickly. "I'm just surprised he'd show up here. I thought it had to be someone else."

"Oh, he's a common enough sight. It's not like he'll be walking down the streets of Dublin, mind, not with every Free Stater in the country wanting to put a bullet in him. But he comes to see how the training's going, boost morale, that sort of thing."

"Have you met him?"

"Can't say that I have. I've seen him, o'course. Father's met him. Says he's a decent man. The right sort of man to lead this fight. He'll never give up, not until the treaty is torn apart and we have what we deserve."

Liam Lynch. The man was a hero to so many of her friends and comrades in Belfast. He was revered as the man who'd won the Tan War—and then fought tooth and nail against his former colleagues after they signed the treaty with Britain. And now Nora would be seeing him in the flesh. She shivered and pulled her coat closer with one hand.

"This area's under Republican control, then?" she asked.

"It is. Can't say that about too many areas, now. But we'll win them back."

No, you won't, Nora thought. But she held her tongue. She wished she'd paid more attention to Eamon, or asked more questions, or read more books. It was hard to keep it all straight—the stories of backroom whispers, the deals and counterdeals made between the IRA, the Free

State, the British, and the Unionists in the North. But she did know it would end badly for her side.

They reached the bottom of the hill and followed the trail for a few more minutes. The desolation was palpable. Then Nora saw a long, single-story thatched cottage, and behind it several outbuildings of gray stone. She saw movement in one of the windows of the cottage.

"The Free Staters know nothing about this place?" Nora asked Pidge, who shook her head.

"The IRA lads found it abandoned only a couple of months ago. Been using it ever since. Some of the officers sleep here. The others kip in the barn." They leaned their bikes against the house and went inside, carrying the bread and butter from their baskets.

The cottage was dark, the only light coming in through the windows. In the kitchen was a long wooden table covered with papers and stubby pencils. An unlit lantern sat in the middle. Maps were pinned up on the walls.

Two women were already in the kitchen. They smiled brightly at Pidge and then looked at Nora in confusion.

"Rose, Lizzie, this is Nora," Pidge said, handing them her armload of bread. "She's from Cumann na mBan Belfast and is staying with us for a wee bit." She nodded to one of the women, who had a round face and plump figure, with deep dimples in each cheek. Her dark curls shone even in the poor light. Nora found her age nearly impossible to guess—she could have been seventeen or thirty-five. "This is Rose, my second cousin," Pidge explained. The other woman was older, her gray hair tied up neatly under a straw hat. She glared at Nora through narrowed eyes.

"Which division?" she asked.

"I'm sorry?"

"My sister is Cumann na mBan Belfast. Which division are you in?"

Ballix. Did Cumann na mBan follow the same organization structure as the IRA? Was there even more than one division in Belfast, or was this a trick to see if she was a spy?

"First Division," she said, meeting Lizzie's eyes steadily. "Falls Road."

Lizzie held her gaze, then huffed and motioned toward the table. "Coogan won't let us use the table, says we can't mess with his papers. Since Rose and I have started cooking, why don't you two get to the laundry? There's a tub and washboard in the back. We've already drawn water, and the kettle's hot." A metal crane held two large iron pots over the fire in the hearth. A basket of potatoes sat on the floor beside bricks of turf.

Pidge put her hands on her hips and huffed. "That's mad, expecting us to make food for a dozen hungry Volunteers with no surface to work on! He can move his damn papers himself if he likes, but we're using that table."

"You talk to him, then," Lizzie said. "He'll not be listening to an old woman like me."

"I will," Pidge said. "We'll see how badly the lads want to eat tonight." She stomped out of the cottage, leaving Nora alone with the two women.

"Go on, then," Lizzie said with a jut of her pointed chin toward the back of the house. "It's not just the laundry that needs doing, either. There are beds to change and rooms to be swept out."

Nora relaxed her jaw and forced her lips into a smile. With the Provos, she'd been just as active as any of the men. She'd forgotten how much times had changed. "Laundry, sure," she said. "But first, do either of you recognize this man?" She showed them her picture of Thomas. Rose only had to glance at it before turning beet red.

"O'course, that's Tom Heaney. What are you wanting with him, then?"

Nora gaped at her. The fingers holding the photograph tingled. He was real. She scarcely believed it, even after everything that had happened.

She found her voice. "My cousin asked me to find him."

Rose visibly relaxed, though her cheeks were still pink.

"Well, he's probably only a few yards away from you."

Nora's throat constricted. "He's . . . here?" She clutched the photo tighter.

"Sure he is, isn't he, Lizzie?"

"As she says," Lizzie said. Her back was to them, and she was up to her elbows in a deep mixing bowl balanced on a wooden chair. "He's around here somewhere, with the rest of them."

Nora kept her eyes on the photo in her hands. The man stared back at her, unsmiling, unblinking. *You're real.*

"You all right, there, Nora?" Rose asked.

"Ach, aye." But she felt rooted to the spot, there in the tiny kitchen. The man she had traveled eight decades to find, the man who'd haunted her dreams for months, was *here*, only steps away. She could no longer wait.

Without another word to Rose and Lizzie, she strode out of the cottage, her eyes fixed on the stone barn ahead. Maybe he was in there. Her heart beat at an unnatural pace, and her hands shook at her sides.

The faded wooden door of the barn was ajar, and she pushed it open. She blinked as her eyes adjusted to the dim light. Two gun racks stood against a narrow wall, but only one of them was full. Several crates were stacked next to them. A man was leaning against them, smoking.

"Oi! What are you doing in here?" he said when he noticed Nora.

"I'm looking for Thomas Heaney," she said.

"What for?"

"That's between me and him."

"You must be new. We're to stay clear of you ladies while you're here. Or should I say *you* should stay clear of *us*."

"It's important."

He shrugged. "Suit yourself. He's out training with the lads. Good luck finding him without getting shot."

She closed the door and walked around to the other side of the barn, determined to find the training site.

There.

He was still far off, but there was no mistaking his gray hair, which glinted in the sunlight that was fighting its way through the clouds. Another Volunteer walked behind him. They talked animatedly, Thomas's hands dancing through the air as he spoke. A large dog ran beside them, tongue lolling. A wolfhound, Nora realized. She didn't move, only stood and watched as he drew closer and closer. He was only the length of the barn away but didn't seem to have noticed her. The dog, however, ran over to her, sniffing enthusiastically. Its shaggy brown head came up to her waist. She gave it a nervous pat.

"Here, Bran," Thomas called, and the dog returned to his side.

"Thomas Heaney?" she asked, her voice wavering. Both he and his companion stopped. Thomas gave her a slight bow.

"At your service."

She leaned forward, searching his face. It was unmistakably the man from her dreams. His voice held the same gentle sway. And his eyes . . . They were the same ocean blue that had begged her to find him.

"I've come," she said, drawing herself up and meeting his gaze with her own.

"So I see, and we're grateful for it," he said, his eyes twinkling. "The lads' laundry is in the brown sacks in the back of the barn. And God knows they're in sore need of washing."

Nora stiffened. "Excuse me?" Was this his idea of a joke?

"Well, you can't expect us to train for a week without starting to smell a bit rare. Especially this one." He jabbed an elbow in his friend's ribs and laughed.

She stared at him wide-eyed, her mind spinning. It was him; there was no denying it. His every feature was familiar. Why was he acting this way? She stepped forward until they were only inches apart. Her lips and nose curled. "I'm not here to do your fucking laundry."

The men stopped laughing, their eyebrows raised. "Ooo, the lady has a mouth on her. Better be careful, Tom," the other man said.

"Well, I don't know why else you'd be here," Thomas said, nonplussed. He took a step back. She frowned. He wasn't joking. Maybe he was just playing dumb in front of his friend. She searched his face for any signs of recognition, but there were none. Unless he was a spectacularly good actor, he had no idea who she was.

This was a scenario she hadn't considered. She needed to get him alone so she could speak more plainly. She was about to tell his friend to bugger off when a bellow came from behind the men.

"Heaney! Casey! I told you to get the sticks, not chat up the ladies." A tall, broad-shouldered man with an imposing mustache glared at them from the far side of the barn. Pidge stood beside him, her brow furrowed.

Thomas and his friend dipped their heads politely to Nora, then swept past her into the barn. They emerged a moment later, each carrying a large sack filled with hurling sticks. Thomas glanced sideways at Nora as he passed her again, his forehead furrowed. Then all three men set off at a jog toward the low hills, the dog at their heels.

"Nora, what on earth are you doing?" Pidge asked, coming up alongside her. "Was that your man from the picture?"

Nora's eyes stayed fixed on Thomas's departing back as it grew smaller and smaller. She wanted to call after him, to demand that he stay and listen to her. But he didn't seem to know why she was there any better than she did.

"Yes. But . . . he didn't recognize me," she said quietly.

"Why should he?" Pidge asked with a scrunched forehead. "You said you'd never met him before."

"Aye. You're right. I don't know what I was thinking." Nora turned away to hide the storm on her face.

"Well, at least you can tell your cousin he's alive and well. Besides, we'll likely be back again. I can always pass on a message for you."

"Is that all you do here? Cook and clean?" Nora knew she sounded harsh, but she was still reeling from Thomas's abrupt dismissal.

"O'course not. In fact, Commandant Coogan has given me an important mission—on Lynch's orders."

"Oh?"

Pidge opened her hand to reveal a folded piece of paper in her palm. "I'm to deliver this to Ernie Hyland tomorrow."

"What is it?"

"Orders. But they can wait. Right now we need to get at that laundry. And Coogan says we can clear the table, as long as we mind to keep everything tidy."

Nora pressed her lips closed and followed Pidge back into the house. But then she asked, "Why the sticks?"

"Pardon?"

"What are they doing with hurling sticks? I thought they were training."

Pidge snorted. "They are. But the Staters got most of the weapons after the Tan War, didn't they? We have more men than rifles, so they use the hurleys for training. Saves the ammunition as well. Honestly, Nora, for someone in Cumann na mBan, you don't seem to know much about what's going on."

Of course I don't know what's going on. This all happened eighty years ago. "I just recently joined up, so I did. After my family . . ." Nora let her voice trail off, and Pidge looked abashed.

"O'course. I'm sorry. You just seem so clever, I'm surprised you don't know more about it, that's all."

"Well, I have you to teach me, don't I?"

Pidge and Nora spent the rest of the day washing sheets and shirts and stringing up drying lines between the buildings, while Nora stewed over Thomas's unexpected reaction. They swept every corner and crevice of the house while Rose and Lizzie prepared strips of cod and jerky and lined up loaves of Mrs. Gillies's dense bread. Nora was no stranger to physical labor but found herself stopping to rest while Lizzie, Rose, and Pidge powered on. Every once in a while Rose and Lizzie would whisper together, then glance at Nora. She ignored them.

Her thoughts were focused on Thomas. If he had the ability to speak to someone in the future, surely he would be able to recognize that person in the flesh. Could it be that he just didn't want to admit to recognizing her in front of the others?

I should just go home, she told herself as she swatted at cobwebs with her broom. But was that even an option?

"The lads are back!" Rose called, leaning out the window. "And Lynch is with them."

"Really?" Nora leaned the broom against the wall and ran out the open door. Two dozen men were marching toward the barn, hurling sticks resting on their shoulders. She scanned the men for Thomas and found him in the second column. Was it her imagination, or was he looking toward the house? "Which one is Lynch?" she asked Pidge, who had followed her into the yard.

"The man there in front, next to Coogan."

Nora squinted. Lynch was a tall, thin man. He wore the suit of a gentleman, not the uniform of a soldier. His trilby sat neatly on top of his head, and he carried a black walking cane. Small round spectacles perched on a long, straight nose. He put Nora in mind of a university professor.

"He looks different than I'd have imagined," she remarked.

"Well, you can't expect him to go around wearing a sign saying 'Chief of Staff of the IRA,' now can you?" Pidge said.

What would Eamon have thought of this? Nora wondered. *Liam Lynch, not fifty feet away from me.*

"Are you ladies going to stand gawking all day, or are we going to serve these lads their tea?" Lizzie glared at them, hands on hips. The women hauled heavy pots of stew and baskets of bread out into the yard. The rain had cleared, so the men gathered around with tin bowls and spoons. Lizzie and Rose ladled up hot bowls of thick stew while Nora and Pidge readied the washing tubs. Nora pulled a large bone from the soup pot and surreptitiously slipped it to the hound, who'd been following her around the yard. She chanced a glance at Thomas and found that he was watching her, too, a thoughtful look on his face. But when she met his eyes, he turned away.

Chapter Twelve

"Honestly, Nora, you're as nervous as a filly about to foal." Pidge and Nora had cycled back to Pidge's house after doing the washing up for the Volunteers' tea. Nora was quite certain she wouldn't be able to lift her arms in the morning after the day's labors, but Pidge had suggested they go to the pub in the next village. "Thomas will be there. Are you certain it's your cousin who was looking for him? You've been absolutely skittish since you saw him." She hid her secret missive from Commandant Coogan inside a roll of stockings in her dresser and then turned to Nora, hands on her hips.

"I have not," Nora protested. "And how do you know he'll be there tonight?"

"Because I asked Jimmy who all was going out."

"Aren't they worried about being caught?"

"What, caught at the pub? No, so long as there're no weapons about, or 'seditious literature,' as they call it, there's nothing they can do. Besides, all the Staters go to the pub in Kildare. My job tomorrow is the dangerous one." Pidge gave Nora a wink, then spun around in a circle. "How do I look?"

"Stunning."

Pidge had changed into a deep red dress that set off her fair skin and dark hair, like a crimson rose in a snowy wood. She beamed at the compliment. "Well, no one will be looking at me, with you along. They'll all be wanting to get to know the new girl."

"Only because they think I'm a spy."

"Only the idiots will think that. You don't think word's gotten around about how you saved Frankie Halpin?"

"How *is* Frankie? I haven't had the chance to check on him."

"He'll be all right. His uncle came and collected him today while we were out. They'll keep him hidden until he's well enough to fight again. I reckon the Staters don't even know he escaped."

Nora had wondered about that. They probably hadn't even bothered to piece together the bodies. The memory turned her stomach. She'd seen a lot of brutality in Belfast and the various armpits of the world where she'd worked, but it never got easier.

"That dress of mine suits you," Pidge said.

"Thank you." Nora had never been much for dresses, but she had to admit the cream lace of the one she wore complemented her red hair. "And thank you for letting me wear it. I promise I'll be off tomorrow and out of your hair."

"Off where?" Pidge looked affronted.

"I'll make my own way. You've done so much for me as it is."

"Don't be ridiculous, Nora! You've no family here, and we'll not be letting you go back up to Belfast with things as they are. You can stay with us for as long as you like."

"That's kind, Pidge, but I'm sure your parents would have something to say about it. Besides, I need to . . . well, there are things I need to look after."

"Suit yourself, but know you're always welcome here."

"Ta."

"Oh, don't look so gloomy," Pidge said, grabbing one of Nora's hands. "Come, let's go have some fun. Lord knows there's precious little of that to be found these days."

Once ready, the women were joined by Stephen, who walked alongside them as they cycled to the nearby village. Nora tried to make conversation with Stephen, but he was as recalcitrant as ever. What had he seen? What had he done? He reminded her again of Eamon—how brooding and distant her brother had been after joining up with the IRA. She could only hope Stephen didn't experience the same dark fate.

The pub was nestled deep in the countryside, off a narrow dirt road. A cat crossed the path in front of them, stopping to hiss before continuing its search for supper. Several bicycles were leaned against the wall, and a couple of horses were tied to a post in the yard. It was dark—the pub had obviously not been hooked up to the electrical grid—and yet the glow coming from the windows and the lantern swinging from the eaves were welcoming enough. They gladly stepped inside.

Nora'd been in her share of Irish pubs before, but this one was . . . magical. There were no big-screen TVs, no blaring Top 40 songs to snuff out conversations, no gambling consoles in the back. No neon signs, no loud tourists, no American beer. The room was filled with the soft hum of conversation, the occasional burst of laughter, and the welcoming glow of fire. The barman was bantering with a couple of older men who leaned against the polished wood bar, each clutching a dewy pint.

Nora followed Pidge and Stephen through the haze of smoke and dim light, her eyes scanning the men dressed in suits and fedoras, the women with their smart hats and curled hair and long coats. Red lips laughed and sipped frothy glasses of dark beer. They found a round table near the back.

"What'll you have?" Stephen asked, his eyes on the floor.

"Whiskey, please," Nora said.

"Whiskey?" Pidge asked in astonishment. Even Stephen lifted his eyes to stare at her.

"Oh," Nora said. "Do . . . do women not drink whiskey here?"

"Do they in Belfast?" Pidge asked, seeming genuinely intrigued.

"Aye. But I don't want to, you know, stand out. I'll have a Guinness, if you don't mind."

"Same, Stephen. Ta," Pidge said. As he walked away, she bent her head toward Nora's. "So? Do you see him here?"

"Thomas? No."

"He'll come. Jimmy said all the lads would come round for a pint after training was over."

"Well, it doesn't really matter." Nora accepted a pint from Stephen and sipped it gratefully. That wasn't fully true, of course. She wanted to get Thomas alone as much as she dreaded it. *I have to explain why I'm here. Maybe then he'll understand.*

"Do you spend much time in Kildare?" she asked Pidge. In a corner of the pub, a fiddler was tuning his instrument.

"Sure I do, though not as much as we used to. Loads of British soldiers, you see, with the barracks being so close. And now the Free State Army has taken over—and you saw what they're capable of. But Ma and I still go to the market there, and sometimes the shops. And Da and Stephen go to the races, don't you?"

Stephen nodded, but his gaze was elsewhere.

"Do you know—have you heard of a group called the Brigidine Sisters?" Nora asked.

Pidge shook her head. "No, can't say that I have. Nuns, are they?"

"Something like that."

"Why do you want to know about them? You're not thinking of joining, are you?"

"Hardly. I just . . . I met someone who was in that society, or whatever it is. I just wanted to know more about it."

Stephen brought them another round, and Pidge described the others in the room for Nora's amusement.

"See that man there? He fancies himself a great poet. We'll no doubt get to hear some of his 'poetry' later tonight. Might give us a song as well." She nodded at a woman's back at the bar and lowered her voice. "Muriel has only been widowed a month, and she already has a list of 'appropriate suitors.' Ma says the man with the most coin will win her hand, but it's a sore deal he'll get in exchange."

Nora eased back into her chair and grinned. Pidge's enthusiasm was infectious, and the Guinness was starting to unknot her nerves. She'd expected it to taste different, but it was exactly the same as the brew she indulged in whenever she was home on R&R. The familiar taste made her homesick, in a confusing, backward sort of way.

"He's been watching you, you know," Pidge said, keeping her eyes on Nora.

"Who?" Nora sat up straighter in her chair.

"Don't turn around. But he came in about twenty minutes ago. Has hardly taken his eyes off you since."

Nora turned around. He wasn't watching her now. But there he was, three tables away, sitting with the two women and the Volunteer he'd been bantering with earlier in the day. One of the women noticed Nora's scrutiny and gave her a questioning look.

Nora stood up, the wooden legs of her chair chafing across the floor.

"What are you doing?" Pidge hissed.

"I'm going to talk to him." She strode quickly, her head held high. When she reached the table, she placed her hands on her hips. "Hello, Thomas. Could I have a word, please?"

Thomas and his companions exchanged glances. Then he pushed his chair back and stood. "Oh, I beg your pardon. I didn't recognize you for a moment. You're the new Cumann na mBan girl, from earlier today, right?"

If you didn't recognize me, why have you been staring at me since you arrived? "I need to speak with you alone," she said, her words clipped.

One of the women at the table said, "I'm so sorry, I'm afraid we haven't been introduced." She held out a pale hand. Nora hesitated, then shook it briefly.

"Nora O'Reilly. I'm a guest of the Gillies family." She tossed her head back in the direction of Pidge and Stephen, who were watching the exchange silently. Pidge was on the edge of her chair, as though poised to come to her aid.

"And how do you know each other, Tom?" There was an undeniable bite in the woman's voice.

"We only met today, out at the camp," he said, looking bemused.

"I need to speak with you. Alone," Nora said. "It's important, so it is."

"Very well," Thomas said. He nodded to his friends and sauntered toward the front of the room, where the tables and chairs had been pushed aside to create a small dance floor. He tossed a smirk back at his mate at the table, then gave a theatrical bow.

"Shall we?" he asked. The musicians—two fiddlers, a guitarist, and a white-haired bodhran player with whistles sticking out of his pocket—were playing a slow and mournful ballad.

"What, dance? No one else is."

"They will. Besides, you're the one who wanted to speak to me alone." He grabbed her right hand firmly in his own and brought it up to his shoulder, then pressed his other hand into the small of her back. She sniffed; he smelled strongly of beer and was in need of a shower. And yet she felt an unexpected rush of pleasure in spite of herself—it felt . . . right to be this close to him, to feel his skin against hers.

"Fine, if that's what will make you talk," she said, stepping awkwardly along with him as they moved into the dance.

"So what do you want, Nora O'Reilly?" He looked genuinely curious, though it did not mask the intensity of his gaze.

"You really don't know? You don't recognize me at all?"

He shook his head, keeping his eyes fixed on hers. "For a moment I thought you looked familiar . . . but no. I wish I did. It isn't every day a beautiful woman demands to speak with me."

Nora ignored this. "But you don't remember seeing me before? In a . . . dream, maybe?"

"I'd like to say yes," he said, gently guiding her through the steps of the dance as other couples filtered onto the floor. "Why do you ask? Do you feel you've met me before?" She was about to tell him about her dreams and demand an explanation, but caution slowed her tongue. The last thing she needed was for him to think she was crazy. She didn't want to end up in an insane asylum, especially in this era. She decided on another approach.

"We've a mutual friend. In Kildare."

She felt his hesitation in the twitch of the hand pressed against the small of her back. But his face remained passive.

"Oh? Who?"

"Brigid."

He stopped dancing.

His hand remained pressed into her palm, but they stood unmoving on the edge of the dance floor while others glided around them.

"You speak of . . . the Lady of Kildare?" His eyes were wary, as though he, too, were now choosing his words with care.

"Yes," Nora said firmly. "That's what I've been trying to tell you. She sent me here to find you. She said you needed my help."

The song ended, and someone tapped on Thomas's shoulder. "May I cut in?" the other man asked.

"No," Thomas said abruptly, pulling Nora in closer. The music started again, and together they moved through the dance, their eyes locked on each other. "Brigid sent you?" he demanded. "Are you certain?" His charming demeanor had dissipated. His eyes were no longer twinkling, but cold and angry.

"Yes, after a fashion." He didn't need to know the Brigidine Sisters had been the intermediary. "I came to help you, in answer—"

"I don't need your help." He jerked her arm as they turned.

"But . . . you asked. You begged me to find you."

"How is that possible? I've never met you before."

"Come with me," she said. She didn't want to create a scene, or worse, be overheard. She stalked out of the pub, trusting him to follow. It was raining, and she'd left her coat inside, but she didn't care. She strode into the dark yard, then turned on her heel. He was right behind her.

"You really don't know? I've been dreaming of you for months. *Months.* Almost every night. At first they were just vague images, impressions, maybe, but I knew you were trying to tell me something. And then you spoke to me as clearly as you did tonight. You told me to find you. You told me to go to Kildare, to find Brigid. And so I did, and she sent me here. And now you're telling me that you don't know who I am, and you don't need my help. What the hell am I supposed to do with that?"

Her frustration poured off her like steam, undampened by the steady rain. She wanted to tell him everything, to tell him she was from the future, that according to the inscription on the back of the photograph he was going to die this year. But his demeanor invited no such confidences. The light of one of the swinging lamps danced across his face, which was hard and somber. He spoke slowly, his eyes never leaving hers.

"Nora. I don't know how you came into Brigid's path. But Brigid is . . . She makes her own choices. She has her reasons for what she does, and I don't pretend to understand them. She gets inside people's heads. I can't do that. It was not *me* who called for you, no matter how it may have appeared at the time. And while I'm flattered—amazed, really—that you would answer the plea of a stranger you only met in your dreams, I assure you, I'm in need of no one's help but my own." His eyes darkened as he said this. He turned to go back into the pub but then stopped. "It would be best for you not to speak of this to anyone. There's nothing but death for dreams in this place."

Chapter Thirteen

Thomas disappeared back into the warmth of the pub. The rain pelted Nora's face. Her cream dress clung to her figure, heavy and cold against her skin.

Had it all been fake, then? Some trick? Or did Saint Brigid put those dreams in her head for some purpose of her own? But why use Thomas at all? *Why make me believe he needs my help . . . and then this? Does he need my help and just not realize it?*

A stone grew in her throat. She swallowed forcefully. She'd been a fool to be swayed by dreams and visions.

But it is real. You're here, in 1923. There's a reason for that. There's got to be. She didn't bring you here for a lark.

"Fuckin' eejit!" she cried, balling her fists. She stalked out of the muddy yard, heading back onto the road. She'd go to Kildare tonight. The Brigidine Sisters were the ones who had done this; perhaps they could tell her why Brigid had *really* sent her back in time.

There was no moonlight, and the road was rough. She stepped in a rut, rolling her ankle. "Ballix!" she yelled, catching herself before she sprawled in the mud. Her ankle throbbed, adding to the maelstrom of frustration that swirled around her. Then she cried out in surprise. Something hairy had leaned up against her.

"Oh! Bran," she said, patting the wolfhound she'd met at the camp. "What are you doing out here? I have no bones for you this time." The dog whined and nuzzled her side. Nora leaned against her gratefully. "Your master is at the pub, needing no one's help but his own." The dog whined again. "That's how I feel, too," Nora whispered.

Resigned, she turned back, knowing she'd not get far on her throbbing ankle in the dark. Bran stayed by her side as she limped along, choosing each step carefully.

Questions swirled inside her head. Why had Thomas reacted so coldly? He'd admitted Saint Brigid was real, and he hadn't seemed all that surprised to hear she had sent Nora to him. But none of it made sense. Someone—or everyone—had lied to her. Either that or Brigid had her own agenda and hadn't felt the need to inform Nora of it. She didn't care if she had to limp the whole way to Kildare. Tomorrow, she would find out the truth.

She found Pidge in a frenzied state outside the pub, keeping dry under the eaves. Bran bounded away into the shadows as soon as they reached the building. "Nora! Where on earth have you been?" Pidge called.

"I'm sorry," Nora said, just now becoming aware of the state of her borrowed dress. "I just . . . needed to go for a walk. To clear my head."

"You went for a walk? In this?"

"Aye."

"Get yourself in here." Pidge threw Nora's coat over her shoulders and dragged her into the pub. Nora ducked her head, avoiding the stares. "Charlie, get this woman a whiskey," Pidge said to the barman as they stalked past him toward their table.

"I'm fine, Pidge, I—"

"What the devil's going on with you and Thomas?" Pidge interrupted. "First the two of you leave together, without a word to anyone, mind you; then he storms back inside only to collect his things and make excuses to his friends. I thought maybe you were just having a chat and wanted your privacy, but when you didn't come back, I started to worry. Then Charlie at the bar said he saw Thomas drive away in his carriage. Well, what was I supposed to think? I sent Stephen down the road to see if he could find you. He'll be drenched through by now."

"Pidge, I'm sorry—"

"Tell me the truth, Nora. It wasn't your cousin who was looking for Thomas, was it?"

Charlie arrived with the whiskey. Nora wrapped her hands around it. She wanted so badly to tell Pidge the truth, but what good would it do? There was no way she would believe her. She'd think she was mad. She couldn't afford that risk, and she didn't want to lose the one friend she had here. But Pidge wouldn't take no for an answer.

"It was an arrangement. Between our parents," she murmured. It was not difficult to look suitably embarrassed.

"An arranged marriage?" Pidge asked with wide eyes.

"Nothing so serious. They thought we would be a good match, so they wanted us to meet. But I only found out about it after my mother died. It was my cousin who told me. So . . . I thought I would give it a try, at least."

"And he turned you away?" Pidge looked scandalized.

"Aye. He did. But it doesn't matter. I've no feelings for the man, if that's what you're worried about. I only just met him today."

"But you came all this way . . ."

Nora nodded grimly. "Aye. So I did. I need to go to Kildare, and soon. We've a . . . friend of the family there who might be able to help me."

Pidge grabbed her hands, which were still icy cold. "Why didn't you say so earlier? We'll go tomorrow."

"It's grand, I can go by myself."

"Don't be silly. It's market day, anyway. Ma's been wanting a new bolt of cloth, and we've some things to post. Besides, I've my mission from Lynch, remember? I have to deliver his letter to a man in Kildare as soon as possible. So we'll do it all at once. Ah, here's Stephen. We'd best be off."

"Stephen, I'm sorry you had to go looking for me," Nora said as the three of them left the pub. "I was grand, so I was. But I appreciate your concern."

"S'all right," Stephen muttered. "I'm glad you're well. We'll have a damp trip home, though."

"Ugh," Pidge said, eyeing the rain with distaste. "Well, there's nothing for it." Then a horse-pulled carriage turned off the lane. The driver hopped down. Thomas.

"Can I offer you a ride?" he said. "You're the Gillies siblings, aren't you? I'm going back that way."

"No, thank you," Nora said stiffly. Pidge and Stephen stayed silent.

"It's a wee bit damp out," Thomas observed. "I'd think you'd be happy for a covered ride."

"I'm in need of no one's help but my own," she said, throwing his words back at him.

"Even on that ankle?"

"How do you—" Nora's jaw stiffened. "Were you following me? Is that why your dog was there?"

"I wasn't following you. Bran was. Weren't you, girl?" Bran ran up to her master, who gave her ears a ruffle. "Thomas Heaney," he said, holding out a hand to Stephen, who shook it.

"Stephen Gillies. This is my sister, Pidge. I guess you've already met Nora," Stephen said.

"Are you sure you're going that way?" Pidge asked. "Our farm is up by—"

"I know where it is," Thomas interrupted. "Won't you get in?"

Pidge gave Nora a pleading look. "We can fetch the bicycles later," she said softly. Rain was dripping off the brim of her hat.

Nora pressed her lips together. "Fine," she muttered. She stalked over to the carriage and climbed awkwardly into the back. Pidge followed her as Stephen got into the front beside Thomas. Bran settled herself on the floor by Nora's feet.

The ride took only a few minutes, the horse picking its way through the ruts and holes in the road. Thomas smoked a cigarette under the canopy of the driver's seat. Nora stared into the darkness. She had so many questions, none of which she could ask for fear of being branded a lunatic. Besides, Thomas was obviously disinclined to help, though she was sure he knew more than he was letting on.

Pidge thanked Thomas warmly when he stopped outside their house. Nora simply accepted Stephen's hand and climbed down without a word.

"You could have said thank you, you know," Pidge said as they hung up their coats near the fire. Stephen climbed the ladder to the loft, and it seemed Mr. and Mrs. Gillies were already asleep.

"You thanked him for all of us."

"Yes, but he came back for *you*."

"He did no such thing. You should have heard him earlier. He wants nothing to do with me."

"You're hurt because he rejected you. I get it. But maybe he was just surprised at first. Maybe he already has a sweetheart, and then this beautiful woman shows up in his life unexpectedly, and he doesn't know how to handle it. Could be he's having second thoughts."

"He made himself pretty clear." Nora scowled. She should have told Pidge something else; now she would treat Nora like a spurned lover. *Better that than her knowing the truth.*

Pidge tossed her a towel. "For your hair. Come, let's change."

Once they were clothed in long flannel nightgowns, Pidge made tea and they sat with their backs to the fire, the heat drying their hair.

Once it was nearly dry, Nora tied her hair into a thick braid and unfolded the settle bed in the kitchen. "Good night. And thank you."

"Sleep well. I'll wake you in the morning."

Sleeping well was not in the cards. Nora lay awake most of the night, replaying her dreams, her conversation with Mary in Kildare, and Thomas's perplexing response to her. A Saint Brigid's cross made from reeds hung above the doorway, just like the one that had hung in her childhood home in Belfast. It was too dark for her to see it well, but she could feel its presence.

"Saint Brigid . . . I need your help. I don't know why you sent me here, or even if you were truly the one who sent me. But if it was you . . . it was a mistake. This isn't where I belong. Please, help me get back home." She followed this up with two Hail Marys, for good measure, and her usual prayers for the dead.

Was Saint Brigid responsible for sending her back in time? Saints could perform miracles, she believed that much. As a child, she'd woven Saint Brigid crosses out of rushes with her classmates every February 1 while their teacher told them stories of Brigid's miracles. When the stingy king of Leinster agreed to give Brigid's abbey only the ground her cloak could cover, she gave each corner of the cloak to one of her nuns and told them to keep running until it covered the entire kingdom. The king relented and gave Brigid a generous portion of land. Nora's favorite story was of Brigid's response to an unwelcome marriage proposal: she thrust a finger through her own eye to make her unacceptable as a bride, then healed it once the offer had been withdrawn. Nora tried to remember everything she'd heard about the saint, in case it would give her some clue into her predicament, some insight into Brigid's design for her. But Brigid had lived 1,500 years ago. What could she possibly want with Nora now?

It felt as though she had barely fallen asleep when Pidge shook her awake the next morning. "Up you get, sleepyhead."

Nora cracked her eyes open. Day four in another century. Pidge was already dressed, and her hair was pinned up. She was adding turf bricks to the fire, and a bucket of water sat beside her.

Nora dressed quickly in Pidge's room and tidied her braid. When she came back into the kitchen, Mrs. Gillies was already mixing another batch of soda bread on the table.

"Ah, Nora! Did you have a good time last night?"

Nora stole a glance at Pidge. "Aye, I did."

"Pidge tells me you found your man."

"Aye, he was at the training camp."

"He must have been pleased to get the message from your cousin, then."

Nora relaxed and gave Pidge a grateful smile. "He was."

"And you've business in Kildare today?"

"A family friend I thought I should try to track down. I don't want to be a burden on you longer than necessary."

"A burden! Don't say such a thing. You're welcome to stay with us for as long as you need."

"Ta, Mrs. Gillies. You're all very kind."

Mrs. Gillies gave Pidge detailed instructions on what kind of cloth to buy, as well as a list of other items to get from the market. She handed her two thin envelopes. "And post these for me, will you, dear?"

Nora quivered with impatience, drinking her tea so quickly it scalded her throat. "Let's go," she gasped, setting the cup down.

The bicycles were in the yard. "Stephen went and fetched them from the pub this morning with the cart," Pidge explained. "I didn't fancy walking to Kildare and back, not with all the things mother wants me to fetch."

The road seemed vaguely familiar to Nora as they cycled. "How's your bottom?" Pidge teased.

"Better today," Nora answered with a grin. Here in the morning sun, her situation didn't seem so dire. She'd find the Brigidine Sisters, explain what had happened, and they would send her back to her own time. She could be back in Darfur before the week was out. With time, she'd forget all about the misleading dreams.

Before long they were passing the barracks outside the town. Pidge muttered, "Traitors." They kept going until they reached the center of the town, near the market, and then they dismounted.

"Right, what shall we do first?" Pidge said, consulting her mother's list.

"I thought I might try and find my family friend while you're doing your shopping," Nora said. Pidge looked up in surprise.

"What, by yourself? Don't you want my help?"

"I'm grand, really. It might take a while, and I don't want to hold you up."

"Are you sure?"

"Aye."

Pidge looked uncertain, but she nodded. "All right, then, shall we meet for lunch, at least? There's a chippy just over there. I should be done in a couple of hours. Does that give you enough time?"

Nora nodded. She felt surprisingly emotional about saying good-bye to Pidge, though they'd only known each other a few days. But if all went well, they'd never see each other again. Making a mental note to look up the Gillies family when she got back to the present, she leaned over and gave Pidge a quick hug. "Good luck. With everything."

She got back on the bicycle and rode in the direction of the cathedral, whose spires were clearly visible from the market. Children and dogs ran across the street, unafraid of the slow-moving horse carriages. A couple of cars and motorcycles puttered past, but the majority of the traffic was of the foot—or hoof—variety. She leaned her bike against the stone wall surrounding the church. The man sitting outside the lace shop was the same one who'd told her what year it was. This time, he didn't spare her a second glance.

She hiked up her long skirt and ran up the pathway to the cathedral. Would they be waiting for her? Mary had said to tell them the code phrase "the bane of Aengus Óg." Surely that meant they were expecting her?

She pushed open the heavy wooden door, which slid across the tiled floor. Sunlight filtered in through the narrow windows, catching dust in its beams. The church was empty, save for a solitary figure in the third row of pews. The woman, who wore a tweed coat and had a dark green scarf wrapped around her head, had rested her forearms against the pew in front of her and was sitting with her head bowed and eyes closed. Nora walked up the center aisle and slipped into the pew behind her. She waited for the woman to finish her prayers. Finally, she lifted her head.

"Welcome, Nora," she said without looking behind her.

Nora's breath hitched. "How do you know my name?"

The woman turned around. Her face was lined with deep wrinkles, though her hair was still a rich, dark auburn set in curls under her green head scarf. "Saint Brigid told me to expect you. I felt your presence just now, as I was praying."

"Are you a Brigidine Sister?"

"I am. My name is Bernadette."

"The other woman—Mary—told me to tell you that Brigid sent me, and that I am . . . I don't know what this means, but she said to say I'm the bane of Aengus Óg. What is that?"

Bernadette nodded slowly. "Those were the words I was told to expect. I have to admit, my faith was weak. The blessed saint, she has spoken to others, but this was the first time I've heard her voice so clearly."

"What does it mean?"

"I was not told. Do you not know?"

"All I know is that Aengus Óg was one of the old gods. The Tuatha Dé Danann."

"Brigid will reveal the truth to you in time, no doubt."

"Well, what *did* she tell you?"

"She said one would be coming to me, a young woman named Nora. That she would be in distress, and I was to comfort her. She also said that you would wish to go home, but that it was not possible. Not yet."

"What?" Panic welled in her throat. Nora rose from her seat and moved into the woman's pew. "You don't understand—there's been a mistake. I'm not supposed to be here."

"Oh?"

"Do you know . . . where I'm from?" She was afraid to say the words out loud.

A glint appeared in the woman's eyes. Was it fear? "You are not from this time."

"Aye, I'm not. One of your Sisters—or Brigid, if you want to believe that—sent me here to help a man. I've found him, but he doesn't want my help. Says he doesn't need it. So unless she's got another plan, I've come here for nothing. I need you to send me home again." The words tumbled out, stepping over each other in her haste to be heard.

"I'm sorry, Nora, but it's not within my ability to do that. You have a job to do."

"How the hell—sorry—how am I supposed to help a man who refuses to have anything to do with me? I can't force him to listen to me, so I can't. If I tell him I know he's going to die, he'll just think I'm crazy. There's nothing for me to do here."

"Is there not?"

"What do you mean?"

"Brigid is the most mysterious of saints. If she sent you here, it was for a purpose."

"Well, it's a bit useless if I don't know what that purpose is. If the relic worked to send me here, it'll work to send me back. Where is it?" She leaned in closely to make her point clear.

Bernadette stayed firm in her seat, frowning. "What relic?"

"There's a relic—a finger bone. It's what I used to get here."

"The relic of Saint Brigid is not here, if that's what you are seeking. It's not been in Ireland for many centuries."

"What? Where is it?"

"Portugal."

"That's not true. I know it's here. Eighty years from now, it's in the basement, in the room with the fireplace." *I'm wasting time.* She ran to the back of the church, to the door that led to the basement. It was locked. "Open it," Nora called out, pulling on the latch with both hands.

Bernadette walked up the aisle toward her, hands folded. "I don't know where you expect to find it, Nora, but this is a Protestant cathedral," she said, her voice calm. "Do you really think we would keep a relic of our most precious saint here, even if we still had it?" Nora let go of the door.

"But . . . it must be here. Mary said the Brigidine Sisters had kept it safe for centuries. I saw it. I held it." Her control slipped slightly. Her hands shook, and her entire chest was clenched tight.

"You *will* see it, you mean. You *will* hold it."

She tried to comprehend what this woman was saying. But it was too much to understand, too much to believe.

"So that's it, then? I'm trapped in 1923 for the rest of my life? There's no way to go back?" A dull ache spread through her entire body, a feeling of helplessness that she loathed and despised.

"That will be for Saint Brigid to decide, I suppose. She is the Lady of Miracles. But there is no way I can help you. I can only pass on her words."

Nora sank down onto the cold stone floor, her head in her hands. What was she supposed to do with no money, no job, no family, here in the middle of a civil war?

"Brigid is not cruel, Nora. If this man will not let you help him, she must have another design for you."

"I don't care."

"I'm sorry?"

"Brigid can go to hell, for all I care. Who does she think she is, plucking people from their own time and throwing them back into the past? I was doing something good; I was saving lives!" Hot tears pressed at her lashes, but she would not let them escape.

The Brigidine Sister laid a callous, wrinkled hand on Nora's shoulder. "We need that here, too. More than ever."

Nora left the cathedral in a daze. Bernadette had given her an envelope of money, a gift from the Sisters to help her in her service to Brigid. She'd reluctantly accepted it and stuffed it into her purse. Then she'd stepped back into the sunlight, squinting after the darkness of the church. If she had no choice but to stay here for an indefinite period of time, she at least needed a plan.

She sat down on the low stone wall of the ruined Fire Temple. Her humanitarian training was kicking in. Her first priority was survival: food, shelter, water. She could find a boardinghouse in town, rent a room. But then she had a second thought. She could pay Mr. and Mrs. Gillies for her room and board. At least, until she found a job. Her nose wrinkled at the thought of the jobs available for women in this era—secretary, nurse, or teacher. Nursing appealed to her most, although her only formal training had been a brief course in emergency field medicine. Perhaps she could get a job with the IRA; at least then she'd be close to the action.

She stood up and brushed off her skirt, pleased that she had a plan. But then what? Bernadette had said Brigid had a purpose for her. She didn't want to merely survive in this new life. If Thomas wouldn't accept her help, perhaps someone else would.

A horrible—and enticing—thought struck her with the force of a bullet. She sat back down on the stone wall, her hands pressed to her mouth. Would her presence in the past change the course of history? She'd never been much for science fiction. She'd certainly never thought about the intricacies of time travel. But there would inevitably be consequences. Had her mere appearance—running into the soldiers, saving Frankie's life, meeting the Gillies family—changed the future?

More importantly, *could* she change the future?

She held her breath, lest the thought escape through her lips. Was *that* what Brigid wanted? For her to change the course of history? And even if it wasn't, what was there to stop her from doing it? She took a deep breath and exhaled long and slow through her nose, trying to remember anything she'd read or heard about this precise moment in history. The end of the Civil War was near, that much she knew. But how close? Was there still a chance to turn things around, to win the war for the Republicans, tear up the treaty with Britain, and keep Northern Ireland with the rest of the country?

She moaned when she realized what this could mean—if the partition never happened, there would be no war in Northern Ireland. No Troubles. And that would mean her brother would never be killed.

That's why she was here. What was it Mary had said as she gave her the relic? *You might be able to help others who are close to you.*

She could change history. *Her* history, and the history of everyone she loved. She could save Eamon's life.

Chapter Fourteen

She had to talk to Thomas again. He had mentioned Brigid, acted like he knew her. Could he be from the future as well? Did he know how this worked? Maybe Brigid had sent him to the past on some sort of mission, but he had failed, which would explain his anger over Nora's interference. Or maybe it had nothing to do with that at all. Maybe he was just a devotee of the saint, like the Sisters. It didn't matter, not now. It didn't matter that he didn't want her help. Now *he* could help *her*.

She ran to the gate and swung onto the bike. Gone was the anxiety in her chest, the blind helplessness. In its place was a lightness that crackled and consumed.

She cycled through the main square, looking for Pidge. Her friend wasn't among the vendors and shoppers in the market, a collection of tables covered in eggs, produce, and barrels of flour and sugar. Nora turned up a side street, curious now to learn everything she could about where and when she was.

She found Pidge standing in the doorway of a narrow brick home. Her bicycle was leaning against the house, a paper bag and bolt of cloth in the large basket. Pidge was glancing over her shoulder when she saw Nora.

"Nora! You gave me a fright."

"I looked for you in the market—what are you doing here?"

Pidge beckoned her closer. "I'm delivering Coogan's message. Come with me?"

"Aye."

Pidge knocked smartly on the door. After a short wait, a young woman in a maid's uniform answered.

"Can I help ye?"

"We're here to see Mr. Hyland," Pidge said.

The maid nodded, keeping her eyes down. "Right this way, if you please." She had a strong Northern accent. *Someone else who's away from home*, Nora thought. They were shown into a parlor, which was sparsely but tastefully decorated. It reminded Nora of her aunt Margaret's house.

"Do you just need to give it—" Nora started, but Pidge hushed her. A moment later, a stocky man with a bristling mustache came into the room, followed by the maid.

"Do you want I should bring some tea, Mr. Hyland?" the woman asked, her eyes still on the floor.

"No, Edna." He was eyeing Pidge and Nora. "That will be all, thank you." Edna left and closed the door behind her. "Three years in my service, and I still can't understand half of what she says," he remarked.

"You're an Englishman!" Pidge declared. Nora bit back her own surprised response. Why would the IRA have Pidge delivering messages to a Brit? Was this a trap? Her eyes darted to the door.

"Yes, and so was Erskine Childers, though I'd like to avoid his fate if I possibly can. Firing squads do not suit me."

"But why—" Nora started.

"English birth and Irish nationalism are not mutually exclusive." His tone was testy, so Nora let it drop. "I understand you have a message for me."

"Oh, yes," Pidge said. She took off her hat and turned it over. With a fingernail, she lifted the inner lining and extracted a folded piece of paper.

Mr. Hyland grunted as he took it. "Have a seat. I may need to send a reply."

Pidge sat with her hat in her lap, watching Mr. Hyland with avid eyes. Nora was suspicious, but she said nothing. Her job was to watch and listen, to try to fill in the blanks in her knowledge of the war. She should have read the message when it was still in Pidge's drawer.

"Hmph. Well, it seems you ladies have another task. I would have thought they'd send men for this, but . . ."

"We can do it," Pidge said eagerly.

"What is it?" Nora asked.

"I'm a collector of handguns. It seems our boys are running out. I told Lynch it was a last resort—some of these pieces are worth a fair amount, you see. But he doesn't care, so long as they shoot straight. Wait here."

"What if it's a trap?" Nora asked Pidge as soon as Hyland had left the parlor.

"What do you mean?"

"What if he means for us to get caught? Isn't it against the law to have a weapon unless you're a Prod or a Free Stater? That's why Childers was executed, wasn't it?"

"We won't get caught. That's why Lynch sent us instead of the lads. Who would suspect two young women, out doing their shopping?"

"You trust him?"

"Liam Lynch trusts him, and that's all that matters."

She's right, Nora thought. This was a real chance to help. She could deliver messages, smuggle arms, maybe even take part in combat. Maybe her involvement would be the tipping point. Wars had been won or lost on lesser things.

"Grand, so," Nora said, standing to pace the small room. "We'll hide them in with the shopping, then?"

"I reckon. What do you think?"

"It should work. I imagine he'll want them taken to the camp?"

"I suppose we'll find out."

They didn't have long to wait. Hyland came back into the room, puffing slightly beneath his mustache. Under his arm was a roll of canvas, which he spread out on the floor, revealing half a dozen pistols. "I've kept two for my own protection," he said. "This is the rest of them—those that still work, that is."

"I'll get the fabric," Nora said. She slipped out the front door and hoisted the bag of groceries into one arm and the bolt of cloth into the other. Edna, the maid, was watching her through the windows. *Surely Hyland trusts where his servants' loyalties lie.*

Back in the parlor, Nora emptied the bag of groceries and wrapped three of the pistols in Hyland's canvas. She stuffed the bundle in the bottom of the paper bag, then covered it with tea, a bag of sugar, and a jar of face cream.

Then they turned to the bolt of fabric. Pidge held one end while Nora worked out the tube in the center. Then they stuffed the other three pistols inside. Nora tore two pieces of the cardboard tube off and stuck them in either end. "It's a little lumpy, but I don't think anyone'll notice."

Pidge lifted the bag of groceries and turned to Hyland. "We'll take these straight to Lynch, then? Or Coogan?"

"I don't think that's wise. There are rumors of an informer in Coogan's ranks. Too many odd coincidences of the Free Staters knowing where our boys are about to strike."

"But then how—"

"Keep them somewhere safe. Lynch will send someone to collect them when they're needed. Or he'll ask you to deliver them."

Nora's eyes narrowed. "Can I see that message? The one Pidge gave you?"

"It's fine, Nora, I have just the place for them," Pidge said.

"I threw it in the fire," Hyland answered, bristling. "But I assure you this is not some trick, if that's what you're insinuating. I've bigger fish to fry than entrapping two silly messenger girls."

Nora's nostrils flared. How dare he, after asking them to take such a risk? "These silly girls could march over to the barracks and turn you in," she spat. "Why aren't you delivering your own guns? God! It's like this in every fucking era. The women are always left to do the dirty work."

"For Christ's sake, Nora, hush!" Pidge said with a panicked look at Hyland. His large face was turning red.

"Are you questioning my loyalty?" he seethed.

"No, not your loyalty. Just your manners," Nora shot back. "Let's go, Pidge. Let's go risk our necks for the rich Englishman while he stays home and enjoys his tea."

"You're only proving my point. You have no idea what I've risked for the Republic. Now get out of here before I send word to Lynch that you're threatening one of his last suppliers."

Nora picked up the bolt of cloth and walked out without a word, Pidge behind her. She put the bolt in the basket on her bicycle. When she turned around, Pidge was staring at her.

"You've quite the temper on you, haven't you? And here I thought it was just Thomas who set you off."

The window curtains split open slightly. Nora pushed her bike down the road, toward the main square. "The man was a sexist eejit."

"A what?"

"A sexist. Don't you have that word? It means he thinks we're less than him just because of our gender."

Pidge looked thoughtful. "Maybe. But everyone thinks that way. And it's not just the women doing the dirty work—most of the time we're not allowed to even fight, except for Countess Markievicz. She does whatever she wants. But it's the lads who do the real dangerous work."

Countess Markievicz—another Republican hero. "I know. I didn't mean that . . . I know it's dangerous for the men. I just wish we had a bigger role, or that the role we do have would be better recognized, that's all."

"I feel the same way, but I'd not hold my breath. And we're not risking our necks for him, you know—the 'rich Englishman.' It's for the Republic. And that's a cause worth dying for."

Once they had passed the market, they got back onto their bicycles and rode toward Pidge's home, keeping a careful eye on the road lest they spill their precious cargo.

"Have you met the countess?" Nora asked.

"Me? God, no. She travels in far different circles."

"But she's Cumann na mBan, right?"

"Sure, but she's also one of them—those at the top. They treat her almost like an equal. O'course, she demands it. Was furious that her sentence of execution for taking place in the Rising was commuted to prison on account of her sex."

Nora raised her eyebrows. "You'd think she'd be grateful to be able to carry on the fight."

"Sure, but she wanted to be treated the same as the men, even if it meant she'd be shot."

"Have they executed any women?"

"Not yet. Doesn't mean there won't be a first, though. They keep threatening it."

They stopped talking as they approached the barracks. Two guards were posted at the gates. Nora nodded to them cordially, trying to keep her racing heartbeat from showing on her face. One of them raised his hand, but not in greeting.

"Hold up there," he said.

Nora brought the bicycle to a stop, clutching the handlebars tight to keep her hands from shaking.

"Pidge," the soldier said, nodding.

"Hullo, Daniel. How you been keeping?"

Nora gave Pidge a curious look. Was she on friendly terms with soldiers on both sides of the war?

"Who's this?" he asked.

"My cousin Nora, down from Belfast. You've heard what's goin' on up there, aye?"

He frowned and nodded briskly. "Aye." Then he glanced at the packages in their baskets. "I'm supposed to search everyone passing by."

"You're not going to steal my mother's tea, are you, now?" Pidge said with a wink and a giggle. Trying to relax her own face, Nora smiled at Daniel with as much warmth and innocence as she could muster.

"Is that all you've got, then?"

"This time, yes. Unless you've got something new for me?"

He blushed and shook his head. "Not here."

"Later, then?"

"Tonight. By the old well."

"Grand so." Without another word, Pidge mounted her bicycle and rode off. After a quick smile and nod at Daniel, Nora followed her.

"What was that about?" she asked once she caught up alongside Pidge.

"Daniel Miller. Joined the Free State Army because he needs the money." Pidge was pedaling fast, and Nora had to work hard to keep up with her. "But he's a Republican at heart. And he's sweet on me, but too shy to ever come out and say it. So he makes excuses to come and see me—tells me things he's learned or overheard. Then I pass it on to our lads."

"So you're a regular Mata Hari."

"What's that?"

"Never mind. I thought I was going to have a heart attack back there. What if it had been someone else?"

Pidge seemed unfazed. "Well, it wasn't. Listen, don't say anything to my parents about these guns, will ye?"

"You're not going to tell them?"

"They've enough to be getting on with. I've my own hiding places, and no one will need to worry about them until Lynch sends someone for them. Can you distract my mother while I bring them in?"

"Aye."

They soon arrived at the farm. Mrs. Gillies was in the back, hanging out sheets on the clothesline. Nora went to talk with her while Pidge brought their goods inside the house.

"How did you make out in town?" Mrs. Gillies asked when she saw Nora approaching. "Did you find the person you were looking for?"

"Aye, I did. In fact, there's something I wanted to ask you."

Mrs. Gillies lowered the sheet so Nora could see her face. "What's that, then?"

"My cousin sent down some money to the friend of the family I met in town. It's enough to get a room in Kildare for a while, until I can find work, but I wanted to ask if you might be willing to have me as a boarder instead. I'd prefer to stay here than by myself in town. I can pay whatever you think is fair, and I'm also happy to help out here at the farm."

Mrs. Gillies's eyes narrowed a fraction. "You wouldn't rather stay with your family friend?"

"He's only got a room himself," Nora said quickly. "And it wouldn't really be appropriate . . ."

"Of course not. I'm sorry, I assumed it was a woman." She continued to hang sheets on the line, her hands moving in swift, practiced motions. "Well, we've only got the settle bed, but Pidge seems to have taken a shine to you. I would hate to charge you, but—"

"I'm happy to pay, really; I couldn't stay otherwise."

"Well enough, then."

"Thanks a mill. Can I help you hang those?"

"I'm almost done. Go on in with you, and we'll start getting tea ready."

Nora nearly skipped back to the house. Now that she'd taken care of her basic needs, she could start planning how best to help the Republicans win this war.

"How'd it go?" she asked Pidge, who was putting away the groceries they'd stuffed on top of the guns.

"All done. What were you and mother talking about?"

"She's agreed to take me on as a boarder. I hope you don't mind."

Pidge's face lit up. "Of course I don't mind!" She grabbed Nora's hands and danced around in a circle.

"I want to see Thomas again," Nora said, grinning at Pidge's enthusiasm. "Could you help me?"

"I was hoping you'd come round. We'll send a message with Stephen; he'll see Thomas tomorrow. He told me their columns are training together."

"You're not going to tell Stephen about the . . . supplies?"

Pidge shook her head. "I'll just tell him to let Coogan know I've got what he requested. The commandant will figure it out."

Nora suspected Pidge didn't want to share the glory of her successful smuggling with her brother. "Can we not go with him?"

"I wish, but there's too much to do here for the next few days."

"I want to help with the war, Pidge. Like, really be involved. I don't want to just be on the sidelines. I want to make a difference. Change things."

"So do I. I wish I could do more, but with Da and Stephen off fighting half the time, it's up to Ma and me to run the farm."

"Are there any jobs you know of? Something I could do to help the cause? I don't need to be paid. Not yet, anyway."

"You could ask Da. He might know of something. Though you heard him at dinner—he thinks we should leave the rebellion to the men."

"Then maybe I can do something more strategic." Nora's thoughts churned. What would it take to change the outcome of the war?

But Mr. Gillies didn't come home that night. Mrs. Gillies didn't say anything, but Nora could sense the worry emanating off her like waves of heat from a radiator. Pidge and Stephen had a hushed discussion in the kitchen after tea. The house was quiet that night, and they all retired early.

"Any word from your father?" Mrs. Gillies asked Stephen when he came in for breakfast after the morning chores. He shook his head.

"Is it unusual for him to be away?" Nora inquired hesitantly.

"Not lately, no," Mrs. Gillies said with a forced smile. "He says it's better for us not to know where he is."

"I'll ask the commandant today," Stephen said, pushing his chair back. Then he looked at Nora. "And I'll pass on your message as well."

"Ta," Nora said, the heat rising in her cheeks. Mrs. Gillies gave her a curious smile.

"What message?"

"Just trying to get in touch with Thomas Heaney again, that's all." Mrs. Gillies made a "hmm" sound and began to clear the table.

Nora spent the day helping Pidge around the farm, her initial excitement turning into frustration. Patience had never been her strong suit, but she hadn't traveled eight decades to pull weeds and muck out stables. And yet she didn't know what else to do. She was one woman—could she really change the outcome of the war?

The next morning Nora was scattering seed for the chickens when Mrs. Gillies wandered over, carrying a large covered basket. "Have you seen Pidge, dear?"

"I think she went to the back field."

"No matter. I'm taking a meal round to Mrs. Lavery. She's been having difficulty getting by since her husband and sons were arrested."

"That's kind of you. Do you want some company?"

"I'll be fine, thank you. If Stephen returns before I'm back, you can give him some of the soup in the pot." There was a note of sadness in her voice, flavored with something else.

She fears it could be her family next.

Nora watched Mrs. Gillies go, her thoughts on the widows and fatherless children she'd known in Belfast. You could always spot them—there was a certain iron in their spine, a simmering anger that never quite left their eyes. It was what she saw when she looked at herself in the mirror.

Ach, stop feeling sorry for yourself. You're a soldier.

"Nora."

The man's voice jerked her out of her reverie. Instinct kicked in, and she brandished her shovel like a weapon. Thomas stood in the doorway of the barn, his hands raised and an amused expression on his face. "Easy, girl," he said. Bran stood by his side, tongue lolling.

She stabbed the shovel into a pile of hay and put her hands on her hips. "That was fast."

"Coogan sent me to collect the, uh, 'supplies.'"

"And did you get my message?"

"That's why I volunteered for the job. Kill two birds with one stone."

"I went back to Kildare."

Thomas's grin slid off his face. "And?"

"And they're almost as frustrating as you are."

"They?"

"The Brigidine Sisters. Brigid's messengers."

"I told you I don't need your help."

"I don't care about that anymore. But if I'm here, I'm going to damn well do something. I need information."

Thomas looked incredibly wary. *He knows something.*

"What kind of information?" he asked.

"Everything. Who is Brigid, really? How do you know her if she's been dead for hundreds of years? Are you a follower or something, like the Brigidine Sisters?"

"I didn't say I knew her. I only said it wasn't me who spoke to you in your dreams. You're the one who said you talked to her."

"It wasn't her, exactly. It was these Sisters—they said she gave them a vision. About me."

"How do you know they weren't just having you on?"

How do I know that? Because I'm here, in the early twentieth century, for starters.

"I just . . . believe them. I have my reasons."

"So they said Brigid wanted you to do something. Maybe they were wrong. Especially if it had something to do with me."

"You don't know anything about that, then? What she might want me to do?"

"I've no idea. But if you want my advice, I'd just forget about it."

"It's not that simple." Why was he being so obtuse? Based on the way he'd acted the other night, he knew a lot more than he was letting on. "The Sister said Brigid must have had a purpose for sending me here. I've an idea of what that might be, but I have to be sure. I don't know how this works or what will happen."

"How what works?"

Nora hesitated. What if she was wrong? What if Thomas was just a regular Irishman, to whom Brigid was simply one of his country's patron saints? Was she just imagining he knew more than he did?

"Where do you come from?" she asked. It was an innocent enough question, if he was no more than he seemed. But if he, too, had been sent here by Brigid, if he, too, had inexplicably traveled through time, he would take her meaning.

"Armagh. But I've lived in the south for many years."

Nora turned away to hide her disappointment. "So you're not . . . Brigid didn't send you."

"No." She chanced a glimpse at him. His expression was inscrutable. She couldn't tell whether he thought she was crazy or had grown bored of her questions. But he was still there. His blue eyes were still fixed on her, like magnets unable to pull away. "Where do *you* come from, Nora?"

She held her gaze steady as she met his eyes. "Belfast. I come from Belfast."

"Right." He looked almost as disappointed as she felt, as though the conversation was not going the way he had hoped, either. "What do you think your purpose is, then?"

"I'm going to help us win the war. At least, I hope I am."

He snorted. "I don't believe in hope. Learned that lesson a long time ago."

"You don't think it's possible?"

He came toward her, his strides slow and long. He stared at her as if she were a puzzle, a riddle to be solved. "Possible? Yes. Or else I wouldn't still be here, I suppose." One corner of his mouth lifted up in a wry smile. "But likely? No. I gave up on that hope long ago."

"Well, *I* haven't given up. There's always time for second chances."

"Good luck to you, then. Try not to get yourself killed, will ye? You're far too pretty for the firing squad."

Nora stared him down, wrestling with whether to tell him his own death was imminent—at least, according to the photograph. "I thought you might be able to help me. But it's every man for himself, is it?"

"It's not that—" he started, but his words were cut off by a low growl from Bran, followed by a woman's scream.

"Pidge," Nora breathed. She grabbed her shovel and ran past Thomas out of the barn. "Pidge!" she yelled. She came around the corner and raced toward the house. Pidge screamed again. A man was dragging her by the hair across the yard. Bran bounded toward them, snarling, but another man swung his rifle butt at the dog, connecting with her skull. Bran whimpered and then fell to the ground, silent.

"Get away from her!" Nora sprinted toward the man, her shovel raised.

"Drop it!" another man screamed, pointing a rifle at her. Three more men surrounded her, the barrels of their guns trained on her head. She hesitated, but then their uniforms registered in her memory. The Free State Army. She threw down the shovel and raised her hands in the air. One of the men advanced toward her, but she stopped him with the blackest look she could muster.

"Don't you fucking touch me. And tell your mate to get his hands off my friend."

The soldier stepped back, looking for direction from one of the others, who jerked his head at Nora. "Against the wall."

She marched over to the wall of the house and put her back to it, her chin held high and her eyes brimming with disdain. The soldier dragged Pidge over and threw her next to Nora. Where was Thomas? Had he done a runner and left them there? Bastard. Nora grabbed Pidge's hand. "Are you all right?"

Pidge spat out a mouthful of blood. "Aye."

"No talking!" shouted the man who seemed to be in charge, brandishing his rifle at her. "Names!"

"Hannah Gillies," Pidge said.

"Otherwise known as Pidge, I reckon," the commandant said with a leer. "I know about you. Tell me, is there a soldier in all of Ireland you haven't fucked? Think I might be next?" Pidge spat again, spraying blood across the commandant's face. He raised the butt of his rifle as though to strike her. She flinched and drew back. "Not so brave now, are you? And who's this whore?"

"I imagine the only women you know are whores. Can't fathom a decent woman wanting to be with the likes of you," Nora said.

Pain flared in her cheek as the back of his hand smashed into it. "Your name," he snarled.

"Nora O'Reilly. What's yours?" Behind him, Nora could see the other soldiers exchange uncertain glances.

"Sir, we found guns hidden in the house," a soldier called out, emerging with Pidge's hidden stash in his arms. "Miller was right."

So it was not the Englishman who'd betrayed them. It was the young man Pidge had mistakenly believed loyal to her.

"Well, well," the commandant said. "It's a shame your men aren't at home. If they were, I would shoot them right here. But we haven't executed a woman . . . *yet*. You still need to be taught a bloody lesson, though, don't you?" he said, bringing himself so close Nora winced from his rank body odor.

"Oh, aye? You gonna teach me how to be a traitor?" she said.

He pressed himself against her, wedging a uniformed knee between her legs. "You're nothing but a useless bitch," he seethed in her ear. "But I'd best search you for more weapons, just to be certain." His hand ran up her leg and over her hips, pressing into her stomach before cupping each of her breasts in turn and coming to rest on her neck. Nora shook with pure rage. She didn't care that four rifles were trained on her. At this moment, she hated this man more than she'd ever hated anyone. She drove her knee into his groin, forcing him away from her with a cry of pain. Then she kicked him in the face as he bent over, sending him sprawling into the dirt.

"You bitch!" he cried out, pressing his hand against his bleeding nose. The men stepped side to side, their rifles wavering. Nora grabbed Pidge's hand and made to run, but her assailant was faster. Her head jerked back as he grabbed her hair and pulled her toward him.

"Pidge, run!" Pidge tried to obey, but she was caught in the arms of another soldier.

Nora's face slammed into a barrel. She tried to get to her feet, but a thick hand held her down. The commandant straddled her, his weight crushing her ribs. Then a glint of metal flashed in front of her eyes.

"I'll . . . show . . . you . . . respect . . . ," the soldier grunted. She waited for her skirts to be lifted, for the chance to grab his cock and twist it off before he could enter her, but instead a searing pain scorched her skull. She screamed, but his grip was firm, and no one came to her aid. Again and again the knife flashed across her skull, and a ragged pile of red hair grew beside her. Then the pressure on her ribs lifted for a moment, and she was roughly turned around. "Not so pretty now, are you?" he snarled. His face was twisted into an ugly grimace. He pointed the knife toward her heart and cut open the front of her dress with a flick of sharp metal.

Then a shot exploded. Pidge screamed. The soldier on top of Nora wrenched around. She pushed him off, but she was shaking so hard, she couldn't find the strength to stand. The soldier who had been holding Pidge was writhing in pain on the ground, clutching his shoulder. Blood oozed between his fingers. The others were wide-eyed and frantic, swinging their rifles in the air toward an invisible opponent. Another crack, and Nora's assailant fell, a bullet in his head.

The shooting was coming from the house. A flash of gray in one of the windows.

Nora forced herself to stand.

Pidge stumbled toward her and clutched at her sleeve while the remaining soldiers advanced on the house. "Let's go," Pidge urged.

"We can't—Thomas is in there." Nora's eyes were fixed on the doorway. Pidge pulled at her arm, forcing her to stumble along with her.

"We can't help him; we need to go *now*."

"No, I can't leave him—" But she didn't have the strength to resist, so she followed in Pidge's wake. They ran behind the barn toward a copse of trees, the sound of gunfire behind them. Once in the cover of the trees, she collapsed onto the mossy ground.

"We have to keep going—they'll come after us," Pidge insisted.

"I know . . . I just need a minute." She could hear more shots—were they coming from Thomas or the Free State soldiers? "They'll kill him," she whispered. Is this how he was meant to die? Had she caused his death rather than prevented it?

"Not if he kills them first," Pidge said. "Let's go."

They stumbled through the trees until they reached the field on the other side. "We can hide at the McCleary farm; it's closest," Pidge said.

Nora strained her ears but could no longer hear the gunfight. Was it over? Who had won?

"He'll be fine, Nora. He can take care of himself," Pidge said, pulling her forward. "Come on. We have to find Ma and then get word to Da and Stephen."

They hovered on the edge of the field. Nora was torn. She wanted to warn Pidge's family, but she didn't want to leave Thomas behind. "We should wait until dark," she said.

Pidge glanced at Nora's bleeding scalp. "That'll be hours from now. We need to get your head looked after."

"They'll search the surrounding farms; no one will take us in."

Pidge's jaw stiffened. "You don't know these people like I do. I say we risk it."

"Your family is safe right now. But Thomas might be hurt; he might need us."

"Nora, Thomas is either dead or captured or on the run like we are. We've no weapons, and you're covered in blood. We've got to get you some help."

Nora turned back into the woods. "No. I shouldn't have left . . . I need to help . . ." Her head swam, and the woods spun around her. Another flash of pain spiked through her head as it hit a tree root. Then nothing.

She awoke with a sharp jostle, her whole body aching. The gray sky moved above her, and her stomach turned. She closed her eyes again.

"Nora!" Pidge's voice whispered in her ear. "Wake up!"

Nora opened her eyes again. Pidge was leaning over her. She struggled to get her bearings. Her head was lying on something soft and warm—Pidge's lap. The sky seemed to be gliding by above her. "Where—?"

"Shh," Pidge whispered again. "We're in a Free State lorry."

"How did they—?"

"It's my fault. You passed out. I tried to drag you across the field, but they followed. I'm so sorry." Pidge's eyes were red rimmed and tight with worry.

Nora stared at the moving clouds. "And . . . ?" She didn't want to say Thomas's name out loud.

"I don't know."

Nora struggled to sit up. Her head felt as though it had been lit on fire. Something was wrapped around it. She reached up to touch it, but Pidge grabbed her hand. "Don't. It's soaked through with blood. They wouldn't give me any bandages." It was then that Nora noticed great strips had been ripped from Pidge's skirt. She also realized they were not alone in the back of the lorry. A soldier sat facing them, his rifle splayed across his lap. Another, his shoulder neatly bandaged, leaned against the side of the carriage, eyes closed. A long, still figure lay in the center of the lorry bed, covered with a blanket.

"Pidge?" Nora moaned. "Who is under there?"

"That's Commandant Kirwin, ye hoore," the bandaged soldier answered, rousing. "Thanks to you, a good man died today."

"A good man wouldn't have attacked two unarmed women," Nora muttered. "Where's the man who shot you?" The soldier with the rifle looked at her with deadened eyes.

"Shut up. You're not supposed to talk."

"Is he dead?"

"I don't have to tell you anything." He glowered at her for a moment longer, then trained his glare on the passing countryside.

"Where are you taking us?"

"Hell."

"Nora, shh." Pidge wrapped an arm around her and pulled her closer. "They're taking us to prison, no doubt. Or the barracks. But for God's sake, don't give them cause to hit you again."

Nora sank back against Pidge's shoulder. "Did he cut it all off?" she murmured.

"Most of it, I'm afraid. He was none too gentle, as I'm sure you felt. Cut you in several places. There was so much blood. I couldn't stop him, I—" Pidge stopped, her words choked off by silent tears.

"It's grand, Pidge," Nora said, closing her eyes again. "We'll figure it out. What about your family?"

"I don't know. I'm just glad they weren't at home."

They embraced each other in the jolting lorry. Nora could tell from the sounds that they were leaving the countryside, but she didn't want to open her eyes. Had Mr. and Mrs. Gillies and Stephen been rounded up, or would they return to a house splattered with blood? Would they know Pidge had just been arrested, not killed?

And Thomas . . . If the soldiers had followed Pidge, that meant only one thing. He was dead. Or captured. Her gut ached.

The lorry lurched to a halt, and the soldier prodded her with the butt of his rifle.

"Up you get. Come on, now."

"She needs to see a doctor," Pidge said as she helped Nora to her feet.

"She can see one in prison," he retorted, shoving them roughly out of the back of the lorry.

A black iron gate loomed in front of them. Through the gate Nora saw five stone dragons, curled above a heavily barred iron door. Kilmainham Gaol. Had it only been a few days ago that she'd been here as an innocent tourist? The outside of the prison was unchanged, and yet the arched doorway with its five twisted dragons held a new, terrifying meaning. There would be no friendly tour guide inside, no brightly colored displays, no memorials to those who had suffered. There would be only suffering.

"Move along!" the soldier barked.

Nora cranked her head around toward the lorry, on the off chance Thomas was in the cab with the driver. But there was only a Free State soldier, one hand on the wheel, leering at her. Pidge grabbed her hand. "I reckoned I'd end up here someday," she said. "We'll be in good company, Nora. The true daughters of Ireland." She lifted her chin and held Nora's hand firmly. They walked into Kilmainham Gaol under the cold stare of the five dragons.

Chapter Fifteen

They were met in the entryway by a short, gray-haired woman in a high-necked black dress. She looked as though she was in mourning, which did nothing to comfort Nora's nerves. Armed Free State guards stood inside the doors. The woman took one glance at Nora's head and rounded on the two soldiers who had escorted them inside. "Who did this?"

They quailed under the matron's stare. "Commandant Kirwin, Miss Higgins."

"And where is Commandant Kirwin? I would like to have a word with him about his treatment of our women."

"He's dead. Shot during the fight."

"Are you telling me one of these women shot him?"

He shook his head. "An Irregular."

She pursed her lips. "So you say. I'll take them from here, lads. Off you go."

She turned sharply and marched into an office off the main hall. "I'm Miss Higgins, one of the wardresses. Your names?" she asked, taking out a leather-bound register.

"Hannah Gillies."

"Nora O'Reilly."

"Sign here." She handed them the register. Nora stared at it blankly for a moment—it was the same book she'd seen eighty years in the future. She took the proffered pen and wrote her name on the line. Some of the names had been written in fine penmanship, complete with delicate swirls and lines. Others were untidy scrawls.

"What are we being charged with? When can we see a solicitor?" she asked.

"You're being charged with sedition under the Emergency Powers Act. Which means you don't get to see a solicitor."

Nora turned to Pidge. "Is that legal?"

"The Free State does whatever they want," she answered, locking eyes with the wardress. "Just like the British."

Miss Higgins ignored this. "And you'll need to see a doctor, I suppose. First Lieutenant Lyons will have a look at you."

"Brighid Lyons? My mother was in prison with her after the Rising," Pidge exclaimed. "Are you telling me she's working with the Free State now?"

"We all want what's best for Ireland," Miss Higgins said, while Nora digested this surprising bit of news about Mrs. Gillies. "I suggest you keep that in mind. Against the wall, now. I have to search you."

"We've already been groped by your men," Nora said.

"Rules are rules. Unless you want me to have you strip-searched."

Nora pressed her lips together and turned against the wall. Miss Higgins patted them down, but it was more perfunctory than thorough. "Right," she said when she had finished. "Come with me. You'll be in the West Wing."

They followed her through a dingy corridor. Gone were the electric lights of the twenty-first century. Gas lamps dimly lit the stone hallway. The temperature dropped the farther along the passage they went. On an archway above them had been painted the words, "Sin no more lest worse shall come to thee." She hadn't seen *that* on the tour.

Soon there were no more lamps, only a faint light emanating from skylights far above them. The smell of human waste wafted down the corridor toward them. Nora wrinkled her nose and breathed through her mouth. Cell doors of solid wood lined both sides of the dark hallway. There were no windows in the doors, only small spy holes covered with metal disks. Finally, Miss Higgins stopped.

"In you go, Miss O'Reilly," she said, twisting a heavy key in the lock and opening a cell door. Nora peered inside. A single window, far above her head, let in a teasing glow of light from the outside. There was no glass in the window, only three thick bars. The floor of the narrow cell was stone. A thin mattress lay in the corner, topped by a small gray pillow and two folded blankets. Also on the bed were an enamel mug and plate, along with a knife, fork, and spoon. If Nora stretched out her arms, she'd almost be able to touch the cell walls.

"What about Pidge? Won't she be with me?" Nora asked.

"No." She handed Nora a long white candle in a metal holder, along with a single match. "You'll get one of these every other day. Make it last. The nights are cold."

Nora looked at the candle in her hand, then back at the wardress. "You're not serious? All we get for heat is a candle?"

Miss Higgins spoke briskly. "Heat and light. There used to be glass in the windows, but your predecessor removed it, complaining of the smell. So you've her to blame, not me. Now listen up, as I'll only tell you this once. Exercise in the yard is from ten to twelve and three to five daily. Roll call at eight, breakfast at eight thirty, lunch at one, tea at five, supper at eight. The lavatory is down the hall. No visitors are permitted, but you may send and receive one single-page letter each week. Until I finish processing you, you'll be locked in your cell, but as a general rule the cells are left open. During daytime hours you are permitted to spend time in the East Wing. It's generally warmer there. As political prisoners, you have a fair amount of freedom here. Cause trouble and you will lose that freedom. Understood?"

Nora gave a stiff nod, then stepped into the cell. Miss Higgins closed the door and locked it. Nora listened at the door as Pidge was shuffled into the cell across the hall. She sank down onto the thin mattress, clutching her candle. With nothing between her and the cold Irish spring, the small, cramped space was already freezing.

I'm not the first to go to prison for Ireland. Several of her friends had suffered long months, even years, in the Maze, Northern Ireland's most notorious prison. A rush of solidarity warmed her a little. She set her candle aside and unfolded the blankets, wrapping one around her shoulders and the other around her legs.

Just survive. Get through today. Tomorrow will sort itself out. She reached inside one of the pockets on her dress and pulled out Eamon's rosary. She clutched the smooth, hard beads as if to squeeze some comfort out of them.

A knock at the door interrupted her thoughts. A key turned, and a tall, blond woman entered the room. She was not much older than Nora, if at all. "Nora O'Reilly?" she asked.

"Aye."

"I'm First Lieutenant Brighid Lyons, the doctor. Miss Higgins sent me. If you'll come with me to the hospital ward, I'll have a look at your head."

Nora tucked her precious candle under her pillow, then followed Lieutenant Lyons out into the hall. The woman led her into a large room—large, at least, compared to the cells—in which there were four beds and a fireplace, which was gloriously lit. A heavy iron kettle hung over the fire from a large hook in the brick wall. Two of the beds were occupied.

"Are we getting a new roommate?" one of the women asked, struggling to sit up. Her face was gaunt, and it seemed as if the effort of propping herself up was almost too much to bear. The other woman opened her eyes and watched Nora but said nothing.

"Thankfully, no," Lieutenant Lyons said. "I've enough on my hands with the two of you trying to starve yourselves to death."

"What happened to you?" the first woman asked Nora.

Nora glanced at the doctor, then addressed the woman. "My friend and I were attacked by Free State soldiers."

The woman shook her head. "See, Brighid? This is the kind of government you're supporting. *This* is why we strike."

"I thought you were striking for your freedom," Lieutenant Lyons remarked wryly.

"That, too." The woman eased herself down on her pillow and closed her eyes. "Have courage, newcomer. No surrender."

Lieutenant Lyons directed Nora toward a bed near the fire. "Are they on hunger strike?" Nora asked.

"Yes. Been almost three weeks now."

Hunger strike. That phrase brought back a powerful memory of a small coffin, flanked by masked PIRA Volunteers, being carried through the streets of Belfast to Milltown Cemetery. Bobby Sands had starved himself to death in protest of his political imprisonment in the Maze, the first of ten such deaths. Nora, Eamon, and their mother had joined the hundred thousand mourners lining the streets that day. Nora, only six at the time, hadn't understood why a man would choose to die and leave his family—especially when hers hadn't been given the choice.

"How long will you let it go on?" she asked the lieutenant.

"It's not my decision, thankfully. The minister of defense, decides when—or if—they'll be released. I send daily updates on their health, but I can't make the decision to release them."

Nora shivered and leaned closer to the fire.

"It's cold in here, to be sure," Lieutenant Lyons said as she took a roll of clean bandages from a low cabinet against the wall. "I was in this wing briefly during the Tan War, before I got moved over to the East Wing."

"I heard you were here before," Nora said. "Must be difficult, holding your former comrades captive."

The doctor was silent for a moment. Then she said, "It is. We don't talk about it much. We all have our reasons for choosing the side we did. At least here I can make sure they are well cared for."

"By freezing them to death, you mean?"

"The candle casts more heat than you would think. And during the day, you're free to do as you please."

"Except leave."

"Except leave. Now let's have a look at your head." Lyons lifted a section of what had once been Pidge's skirt. It pulled hard, and Nora winced. "It's dried on to the wound," Lyons said. "I'll need to soak it." She lifted the kettle with a pair of heavy oven mitts and poured hot water into a ceramic basin on top of the cabinet. After soaking a strip of cloth in the water, she set it on Nora's head. The heat made the knife wounds sting, but the warmth almost made it worthwhile. The doctor slowly soaked each section of makeshift bandage and then peeled it from Nora's ruined scalp.

"So what are your reasons?" Nora asked.

"Pardon?"

"Why are you supporting the treaty? If you were in here for fighting against the British, why join them now?"

"I suppose it's like Michael Collins said: the treaty gives us the freedom to *get* freedom. And Lloyd George made it clear during the negotiations that it was either the treaty or 'an immediate return to war.' I used to go with one of the lads in the IRA. He told me they couldn't win another war with the British. They had no ammunition, no weapons left. And Britain's not recovering from the Great War anymore, like they were then. They'd be free to crush us—and crush us they would. So I'd rather take the treaty and work toward full freedom than lose a war and stay under England's thumb. Where would that leave us? At least now we've our own government. And we'll have the Republic someday, I truly believe it."

Nora kept her eyes down. Mick had always said the Free Staters were naught but traitors, giving in to British demands without putting up an honest fight. Even if the only alternative had been war, it was better than kowtowing to the might of the British Empire . . . wasn't it? It had seemed so black and white when her only friends were hard-line revolutionaries. How would Eamon have responded to Lieutenant Lyons's argument?

"And you? Why do you still fight?" Lyons asked. "Surely you must know it's a lost cause. If you defeat the new Free State, which you have to admit is unlikely given the number of Irregulars who've been captured, you'll have the Brits to deal with next. I don't understand it. Is it just stubbornness that drives you on?"

It's the knowledge of what happens next, Nora thought. She could tell that the doctor believed what she was saying, that she truly thought there was no choice between annihilation and dominion status within the British Empire. But she hadn't lived through the Troubles.

"I'm from Belfast, so I am. And I'm afraid of what will happen when—if—the country is divided. Permanently. The Unionists, the Prods, they hate us so much. I know that if we let the partition happen, the fighting won't end. It'll go on for years, ruining lives and families . . . like mine. I've a chance to stop it, so I must."

"You sound like it's written in stone."

"Not if I can help it."

"We've all lost people we love. And I don't doubt that things will be difficult for those in the six counties." There was a hint of steel in the lieutenant's voice. "But think of how many more will die if we take on England again. We barely survived the last war. I fear we won't survive another one."

Nora clenched her jaw, remembering the sight of Eamon's broken body on that hospital bed. "I'd rather die than get in bed with the British. No surrender."

Lyons was wrong. There were other options—there had to be. The British had to be as tired of war as the Irish. If they could overturn the treaty, if they could win the war here on Irish soil, the British would not be so keen to renew hostilities. They, too, had suffered greatly during the Tan War. And Nora knew better than anyone that the Irish were perfectly capable of bringing the war to England.

The doctor bit her lip. "Whatever side you're on, you can't deny it's a tragic outcome. The first thing we do after we finally get the British out is to start killing each other. Makes me wonder if we really deserve independence. Just look at you . . . I'm ashamed of the men who did this."

Nora gingerly touched her head. What would have happened to her if Thomas had not shot Commandant Kirwin? And where was he now? Did they even bury the Republican men they executed? Did he have any family who would claim his body? Or was there a chance he was still alive? "Do you have a mirror?"

Lyons rummaged around in a drawer and pulled out a small hand-held mirror, which she passed to Nora. Nora took a deep breath, then looked.

"Jesus Christ," she said softly. One of her eyes was turning purple around the outer edge. Her left cheek was scored with red lines spotted with splinters from the wooden barrel she'd been shoved against. Her bottom lip had been split by Kirwin's backhand. A trickle of blood had dried on her chin. But the most shocking sight was the matted, ragged tufts of red hair between the deep red gashes made by Kirwin's knife.

"It'll grow back, and you'll never know the difference," Lyons said. "Here, let me clean the wounds. I'll shave the rest to even it out; then we'll bandage it up. I've a scarf you can wear over the bandages. It's quite pretty."

"No."

"I beg your pardon?"

"Clean the wounds, please. But I don't want to cover it up." What she wanted was to show the Irish people how she'd been brutalized by Free State soldiers. Her heart raced at the possibility. It had worked in 1916, after all. The British had executed the leaders of the failed Easter Rising. That had been the last straw—the one merciless act that had finally turned the beaten-down, dispassionate Irish people into a revolutionary force to be reckoned with. Surely the beating and molestation of a woman in this otherwise genteel age would help turn the Irish people against the Free State. Just because she was behind bars didn't mean she was helpless. She could still have a role to play in this war.

"No one will believe you," Lyons said softly, as though reading Nora's thoughts.

"You think they'll believe I hacked off my own hair?" Nora winced as the doctor ran a razor over her scalp, trying to avoid the knife wounds.

"Listen to me, Nora. I know you're in here because you're a revolutionary. I know what that means, how it feels, believe me. But we finally have our freedom. Don't you want to be around to taste it? Don't go causing trouble for yourself."

"I've been causing trouble for myself since I was fifteen years old. I'm not about to stop now." She returned her gaze to the flames and tried to ignore the pain. It could work. But she had to be bold; she had to act now. What she needed was a camera. She was certain their letters in and out would be read by a censor, but there had to be a way she could contact a sympathetic newspaper and get the story out. Small, seemingly inconsequential actions had changed the course of history before, she mused. Maybe this would be one of them.

Nora stood the moment the doctor finished.

"You must let me cover those wounds. They'll become infected otherwise," Lyons urged.

"Fine." Nora sat down again, tapping her hands against her legs while the doctor wound a clean white bandage around her scalp. Then she wrapped a pale blue scarf over the bandages and tied it at the nape of Nora's neck. "Thank you," Nora said. "Miss Higgins said we're free to move around the prison? So I can go to the other wing, then?"

"You can. But mind yourself, Nora."

Nora caught the eye of the silent bedridden woman as she left the room. The woman said nothing but nodded at Nora in a way that bolstered her determination. The fire she'd felt after visiting Bernadette, the Brigidine Sister, was rekindled in her chest. The arrest was a set-back, but she could still change the future. She banged on Pidge's cell door. "Pidge! Are you in there?" There was no answer. She headed down another hallway, which was strangely empty, trying to remember the way to the newer wing from the tour she'd taken with Liz. As she walked, she untied the knot of the scarf and wrapped it around her neck, then unwound the bandage before it had a chance to fuse to her injuries. She folded it neatly and tucked it inside a pocket. She'd put it back on after everyone had seen what the Free State had done to her.

Finally, she encountered a guard, who barked, "You there! Get outside with the others."

She frowned, then realized the others must be out in the exercise yard. Her stomach ached, but she had no idea when the next meal would be served. She went through the doorway the guard had indicated, hovering a little before stepping into the courtyard. The sky was overcast but dry. The courtyard was surrounded on all sides by high stone walls that soared up thirty feet above her. She'd been here before, on the tour, on the way to the smaller courtyard she'd seen in her dream.

Women stood in groups, chatting, some smoking. Most wore dresses. Some even had on hats and gloves, as though they were en route to a cocktail party and not languishing in jail. A few of the women wore trousers. A game of some sort was taking place on one side of the courtyard—the women were throwing a small white ball to each other, trying to hit it with what looked like a broken chair leg.

Nora stepped forward. Several of the prisoners closest to the door turned to look at her and gasped.

"Christ have mercy!" an older woman exclaimed, rushing forward. "Who did this to you, child?"

They gathered around her, exclaiming at her wounds and pressing her with questions. "Nora!" Pidge called out, shouldering her way to Nora's side. "See, I told you what they did to her."

There were shocked gasps and clucked tongues. Nora—with Pidge's constant interruptions—told the story of their arrest. She hesitated when she reached the part about Thomas.

"Then a man, one of ours, came out of nowhere and shot the bastard. We tried to run, but they caught up with us."

"Who was he?" one of the women asked.

Nora glanced at Pidge. "I don't know. I didn't recognize him." If there was even the slightest chance that Thomas was alive, she didn't want to be the one to lay the charge of murder at his door.

"How'd they find you?" another asked. "How did they know about the guns?"

Pidge looked down at her feet. "It's my fault. We ran into a Free State soldier on the way home. The guns were hidden in the goods we picked up at the market. I talked him out of searching us, but he must have been suspicious." She scowled. "And here I thought he was one of the good ones."

"Have a fag, both of you. It's the least we can give you," one petite brunette said, handing them each a cigarette.

"Unless Betty's smuggled in more whiskey!" another said with a giggle.

"You drank it all!" The indignant response came from another woman who could only be Betty.

"Keep it down," the brunette warned with a nod toward the guards at the doors.

"Do any of you have a camera?" Nora said quietly. "I thought if we could get a photograph to the papers. Build some sympathy."

The women looked at each other, but no one said anything. Those who had been playing the game on the other side of the courtyard filtered over, curious about the newcomers. Nora was about to launch into a repeated description of what had happened when two of the guards walked over and broke up their huddle. "Time's up, ladies. Back inside."

"We'll talk more later," the petite brunette said, squeezing Nora's hand before filing in with the rest of them.

"You're a quick thinker, Nora," Pidge said as they headed inside together. "I'd have been more worried about the state of my hair if it were me. But you're right: we need to make sure the country knows how the Free State treats its women. They can lock us up, but they can't shut us up."

"Yes, but how do we manage it?" Nora muttered.

"We'll talk to the OC. She's the one of us who's in charge here, and she'll have some ideas."

"The OC?"

"Officer Commanding. Woman called Mrs. Humphreys. The others call her OC God; she's very religious. I've been asking around while you were with the doctor, trying to get the lay of the land."

Nora turned her head sharply. "Mrs. Humphreys? Annie Humphreys?" That name had come to her unbidden while standing in a cell on her tour of Kilmainham. Could it be this OC woman?

Pidge shrugged. "No idea. Why, do you know her?"

"No . . . I've just heard the name, that's all."

"I guess we'll find out. But what about this doctor? Did she not bandage you?"

"I took it off. Better that they see me this way."

"Until it gets infected and your head falls off."

"Aye, mother. I'll wrap it up again after we've seen this OC."

"It's almost time for tea," the petite brunette said, turning back to look at them. "Go and grab your mugs, and meet me in cell 243 in the East Wing. I'll fetch Mrs. Humphreys to join us. She'll get an eyeful at the sight of you—and an earful, from the sounds of it."

"Thank you . . ."

"Jo O'Mullane."

"Nora O'Reilly. This is Pidge Gillies."

"I've heard about you, Pidge. Grand family you've got. Are they well?"

"I don't know," Pidge said, her forehead creasing. "They weren't at home when I was taken. I've been worried sick about them."

"They'll find you. Word travels fast. And you can write to them. Post goes out tomorrow."

Nora and Pidge walked down the long corridor toward their cells. Other women joined them, grabbing their own enamel mugs.

"Welcome to the West Wing," one of them said. "It's as miserable as it seems."

"I heard the girls in the East Wing are going to protest until we get proper beds," said another. "I'm Julia O'Neill. Here's my sister Frances."

"Hullo," Frances said. "Don't hold your breath for the beds. No one will risk the fuss of a protest while Mary and Kate are still on hunger strike."

Nora collected her cup and followed the others. They emerged into the bright open horseshoe of the East Wing. Light filtered through the glass ceiling high above them. Three levels of cells surrounded them. The prisoners moved freely—some on the narrow landings that curved outside the cell doors, some down on the main floor. Several women arranged themselves onto the benches that sat in rows to Nora's left. It looked like some sort of class was about to be held. She and Pidge climbed the narrow metal staircase and looked for cell 243. Then they heard a voice beckoning them from the other side of the horseshoe-shaped landing.

"Pidge! Nora! Over here!" Jo was leaning over the railing and waving to them. They passed several cells, none of which were as austere and gloomy as their own. Above Jo's cell door was carved the words "The Invincibles."

"What's that?" Pidge asked, pointing.

"It's our cell name," Jo said proudly. "Me and my friend Lena share it. Come in, then. The tea will be around shortly."

"Where's Lena?"

"Irish lessons." Jo laughed. "Downstairs. May Kelly runs them. God knows I'd love to speak our mother tongue, but I've no memory for it. I do like the history lessons, though. They didn't teach us any proper Irish history in the British schools, that's for sure. And there's French and German and dancing and whatever else you might want to learn. We're a regular university in here."

Nora smiled. Her mother had insisted she learn Irish from a young age, but she hadn't spoken it in years. Perhaps she could practice with Lena.

Jo's cell was positively luxurious compared with those in the West Wing. There was a small wooden table and two chairs in addition to the two beds. A tricolor flag embroidered with the initials "CnamB" had been pinned to one wall. On the other wall, "Up the Republic!" had been written in large letters in pencil. A small box sat on the table. Beside it was an autograph book that resembled the ones Nora had seen on display on her first visit to Kilmainham.

"Here comes the tea. Get your cups ready," Jo said. Nora peered out the door. A thin, haggard woman wearing a dirty smock was going from cell to cell, holding a bucket.

"Is she a fellow prisoner?"

"One of us, you mean? No, she'll be a regular convict. They send them up from Mountjoy to do the cooking, cleaning, serving, and all that. Must be hard for them to see us enjoying our smokes and food packages, especially since we don't have to do any of the dirty work. But we've committed no crimes, either."

The woman arrived at their cell door. "Hullo, Marge," Jo said to her, then dipped her cup into the bucket.

"The tea is served in a bucket?" Pidge said indignantly.

"No fine china here," Jo said cheerfully. "But it tastes decent. Go ahead."

Nora and Pidge dipped their cups into the liquid. Though Nora made a point of smiling kindly at Marge, the other woman merely scowled back before hobbling to the next cell.

"What do you think she did?" Nora asked, sipping her tea. Milk and sugar had been added to the bucket. Jo was right: it was quite palatable, despite the lukewarm temperature.

"Who knows? Stealing, most likely. How's your head?"

"Sore, but I'll live."

"Here comes the OC now." To Nora's surprise, Jo stood and saluted as a short, plump woman with salt-and-pepper hair entered the cell. Jo prodded them with her foot, so Nora and Pidge also stood and saluted.

"May I present Mrs. Annie Humphreys, officer commanding of Cumann na mBan Kilmainham Gaol," Jo said with aplomb. "These two are Nora O'Reilly and Pidge Gillies, our newest arrivals."

Mrs. Humphreys gave the girls a sharp look, then sat down at the table. Nora sat on the edge of Jo's bed, beside Pidge. "Pleasure to meet you," Nora said. "I understand you might be able to help us—"

"Where do you come from, Miss O'Reilly?" Mrs. Humphreys interrupted.

Nora hesitated. "Belfast."

"And you were a member of Cumann na mBan there?"

"Aye."

"I'm always very interested in our new arrivals, so I've already made some inquiries. Lizzie Whelan tells me she met you for the first time earlier this week, at one of the training camps. Tells me you were making inquiries about some of the Volunteers."

"Is Lizzie here, too?" Pidge exclaimed.

Mrs. Humphreys ignored her, her eyes trained on Nora.

Nora stiffened, the implication clear. "Yes, I was helping Pidge—"

"How exactly do you know Miss Gillies?"

"She saved Frankie Halpin's life, that's how," Pidge interjected.

"I'm talking to Miss O'Reilly," the OC said coldly.

"It's true," Nora said. "I came across an ambush by the Free Staters. Frankie was the only survivor. I ran to the closest house for help. That's how I met Pidge and her family."

"So I've heard. And what was a young woman doing on a country road with the National Army in the middle of the night?"

Nora narrowed her eyes. "Why don't you just come out and say you think I'm a spy?" She clutched her cup tightly.

"It's my job to know who's in here—who's listening to what we say," Mrs. Humphreys said steadily. "Your story doesn't quite line up."

"Can't you see her face? Her head?" Pidge exclaimed. "Do you think the Free State would do that to one of their own?"

"I have no idea what they're capable of," Mrs. Humphreys said. Jo watched the exchange with round eyes.

"I came from Belfast to look for my uncle after my family was murdered," Nora said through clenched teeth. "His home in Kildare was deserted. Some Staters harassed me, so I ran. I lost my way. I decided to wait in a wooded area until daylight, but then the massacre happened on the road near me. I ran to get help."

"Are you telling the truth, Nora? That's quite the story you've got," Jo said, looking impressed.

"O'course it's the truth."

"Then why've none of our Belfast girls here heard of you or your family?" Mrs. Humphreys asked.

Nora set her cup down on the table, keeping her hands steady. "I signed up recently."

"Hmm. Well, that may be. But you'll have to forgive me for having my suspicions. You see, one of the guards here is called O'Reilly, and judging from his tongue, he is also from Ulster. Any relation to you?"

Nora stared at her, suddenly remembering what Aunt Margaret had said—her great-uncle had worked as a prison guard in Dublin until he was killed during the Civil War. Could this be the same man?

"I don't—no, I don't have any relatives in Dublin. And all my relatives are Republicans."

"But you and he are both from Ulster, are you not?"

"Look, I don't know who you're talking about. O'Reilly's a common enough name. But I'm not a spy, so I'm not. And I don't take well to people questioning my loyalty after all I've done for the cause."

Mrs. Humphreys stood up. "That sounds like a threat."

"What does it matter?" Nora stood as well, towering over the squat woman. "The question is, what are we going to do about this?" She gestured to her head. "Are we going to use it to help turn the people in our favor? Or are we going to sit in our cells talking about where we're from and who we know?"

There was a heartbeat of silence; then Mrs. Humphreys said, "So that's your plan?"

"If we can get the story of our mistreatment out—better yet, a photograph—it may well spark an outcry. It might encourage others who have been mistreated by the Free State to speak out. Who knows what kind of ripple effect it could have?"

Mrs. Humphreys pursed her lips. "There's a wardress, Miss Wilson, who will likely take the story out for us. She's helped by smuggling in food packages during the bans and bringing in the bulletins. Can you write down what happened?"

"Aye. What about a photograph?"

The OC shook her head. "No cameras in here, far as I know."

"Can this Miss Wilson bring one in? Disguise it as a food package or something?"

"It would be a coup, for certain. I'll speak with her. But I want Miss Gillies's name on the letter. Whether or not you're telling the truth about where you come from, the Gillies name will carry more weight."

"I don't care whose name is on it, as long as the truth gets out," Nora said, picking up her cup of tea again. They seemed to have arrived at a truce—for now.

Mrs. Humphreys nodded stiffly at them and left the cell.

"Well, that's not what I expected," Jo said, staring after the OC.

"Me, neither," Nora said. "Is everyone in here Cumann na mBan?"

"Not officially, no. O'course, everyone was caught doing something the State deemed 'revolutionary.' Either that or their menfolk are known Republicans. Except Peggy Murphy, I suppose. She says she was picked up because she crossed the street to talk to Jennie Nagle while she was being arrested. Bit stupid of her, really. But most are Cumann na mBan, aye. I'm on the Prisoners' Council."

"What's that?"

"The way we organize ourselves in here. The quartermaster's in charge of distributing any food packages that arrive, making sure the girls have enough soap, candles, things like that. The adjutant's in charge of distributing the post. May Kelly runs the lessons. And the OC is the go-between with the wardresses and the prison governor. She also makes sure we go to church." She rolled her eyes at this last statement.

"Church?"

"There's a chapel here, but we're not allowed to use it. So we've set up an altar. It's in the corner of the landing on this floor."

"Why can't we use the chapel?"

Jo made a face. "Because our fine clergy believe we are waging a 'war of wanton destruction, murder, and assassination against the people and the people's government.' No confession, no communion, until we repent of our sins and sign the Form of Undertaking. That's a form promising you won't do anything to hinder the new Free State government. You get to leave, and you're welcomed back into the church with open arms."

Nora stared at her. "Are you dead serious?" She felt automatically for the rosary beads in her pocket. Most priests in Belfast had supported the Provos' activities, even if they couldn't say so publicly. It was a priest who had swayed her to join the cause in the first place.

"I am. Some of the girls find it a bit rough, not being able to go to Mass and all. But we've managed. The Lord knows we're in the right. Now who's for a game of whist?" Jo pulled a deck of cards out of the box on the table. Before she closed it, Nora glimpsed a delicate pair of cream gloves and a stack of letters wrapped in a green ribbon.

"Ta, Jo, but I'd best be getting back to my own cell. Need to write that account and all." In truth, she didn't know how to play whist, and the last thing she needed was for more suspicion to be cast her way.

"Stay here and do it," Jo urged. "You don't want to go back to that dungeon until you need to. Here, you can use some of my paper." She opened the box again and pulled out a single sheet of paper and a pencil only two inches long. "We're trying to get more, but O'Keefe's in one of his moods," she explained.

"Who's O'Keefe?"

"Deputy governor of this fine establishment. Also a right bastard."

Nora accepted the pencil and paper and began to set down an account of their assault, making it from Pidge's point of view. Once again she left nameless the IRA Volunteer who had saved them. The Free State would counter with its own version of events, but hopefully the damage would be done by then. She passed the paper to Pidge, who scrutinized it.

"You're not going to say—"

"No."

Pidge nodded and signed the bottom.

"Can you give it to the OC?" Nora asked. "I need to lie down."

"Do you need to see the doctor again?" Pidge asked, her forehead wrinkling.

"No, but if you could help wrap me up . . ." She pulled the bandages out of her pocket and handed them to Pidge.

Jo laid a hand on her arm. "Don't give up hope, Nora. We'll get the story out."

Nora returned to her cold cell, exhausted by the day's many traumas. She wished she had half as many answers as she had questions. What would happen to her if she managed to change the past? Would she be able to go home? Was she still expected to help Thomas? And how could she do that . . . if he was already dead?

She lit her candle and moved it close enough to the bed so that she could feel its heat, but far enough away so that she wouldn't light herself on fire. The dying light of the cloudy day eased in through the open window above her. She wrapped her blankets tightly around her and closed her eyes, trying to shut out the world.

Chapter Sixteen

The next morning she woke up shivering. Her candle had snuffed itself out during the night, and the air was moist with the morning rain. Outside her door, a voice bellowed, "Roll call! Out of bed!"

Nora gripped her blankets tighter, unwilling to relinquish what little warmth they offered. She was rewarded with a loud bang on her cell door, which flew open a second later.

"Get up! Outside your door, now!" a guard shouted at her. Nora considered ignoring the order, but it wouldn't do to make enemies. She stumbled into the corridor, still wearing her blood-splattered dress and thin black shoes. On both sides of her, girls were shivering and yawning. Miss Higgins walked up and down the corridor, calling out names and checking them off on a clipboard whenever a girl shouted "Present." She stopped at Nora's door last.

"Nora O'Reilly."

"Aye."

"Do you have anything clean to wear?"

"No."

The wardress's face softened. "Make sure you send away for something. How are you feeling?"

Nora fingered the bandage. "Fine."

Miss Higgins's eyes lingered on Nora's bruises. After she left, some of the prisoners returned to their cells, while others stumbled down the hall toward the lavatory. Pidge crossed the corridor to Nora.

"Sleep well?" Pidge asked.

"Hardly. You?"

Pidge shrugged. "I wrote a letter to my parents last night. Jo loaned me one of her papers." Her eyes drifted past Nora to the window in the cell wall. To the world outside.

"I'm sure they're fine," Nora said, trying to sound as if she believed it. "If your mother had been arrested, she'd be in here with us, right?"

"It's not her I'm worried about, not really."

"I know." Nora tried to change the subject. "So, shall we name our cells, like Jo and Lena?"

Pidge smirked. "I was thinking, 'The Hidden Room.' You?"

"Good choice. I thought maybe . . . 'The Bane of Aengus Óg.'"

Pidge raised her eyebrows. "What's that supposed to mean?"

"I don't know . . . just something someone told me once."

"Fair enough. Listen, let's go up to the East Wing after breakfast. Jo told me you can see the street from some of the third-floor windows. Maybe my parents will be down there, looking for me. If nothing else, we can shout down for news."

They heard breakfast being delivered and grabbed their bowls. The prisoner on delivery duty today ladled them each a serving of watery porridge. Nora poked at hers with her spoon, then lifted a small amount to her mouth. She'd had worse in the camps . . . but not by much.

Pidge was equally unimpressed. She set the bowl aside. "When I wrote to Ma, I asked her to send some food packages. Seems we'll be needing them."

Nora was touched that Pidge seemed to think of her as one of the family. It had been a long time since someone had thought to look out for her. "Come, let's go find this window." They followed the example of the other prisoners and set their bowls and cutlery outside their cells, presumably for washing by the convicts.

The air warmed as they climbed the staircase to the third floor. The cells were the same as on the other floors, arranged in a horseshoe shape that could easily be watched by the guards and wardresses. They didn't have to ask which cell had the best window—there were already half a dozen women crowded around it, waiting their turn. Nora stood on tiptoes to look inside the cell. The bed had been shoved under the window, and a small table was balanced on top of it. A prisoner was standing on top of the table, leaning out of the glassless window. She shouted to someone down below, "Come back and tell me if you find him, will ye?" There was a muffled response. She stuck her arm out and waved frantically, then climbed off the stack of furniture and hurried past them, her cheeks wet.

A few minutes later, it was Nora's turn. The view was spectacular. To the left was the top of the Guinness brewhouse, and beyond that she could see soaring church spires over the tops of the trees. The majesty of the Wicklow Mountains loomed straight ahead of her. But closer still was a crowd of people standing on the banks of a small river, in front of a large billboard plastered with brightly colored waybills and advertisements. It was hard to make out the faces of the people down below.

Out of the corner of her eye she could see Pidge bouncing up and down on the cell floor. "Do you see anyone you know?" Pidge asked.

Of course not. Everyone I know hasn't been born yet. "No. Here, you have a go," Nora said, helping Pidge up beside her and then shifting over so the younger woman could see out of the tiny window. Pidge's eyes were anxious as she scanned the distant figures.

"There!" She pointed to a figure at the back of the small gathering. "Ma!" she bellowed, leaning out of the window and waving. "Ma! Kathleen Gillies!"

Mrs. Gillies, clad in a long, dark coat and brimmed hat, pushed forward and waved a gloved hand. "Pidge! Oh, thank God! Are you well?"

"Grand! And so is Nora!" Nora stuck her face in the window and waved down at Mrs. Gillies. "Are you all right? I've been so worried!" Pidge yelled.

"I'm fine! Your father and brother are still away visiting your aunt and uncle." Pidge gave a whimper of relief. At least they'd not been killed. Yet.

"Ma, I'm sorry!" Pidge cried out, her voice breaking. "It's my fault, I—"

"Hush, Pidge," Mrs. Gillies cut her off. "I know what they found. What's done is done. They've been looking for an excuse to come after us for a long while now."

Pidge shook her head, tears wetting her cheeks. "I'm sorry," she said again, but just loud enough for Nora to hear her.

"Ask her about Thomas," Nora said. "But don't say his name."

"Did you see Nora's friend? Is he all right?" Pidge yelled.

Nora wished she could see Mrs. Gillies's face more clearly. "No," Mrs. Gillies called up. "The neighbors told me what happened—I've done nothing but pray that the two of you were not harmed. Are you sure you're all right?"

"Aye, we're grand, other than being in prison!" Pidge shouted, recovering her normal good cheer. Nora processed Mrs. Gillies's news. If they'd killed Thomas, would they have left him there for Mrs. Gillies to find, or would they have taken the body with them? But there'd only been one body in the lorry . . . The pressure in her chest lessened slightly. There was a chance—a small chance—he was still alive. "What about the dog?" she asked.

"There was a dog, badly hurt, but she ran off as soon as she was well enough," Mrs. Gillies answered. "Tell me, what do you need?"

"Everything!" Pidge shouted. "Cakes and candles and bread and paper and my sewing kit and hairpins—" She stopped to take a breath. Nora grinned and took over.

"And a proper bed and a fireplace and some books and a telephone, please!"

Mrs. Gillies smiled broadly. The sight of it sliced into Nora's heart. How horrible it must have been for her to have come home to find her house ransacked and her daughter missing. Hopefully the sight of them, smiling and in the company of others, would give her some peace. How long would Mr. Gillies and Stephen have to stay in hiding? Nora felt an awful burden of responsibility. She should have either talked Pidge into hiding the guns elsewhere or refused to smuggle them in the first place.

"Don't be keeping those windows all to yourself!" someone shouted from behind them. A burly woman missing two teeth shoved in next to them.

"Hey, that's my mother down there!" Pidge said, shoving back.

"You've had your turn. There's over two hundred of us, and only three windows that can see down to the river."

Pidge pinched her lips together but then turned back to the window. "I have to go! I wrote you a letter. Will you come back?"

"As often as I can!" Mrs. Gillies cried. "Be safe, Pidge!"

"Don't forget to send food!" Pidge shouted. She waved wildly, then turned back to Nora. They jumped off the table and left the cell. The corridor by the windows was beginning to fill up now. *Not a bad distraction, I suppose*, Nora mused.

"There, you know they're all right," she said, a hand on Pidge's shoulder.

Pidge nodded, her face somber. "Mother is safe, at least."

"I'm sure your father and brother are just laying low. It's not like they can go back home so soon after what happened."

"I know. Sorry there was no news of Thomas."

"Aye. I just wish I knew what happened to him—if he's dead or alive."

Pidge gave her an encouraging smile. "Did you . . . resolve things with him?"

Nora huffed. "No. We were arguing in the barn when I heard you scream."

"You've an odd idea of how to go about courting a man, Nora. You might try being kind to him instead of fighting every time you see him." Pidge laughed.

"If he's still alive."

"Don't think like that. If he was dead, they'd have thrown him in the cart with that other fella. And I bet they'd have enjoyed telling us what they'd done. Let's hope for the best. Maybe you'll get another chance."

Nora nodded, heartened slightly.

Jo O'Mullane met them at the top of the staircase. "Come on," she whispered, gesturing with her hands. "It's here!"

Nora's heart thumped. *It* could only be the camera. She followed Jo down the stairs and into a cell near the end of the corridor. Inside sat OC Annie Humphreys, her face grim.

"Close the door," she said. "Jo, you're on guard."

Jo stood next to the door and fixed her eyes on the corridor through the small barred window.

"How'd she find one so quickly?" Pidge asked.

"I spoke with her yesterday," Mrs. Humphreys said. "Turns out her mother had recently been given one as a gift. She brought it in this morning. Now, it's important that we do this quickly. We've heard another report that they plan to execute one of the female prisoners. This might be enough to stop them."

"They wouldn't," Pidge seethed. "The people of Ireland would never stand for it! There would be another rising!"

"There are over ten thousand Republican men and women in captivity, Miss Gillies. There aren't enough of us left to revolt. If they start executing women, Lynch and his lads will have no choice but to surrender. They'll put the blame on them for continuing to fight while women are being killed."

"You think the people will blame the rebels if the Free State starts executing women?" Nora found this hard to believe.

"The State controls all the newspapers except for the *Eire*, which it constantly tries to shut down. The people already want an end to this war. I fear an execution would push them over the edge."

"Then why is this any different?" Nora gestured to her face and scalp.

"Because you're still alive. And it will be hard for the papers to position the brutal beating of a woman as a politically necessary act of war. It's a long shot, to be sure, but it's a sight better than doing nothing at all."

"Who do they plan to execute?" Jo asked from her post at the door.

Mrs. Humphreys shook her head. "It's just a rumor at this point. Let's pray it stays that way."

Pidge stood straighter. "I'm ready to die for the Irish Republic."

"Pidge, don't say such things. Think of your family," Nora urged.

"Enough," Mrs. Humphreys said. "Miss Wilson took a great personal risk by bringing this in for us." She reached under the blankets on the bed and took out what looked to be a flat leather purse. She undid the buckle and pulled gently. The "purse" expanded into an accordioned camera the size of a shoebox.

"She tells me it's the newest model. Should take a fine photograph."

"And then what do we do with it?" Nora asked.

"She'll take it back out and pass it to one of our girls on the outside, who will bring it to the *Eire* with your letter."

Nora stood against the white wall of Mrs. Humphreys's cell while Pidge removed her bandages.

"Your bruises are darkening," Pidge said. "Should show up nicely."

The OC photographed Nora's wounds from several angles before folding up the camera.

"So I guess it's up to the *Eire* now," Nora said as Pidge bandaged her back up. "And the Irish people." The OC was right: it was a long shot, but one they had to take. "How long before it's published?"

"Might be a few days. The *Eire* is published in Scotland, to avoid the censors."

"Someone's coming," Jo said. The camera disappeared. Mrs. Humphreys shoved several playing cards into each of their hands.

"Hello, Miss Higgins," Jo said to the wardress as she entered the cell.

"Miss O'Mullane. There you are, Miss O'Reilly. I've a clean dress you can wear until you manage to send for one of your own." She handed Nora a folded bundle of navy fabric.

"Ta." Nora accepted the dress and unfolded it.

"Mother will send us another for you," Pidge said. "Poor Nora, you've lost everything, haven't you?"

Nora thanked the wardress again. "I'm going to go change," she told the others, pushing past Jo into the corridor. She clutched the bundle to her chest as she made her way back into the gloom of the West Wing.

There was nothing to do but wait . . . and pray.

Chapter Seventeen

Excitement danced through the air the next morning. "What's going on?" Nora asked the girl in the cell next to hers after roll call. She stamped her feet on the ground in an effort to warm them up.

"Delivery day," the young girl told her. "I'm dying for some cake, and my mother promised she'd send me a new crochet hook."

Nora visited the lavatory, then stuck her head in Pidge's cell, but it was empty. She went to the East Wing and started the long walk up the stairs to the third floor, planning to look out the windows while the others were distracted with their packages. The same questions that had burdened her all night still ran through her head. Had Miss Wilson gotten the camera out of Kilmainham? Were the pictures of her wounds being developed this instant? Where was Thomas?

The third-floor windows were almost vacant, with everyone waiting for their letters and packages down below. Nora stood on the table and looked out, soaking in the view. A few people were gathered by the river, looking up at the windows. One of them was a small boy in a cap. When he saw Nora, he yelled, "Is Dorothy MacKinnon there? Can you fetch her?"

"I'm here," came a breathless voice from behind her. The skinny, red-haired girl gave Nora a quick smile as she stepped down to make room. "Ronan!" Dorothy yelled.

Nora wandered out of the cell and along the corridor, thinking again of Thomas. She hated to admit it to herself, but she had been hoping to see him down by the banks of the river, looking for her. *Don't be daft. If he got away, he'll not be coming after you.*

"But where are you?" she whispered. The wounds on her head itched, and she pressed her hands against the scarf the doctor had given her. Restless, she wandered back toward the staircase, where she met Pidge.

"There you are!" Pidge said, her eyes dancing. "Come on, our parcel's arrived."

"*Our* parcel?"

"From Ma! I opened it already, and she's sent some things for you. I've got it all up in Jo and Lena's cell. They've got a lamp, and we're using it to make tea."

Jo and Lena, a plump young girl with cherubic blond curls, were so caught up in examining the contents of their own packages that they barely noticed when Nora and Pidge arrived. A tin cooking pot was balanced on a gas lamp affixed to the cell wall.

"She's sent us some of my clothes—you can share, o'course," Pidge said. "And some biscuits and strawberry preserves. And my sketchbook. Did you know I've a fair hand at drawing? Rosary beads, obviously. Pencils, notebooks, everything we need to be comfortable. Well, as comfortable as possible in this dungeon."

"Whiskey?" Nora asked with a grin.

"As if that would make it past the censor without a bribe!" Lena exclaimed, looking up from her embroidery set. "My mother sent me a birthday cake last month for my sixteenth, so she told me in the letter, but the cake never arrived. Ate it himself, I'm sure, the pig."

"How long have you been here?"

"Three months," Lena said, her chin held high. "And I'm still as stubborn as ever."

"Here you go." Pidge passed Nora a box. Inside was a tin of tea, a tub of salve, two colored scarves, and a white envelope with Nora's name on it in thin dark ink. The seal had already been broken. Nora unfolded the letter.

> *Dear Nora,*
>
> *I am so sorry this has happened to you while you were staying with our family. I feel that perhaps we have been thrust together for some reason only known to our Lord. Pidge's letter to me was largely blacked out, but I've heard the talk and can guess the rest. It seems we are in your debt once again.*
>
> *I know they have a doctor there in the jail, but I have sent along some of my own salve, which I've used for many years on the injuries that have come through our door.*
>
> *We have still had no word of your friend, I'm afraid. I will write if I hear news.*
>
> *I hope you will forgive me, but I went through your things, in the hopes of finding some personal effects that might comfort you in your imprisonment.*

Nora's eyes staggered. She gripped the letter tighter and angled it away from the other girls.

> *I think they will be better left here for the time being, but I hope we can talk soon. I must admit I am most curious. Until then I will not mention it to anyone.*

You have shown great courage in the short time I have known you, Nora. Continue to be strong, both for yourself and for Ireland. Look after Pidge. I do worry about her.

Yours,

Kathleen Gillies

Nora folded the letter with shaking hands and slipped it back inside the envelope. Then she tucked the envelope inside her dress, next to her thumping heart. Mrs. Gillies knew—or at least suspected—her secret. How would she react? Would she think Nora was a spy? A witch? A lunatic? It seemed impossible that she would believe the truth, though the letter had sounded almost . . . accepting.

"What did she say?" Pidge asked. "Did she have word of—"

"No," Nora said quickly, pretending to take great interest in the other contents of the box. "She just wanted to make sure I was well. Wants me to keep an eye on you, too."

Pidge snorted. "That's what I thought! There's not much trouble I can get up to in here!"

"Oh, I don't know about that," Jo said. "Remember, Lena, how much trouble Anne Callaway first caused when she got here?"

"Wrecked her cell and barred the door," Lena said. "Made so much noise they banned letters and packages for a week, for all of us! She ended up getting a month in solitary."

"They tried banning our parcels last month as well, just because we wouldn't be their charwomen and clean the corridors. We got them back by going on hunger strike," Jo said proudly.

Nora raised an eyebrow. "How long were you on strike?"

"Less than a week until they caved and gave us our parcels back," Jo said. "*And* sent the convict women in to do the cleaning."

"Did everyone do it?" Pidge asked breathlessly, as though they were discussing a daring fashion trend and not group starvation.

"No, less than half of us," Jo said with a wrinkled nose. "Lena didn't, did you?"

Lena shook her head. "Not worth dying for parcels and letters, in my opinion. If it would stop the treaty, then maybe I would. But even then, I don't think I'd have the strength."

"What was it like, Jo?" Pidge asked.

"Awful. I thought I was going mad after the third day. I'd not be in a rush to do it again. But there's a certain solidarity in it, you know?"

Pidge nodded soberly, as though she perfectly understood.

"Is that why the women in the hospital wing are striking? They really think they can overturn the treaty that way?" Nora asked. She'd always viewed hunger strikes with a sense of horror, but if it could help prevent partition . . .

To her surprise, Jo laughed. "Goodness, no. They just want their freedom. We're unjustly imprisoned by a false government, after all. At least, that's what they keep saying."

"But they must be suffering horribly. The doctor said they've been on strike for nearly three weeks."

Jo sobered up. "Yes, I imagine they're having a very hard time of it at this stage. Won't be long before they get released, no doubt."

"You know, I remember hearing loads about it the first time Mary MacSwiney went on strike, last year. There were protests and everything. But I've not heard so much about it this time," Pidge said sadly. "Do you think, if there were more of us . . . ?"

"Let's just . . . wait," Nora said quickly. "Let's see if releasing our story leads anywhere."

Raised voices in the corridor distracted them. Jo went to the door and peered out. "What's going on?" she called down the hallway.

"Dorothy MacKinnon's signed the form," someone called back.

Nora moved toward the commotion. From the railing she could see the young red-haired girl who'd stood at the window with her this morning. She was clutching a small carpetbag to her chest and crying.

There was a guard on either side of her. Jeers and shouts of "Traitor!" echoed off the walls from the women who were now crowded around the railings.

"She was talking to someone out the window this morning, a child . . . ," Nora said.

Jo nodded. "Her brother. He's had a hard time of it, to be sure. She's the only family he's got left. Still, I wouldn't be able to live with myself. They'll stand me before the firing squad and pin a white cloth to my chest before I'll sign the form."

"But surely you could just sign it and then go back to work for the Republic, couldn't you?" Nora asked. Perhaps people took oaths more seriously in this decade.

"Sure, and some have done just that, but when they get arrested again, they're either thrown into solitary or sent off to the NDU. North Dublin Union makes this place look like a palace."

"Here comes Mrs. Humphreys," Lena said. "Let's ask her what happened." But before they could blurt out any questions, Mrs. Humphreys jerked her head toward Jo's cell door and marched inside. Nora's heart sank. This was not a good sign.

"Miss Wilson was caught taking the camera out," Mrs. Humphreys said in a hushed voice as soon as Jo closed the door.

"What? How?" Nora asked, aghast.

"I thought you might be able to answer that. It was your man O'Reilly who caught her. Seems to me someone must have tipped him off."

Nora's cheeks burned with indignation, and she fought to control her voice. She wanted to tell them everything she had done for the cause of the Republic, then dare them to call her a traitor to her face. "Fuck you. I told you, I don't know the man. This was my idea. Why the hell would I want to sabotage my own plan?"

The other women stared at her in shock.

"God! Does anyone have a fucking cigarette?"

Lena reached into her pillowcase and drew out a small tin, from which she produced a cigarette and a book of matches. She handed them to Nora wordlessly.

Nora kept her eyes on the flame as she lit the smoke. Then she closed them and took a long draw, imagining she was smoking behind her old school in Belfast—before her life had been ripped apart. The others remained silent. "So, what happened to her?" Nora asked.

Mrs. Humphreys cleared her throat. "She was released from her duties. The camera was confiscated. It will be a few days before they develop the film, no doubt, if they do at all. They already know what's on it."

"The letter?"

"Also taken."

"Fuck."

"Miss O'Reilly, I must tell you we don't tolerate such language. Obviously, you are upset, but—"

"Aye, it's grand. It was just . . . this was my one chance."

"Your chance for what?"

"To do something about this fucking—sorry—war."

Mrs. Humphreys inspected Nora through narrowed eyes. "I'll take your word for it. I suppose it could have been someone else who informed on us . . . and I mean to find out who." She cleared her throat and addressed the other women. "We've had a few new arrivals, so I've updated the new prayer schedule. It's posted down by the yard, but Jo and Lena are on from nine until eleven p.m. this week. Nora and Pidge, you drew the short straw. Two until four a.m."

"What prayer schedule?" Pidge asked, looking thoroughly confused.

"We keep a twenty-four-hour vigil for the hunger strikers, Miss Mary MacSwiney and Mrs. Kate O'Callaghan," she said sternly. "And you are expected to visit them once a day. I'm surprised the other girls haven't told you."

Jo and Lena looked at their feet. "There's been a lot going on," Jo said.

Mrs. Humphreys huffed. "Well, we tried, and I don't fault you for it, Miss O'Reilly. Perhaps you'll come up with another idea. We're still Republicans, even in here."

After she left, Nora sank down onto Lena's bed and took a final draw on the cigarette. She snuffed it out on the bottom of her shoe.

"Cheer up, Nora. It was a good idea," Lena said.

"Probably wouldn't have worked as well as we'd hoped, anyway," Jo said. "If the people don't care about Kate and Mary starving themselves, then they probably wouldn't care about one of us being beaten."

Nora looked up at her. "You really think that?"

"Ah, Nora, don't look that way. Who knows, maybe that photograph would have done some good. But now we won't know either way."

Nora stood up. "I'll think of something else."

"Sure, you can think about it at two in the morning while you're at prayers," Lena said with a giggle.

"Do they really expect us to pray for two hours?" Pidge asked, shaking her head.

"We cheat a bit. Lena does the first hour while I do the second," Jo said. "I mean, I don't think God minds, does he?"

"I'm sure it's just fine by him," Nora said. "There weren't any visitors sitting with the hunger strikers while I was in with the doctor. Are we supposed to just pop in?"

Lena and Jo shared guilty looks. "Well . . . it's getting hard to see them. There was this horrible spell when they were vomiting all the time. Poor Kate looks more like a doll each day. Sometimes they moan—they can't help it. It's just . . . difficult to see them like that, is all, when we're out here eating cakes and playing games."

"I can imagine," Nora said. The mood in the room was morose.

"Enough of this depressing talk. Here, will you sign my new autograph book?" Pidge asked.

Nora took it from her. Was this one of the books in the display case in the Kilmainham of the future? They traded books and spent a few moments writing in them and exchanging idle gossip.

Pidge was strangely withdrawn. "You all right?" Nora asked after a few minutes.

"It's just . . . We can't sit here, drinking tea and playing whist, while our men are being executed and the treaty is forced through an illegitimate parliament."

"You're right, we can't," Nora said firmly. "That's why we tried to get our story out. I meant it. I'll come up with another plan, there must be—"

"*I* have a plan."

"What?"

"I think . . . I'm going to join the hunger strike."

"Ah, Pidge, you don't know what you're saying," Jo said. "I've done it, remember? It's not an easy task."

"I didn't say it would be easy! It hasn't been easy on Kate and Mary, has it? But it works. Nell Ryan, Maud Gonne, Kitty Costello, they all got released, didn't they?"

"Yes, but think of how they suffered!" Lena said. "They had to carry them out on stretchers, and they were brought straight to hospital."

"Nora, surely you agree with me," Pidge said, her eyes pleading. "You'll join me, won't you?"

Nora hesitated. Would two more hunger strikers really be enough to turn the tide? "I don't know, Pidge. It doesn't seem . . . *enough*, somehow, if that makes any sense."

"Not enough? What more could we do than lay down our very lives? You're not afraid, are you?"

"I'm willing enough to die for Ireland, if that's what you're asking. But if what Jo says is right, and no one seems to care about what Kate and Mary are doing, what makes you think they'll care about you? How d'you think it will change anything? The most you can hope for is release, and then what? You'll be so weak and sick you won't be of any use to the Republic. You'll be free—but for what?" The thought of Pidge's healthy figure wasting away, week after week, was horrible to imagine. *Look after Pidge*, Mrs. Gillies had written.

"It's solidarity, that's what it is," Pidge said. Pink blotches were forming on her pale cheeks.

"Have you ever actually been hungry? For more than a few hours, that is?" She shut her eyes, trying to block out the memories. Emaciated men, women, children trickling into the refugee camps. People dropping dead by the side of the road, only to be carved apart by vultures. "I've *seen* people starve to death. It's the worst way to die, Pidge. We know they're thinking of executing one of us. What if they decide to let one of us die of hunger? Are you willing to take the chance, just for the sake of solidarity?"

"I'm surprised at you, Nora. For all your talk of being a revolutionary . . ." Pidge glowered at her feet.

Nora couldn't blame her. Ten years ago, she'd have felt the same way. "If it would change things, then I'd be the first to do it. But you're right: I don't want to starve myself just to be released and sent to hospital for weeks. I want more than freedom from this jail. A hunger strike won't achieve that."

"Then what will, Nora?" Jo asked softly. Pidge was still avoiding her gaze.

Nora shook her head. "I wish I knew."

Nora spent the rest of the day getting a feel for the routine of Kilmainham. She understood Pidge's frustration—she felt it herself— but if the memory of the H Block prisoners in the Maze had taught her anything, it was that the British were more than happy for Republicans to starve themselves to death. It had never seemed a particularly effective tactic, considering the cost, but she could tell Pidge was still thinking about it. The younger girl spent most of the afternoon in her cell in the West Wing. Nora watched her chew her biscuit at lunch slowly, methodically, as though savoring every bite. They didn't speak of it again, but something had changed between them. It made her feel strangely lonely. Her thoughts flitted from Thomas to Mrs. Gillies's letter to the Brigidine Sisters . . . and finally to Eamon. He'd been a reluctant revolutionary if ever there was one. He would have scoffed at the idea of going on hunger strike, she was sure of it. He had been far too practical for such things.

She forced herself to join the others in the exercise yard for a game of rounders. No one seemed to mind that she didn't know how to play; she blamed it on being a city girl. It was simple enough, much like the baseball games she'd seen on the telly. A bowler threw the ball to a batter, who tried to hit it with a wooden chair leg. Other women tried to catch it and tag the batter before she reached one of the posts around the yard. It felt good to do something active, and the camaraderie of the other women helped soothe her own bitter disappointment over the confiscated camera. She avoided the girls from Belfast, lest they ask too many questions, and instead stuck close to Jo and Lena and their friends from Cork. The competition in the game was heating up when Julia O'Neill sent the ball soaring over the wall and out onto the street. A collective groan rose from the players.

"That was our last ball!" one of the Cork girls cried.

"I'll write for another one right away," Julia said, her face turning pink.

"Ach, it was a good shot, so it was," Nora said. "I think this means you won the game."

After supper, some of the girls gathered in the corridor outside the hospital room to sing hymns. Nora stood a little way off, listening to their soft voices. She wanted to offer her support to the hunger strikers, but she didn't want to intrude on this intimate moment between those who truly belonged here, in this time. *Let us carry your cross for Ireland, Lord,* they sang. Her chest ached. She missed going to Mass with her mother and Eamon. She'd say extra prayers for them tonight.

She followed the stone walls back to her own cell, letting the voices fade behind her.

She woke hours later to a knock on her cell door. She picked up her burning candle and, keeping a blanket around her shoulders, opened the door. It was Julia O'Neill.

"I saw you were next on the prayer schedule, so I thought I'd wake you. Shall I wake Pidge as well?"

"No, I'll do it," Nora said quickly. "So we just . . . pray by the altar? On the landing? This is my first shift."

"Yes, second floor of the other wing. You'll see it—Grace Plunkett painted a beautiful picture of Our Lady. Just try to stay awake. That's why there are two of you. Monica Doyle fell asleep last week, and the OC was ragin'."

"Ta," Nora said. "Good night." She watched Julia pad down the hallway, then grabbed her rosary beads. She'd let Pidge sleep for another hour, then wake her.

Julia's sister Frances was still kneeling in front of the altar when Nora arrived. She cleared her throat softly.

Frances didn't say anything—she just smiled and got to her feet, then walked past Nora and down the stairs.

Nora shivered. The tour guide in the future had told her Kilmainham was said to be haunted. Alone in front of this altar, surrounded by the cells of women who had been long dead on her first visit to this place, the idea of ghosts seemed all too possible. The entire jail seemed to be holding its breath. Were Kate O'Callaghan and Mary MacSwiney meant to die here? Was something else afoot?

The altar was simple enough, a small wooden table covered in a white cloth embroidered with fine blue and yellow flowers. A painting of two saints decorated the wall behind it, the Virgin Mary presiding above them. Nora picked up the lit candle from the altar and held it closer to the painting. The two figures were identified in small black letters at the bottom of the image: "Saint Colmcille" and "Saint Brigid."

Well. Perhaps this was the right place, after all.

Kneeling, Nora crossed herself and clutched her rosary beads. She prayed the Our Father and a couple of Hail Marys, feeling guilty that she'd let her devotion slip amid the chaos of the past few days. She stared at the painting of Saint Brigid as she recited another Hail Mary.

"If you have a plan, could you just tell it to me already?" she muttered.

The silence of the jail closed in on her.

"Or if you have any ideas, that would be grand as well."

Nora stood and rubbed her knees. When she turned around, a guard was watching her from near the top of the staircase. She stiffened, then raised her chin and walked toward him, planning to tell him to leave her alone. But as she drew closer, those thoughts were pushed from her mind. His face was thin, with a long, straight nose and eyes just a little too close together. The same red hair as hers peeked out from under his cap. He looked young. Eighteen or nineteen, maybe.

"What are you looking at?" he asked.

"You're . . . you're Roger O'Reilly, aren't you?"

"Aye. What's it to you?"

"Nothing. You just . . . you look like my brother, is all. I'm an O'Reilly as well."

"Oh, aye, you're the one who caused all the trouble with your smuggled camera, are you not?"

"Just trying to tell the truth." She kept her gaze steady. "You're the one who got Miss Wilson fired."

"'Twas her own doing, so it was."

"Why do you work here, Roger? You come from a family of Republicans."

His eyebrows twitched. "How do you—you don't know what you're on about."

"Don't I?"

"What, you think because we have the same surname you know my family?"

She regarded him silently, struck by the family resemblance. He looked away from her gaze—maybe he could see it, too. It was definitely the young man in the photograph she'd seen at Aunt Margaret's, the one of her grandfather and his brother laughing, their arms slung around each other. "Is your brother here as well?" Her grandfather had died when she was a little girl, and she could scarcely remember him. The thought of meeting him here filled her with excitement. Might he believe that she was his granddaughter, come from the future?

"How d'you know about my brother?"

What was she supposed to say? *Mind yourself.*

"I just thought maybe we were distant relations. Both of us being from Belfast and all. I can tell from your accent," she added hurriedly.

"Aye, well, I've loads of relatives I've never met, so I suppose it's possible. But that doesn't mean you'll be getting special treatment, y'hear?"

"I wouldn't dream of it."

Nora was about to ask why Roger had come to Dublin, but then she remembered the date on the back of the photograph at Aunt Margaret's, and her blood chilled. April 4, 1923. The date of Roger O'Reilly's death.

"What's the date, Roger?"

"April 1, I reckon. Or April 2, I suppose, seeing as it's past midnight. Why d'ye ask?"

"Nothing. I just . . ." She couldn't take her eyes off him. It was as though she were already seeing a ghost stalking the halls of Kilmainham. On an impulse, she reached out and laid her hand on his arm.

He jerked away. "Houl on! What are you playing at?"

"Nothing," she said quickly, drawing away. "I just . . . I'm sorry." She ran back to the altar, pressing the rosary beads into her chest. Should she warn him? Would it even work? Or would he, like Mrs. Gillies and Mrs. Humphreys, suspect she was not as she seemed? *I don't even know how he dies, let alone where. What if I tell him to stay inside all day, and his house catches on fire? What if I'm the one who causes his death?*

She squeezed her hands together, the beads pressing into her palms. "Holy Father, Mary, Brigid, anyone who is listening, this isn't what I signed up for. I don't want this man's death on my hands. What should I do? What should I do?"

She stayed at the altar until a voice softly said her name.

"You've gone and done the shift for both of us," Pidge said, pulling a prison blanket tighter around her shoulders. "Why'd you not wake me?"

"I planned to, after an hour. I suppose I just got into it." She checked over her shoulder. Roger was still at his post, watching them.

"Well, it's Cis and Una's turn now. They're on their way up. C'mon." They tiptoed together back to their cells, nodding at their replacements on the way. Nora's knees ached, and she was shivering.

"Have time for a talk?" Pidge asked.

"Aye, o'course." Pidge followed her into her cell. They sat close together on the mattress, both clutching their candles.

"I've decided I'm going to do it." Pidge didn't look at her but stared into the flame in her hands.

"Join the hunger strikers? Do you really think that will bring about Ireland's freedom?"

"All I know for sure is that sitting here doing nothing certainly won't."

Good Lord, was she really willing to die out of sheer stubbornness? "If it's your freedom we're talking about, just sign the form, like Dorothy MacKinnon. You'll be back with your family by nightfall."

"And have everyone think I'm a traitor? I'd rather die."

"That's just the problem—you might. Think about your family, for Christ's sake. Do you think your mother can stand to lose another child?"

Pidge stood up and crossed to the other side of the cell. She leaned her back against the wall and glared at Nora. "Why are you so against this?"

"I'm trying to save your life!"

"Did you even read what I wrote in your autograph book?"

Nora frowned. "No . . . I've not had a chance yet."

Pidge went to the door. "Read it. It sums up everything. And if you still can't understand why I'm doing this, then you're not who I thought you were." She opened the door and walked out. Nora heard the cell door on the other side of the corridor open and close.

Ballix. She grabbed her autograph book and opened it to the first page, where Jo had written:

> *Now, Nora, my dear, always be of good cheer,*
> *And don't let the 'Union' oppress you,*
> *There are great times ahead when the Slave State is*
> *dead,*
> *And an Irish republic will bless you.*
> *— Jo O'Mullane, Kilmainham Gaol April 1923*

She turned the page to see Lena's signature.

> *Here's to the girls in Kilmainham.*
> *Here's to the girls on the run.*
> *Here's to the girls who are active,*
> *And to girls who can carry a gun.*

Had Lena, with her blond curls and rosy cheeks, ever carried a gun? Had she ever taken a life?

She turned the page again.

The date was neatly written in the top corner, underneath the words *Kilmainham Gaol*. Delicate scrolls and knots wove their way around the outer border of the page. In the center was written, in a curving, delicate hand:

> *Far better the grave of a rebel, without cross, without*
> *stone, without name,*
>   *Than a treaty with treacherous England that can*
> *only bring sorrow and shame.*

"Those aren't the only two choices," Nora whispered to the empty cell. She lay down on her mattress, with the autograph book splayed open on her chest. She'd told Pidge she'd think of something else, something that wouldn't put her life at risk. Pidge's life . . . Roger's life . . . how many more would be put in her hands? Would death follow her everywhere she went?

At least she could do something about one of them. She picked up her candle and returned to the altar. Two girls were kneeling beside it, their hands busy with their rosaries. As before, Roger stood a way off, in the shadows, watching. She hesitated, remembering the OC's suspicions, which would surely be confirmed if she were seen talking to the guard. But if the alternative was letting him die . . .

She marched over to him. "I need to talk to you."

"What are you doing back here? You're supposed to be in your cell."

"It doesn't matter. Listen, I know what I'm going to say will sound crazy. But while I was praying, I had this . . . strong premonition about you."

He took a step back. "About me?"

"Aye, just hear me out. It's going to sound—well, here it is . . . I had this feeling that you're going to, well, die. In three days' time."

"What are you on about? Is your head cut?" The girls at the altar glanced back at them.

Nora kept her voice low. "I told you it would sound crazy, but I'm quite serious. On April 4, you're supposed to die."

"Is that a threat?"

"No, it's nothing like that! Believe me, this doesn't have anything to do with the war or which political side you support. It was just a sense I got. When I was praying. Do you pray?"

"O'course I pray," Roger muttered. "But I don't have no feelings about people dyin'."

"Neither do I, usually. And I wasn't going to say anything. But it didn't seem right to keep that from you. I'd want to know, if it were me."

"You're off your head. Go on with you, or I'll report this to the matron, so I will."

"Fine. I'm going. All I know is what God showed me. And I don't know what you can do to stop it. Or if you even can. But I'd at least try if I were you."

"Get on with ye!"

Nora turned and hurried down the staircase. Maybe it would do nothing, but at least she'd followed her conscience. Besides, this was an important test. In three days she'd know for certain if the past really could be changed.

She lay awake in bed, her mind racing with questions about Roger and his coming fate.

Then a sudden realization struck her.

Roger O'Reilly wasn't the only man who was meant to die in the coming days.

"Liam Lynch," she whispered into the darkness. "April 10."

It was April 10, she was sure of it. Her Provo mates had made a big deal out of it when the Good Friday Agreement was signed on the exact anniversary of Lynch's death. "Like spitting on the grave of one of Ireland's greatest heroes," one of them had said.

She sat up and stared at the lone flame flickering on the floor beside her. Those same friends claimed Lynch's death had effectively ended the Civil War. He'd been shot by the Free State Army during a skirmish in the countryside. The Staters hadn't even known they'd shot the chief of staff of the IRA until he told them who he was. They took him to a hospital, but it was too late. Without their leader, the IRA had lost its nerve and surrendered to the Free State, leaving the six counties of Northern Ireland to fend for themselves.

This was it. This would be so much bigger than a propaganda coup, so much bigger than saving a single man's life.

If she could save Liam Lynch, the IRA would fight on. They wouldn't give up until the treaty was rejected. There would be no surrender.

Chapter Eighteen

To Nora's dismay, Pidge announced her decision to the prison matron and a crowd of fellow prisoners the next morning. She told them she planned to stay in her cell for as long as possible, only moving to the hospital room when her condition required it. She pledged to let no food cross her mouth until she was a free woman.

As soon as they were alone, Nora tried again to talk her out of it. Pidge was adamant, and Nora reluctantly dropped it. Pidge was a grown woman, entitled to her own mistakes. And she'd need support, not censure, if she were to survive this ordeal. Nora just hoped the authorities would cave and release her sooner than later.

At mealtimes, Pidge shut herself into her cold cell, so as not to be tempted, she said. Jo and some of the others who'd been on strike before gave her advice on dealing with the cravings—and the pain—that accompanied the first few days.

"The first days are the worst," Jo said. "Try to keep busy for as long as you can, and whatever you do, don't let your mind dwell on food."

Nora passed the news on to a stricken Mrs. Gillies from the third-floor window. A letter arrived for Pidge the next day, begging her to reconsider. Pidge set the letter on fire.

April 4 arrived. The day of Roger O'Reilly's death. Nora spent the day in nervous anticipation. If she had successfully changed Roger's fate, that meant she could change Lynch's as well. He wasn't stationed by the front doors as usual. Nor was he in the exercise yard when the women were allowed out for their rounders game. Nora began to pace around the halls of the jail. His red hair and gangly form were conspicuously absent. At noon she joined Pidge in her fast, her stomach too tight to eat. At dinner, she had a few spoonfuls of potatoes and onions but could not sit still long enough to finish her bowl. She went on another circuit around the East Wing, walking up and down the stairs and returning repeatedly to the altar.

She'd mercifully been moved to a midday prayer shift. It was hard enough on her, Mrs. Humphreys said, to have her closest friend on hunger strike. That same afternoon she and Pidge were moved to Dorothy MacKinnon's old cell in the East Wing. Nora was grateful for the shared quarters. It would be easier to keep an eye on Pidge this way.

By the time night fell, Nora succumbed to exhaustion and curled up under her blanket. But sleep would not come. Had Roger merely taken her advice and stayed home . . . or was he dead? If so, how had it happened? Had he thought of her warning as he lay bleeding out from a bullet wound or a mangled leg? She tried to tell herself that she'd done everything she could, that if he'd believed her he might still be alive . . .

But as the day wore on, her feeling of dread grew. Perhaps Ireland was set on a tragic course from which it could not be derailed.

No, it had to be possible. Even being here had changed the future for some. Frankie Halpin. Pidge. Thomas. She cringed into her pillow. Yes, she'd probably saved Frankie Halpin's life, but what of the Gillies family? What of Thomas? They were worse off now than before she'd met them.

She drifted to sleep, haunted by thoughts of Roger O'Reilly's face, bloodied and still . . . who then became Frankie Halpin . . . who then became Eamon . . .

The morning brought gray light through the bars of her window. Another day of uncertainty. Pidge was tight in a ball on her mattress, arms wrapped around her knees. Nora knelt beside her and rubbed her back.

"Stomach cramps?"

Pidge nodded. "It hurts."

"I know."

"I'm afraid. What if I can't bear it?"

"There's no shame in going off the strike."

"Jo says the pain goes away after a couple of days."

"Yes, I suppose it does. But that doesn't mean it gets easy."

"You said you've seen people starve. Who?"

Nora hesitated. Africa was too exotic of a destination for a poor Catholic girl from Belfast. She couldn't say she'd worked there, in feeding clinics and refugee camps where daily grave-digging was a tragic necessity.

"Children. Orphans and street children. A friend of my mother's ran a home for them. I helped out when I could."

"How horrible."

"Aye, it was."

"What . . . what was it like? For the people who starved?"

Nora shook her head, remembering going from bed to bed in the feeding center, checking to see who was still alive—and who had arrived too late. "It's not pretty, so it's not. Someone explained to me once how it works. Your body uses up all the energy it's stored . . . and then it basically starts eating itself—getting energy from your muscles and tissues. Eventually, there's not enough energy to keep the organs functioning, and your body shuts down. You get infections, or have a heart attack, or the brain just stops working."

Pidge grimaced. "That's an awful way to put it."

"Aye, but it's the truth. Don't you think—"

"Don't. Don't say I should reconsider. I only wanted to know what's ahead, is all. So I can be ready for it."

"All right." Nora stood up. "I'm going to see if there's any news."

"News about what?"

"About anything."

Nora quietly ate her breakfast with Jo and Lena so as not to torture Pidge with the smells. "Has any news been brought in today?" she asked.

Jo was bent over a crochet hook, biting her lip. "The war rages on."

"Anything specific? Any . . . deaths?"

Jo looked up. "Last night at the window we got word of an ambush, if that's what you mean."

"Our side or theirs?"

"Ours, o'course. On the Ballystodden Road. Didn't lose a single man. Two of theirs were killed, though."

"Do you know who they were?"

"The men who were killed? No. Why?"

"Doesn't matter. I just heard someone had been killed, that's all."

"I heard they're going to move us," Lena said.

Nora frowned. "Where?"

"North Dublin Union, most like." Lena wrinkled her nose. "I don't fancy being there; it's more of a workhouse than a prison. But I suppose we'll adapt."

"When?"

She shrugged. "It's just something I heard. They need to make room for the men in here."

Jo scowled. "They can't arrest all of us, but they sure are trying."

Nora went to the lavatory and took a hot bath—a prison luxury she hadn't been expecting—then returned to the altar on the second-floor landing. Two Kerry girls were there, their lips moving silently as their hands moved around the rosary. She remembered the children's rhyme she'd sung as a small child.

Ring around the rosary
Pocket full of posies
Ashes, ashes, we all fall down.

One of her colleagues had tried to teach it to the children in Haiti, but he stopped after Nora told him it was a song about the plague. Tragedy as seen through the eyes of children.

"Miss O'Reilly."

Roger O'Reilly strode toward her. There was no translucence to his form, no blurred edges. He was as solid and alive as when she'd first seen him.

"Good God, Roger!" she whispered. Without thinking, she ran to him and flung her arms around his neck in relief and joy and astonishment. "You're alive!"

He disentangled himself from her embrace, blushing furiously. He stepped back but then said softly, "Thanks to you . . . I think."

She didn't care who he thanked. She grinned back at him, then punched him on the arm. "You're welcome." A laugh bubbled up from her throat. "It worked!"

"What worked?"

"I'm just so relieved that you're still alive," she said, bouncing up and down on her toes. It could be changed—*everything* could be changed.

He moved in closer to her. "Nora, you knew that ambush was coming, didn't you? I was supposed to be there, on the Ballystodden Road. But I begged off sick. Are you . . . are you wanting to switch sides? Is that why you told me?"

She stopped bouncing, suddenly serious. "I am most certainly not wanting to switch sides, Roger O'Reilly. That's something *you* should be considering, not me." Then she smiled again. "Because *we* are going to win this war."

She scampered back to Jo and Lena's cell, where she found Pidge sitting on Lena's bed.

"Nora!" Jo called. "Come on in, Lena's going to tell us our futures."

Lena was shuffling a deck of cards, grinning broadly. "Don't be nervous; I foresee happy futures for us all. I'll tell you how many babies you'll have."

Nora snorted, then sat on the edge of Lena's bed beside Pidge. "How are you feeling?"

"Better," Pidge said. "The cramps are gone. For now."

Nora rubbed her back. "Listen, I need to tell you something. Don't get upset."

Lena stopped shuffling. The three women looked at her expectantly.

"I'm going to sign the form."

"*What?*" Jo stood so fast her chair toppled over behind her. Lena's mouth hung open, her hands frozen around her deck of cards. Pidge's lower lip trembled and her nose wrinkled, as though Nora had just passed her the chamber pot.

"It's not what you think. I have a plan," Nora said quickly. She laid her hand on Pidge's arm, but Pidge jerked it away.

"What are you talking about?" Pidge demanded.

"I can't tell you why, but I need to get out of here."

"We *all* need to get out of here," Jo retorted. "You think we don't have families waiting for us, mothers worried that we'll be the first to die in here, sweethearts to see, a cause to fight for? But you don't see us signing the form, do ye?"

"It's treason, Nora. Treason against the Republic," Lena said.

"It's not," Nora said quietly. "I'm going to help the Republic. Save it, if I can."

"How?" Jo asked.

"I can't say. I'm sorry."

"So you're going to leave me? And Kate and Mary? You're going to go back to your old life while we're starving ourselves for the cause?" Pidge kept her gaze fixed on the cell floor as she spoke.

Nora swallowed a stone that had lodged in her throat. "I don't want to leave you, Pidge. But I have to. I have to do this."

"Does this have anything to do with Thomas?"

"Who's Thomas?" Lena asked.

"No," Nora retorted. "It has nothing to do with him. I don't even know where he is—or if he's still alive."

"Then what? What could be so important that you would betray your sisters?"

"I'm not—"

"You know what? I don't care." Pidge got to her feet, hands on her hips. "You want to leave? Fine. Maybe the OC is right; maybe you're a spy, after all. Did you tell those Staters to come to my house? Did you lead them to the training camp, too? Are all those lads in prison now because of you?"

"You're talking rubbish!" Nora shot back. "You have no idea what I've done—what I've lost—all for the sake of a free Ireland." She stopped herself, clenching her teeth together. Then she reached out a hand. "Pidge, you have to just trust me on this."

Pidge slapped away her hand. "I can't believe I let you into my home. Into my family. Get out. Just get out!"

Nora pressed her lips together. "Fine. But you'll see that I'm right in the end." She stalked out of the cell, ignoring the stares of the other prisoners as she hurried down the corridor. She went straight to the wardress's office.

"I want to sign the form."

Miss Higgins looked up from her desk. "Is that so?"

"Yes."

"I have to admit I'm surprised, Miss O'Reilly. But I'm always pleased when one of my girls makes the decision to support our government."

"So, can I sign it now?"

"I'm afraid not."

"Why the hell not?"

Miss Higgins cleared her throat. "Language, please. Because it must be witnessed by the prison governor. Mr. O'Keefe won't be here until tomorrow, to oversee the transfer. You'll have to wait until then."

"What transfer?"

"Kilmainham has become too crowded. The women are being moved to North Dublin Union. The State needs Kilmainham for more male prisoners."

"Even the hunger strikers? Surely they're too weak to be moved."

"They could always eat something," Miss Higgins said, closing the book on her desk with a thud. "I'll send for you tomorrow when the governor arrives."

Nora returned to her cell and closed the door. She had to stay focused on the job at hand. Find Lynch. Warn him about the gunfight that would lead to his death. Protect him. That was her job.

She didn't know where or how she would find him. But first she had to get out.

She stayed in her cell the rest of the day, thinking, planning—and avoiding the other prisoners. But she couldn't stand the idea of Pidge thinking she was a traitor. Maybe she could earn her trust by telling her only part of the truth.

"Hey, I've been waiting for you. We need to talk," Nora began when Pidge finally returned to their cell.

"There's nothing to talk about." Pidge picked up her box of belongings and put it under her arm.

"Where are you going?"

"Hospital wing. Lyons says it's time."

"But . . . you're not that weak, yet . . . are you?"

"What do you care? You're leaving anyway." Pidge shoved the heavy door shut behind her, letting the sound reverberate through Nora's body.

The next morning she lay awake in bed, waiting for Miss Higgins to bellow for roll call. A faint scrape at her door made her sit up. Then a click. She crossed the room and pulled on the door handle. It was locked.

"Hey!" she said, banging her palm against the door. "Hey!"

Through the tiny grate she could hear other cries of protest down the corridor. Then a man's voice boomed out.

"Listen up, ladies! You are being moved today to another facility. When your door is unlocked, you may proceed in an orderly fashion to the entrance, where our men will escort you to the transport vehicles. If all goes smoothly, no one will be shot."

His speech was met with boos and jeers through cell doors. After half an hour had passed, the commotion in the hall told Nora they were being released. The lock in her door turned. Miss Higgins stood on the other side.

"Do you still wish to—"

"Yes."

"Then you may go down to my office and wait for me there."

Nora fell in step with the other prisoners. When would they move the hunger strikers? Had they done so already?

Two dozen women were gathered at the top of the stairs. OC Humphreys stood on an overturned chamber pot. "The governor has rejected our demand that the hunger strikers be released," she said. "And so now we must resist. Until they are given their freedom, not one of us will leave willingly." Her eyes fell on Nora. "Except for Miss O'Reilly, who has consented to sign the form."

Dozens of shocked, angry eyes turned on her. Guards stood within easy earshot; she couldn't well explain that she had a job to do for the Republic.

"She's sweet on one of the guards!" someone called out. Nora pinpointed the voice in the crowd—one of the Kerry girls who'd seen her hugging Roger. "I saw them necking!"

A low murmur swelled around her.

"On your way, Miss O'Reilly," Mrs. Humphreys said. "One less Stater in our midst."

Nora walked mechanically through the crowd of women toward the staircase. Behind her, Mrs. Humphreys continued. "As you know, we have three hunger strikers in our care. Miss MacSwiney and Mrs. O'Callaghan in particular are in a very bad state. No matter what happens, no matter what they do to you, do not cry out. Their nerves will surely not stand it. Now, everyone link arms. They'll have to remove us by force. We will not desert our sisters."

Nora's every step echoed on the metal stairs. *Save Liam Lynch. Save Liam Lynch.* She repeated this mantra over and over, driving herself forward. A dozen soldiers stood to attention in the entrance, waiting for orders, their eyes fixed on the defiant women above them.

Miss Higgins was waiting in her office. Beside her stood a man with a large mustache and salt-and-pepper sideburns. A Webley hung from a holster around his broad waist.

"Ah, Miss O'Reilly," Miss Higgins said. "Deputy governor, this is the woman I was telling you about."

"Ready to turn your back on these devils, are you?" he grunted.

"Just give me the form."

Miss Higgins slid a piece of paper across the desk and handed her a pen.

> *I promise that I will not use arms against the Parliament elected by the Irish people, or the Government for the time being responsible to that Parliament, and that I will not support in any way any such action. Nor will I interfere with the property or the person of others.*

Out in the entryway, the soldiers' boots thundered up the stairs.

"Be glad you're not still with them," the governor muttered in her ear, his hand resting on the small of her back. She flinched away.

"Right there, dear." Mrs. Higgins pointed to the bottom of the letter.

Nora stared at the hateful words. *Save Liam Lynch. Save Eamon.* She signed.

"Excellent." Deputy Governor O'Keefe rubbed his hands together, then took the paper from her and signed below her name. "One less mouth to feed. I'll get one of the lads to show you out."

Nora shrugged off his proffered arm and marched back into the entryway. She slammed to a sudden halt at the sight before her. On the stairs, soldiers grappled with the women prisoners, who clung to the railings like children to a mother's leg. It was the vision she'd experienced when she came to Kilmainham as a tourist. Some of the women moaned quietly, but they were all following the OC's orders not to cry out.

"Let go, you Irregular hoore!" one of the soldiers yelled in Julia O'Neill's ear, his arms wrapped around her waist. He ripped her arms free of the railing and threw her down the remaining dozen stairs. Nora ran to her. "Stop it! What's wrong with you?" she cried up at the soldiers. One was beating on the hands of one of the Kerry girls. Her face was contorted with pain, but she still didn't cry out. Jo came to her rescue. The soldier kicked her in the head, and Jo crumbled onto the stairs, rolling down three of them before coming to rest on the landing.

"No! Stop it!" Nora yelled. She rushed at one of the soldiers near the bottom who had ripped Lena's dress half off and was pawing at her while she cried. Nora grabbed his arm and shoved him away. "Don't you touch her," she snarled.

Rough hands grabbed both of her arms. She fought against them. Then a bored voice beside her said, "You're no longer a prisoner here, Miss O'Reilly. It's time for you to leave." O'Keefe shoved the form into her hands; then two soldiers dragged her toward the main doors.

"Let go of me!"

"Wait until you see what we do to the hunger strikers," one of the soldiers whispered before they shoved her onto the cobblestones and closed the door.

Nora scrambled to her feet. "Hey!" She slammed her hand against the door. She wrenched at the iron handle with both hands, but it was locked solid.

"Do you need help?" A soldier stood behind her, bewildered.

She shoved the form at him. He read it, then handed it back. "They're beating those girls in there," she snarled. "Are you just going to stand here and let that happen?"

He looked taken aback. She stormed past him, weaving between the military vehicles waiting to take the prisoners to NDU. The sooner this was over, the better.

She walked for several minutes before realizing she had no idea where she was headed. A large park was on her left. She wandered into it, her rage cooling.

If she could find her way back to the IRA camp where she'd first seen Lynch, maybe she'd find him—or someone who knew where he was. She sank onto a bench and rubbed her temples. She was running out of time. Lynch would be dead in less than a week. If only she could remember where he'd been hiding before the skirmish broke out. Why hadn't she paid more attention?

A woman sat down next to her. She was finely dressed, in a long, elaborate gown of cream and burgundy, buttoned ivory gloves, and a brimmed hat dripping with lace and ribbons.

"Trouble, child?" Her voice was deep and coated with honey.

"I'm grand." Nora stood. She'd accomplish nothing by chatting with a rich woman in a Dublin park.

"Sit down, Nora." It was not a request. Nora looked at the woman more closely. Did she know her? No, she would have remembered this face, the high cheekbones and deep, dark eyes that glittered from under long lashes. Her hair was black and glossy, arranged in tight curls under her hat, setting off the smoothness of her pale skin. Her wide mouth was spread in a taunting smile. Nora felt a jolt in her stomach but didn't understand her reaction.

She stayed where she was. "Who are you?"

"You know who I am."

Nora narrowed her eyes. "I'm quite sure I don't."

"You asked for my help."

"I—" She hesitated. There was something different about this woman. Something . . . ethereal. But no. Impossible.

"As impossible as moving through time?" The woman's smile broadened.

"How did you—"

"Know what you were thinking? It's a special talent of mine. Getting inside people's heads. And I really do think you should sit down."

Nora sat.

"Are you . . ." She felt ridiculous saying it. "Saint Brigid?"

The woman threw back her head and laughed, a deep, throaty laugh that filled the air around them. "Oh my child, no. Well, yes *and* no."

"I don't understand."

"Of course you don't! Oh, fine, I'll spell it out, shall I? I was, for a time, the woman you call Saint Brigid. But I am so much more than that."

A wave of dizziness washed through her. Nora grabbed the back of the bench to steady herself. She wanted to believe . . . but something inside her still rebelled, even after everything she'd experienced. *Have faith*, she urged herself.

"But you . . . you have all your fingers," she blurted out. "The relic—"

The woman laughed again, then wiggled her fingers in their ivory casings and leaned forward. "They say I once grew back an eye. If that's true, a finger shouldn't be much of a problem, should it?"

"Did *you* give me those dreams? Was Thomas telling the truth?"

The woman winked at Nora. "*Thomas.* Oh, yes, he was. I thought some of his stubbornness would have worn off after all these years, but he's still as obstinate as a mule. Until now, that is."

"Do you know where he is? Is he okay?" Nora pushed aside the tornado of thoughts in her head—was she really speaking with a saint who had been dead for hundreds of years?—and forced herself to focus.

Brigid—or whoever she was—patted Nora's knee. "He's fine. For now."

Nora exhaled loudly. "Thank you."

"Oh, I had very little to do with it. *Thomas* always wants to do everything himself. But . . . he needs you, Nora. Whether he likes it or not."

"Let me get this straight. Let's say you *are* Saint Brigid—and I want to know how that works, but not right now . . . though how else would you know about the dreams and the time travel? But let's say you are the one who started all this. Why did you send me here?"

"Why do you think?"

"I have no idea. I thought it was to help Thomas. But he doesn't want my help. The woman at the church said you have a plan, that you sent me here for a reason. *What is it?*" Nora leaned forward hungrily, lest Brigid disappear if she took her eyes off her for a second.

"Let's just say you and Thomas can help each other."

"I told you, he doesn't want my help!"

"Do any of us want what we truly need?" Brigid said.

"Tell me the truth. I deserve at least that much."

"The truth is not mine to tell, Nora."

"Then who can?"

"You can. You can discover it for yourself. Now stop with the questions. You've been given a second chance. Do you know how many people would do anything for that?"

Nora glared at her, breathing heavily. A second chance. The only thing she had ever wanted since she was fifteen years old. Then a glorious thought swept the breath from her lungs. "Can you send me back?"

"Back where, dear?"

"Nineteen ninety-one. When Eamon was killed. No, the year before—when I fucked everything up by trying to sell those drugs. If I didn't try to sell them, Eamon would never sign up. He would—"

"I can't send you back there, Nora." Brigid's eyes were cloudy.

"Why the hell not? If you can send me to 1923, you can send me to 1990!"

"Because that's not where you're meant to be. You're meant to be here. Now."

"That's shite, so it is! I don't know what I'm supposed to do here." Her stomach ached, and her chest seared with loss. She'd hoped saving Eamon would be as easy as saving Roger.

"You know exactly what you are supposed to do. What you need is a guide. *Thomas* knows how to find Liam Lynch."

She sat up straighter. "How do you—never mind. Do *you* know where Liam Lynch is?"

Brigid pursed her lips. "I don't."

"Well, where the bloody hell is Thomas?"

"As I understand it, he's being transferred to Kilmainham Gaol this afternoon, once all of your fellow prisoners have been removed."

Nora closed her eyes. "And how am I supposed to help him in there? I just got out myself."

"You'll think of something."

"I can't force him to accept my help."

"You won't have to." Brigid reached inside a pearl-adorned handbag and handed her a folded sheet of paper. "He asked me to give this to you."

Nora took it without opening it. "How do I know you didn't forge this? Like you put those dreams in my head?"

"I put those dreams in your head to get you here. And it worked. But now you're on your own. Both of you. I'm just the messenger."

Nora unfolded the paper. It was a letter, written in the most elegant penmanship she'd ever seen.

Dear Miss O'Reilly,

It is with a humble heart that I must ask for your forgiveness. My behaviour has been appalling, especially in the face of your honest willingness to offer assistance to a stranger. I offer no excuses, only that I was taken aback by both your ferocity and your beauty.

If our mutual friend has indeed delivered this letter, then you are aware of my present confinement. I would very much like to see you, if you are willing to overlook my boorish past behavior. Perhaps in person I can answer some of your questions—and ask some of my own.

My dear Miss O'Reilly, I will speak plainly. I was wrong. I would very much like to accept your offer of assistance, if the offer still stands.

Yours,

Thomas Heaney

Nora read the letter through twice, her heart rattling around in her rib cage. He was alive. And he wanted her help.

"Well?" Brigid asked, leaning forward.

Nora opened her mouth to speak, then stopped. "You say he knows how to find Lynch?"

Brigid made a noncommittal noise, but her eyes sparkled.

Nora stared down at the letter, then folded it and stuffed it up her sleeve. "I suppose I can go see him. But prisoners at Kilmainham aren't allowed visitors. So I don't know—"

"Some prisoners are allowed visitors," Brigid interrupted. "Under certain tragic circumstances. If you said you were his wife . . . or fiancée, even. They would have to let you say good-bye, after all."

"Good-bye?"

"Didn't he tell you? The day after tomorrow he's going to be executed."

Chapter Nineteen

Brigid gave Nora a purse of money and the name of a friendly hotel. "Tell them Countess Markievicz sent you," she said with a wink.

"You're not—"

"She's a dear friend. Won't mind in the slightest. And Nora?"

"Yes?"

"Go easy on Thomas, will you? He's not used to accepting help from others. Believe it or not, he's even more stubborn than you are."

Brigid swooped down and kissed both of her cheeks, then walked away through the park. Nora watched her step behind a large stone monument, but no one emerged from the other side. She shook her head. *Anything's possible now.*

She checked into the hotel, where they upgraded her to a suite at the mention of the countess. On a glass table in the front room was a bottle of wine, a bowl of fresh fruit, and a packet of cigarettes. She tipped the porter and waited for him to leave. She uncorked the bottle and took a swig, forgoing the glass. Not bad. She took the cigarettes and wine into the bedroom, intent on collapsing on the bed for the rest of the day.

But there was something on it. A dress. Hat. Shoes. Stockings. Gloves. Handbag. Hairbrush. A makeup palette. She set the wine and cigarettes down on the nightstand. Gently, she picked up the dress. It seemed so delicate it might fall apart in her hands. A cream under-dress covered in delicate gold lace and embroidery. A cluster of pearls gathered the material together at the waist. More pearls decorated the shoulder straps and the bodice.

So this is what Brigid wanted her to wear to meet Thomas. She supposed it was better than what she had on now—a shapeless navy bag of a dress in sore need of a washing. She shed the navy dress and draped it over a chair. Then she gently hung up the cream dress in the closet and draped the stockings and gloves over a chair.

She crawled into bed naked and lit up a smoke.

Kilmainham felt like a different place when she arrived the next day. She made herself known to the sentry at the gate as Mr. Heaney's fiancée. He gave her a pitying look, then showed her inside. *Welcome back,* the dragons whispered above her head.

The jail was eerily silent. There were no prisoners milling about, no shouts across the corridor, no balls thudding against the walls in the exercise yard. No Julia, lying crumpled at the bottom of the steps, no Jo, fighting valiantly to protect her sisters. No Pidge.

The guard knocked on Miss Higgins's door, but it was not Miss Higgins who answered, thank God. Instead, a stern-faced man with thick eyebrows looked up from his desk when they entered.

"Mr. Heaney's fiancée, sir," the guard said. "Here for her visit before . . ."

"Before he is executed for being a worthless traitor," the new warden said, standing. He gave Nora a cold stare. "Your name?"

"Miss . . . Ryan. Nellie Ryan."

"All right. Show her up. You have ten minutes, Miss Ryan."

Nora hurried behind the guard up to the third floor. "It's so quiet. Where are all the prisoners?" she asked.

"Locked in their cells, o'course," the guard answered.

"Why? The women were allowed to move about freely."

"The men are more dangerous, I suppose."

I doubt that.

He stopped outside a cell and knocked. Nora took a deep breath.

"Yes?" called a voice from within. She recognized it even through the metal door.

The guard answered. "A visitor for you. Your fiancée."

"You're the one with the keys. Let her in."

The guard turned the key in the lock and pushed open the door. Thomas was sitting in a thin metal chair in the corner of the room, one foot resting on the other knee, a cigarette dangling from his fingers. "Hello," he said. He stood and doffed his hat.

The guard made to enter the room as well, but Nora gave him a pitiful look. "Could we have privacy, please? It's the last time I'll see my fiancé, after all."

The guard ducked his head. "Of course, miss." He stepped into the hallway, closing the door behind him.

For several seconds, they just stared at each other.

Thomas broke the silence. "Fiancé?"

"It was the only way they'd let me see you."

"You look stunning."

She rolled her eyes. "I had a visit from our mutual friend."

He nodded. "She believes I'm a bit of an arse, if you'll excuse my language."

"You *are* a bit of an arse. But I still owe you. For what happened at the farm."

"I'm sorry I didn't step in sooner," he said quietly. "I was trying to get into a position to shoot them all. I had no idea they'd take it as far as they did." He closed the distance between them and gently lifted her hat, laying it on the bed. "May I?"

She ducked her head ever so slightly. He reached behind her neck and untied the knot of the scarf she still wore. He folded it in half and set it aside. Then he touched her scalp with tender fingertips, taking care to avoid the wounds.

Nora stood perfectly still, her only movement the rapid rise and fall of her chest. His fingertips brushed her cheek. The bruising had faded, but his thumb traced its outline.

She stepped away. "Thomas. How can I help you? Your letter said—"

"Yes. I know what I said. Brigid assured me I could trust you."

"Is she for real? I asked if she was the saint, and she just laughed and laughed."

Thomas sat on the edge of the bed and motioned for Nora to take the chair. She picked up her scarf and retied it, then sat.

"She didn't tell you?" he asked.

"I have a feeling there's a lot she's not telling me."

He took a deep breath and looked toward the door. Then he leaned forward and lowered his voice. "What I'm going to say will sound impossible, but you must believe me."

"More impossible than—" *Going back in time eighty-two years?* But instead she said, "A saint appearing to me in the park?"

"She's not a saint. She's a god."

"What?"

"She is the goddess Brigid of the Tuatha Dé Danann. I'm sure you've heard the stories."

"In children's books, yes." *Anything is possible . . . right?*

"She enjoys injecting herself into the lives of humans. Sometimes it's helpful. Other times . . . In any case, it doesn't matter."

"It doesn't?"

"She seems convinced you can help me. Though I admit I cannot see it, I trust her. And so I trust you. You know about the execution order, I suppose?"

"Yes, which is why we need to figure out a way to get you out of here."

"It won't happen."

"What d'you mean?"

"The truth, Miss O'Reilly, is that I cannot die. I am under a curse. I will not die until I have saved Ireland from her enemies."

Nora struggled to make sense of this. "You mean . . . you literally will not die? Or is this some kind of new Republican slogan?"

"No, I literally will not die. Believe me, I've tried. I've thrown myself off the cliffs at Dun Aengus, I've tried to force a sword into my own heart, I've fashioned a noose out of every kind of material. And each time, I am defeated. The wind slows my fall, the sword shatters against my breast, the rope breaks. And tomorrow, when they try to shoot me, the guns will jam, or there will be an eleventh-hour postponement."

"But . . . why?"

"Why?"

"Why do you want to die?"

He folded and unfolded his hands in his lap. A lock of gray hair fell into his eyes, and he pushed it away. "Because I have lived a very, very long time. I just want to go home. I don't belong here anymore."

"How long?"

His blue eyes met hers. "Over eighteen hundred years."

Nora snorted and stood. She paced the small cell. "That's impossible. No one can live that long."

"No one *should* live that long. I told you: it's a curse."

"And who put this so-called curse on you?"

"Aengus Óg."

Nora stopped pacing. "Aengus Óg?"

"Yes." She stared at him, her mouth open. "What is it?" he asked.

"Nothing. It doesn't mean anything. It's just . . . This woman I met before I came here, the one who told me about Brigid. She said I was the 'bane of Aengus Óg.' I didn't understand what it meant. I still don't."

He exhaled slowly. "It means you are meant to help me break this curse."

Is that what this was all about? The dreams? Her arrival here in the past?

She sat down and met his eyes. "I think, perhaps, we can help each other. Now it is time for *you* to believe *me*."

"I'm listening."

"I come . . ." *Oh, God, this is going to sound crazy. But no crazier than living for almost two millennia.* "I come . . . from the future."

His eyes narrowed, but he remained silent.

She cleared her throat. "Two thousand five, to be exact. Like I told you, I've had several dreams about you. In the clearest one, you asked me—begged me—to come to Kildare and find Brigid. I thought she might just be an ordinary woman. Anyway, I just happened to be in Dublin, so I figured I might as well take a short trip to Kildare. I had a photograph of you that I'd found at my aunt's house. It said . . . It had the date 1923 written on the back. It also said you were killed in action. Which according to you is impossible, right?"

He nodded.

"So . . . I went to the church, and I met this woman—a Brigidine Sister. She told me to hang on to one of Brigid's relics, a finger bone of all things, and to think about you. It sounded crazy, but I did it. And then I blacked out. When I woke up, I was still in the church. But it was 1923."

She pressed her hands against her mouth. It was too much, to say this out loud, to acknowledge what had happened.

His hands wrapped around hers. He brought them down to her lap and held them there. "Miss O'Reilly," he whispered. "I believe you."

Tears—stupid, ridiculous tears—rose to her eyes, but she battled them back and forced her lips into a smile. "Call me Nora, please. And I believe you, too." And why not? Was there anything she wouldn't believe at this point? Reality was a different beast than she'd believed it to be.

"So . . . you were right. And I behaved—" He shook his head.

"Exactly as one would expect you to behave, given that a strange woman showed up out of nowhere and said she'd been dreaming about you."

He leaned back on the bed. "So what happens next?"

"I think we both want the same thing. You want to save Ireland, right?" He nodded. "So do I. In my world, or timeline, or whatever it is, the Free State wins. And Ireland does become a republic eventually, which is grand, so it is. Except for—"

"The North," he finished. "The North stays with England, don't they?"

"Yes. The partition becomes permanent. And the war doesn't stop. Not in the North, at any rate."

"And you're a Volunteer in that war."

"I used to be. It's over now. We lost."

"So you want to change history."

"Aye."

He pondered this for a moment. "How does the Free State win?"

She pinched the bridge of her nose. "That's the problem. I'm a little sketchy on the details. If I had known—well, it's too late now. All I know is that Liam Lynch will be killed in action on April 10. His successor gives the order to dump arms, which more or less ends the war. Lynch would have kept fighting."

"Good Lord," Thomas breathed. "The Chief is going to be shot?"

"Aye."

Thomas glanced at the door again, then leaned forward. "No one else knows this. The Chief has made a deal with Cosgrave, the president of the Free State Executive Council, to scupper the Boundary Commission that's in charge of partition. It's absolutely top secret. Lloyd George would have a fit in London if he knew they were even discussing it."

Nora gaped at him. "How do you know this?"

"I have ears outside this prison. Lynch has agreed to call off the fighting and accept the treaty, but only if the six northern counties remain part of the Free State. Cosgrave has agreed. Says they'll take up arms against the British again if that's the only way. And Lloyd George doesn't have the stomach for another war, not when we've already gained so much. He'd rather lose Northern Ireland than send his country to war again."

Nora's heart leapt. A deal to keep Ireland together? Then the implication struck her. "But if Lynch is killed . . ."

"The deal is off. Cosgrave trusts Lynch. He knows he'll be able to rein his men in. He won't make this deal with anyone else, not when he's already this close to winning the war. Everything hangs on Lynch."

Nora resumed her pacing. "We have to warn him. Get him to change his plans, his location. Brigid said you know where he is."

"I do."

"How?"

"Bran is with him."

"Bran? Your dog?"

"She's . . . a very special dog. She can communicate with me."

Nora shook her head. "This is getting weird."

He shrugged. "You get used to it."

"We still need to get you out of here. I'd prefer you not take your chances with the firing squad."

"I'm telling you, they won't be able to kill me."

"And I'm telling you, I don't want to test that theory."

"Are you planning to smuggle me out under that dress?"

"No. I've a better idea. Someone owes me a favor."

The guard knocked, then opened the door, looking apologetic. "I'm sorry, Miss Ryan, but I've already given you extra time. I need to escort you out now."

Nora stayed where she was. What if this really *was* good-bye? What if he was wrong? The guard cleared his throat. "If you want to, ah, say a final farewell, I'll be just outside the door."

Thomas stood and held out his arms. "Good-bye, darling. Be brave for me."

"I'll see you soon," she whispered as he wrapped her in his arms. "Kiss me."

"What?" he whispered back.

"The guard is watching through the spy hole. I'm your fiancée. Kiss me."

He ran his thumb over her lips, then bent and brushed them with his own. His hand lingered on the nape of her neck where the scarf was knotted. Her pulse quickened and her heart fluttered in her throat. How long had it been since she'd kissed a man? Relationships among humanitarian aid workers were fleeting, to say the least. And she was a pro at keeping people at a distance. But Thomas . . .

"Now act distraught," he said softly into her ear, interrupting her dangerous thoughts. "I'll tell Bran to find you. She might be able to help."

She nodded and touched his cheek lightly with her fingers, still aware of his hands on her waist. The guard cleared his throat again from outside the door.

"Good-bye," she whispered.

She kept her head down as she left the cell, but a glimpse of red hair caught her eye. Roger.

"I can make my own way out," she said to the guard outside Thomas's cell.

"I'm afraid I have to—" he began, but a voice behind them cut him off.

"I'm going down, Billy; I can escort her," Roger O'Reilly said, giving Nora a cursory glance.

"You're a brick, Rog, really," the other guard said. "I'm due for my break."

"Follow me," Roger said curtly to Nora as the other guard sauntered off in the other direction. Once they were alone, he whispered, "What are you doing here?"

Nora spoke fast as they descended the stairs. "I need a favor. But I can't talk about it here. When's your shift over?"

He frowned. "I can't—"

"You owe me, Roger. I saved your life."

He looked away. "Grand. I'll meet you at seven at the bar at the Shelbourne. But for God's sake don't tell anyone. It's my job on the line, so it is."

"Thank you," she whispered as they reached the entrance. She cast one last look up at Thomas's cell before she was escorted out into the cold Dublin sun.

By the time seven o'clock arrived, Nora had developed a plan and paid a trip to a hardware store. All she needed now was a massive amount of luck—and Roger's cooperation. She hoped she was doing the right thing. If he was caught helping her, he'd likely be arrested and imprisoned himself. But if they could change history, it would be worth the risk . . . wouldn't it?

The Shelbourne wasn't far from her hotel. She hurried along the cobblestones under the dim light of the streetlamps, her pearled handbag and a brown paper package clutched under her arm. As she passed a laneway, a dog barked. She hesitated. "Bran?" she called out softly. The wolfhound trotted out of the laneway and nuzzled her leg. She scratched Bran behind the ears. "So, you're a 'special' dog, are you? As long as you can lead us to Lynch, I don't care what you are. Wait for me?" She lowered her voice to a whisper. "I'm off to meet Roger. We're going to bust your master out of jail."

She grinned at the ridiculousness of talking to a dog, but Bran almost seemed to understand. The wolfhound padded along beside her until she reached the Shelbourne, then slunk into the shadows of the lane next to the entrance. She could still see Bran's eyes watching her as she entered the brightly lit lobby. A polished mahogany desk wrapped around half the entryway. Fresh, fragrant flowers graced small tables beside enormous wingback chairs. She nodded to the doorman as though she'd been here a thousand times and made her way through the lobby to the lounge, an expansive, airy room with a high arched ceiling and immense windows. She scanned the room. He wasn't there.

He'll come. Unless this was a setup. No, she'd said nothing incriminating. All she'd done was ask for a favor. He had no idea what she wanted. She took a seat at a small table near the back of the lounge, as far away from the clusters of other patrons as possible.

She kept her eyes on the door. She almost didn't recognize him at first. He was dressed in a three-piece suit and top hat. She stood and smiled, hoping to put him at ease. To her surprise, he bent and kissed her hand in greeting.

"You look wonderful," he said.

"As do you. I almost didn't recognize you."

"Well, one can't wear a uniform all the time."

"Indeed not."

A tuxedoed waiter appeared, and they ordered drinks. She allowed Roger to order for her in the hopes it would put him in an agreeable mood.

"So you were visiting Thomas Heaney, today," he said, his eyes fixed on the waiter's back.

"I was."

"Which can only mean one thing: you're his fiancée."

"Oh . . . aye. I am."

"I don't see a ring."

"It's been a little difficult for him to procure one from prison."

"So it's a recent engagement. I should offer my congratulations."

"Ta."

"And he's meant to be executed tomorrow."

"Aye."

Their drinks arrived. Nora took a sip of her sherry, eyeing Roger's whiskey with envy. He leaned forward. "Did you really have a vision from God that told you I was going to die?"

She kept her gaze steady. "Aye."

"You're sure it wasn't just a message from your fiancé? Or one of your other Irregular pals?"

"Does it matter? I saved your life. Do you wish I hadn't?"

He took a swig of whiskey. "O'course not."

"Then I need your help." He didn't reply, just regarded her coolly over the rim of his glass. "I want you to help Thomas escape."

"Impossible."

"It's *not* impossible. I've thought it through. There's *very* little risk to you."

"I doubt that. But just out of curiosity, what's your plan?"

"The gate is locked at night, when there's no sentry on duty."

"I don't have the key for that."

"I didn't think you would. But you do have a key to Thomas's cell, right?"

He swallowed. "Maybe."

"All I need you to do is leave his cell unlocked tomorrow night. And give him something he can use to cut the lock at the gate."

"You want me to give something to a prisoner? There's no way. There's always at least two of us to a floor—the other guard would notice if I went into his cell."

"Then leave it somewhere he can find it," Nora insisted.

"And what do you suggest I leave him? Assuming I'm fool enough to agree to this plan?"

"Something strong enough to break the lock. Like a bolt cutter."

Roger took a deep breath. "I suppose that would work. But how am I supposed to smuggle something like that in?"

"I've already taken care of it." She pushed the parcel at her feet over to him. "I had the man at the shop take it apart at the hinge. He took off the handles as well, so it should be easy enough to fit it inside your jacket now. Just leave him the tools to reassemble it—they're all there."

Roger stared at the package on the floor but didn't pick it up. "They told me Cumann na mBan had talents. But I thought it was more in the"—he reddened—"gathering-of-information department, if you'll pardon me. But this—" He nudged the package with a polished shoe. "How does a lady such as yourself know these things?"

Nora's jaw tightened. "It's easy. I'm no lady."

Smoke. Screams. Shots being fired, but by whom? Mick had broken the lock on the police station door, told her to grab the bolt cutters and run. But she hadn't wanted to leave him. The explosion had left her ears ringing for days. And the screams . . .

"Miss O'Reilly," Roger was saying. The waiter had reappeared and was regarding her impatiently. "Would you like another?"

"Oh. No, thank you." She turned back to Roger. "Will you help me?"

He stared into his glass for a long time. "After this, we call it even? A life for a life?"

She leaned over the table and covered his hand with her own. "A life for a life."

Chapter Twenty

Bran was still waiting for her when she left the Shelbourne. Roger insisted on walking her back to her hotel. "Is that your dog?" he asked in alarm when Bran followed at their heels.

"She's Thomas's, aren't you, girl?" Nora scratched Bran behind the ears. "But she's staying with me for now."

The clerk at the hotel desk wrinkled his nose at Bran but didn't try to stop her. The countess's name had to count for a great deal.

"Thank you grandly, Roger," Nora said, holding out a hand.

He took it and bent low, brushing his lips over her knuckles. When he stood, he didn't let go. "Are you really engaged, Miss O'Reilly? Or is that just another part of your plan?" His eyes were far too hopeful.

Nora hesitated. Would he be more apt to help them if he thought he had a chance with her? She'd done worse things for the cause. But of all the Free Staters she'd encountered, Roger had been the kindest. And he was risking his life to help her. She couldn't lead him on. Besides, he was her great-uncle. Ew.

"I am," she said. "I'm sorry."

His face tightened. "Will I see you again?"

"I don't know. Probably not." *Not unless you live to be a hundred . . .*

He removed his hat. "Then allow me to thank you, once again, for saving my life."

"O'course. And Roger?"

"Aye?"

"Good luck tomorrow."

He patted the inside of his jacket, then nodded at her and walked back into the night. She stared after him, hoping she'd done the right thing. Would he be caught? Would Free State soldiers break down her door in the middle of the night? Would they shoot Thomas on the spot if they found him trying to escape?

"C'mon, Bran," she whispered. She climbed the stairs to her room, took off her hat and shoes, and then collapsed on the bed. Bran curled up beside her. She wrapped one arm around the dog's shaggy back. And waited for morning.

"Were there any executions last night at Kilmainham?" She had hurried down to the front desk first thing, still dressed in her clothes from the night before.

The clerk looked at her in alarm. She'd forgotten her head scarf. "No, I don't believe so."

"Are you sure?"

"Our bellboy lives in one of the tenements across from the jail. He says he's heard every one, always in the middle of the night. But all was quiet last night, so he says."

Nora let out a breath. "Thank you." Thomas had one more day . . . time enough to put her plan into action. She turned to go back upstairs.

"Shall I send up some breakfast?" the clerk called after her.

"That would be grand."

Bran pouted at her when she reentered the room. "Don't give me those eyes," she told her. "It's going to be a long day."

She ran a bath, soaking her sore head under the water. There was a knock at the door just as she was getting out.

"Your breakfast, Miss O'Reilly."

"Just leave it outside the door, please," she called, grabbing for a towel.

"What do you think? Is it really breakfast? Or soldiers?" she whispered to Bran, who sniffed at the door and then panted, her tongue hanging out.

Nora opened the door and wheeled in a silver cart. Eggs, sausages, and thick slices of buttered bread. She poured tea from the silver urn, then gave Bran her sausages.

After breakfast, she and Bran headed out onto the street and hailed a taxi. "North Dublin Union," she told the driver.

"They're not accepting visitors," he told her.

"Go anyway."

The driver was right. The sentry at the gate refused to even let her inside to speak with the wardress. Nora walked around the entire former workhouse, looking for a window that opened onto the street, or some way to communicate with the women inside. But there was nothing.

"Will you take a letter, at least?" she asked the sentry at the gate, handing him several pound notes. He nodded stiffly.

She'd brought along some of the hotel stationery, worried this might happen. So she sat on the low stone wall that bordered the gate and wrote her letter.

> *Dear Pidge,*
> *I hope you are well. I know you are angry with me right now, but trust me when I say I'm doing the right thing for Ireland.*

She paused and nibbled on the end of the pen.

I hope I will soon be going back home. You're very brave, my dear Pidge. Never change. Ireland needs more women like you.
   I will never forget our friendship or the adventures we shared.
   With love,
   Nora

She folded the paper and gave it to the sentry. She only hoped Pidge would read it.

When darkness fell, Nora returned to Kilmainham. Three women sat on a bench outside the gate, praying. They nodded to Nora, who was carrying her rosary. She sat next to them and moved her fingers around the beads, a better alternative than letting them quake in her lap. Bran lay still at her feet. What had she been thinking? This kind of operation took weeks to plan. It needed to be rehearsed; the equipment needed to be tested. They needed maps and code words and exit strategies. And here she'd planned it all in an afternoon, with the help of a Free State soldier. Thomas didn't even know what he was supposed to do.

But it was the best plan she had. She'd considered improvising a bomb to blast the door open, but she was no explosives expert. That had been Paddy Sullivan's job. And she would have needed either shaped charges or a large quantity of gunpowder—two things she couldn't obtain in an afternoon. Besides, setting off an explosion in a town crawling with soldiers was the perfect way to get rearrested.

The hours slid past. One by one, the praying women left. Nora saw the sentry close up his station and walk down the road, whistling off tune. She stood slowly, her legs stiff. Without a sound, Bran lifted herself up and followed Nora as she walked around the wall, the rosary still clutched in her hand. *If any of my prayers have meant anything, let them work now.*

The side gate was locked from the inside with a heavy chain and a padlock. She'd observed it several times while in the exercise yard. This is where Thomas would bring the bolt cutter. Then it would just be a simple matter of assembling it, cutting the lock, and opening the door.

"Excuse me, miss? Are you all right?"

Nora tensed and swung around. Four Free State soldiers sauntered toward her. Their jackets were unbuttoned, and cigarettes hung from their lips and fingers. One of them held a half-full pint glass in his hand. "What are you doing, skulking about here? It's past closing time."

"I'm not drinking; I'm praying," Nora said, holding out her rosary beads. "For the poor souls inside Kilmainham."

"Did you hear that, lads? The 'poor souls inside Kilmainham.' They weren't so poor when they were shooting our men, were they?"

"Come on, Pete. Let's move along." One of the men gave his friend a good-natured shove, but he stumbled, sloshing beer into the street.

"Look what you've done!" He staggered over to Nora. "Now you'll need to buy me a drink."

Bran tensed beside her, and Nora put a steadying hand on the dog's head.

"Leave her alone, Pete. She said she's praying. *You* wouldn't want to be locked up in there, I reckon."

"Maybe she's planning a breakout," Pete slurred. "We should search her."

Nora's hands tightened on her bag. Inside was the handgun she'd acquired in a small shop in north Dublin—the result of a few discreet inquiries. She couldn't possibly take out all four of them, even in their inebriated state. And the shots would ruin Thomas's chances at escape.

She drew herself up. "I think you should listen to your friend. I'm doing no harm here, and I've my dog to protect me." As if on cue, Bran growled long and low. "Besides, I would hate to have to report to your superior how you harassed a pious woman while under the influence of that vile drink."

Pete looked like he wanted to argue, but his friends had better sense—or perhaps it was the size of Bran's teeth that put them off. "We'll leave you, miss," one of them said. "But it's not safe for a woman to be out this time of night. Praying or no."

"I can take care of myself. *You* take care of *him*." They caroused around the corner. Nora leaned against the door in the prison wall with relief.

"Nicely played," a voice whispered through the door. She spun around.

"Thomas!"

"I thought they'd never leave. Hang on while I put this damn thing together."

She kept her eyes on the road, listening to the clanking of metal and Thomas's occasional grunts.

"Keep it down," she whispered.

"You couldn't have sent me something quieter?"

"Just hurry."

There was a crunching, grinding sound. Then a snap.

"Gods be damned!" Thomas hissed. "It broke."

"What? The padlock?"

"The bolt cutter. Handles snapped clean off. I can't get enough leverage. I'll have to try again tomorrow."

"You can't! They're going to execute you in less than two hours!"

"I told you: it won't happen. I'll be grand."

"*I* won't be grand! We have to get you out of here and find Lynch! He'll be dead in two days!"

"Well, I can't very well climb the bloody wall, can I?"

"Jesus. How have you managed to stay alive for hundreds of years?"

"I told you: it's—"

"Aye, the curse, I know. Now stand back."

She knelt down and opened her bag. Underneath the gun was the only backup plan she'd been able to come up with at the last minute—besides shooting her way into the jail, of course. A tight coil of rope. She only hoped it was long enough. She tied one end to a rock the size of a rounders ball. Then, after casting a glance about for any straggling revelers, she took several steps back and threw it as hard as she could over the wall.

She cleared it—just. The absence of a thud against the other side of the wall hopefully meant Thomas had caught it. She kept hold of her end and hurried back to the door. "Did you catch it?"

"Yes. Can you tie it to something on your side?"

Nothing was within reach. "It's not long enough. Just climb already! I'll hold it." She quickly tied a loop in her end and then stepped into it. She sat back on the rope and braced her feet against the prison wall, hoping her weight would be enough.

His first pull nearly tore the rope out from under her, but she tightened her grip and leaned back, praying the knot would hold. Bran wove around her legs, whimpering. "Come on . . . ," she muttered. Sweat ran into her eyes, stinging. She craned her neck upward. Finally, there was a flash of white hand; then Thomas's face appeared. He slung his body on top of the wall, panting. Then he hauled up the rope and wedged it into a crack at the top of the wall, the rock holding it firm.

"You can let go now," he whispered down. She lifted the rope over her head and stepped back. Thomas rappelled down the side of the wall, jumping the last few feet to land beside her. Bran ran up to him, tail wagging.

"Hey, girl," he whispered, giving her a pat. "Let's get out of here."

They set off down a nearby lane, staying clear of the flickering streetlights. After they'd crossed a couple of streets, Nora stopped. "Keep dickie for me, will ye?" The street was mostly deserted, except for a couple of rickety topless cars parked outside a pub that still had its lights on. The sound of voices and a lone fiddle trickled out under the door. She tried the door of one of the cars, which looked like a Model T. It was unlocked.

"Get in!" she whispered, slipping into the driver's seat. Instead, Thomas leaned against the side of the car, his eyes sparkling with amusement.

"Ever driven an automobile before?"

"O'course I have! Jesus! Just not . . ." She stared blankly at the dash, then bent over to look for the starting wires. Hot-wiring a car in the nineteen nineties had been easy. But this contraption . . . Did it even have wires? Where was the ignition?

"I think this is what you're looking for," Thomas said, lifting the hinged cover off the engine at the front of the car. Nora jumped out and peered around him.

"Those wires," she said, pointing. "We need to connect them."

"I'll do it," Thomas said. "You hit the starter. It's on the floor. On my signal."

Nora climbed back into the cab and found a lever on the floor. She craned her neck out the window and watched him fiddle with the wires. When he gave her a thumbs-up, she pumped the lever and the engine came to life, uncomfortably loud. Thomas quickly closed the engine cover and let Bran into the back of the car before climbing into the passenger seat. Nora gripped the steering wheel.

Sweet Jesus. What would Eamon say if he knew she was stealing a vintage Model T?

"You do this often?" he asked as they turned down a laneway, away from the pub. "Break people out of prison? Steal automobiles?"

Nora huffed. "Only when necessary."

She could feel his eyes on her. *The road. Look at the road.*

"Who *are* you?" he asked.

"I told you. I'm no one. Just a messed-up kid from Belfast who got sent to 1923. Maybe I'm being punished."

"For what?"

"Nothing. It was a joke."

He directed her through a maze of side streets and laneways. The streets were empty, save for the odd dog or drunkard. The car was slow and jerky, and she could feel every pebble under the wheels. But the farther they drove, the more she relaxed. Thomas was free. Would they go looking for him? Was one lone Republican worth a manhunt?

"Where are we going?" he asked.

"To Lynch, of course. I thought you knew where he was."

"I know he's somewhere in the Knockmealdown Mountains. But it's a big place."

"So we look until we find him."

It didn't take long to get out of the city. The headlights of the car were dim, and Nora could barely make out the road.

"We're almost there," Thomas said. "Take the next road to the right."

Nora slowed. Then headlights blared in their eyes.

A large metal barrier and an army lorry loomed ahead of them. Nora killed the headlights and swore, then threw the car into reverse but didn't step on the gas; she was frozen with indecision. Should they try to bluff their way through, or would it be safer to make a run for it?

"It's too late, they'll have seen us," Thomas said. His eyes were wary. Bran growled in the backseat. Two soldiers walked toward them, weapons drawn.

"Thomas, we *cannot* get arrested. There isn't time."

She scanned the area around them, but it was too dark to see anything. *We'll use that to our advantage.* She stepped on the pedal and backed away from the roadblock. The army lorry's engine started. "Let's run." She slammed on the brakes and threw open the door. Thomas was already at her side. He grabbed her hand, and they plunged off the road, Bran racing after them. They were in a field of some kind, but it was too dark to see anything. Tall grass whipped at their hands. Shouts chased them, and the thunder of boots, but then they were in the trees,

Thomas pulling her along, this way then that, lifting her over roots and stones as though it were broad daylight. The shouts faded. The soldiers were going the wrong way. She clung to Thomas's hand, sure that if they lost each other they would not find their way back together again. They ran. And ran. And ran.

Finally, he slowed. A stitch in her side made her double over. Bran pushed her wet nose against Nora's cheek.

"It's safe. We can rest for a while," Thomas said.

"How did you . . . ? It was like you could see," she panted.

"I've spent a lot of time in these fields and woods. There's a patch of dry moss over here. Let's sit."

They listened to each other breathe for a long while. Then Nora put her face in her hands. "Ballix!" Lynch would be killed the day after tomorrow, and here they were lost in the middle of nowhere, with no car and with Free State soldiers at their heels.

"We'll find him, Nora. I want it as much as you do."

Do you? "Even if we find him—which would be a miracle at this point—and save this secret deal between him and Cosgrave, then according to you, the curse will be broken."

"Aye."

"Are you so anxious to die?"

His breath hitched. "I am."

"I have a lot of questions for when this is over."

"I imagine you do. I've my own questions as well. I've met a lot of strange and interesting people, but never someone from the future. But let me ask you just once, right now: Why is saving Lynch so important to you? Are you really such a patriot?"

A patriot. Was she? At one time in her life, she'd have answered yes without hesitation. She'd fought for her country. Bled for it. *But would I have done the same if Eamon hadn't died?*

"I love Ireland. I do. And she deserves to be free and whole."

"But?"

How could she tell him the truth? He was practically a stranger. And yet he'd been inside her head for months, and besides Brigid and the Brigidine Sisters, he was the only person in 1923 who knew who she really was. She *wanted* to tell him—a realization that both confused and frightened her. How would he view her once he knew the truth?

She buried her hands in Bran's brown fur. "I told you the war continues in the North. My father was a Volunteer. He was killed when I was very young. My brother Eamon, he only wanted peace. But I was stupid. Selfish. I got in trouble with the Provos—that's what the IRA becomes. They wanted him to sign up. He did it, but only to protect me. He never wanted any of it. And then . . ." Thomas's arm settled around her, and she stiffened. But he left it there, warm and accepting, inviting her confidence. She softened and rested her head against his shoulder.

"He died?" Thomas asked softly.

"Aye. Beaten to death by Protestant paramilitaries." Even as she said it, the rage flickered inside her.

"And you want to avenge him."

"I want to fix it. Make it so it never happens."

"You've buried your dead, Nora. Don't try to bury the living as well."

"What's that supposed to mean?"

"It just means that I know a thing or two about regret. About moving on without the people you love. Sometimes it's hard to remember that you're not the one who died."

She shrugged off Thomas's arm. "We should keep going. Maybe we can get back to the car."

"They're still out there, looking for us," Thomas said. "We need to be careful."

"If we're careful, Lynch will die . . . and so will my brother."

"Bran." Thomas jerked his head, and Bran slunk into the woods.

"Where's she going?"

"To find Lynch's exact location for us. It'll make our path easier in the morning. Save us some time."

She shivered. Thomas wrapped his arm around her again. "We'll make better time in the morning. We're less than a mile away from the Gillies farm. I reckon it's safe to go that far, so long as we're careful."

Her heart warmed at the thought of seeing Mrs. Gillies, and she had to admit Thomas was right. If they blundered their way back to the car now, they'd almost certainly get caught. She got to her feet and waited for him to point the way. He offered his arm, which she could barely see in the impenetrable darkness. She wrapped hers through it, and he led her like a blind person around rocks and hedgerows.

They smelled it before they could see it. The unmistakable scent of burning wood. She tensed as the first whiffs reached them. They picked up the pace.

"It's just over the next rise," Thomas said.

Maybe it was a bonfire. Maybe a farmer clearing his field. Maybe . . .

They crested the hill. The darkness was pierced with the red glow of coals. It was all that remained of the Gillies family home.

"No," Nora breathed. She let go of Thomas's arm and plunged down the hill, her eyes fixed on the embers.

"Wait!" Thomas whispered. But Nora ignored him, her heart pounding in her ears, driven forward by the fear of what she might find.

The home was a blackened shell. Most of the thatched roof was gone, and scorch marks lined the windows. Broken furniture and crockery spilled into the yard. Scraps of books, a shattered mirror, and a soot-covered teakettle. "Mrs. Gillies!" Nora called, wheeling around wildly. "Mr. Gillies! Stephen!" For the first time, she was glad Pidge was in jail. At least she was safe from whoever had done this.

Thomas arrived at her side, his face grim. There was movement in the doorway of the stone barn, which looked untouched. Thomas grabbed her arm. "Stop. Whoever did this might still be here."

She wrenched her arm out of his grip. "Then they'll have me to answer to, won't they?" She drew her pistol from her beaded bag and stalked toward the barn. "Whoever is in there, come out slowly!"

A figure emerged. Mrs. Gillies stood trembling in the doorway. Her skin was blackened with soot, her hair wild and frizzy in the dim light of the embers of her home. Nora stashed the gun and rushed over to her. "Are you hurt?"

Mrs. Gillies shook her head. Her eyes were rimmed red and her lips cracked.

"I think she's in shock. Thomas, your jacket." Thomas had already shrugged off his jacket, and he gently settled it around Mrs. Gillies's shoulders.

"She should sit down." Thomas led them to a large stump in the front yard. Nora lowered Mrs. Gillies down and sat beside her, her arm around her shoulders.

"What happened?" she whispered. "Where are the men? Are they okay?"

Mrs. Gillies tried to speak, but nothing came out except for a dry rasp.

"Thomas, see if you can find an unbroken cup in there," Nora said. "The water pump is behind the barn."

Mrs. Gillies swallowed hard and tried again. "They took them."

"The Free State?"

Mrs. Gillies nodded, her lips clamped shut.

"Oh no." Nora felt a great wave of nausea. "I'm so sorry. I should have . . ." Her apology hung limply in the air between them, useless.

Mrs. Gillies didn't meet her eyes. "They were hiding out on the Hill of Allen with some of the other lads. Staters picked them up earlier today, then came round and burned all the houses."

Nora stayed silent. How could she and Pidge have been so reckless? Mr. Gillies and Stephen would be lucky to escape the firing squad. It wouldn't matter to the Free State that the weapons they'd found here last week had been smuggled in by Pidge without her parents' knowledge.

"Mrs. Gillies, I—" But what could be said?

Mrs. Gillies patted her knee, then moved her hand away rather quickly. "What's done is done. I signed up for this life when I married Sean. How could our children be anything but revolutionaries? I just hope . . ." She stared at the blackened remains of her home. "I tried . . . I tried to put it out. But I couldn't."

Thomas returned with a chipped mug full of clear water. Mrs. Gillies sipped it. "Is this your young man? The one you were looking for?" she asked, cradling the mug in her lap.

"Aye."

"I see. And Pidge? Do you have any word from her?"

Nora had to look away. "Not since they moved them. I went to North Dublin Union, but they wouldn't let me in. I sent her a letter."

Mrs. Gillies nodded. The water seemed to have revived her somewhat. "She wrote to me. Told me you'd signed the form."

"I'm not a traitor. I have my reasons. There are things that only I can do . . . and not from inside a prison."

Mrs. Gillies patted her knee. "I know there are things you can't speak of, Nora. I won't ask you. But Pidge is young. She doesn't understand. She's angry, and who can blame her?"

"I know." Nora stared at the embers, the way she might have done around a dying campfire. But this was a family's home. A family's life.

"I don't want her to know what happened here," Mrs. Gillies said. "She might not be strong enough to take it."

"I tried to talk her out of the hunger strike. I did everything I could, but she was set on it."

Mrs. Gillies sniffed, and her mouth grew tight. "Pidge has a fire in her. I'm not sure it will be quenched until she's given her life for the Republic."

"It won't come to that. They'll release her."

"They released Brenda Moynihan last month, after twenty-seven days on strike. She died this past week. Influenza. Too weak to fight it off."

Nora struggled with what to say. How could she promise this woman that she wouldn't lose her entire family? She couldn't predict the outcome. "It will end soon. The war. I can't say what will happen next, but this war—Irish against Irish—it's going to be over soon."

"I wish it were true, Nora."

"It is. Trust me."

Thomas knelt down beside them. "She should get some rest. Do you have somewhere you can go?" he asked Mrs. Gillies. "We can take you there."

She shook her head. "I'll be fine in the barn for now. The McQuarrys will take me in in the morning, I reckon. At least until the men are back."

"We'll stay with you until morning," Nora said, her voice tight. She wanted to find Lynch, she wanted to keep going, but she couldn't leave Mrs. Gillies here all alone. Besides, it was well past midnight. She wouldn't get far without some sleep.

Thomas wrapped a stick in some ruined curtains and made a torch. Inside the barn they found extra blankets for the horses. They made Mrs. Gillies as comfortable as possible on a bed of hay. Nora sat beside her.

"I'm sorry about your things, Nora," she whispered.

"Don't worry about it. It's grand," Nora said. None of that seemed to matter now.

"What was it all, if I may ask? Some of it seemed so strange. That pamphlet about Kilmainham . . ."

Nora adjusted the blanket around Mrs. Gillies's shoulders. What would tomorrow bring for this brave soul?

"It was for a play. I was in a theater company in Belfast. We were . . . imagining the future. I guess I had some of the props in my bag when I left."

"Ah. I see."

Nora was glad she couldn't see the older woman's eyes.

She waited until Mrs. Gillies's breath slowed to a steady, deep rhythm. Then she went back into the yard. Thomas had started a fire near the stump. She sat next to him and stared wordlessly into the flames.

"It was kind of you to offer to stay," he said.

"When I first arrived here, from the future . . . she was the first person to show me kindness. I think she suspects—I think she's always suspected—that there's something not quite right about my story. But she's given me her trust anyway. I couldn't just leave her here."

After several silent minutes, she asked what she'd been wondering for the past two days.

"Why did Aengus Óg curse you, Thomas?"

"You won't believe me."

She tore her eyes from the flames to look at him. His profile stood out against the fiery backdrop. The long, straight nose. The determined set of the jaw. The furrowed brow. For all his lighthearted banter, for all his nonchalant demeanor, there was a great heaviness on him.

She tried to tease it out of him. "It must have been bad, to make a god so angry with you. That's who Aengus Óg is, right? One of the Tuatha Dé Danann? Like Brigid?" The Catholic in her rebelled at the thought of other gods, but she couldn't rule anything out now. She'd have to sort it out with the priest later. If there was a later.

"He is."

"Look, I'm here, aren't I? You didn't bat an eyelash when I told you I was from the future. So you've been cursed by a god. That's no more unbelievable."

"I've never told anyone."

"In eighteen hundred years? Now *that's* something I find hard to believe."

"You're right. I did tell a few, at first. But then they tried to kill me . . . so I had to kill them instead. Is that what you want to hear?"

"That's what you're worried about? That I'll try to kill you?" He shook his head, the gray strands glittering in the firelight. "We're in this together, remember? We want the same thing."

He picked up a long stick and poked the fire, sending sparks into the air. "I suppose we do."

"Then let's be honest with each other. I told you about my brother. I haven't told anyone that, not since I left Belfast. Tell me why you were cursed."

"Do you know the story of Diarmuid and Grania?"

Was he trying to change the subject? "Not really. I mean, I've heard the names, but I can't remember the story."

"It's part of what they call the Fenian Cycle. Stories about Fionn mac Cumhaill and his band of warriors, the Fianna."

"Yes, I've been to the pub."

"What?"

"Finn McCool's. A cheesy, fake Irish pub in America and London."

He stared at her, nonplussed.

"Sorry. Go on," she said.

He turned his attention back to the flames. "Diarmuid was one of Fionn's men. They were as close as brothers. He was handsome, skilled with both bow and sword, could turn your eyes to rivers with his poetry. And that was before the love spot."

"The what?"

"A hag gave it to him one night, on account of his kindness to her. You couldn't see it, but it was in the middle of his forehead. Made every woman who set eyes on him fall madly in love."

"Lucky him."

Thomas shook his head. "Not so."

"What did he do?"

"He wore a cap to cover the love spot. So long as the women could not see it, they regarded him as no more than any other handsome warrior. Until his leader, Fionn mac Cumhaill, decided to remarry. His wife Maighneis had died, and after the grieving period was over, he sent one of his men and his son Oisín to find a suitable wife for him. They found *her*. Grania. The daughter of Cormac mac Art, High King of Ireland. She was young, beautiful, and from a noble family—everything a man could want in a wife."

Nora snorted. Thomas gave her a half smile. "You have to understand this was another age," he said.

"Sadly, not much has changed." Nora took the stick from him and rearranged the wood in the fire.

"The date of the wedding was set. Fionn and his men went to the house of Cormac at Tara for a week of feasting before the wedding. He and Grania spoke many times. She was charming, gracious, and kindhearted. He loved her almost at once.

"The day before the wedding was the grandest feast of all, in the long hall. Hundreds of men, women, dogs."

"Dogs?"

"The hunting dogs, like Bran. They rarely left the warriors' sides. There was plenty of wine and ale. The dogs were fighting over the scraps. When Diarmuid intervened and tried to separate them, his cap was knocked off."

"Ahh. And someone saw his love spot? It wasn't . . ."

"It was. Grania. Fionn's betrothed. It wasn't anyone's fault. It was Diarmuid's own curse; I see that now. I was so blind . . ." He broke off and put his head in his hands.

Oh dear God. So *this* was why he was telling her the story. The truth stunned her as surely as if he'd cracked her head against a stone wall. "Wait. Thomas. Are you saying . . . ?"

He stood up, putting the fire between them. "I don't expect you to believe me. But yes. I am Fionn mac Cumhaill."

Brigid . . . time travel . . . and now Fionn mac Cumhaill. She would have laughed at the absurdity of it all if there hadn't been so much at stake. "Tell me the rest. Tell me what happened."

She couldn't make out his face behind the flames. But then he started pacing on the other side of the fire.

"Grania forced Diarmuid to run away with her that night. There were different customs in that time. She bound him, not with ropes, but with words. A *geis*, it's called. He had no choice but to do her bidding. So they ran. And for years I hunted them."

"*Years?*"

"I had already lived a long life. Grania was to be my last queen." The words hung heavy in the air. "I was a different man. I was arrogant, proud. I wouldn't listen to the counsel of those around me, not even my own son. I became a man obsessed."

"Did you find them?"

"Yes. We made peace, after many years."

"Well . . . that's grand then, isn't it?"

"And then I killed him."

"But—"

"I wish I could say it was an accident. But it was not. Even though we had made peace, I saw my chance for revenge, and I took it. I tried to save him at the last minute, but it was too late."

"Is that why you were cursed?" she asked softly.

He walked around the fire and stood beside her, still staring into the flames. She said nothing. Waited.

"Aengus Óg had fostered Diarmuid as a child. He had helped Diarmuid hide from me for years. When he found out I had killed his beloved foster son . . . his anger would not be quenched. I was very powerful then. My mother was the granddaughter of the great Nuadu Airgetlám, High King of the Tuatha Dé Danann. At the time, many warriors had *sidhe* blood in their veins, and it gave us great strength, skill, and longevity. I was the greatest of them all. But even I did not have the power of the old gods. Aengus Óg took my power, making me as weak as any other mortal man, and then he cursed me. I would not die until I saved Ireland from her enemies. And so I have lived. And lived. And lived. And watched everyone I've ever loved grow old and die. Century after century after godforsaken century."

Nora reached up and grasped his hand. It was cold, and his fingers twitched in surprise. She pulled him down beside her onto the stump. "Then what does it take to save Ireland? Every country will always have enemies, so what exactly did Aengus Óg mean? Did he tell you?" She kept his hand tight in hers, as though she could siphon off some of his pain.

"The gods delight in being oblique. If I knew exactly what Aengus Óg wanted, perhaps I would not still be here," he said in a voice so soft she could barely hear him over the crackle of the flames. "I tried everything . . . I fought the Vikings, then the Normans. Cromwell. The 1798 Rebellion. The 1916 Rising. No matter how hard I fought, it only got worse. I thought—I dared *hope*—that when we won the Tan War, when we beat off the British after over seven hundred years, the curse would be broken. But . . ."

"But the treaty doesn't include the North."

He squeezed her fingers; then his hand slid away, leaving her hand cold and alone in her lap. "I'm not a hero, Nora. I'm not who I used to be. I'm just a soldier. An ordinary man with an ordinary man's strength."

"Maybe that's all it will take." Wasn't she also just an ordinary woman, trying to do the impossible?

"Or maybe I need to take my head out of my arse—pardon my language—and accept someone's help. Those were Brigid's words."

"You and Brigid have known each other for a while, I gather?"

"Aye. She's always been fond of me. But she can't interfere directly. Not with the curse. There's no love lost between her and Aengus Óg, but I know she won't act directly against him."

"So she sent me to you."

"So she did. And I'm glad, though I know I didn't act it at first. I'd have had no clue about Lynch if you hadn't come here. You've given me another chance."

She leaned her head against his shoulder. "Let's hope it works."

Chapter Twenty-One

When Nora opened her eyes, the sky was lightening, a pale gray rimmed with pink, blending together with wisps of cloud. A bird chirped nearby. The ground beneath her was hard, and her back ached. Half her body was cold. She turned her head, ignoring the protest of her neck. A pile of black ash in a circle of stones. Right. She didn't want to know what the house looked like in the harsh reality of daylight. Her other side was warm, and she turned toward it instinctively, drawing closer to the source of heat. Thomas—no, Fionn—lay next to her, eyelashes resting on his cheeks, his mouth slightly open. Stubble grazed his jaw.

Fionn mac Cumhaill. Impossible. He was just a soldier, an actor, spinning a wild tale so that . . . why? What could he possibly gain from such an outlandish story? Unless he wasn't acting alone. Brigid could be playing with her.

But if she believed in Brigid, was it really such a stretch to accept that Thomas was Fionn? Being Catholic and believing in the gods and warriors of legend weren't mutually exclusive. She certainly wouldn't be alone in that. Plenty of old women in Belfast went to Mass every day, clutching their rosary beads and their Bibles, but still tried to keep the fairy folk happy by tying ribbons to trees and pouring a little bit of whiskey onto the ground. In 2004 the government had diverted a new motorway to avoid cutting down a fairy tree in Clare. Would Father Donovan accuse her of idolatry, or did he harbor the same secret belief in the old ways?

Her father had told her some of the stories of Fionn and his Fianna. At least, that's what Eamon had once said. She'd been too young for the stories to stick, but she'd heard them later, at school. Fairy tales, so they were called. Fionn and the Salmon of Knowledge. Fionn and the Giant's Causeway.

How many women has he been with over the centuries? The thought came unbidden into her mind. *What does it matter? He can take you to Lynch. Then you can go home, and your father and brother will be alive and well.*

Besides, the women he had loved were all dead now. And how about his children? How many children had he watched grow old and die? She reached out a hand to touch his cheek, moved by the magnitude of sorrow he must have suffered in his long life. But she hesitated and withdrew it. Rolling onto her back, she stared at the sky. She could contemplate his past later. It was time to reinvent the future.

When she reached over to wake Fionn, his eyes were open. "Good morning," he whispered.

She stood and brushed soot off her dress. "I'll go check on Mrs. Gillies. Then we need to go. Can you . . . talk with Bran? Find out where Lynch is?"

He sat up and wrapped his arms around his knees. "Aye. Go on and make sure she's all right."

Nora gently shook Mrs. Gillies, who looked at her wildly for one moment before her eyes softened in recognition. "Nora. You're still here. Is it morning already?"

"Aye. How are you feeling?"

"Oh, I'll be fine, no doubt." She pulled herself up from the hay and got stiffly to her feet. "I appreciate your concern, but you don't have to stay, Nora."

"We'll take you to the neighbors, then we'll be off. We could really use a car. We have a long way to go, and not much time. Do you think . . . ?"

She shook her head. "I don't have anything for you here. But the McQuarrys have a motorcycle, I believe. I'll ask them for you once we get there."

The three of them walked in silence through the back field and onto a little dirt road. After about half an hour, they reached the McQuarry home. A middle-aged woman rushed out to greet them. "Kathleen, are you all right? What's happened?"

Nora took Fionn's arm, and they fell back, letting the two women talk in hushed voices. Mrs. McQuarry kept looking over her shoulder at them. Finally she nodded and addressed them. "Owen is away, but he took the pony and trap. He'll not be happy, sure, but you can take the motorcycle. I know Kathleen wouldn't ask if it weren't important."

"Thank you," Nora said.

Fionn brought the motorcycle out of the shed while Nora helped Mrs. Gillies get settled in the house. When she came out, he was waiting for her. She climbed awkwardly onto the back and wrapped her arms around his waist.

"How far to the Knockmealdown Mountains?" Nora asked.

"A couple of hours, maybe."

"Do you know exactly where he is?"

"As long as Bran stays with him, we'll find him."

Nora couldn't help but look behind, through the strands of hair whipping in her face. "God, I hope she'll be all right. And the rest of them."

"You can't take care of everyone, Nora."

"I can try."

"You'll only get yourself hurt that way. Believe me, I've learned that lesson."

"What's that supposed to mean?"

"It means people are usually best when left to their own devices."

"That's ballix, so it is. Everyone needs help sometimes. Even you."

He gripped the handlebars tighter. "You'll learn. Someday."

She scanned the awakening countryside for signs of roadblocks.

"So how does it work with you and Bran? You can speak with her, even if she's not here. How does that work?"

"It's always been that way. It was one of the few mercies Aengus Óg left me. Her life is tied to my own."

"You mean she's been with you all these years?"

"We've been separated a few times, but for the most part, yes. I don't suppose your children's stories tell you how she came to be?"

"Maybe they do, but I don't remember them."

"She was born to my mother's sister, after one of the sidhe—the Tuatha Dé Danann, that is—turned my aunt into a hound."

"Now you're just messing with me."

"It's true. Tuiren, my aunt, married one of my men. Only his lover, who was one of the sidhe, didn't appreciate him taking a wife. You'd think he would have considered that. Anyway, the lover paid the new wife a visit and turned her into a hound. But Tuiren was already with child. Two whelps, actually. Bran and Sceolan."

"And they were born as . . . wolfhounds?"

"Aye. Tuiren eventually regained her human form. But the pups remained as they were, though with the minds of humans."

Nora grappled with this. "Bran has the mind of a human?"

"And the instincts of a hound."

"So she's your . . . cousin?"

"That she is."

"What happened to the other one?"

"She died. While we were hunting Diarmuid."

"Oh. I'm sorry." They rode in silence for a while. "Is that how you know about the deal with Lynch and Cosgrave? Bran's your spy?"

"You could say that. She's very observant, for a hound."

"A hound-woman." A sudden thought struck her. "So she can understand what I'm saying?" She racked her brain, trying to think of anything embarrassing she'd said or done while Bran was around.

"She can. But don't worry; she's very discreet."

Nora resolved to be more circumspect when Bran was in earshot. "And you can understand her?"

"It's not as simple as communicating with another human, but we've figured it out over the years."

"They're true, then? All the stories?"

His hands twitched. "Not anymore. The sidhe have withdrawn. All save Brigid. I don't think she'll ever leave. But the druids, the bards . . . everything you would call magic. Gone. All we have left now are our mortal selves. And our guns and our hatred and our base desires. It's a different world you live in."

"You live in it, too."

"So I do."

"What if Lynch doesn't believe us?" Nora asked.

"He'll sure as hell want to know how we know the Free State is in the area. How will you explain that?"

"I don't know . . . I'll say I have a lover in the Free State Army."

Fionn glanced back at her and raised an eyebrow. "Do you?"

"Oh, aye, I've had loads of time for dating lately."

"They'll want a name."

"Fine. Daniel Miller."

"And who's that poor sod?"

"A friend of Pidge's. At least, he used to be. He's the one who got us arrested."

Nora craned her neck over Fionn's shoulder and kept her eyes on the road, looking for a cloud of dust or any other telltale signs of a roadblock. They passed only two other people, a man on foot and a farmer with a horse and cart filled with milk canisters. But neither gave them a second look.

She had so many questions about this strange, ancient man fate had delivered to her, but she couldn't handle any more right now. Her mind was stretched thin enough as it was. When would the deal be made with Cosgrave to get rid of the Boundary Commission and keep Ireland together? She would need to keep Liam Lynch alive until then.

Finally, Fionn directed the bike off the road and stowed it behind a cluster of dense brush. "We'll walk in from here." The ground was covered with gorse and stone. They pushed their way through it, heading toward the base of the mountains.

"Where is he?" Nora asked.

"He's been on the move—traveling toward Araglin." He frowned. "Maybe that's where he's meeting Cosgrave to sign the deal. But right now he's at Goatenbridge."

Nora moved faster. "What if he leaves before we get there?"

"Then we'll follow. We'll find him before they do, Nora. This way." Fionn veered to the south. "If we stay off the road, we should avoid the scouts."

"Scouts?"

"If the Chief is in the area, they'll want to know who else is around."

Nora huffed. "It wasn't enough last time. I mean . . . tomorrow. *Jesus*. This is messed."

Finally they came in sight of a small thatched cottage in a glen near the foot of the mountain. Fionn stopped. "That's it."

Nora's heart pounded. "We made it." She took off at a run, not wanting to waste another second.

"Wait," Fionn called out, but she ignored him. Liam Lynch was inside that building, and he was going to die unless she did something about it.

The click of a barrel stopped her in her tracks.

"Hold it right there," a man said, pointing a rifle at her head. Another directed his Thompson at Fionn, whose hands were in the air.

"We have to see the Chief," Nora said. "I have important information for him."

"The Chief isn't here," the man said, circling her slowly.

"Like hell he's not. I don't care if you shoot me; just let me talk to him first."

The two guards exchanged glances.

"She's telling the truth," Fionn said. "She really doesn't care if you shoot her."

"What kind of information?" asked the guard pointing the rifle at her. "If we happen to see him, we'll pass the message along."

"My message is only for him." Nora folded her arms. "And you're holding that wrong," she said to the man with the Thompson.

"Both of you, against the wall," her guard said, jabbing toward the side of the house with the rifle. Nora and Fionn stood facing the wall, their hands pressed against the siding. The guard with the rifle went inside the house, leaving his comrade behind to cover them.

"Bet this didn't happen back in the day? With the Fianna and all?" she asked Fionn, watching his face for his response.

He gave her a sideways glance; then a corner of his mouth lifted in a wry smile. "No. It most definitely did not."

"They say humility's a virtue, you know." He gave her another look, but this time said nothing. Nora's nerves sparked with excitement. In a few minutes, this might all be over. But she felt a twinge of hesitation as well. What would happen to Fionn once the curse was lifted? Would he die immediately, or just become mortal like the rest of them? Maybe he would shrivel up into an old man, like the story of Oisín after his return from Tír na nÓg after three hundred years away. She realized with a start that if the stories were true, Oisín had been Fionn's son.

The first man returned and nodded to his comrade. "He says he'll see her. Not you," he added as Fionn turned to follow Nora.

"I'm going with her," Fionn insisted.

"Chief's orders. Only the lady."

Nora made to follow the guard inside. Fionn started after them but was stopped by the barrel of a rifle pointed at his chest.

"Nora, are you sure—" he said.

"Just wait here. I'll be fine," she said. But in truth, she'd been counting on Fionn to lend her story credibility. He was an IRA man. He'd fought with Lynch before. But she didn't argue. She couldn't lose her chance, not when she'd come this far.

The guard led her into the house, where a group of men sat around a long wooden table. Plates of biscuits and mugs of tea littered the table, along with ashtrays, sheaves of paper, and a large map. She recognized Lynch at once. He was thinner than he'd looked at the training camp, but he had the same studious, handsome face, the same strong jaw and perfectly shaped lips. It struck her that he was younger than she was.

"So here's the woman who says she has information for us," he said genially, leaning back in his chair. "What's your name, dear?"

"Nora O'Reilly."

"You're Cumann na mBan?"

"No. I mean, yes, but that's not why I'm here."

"Then tell us." The other men regarded her with interest, casually smoking or sipping their tea.

"I'd like to speak to you alone, sir."

He lifted an eyebrow. "Alone? That would hardly be appropriate."

"I insist."

"As do I. Whatever you have to say can be said in front of my men."

Nora hesitated, then gave in. She didn't have time to argue. "You're in trouble."

At this, all the men looked up. A man with a thick bristle-brush mustache pushed back his chair and stood, one hand on the revolver at his waist. Lynch took a long draw on his cigarette. "Sit down, O'Casey." He turned back to Nora. "What kind of trouble?"

"There's going to be a gunfight, a skirmish. Tomorrow. Free State soldiers are headed this way, and they'll intersect you on your way to Araglin."

Lynch raised an eyebrow. "And how do you know we're headed to Araglin?"

"It doesn't matter. What matters is that the Free State knows it. You have to get out of here."

"That's impossible," one of the men said. "Our scouts would have heard if Staters were in the area."

Lynch didn't take his eyes off Nora. "Are you certain?"

"Aye. I know . . . I know you'll run, take to the mountains. But they've a column coming from either direction. They'll box you in. You'll be outnumbered."

"Hogwash!" O'Casey said.

Lynch remained calm. "Go on."

"It can be changed, so it can. If you leave now, you'll be able to get out in time." Nora pleaded with him with her eyes. *You have to believe me.*

"I think I *will* have that private word, Miss O'Reilly." He pushed his chair away from the table and indicated that she should precede him into the next room, a small office. He closed the door behind them.

"How do you know this?" he asked.

"I have a, uh, friend in the Free State Army," she said.

"And he gave you this information?"

"No. I overheard him talking to his superior and did a little snooping. I saw some memos about troop movements."

"Did you make copies?"

Nora grit her teeth. "No, there wasn't time."

"But you're certain of what you saw."

"And heard. Yes."

He lit another cigarette. "What battalion is your 'friend' in, may I ask?"

She hesitated. "Kildare."

"Kildare. And why would a soldier in Kildare know about troop movements in Tipperary, I wonder?"

Her hackles rose. If he suspected her of lying, he might ignore her advice. "I have no idea. What does it matter? I know what's going to happen. You can't go to Araglin. Not tomorrow. If you die—" She stopped, choosing her words carefully. "If you die, we'll lose the war. You know that."

"You put too much faith in me, Miss O'Reilly. I'm only one man."

"You're the most important man on our side."

He tapped an inch of ash into a tray on the desk. "Whether or not that is the case, I'm inclined to not take unnecessary chances with my life at this point. But it does put me in a certain . . . predicament."

"What does it matter if it saves your life? This country needs you alive." *I need you alive.*

"I have a meeting in Araglin. A very important meeting."

"I know."

"You know?"

"Why else would you go there?"

He drew close to her and dropped his voice. "My own men do not even know the reason for this meeting. I need to keep it that way, until everything is settled. But I'll need to send a message to my . . . counterpart to change the location. I'll need a messenger."

It was working. "We came here by motorcycle; I can take your message—"

"I'm not about to send a woman alone into the mountains, Cumann na mBan or not."

"My friend . . ." She corrected herself. "My fiancé, Thomas. He's just outside, with one of your guards. Let him deliver your message." The necessity of it struck her as she said it. It had to be Fionn, didn't it? He had to play a part in order for the curse to be lifted. "You know him—Thomas Heaney. He's one of you. You can trust him."

"Thomas Heaney . . . Ah yes, I remember him. One of Coogan's men. In fact, it's his dog that's been hanging about, isn't it? The large hound?"

She pretended she didn't hear. "He'll find your counterpart and deliver your message. The meeting can still happen—just somewhere else."

"And what about your friend in Kildare? Does your fiancé know about him?"

Nora gritted her teeth. "We all do our part for the war effort," she said pointedly.

Lynch muttered something that sounded like "love and war," then opened the door and called toward the kitchen. "Bring in Heaney—the lad outside."

A moment later Fionn was shoved through the door and into the small room. "Are you all right?" they asked each other, speaking at the same time. Nora reddened. Lynch gave an amused smile.

"I have a message for you, Heaney," he said. "One that must be delivered to William Cosgrave—and only to him, am I clear? No one else is to know of this."

"Yes, sir," Fionn said. What was it like for him to take orders after being a leader for so many years? But he'd probably been taking orders for centuries now. Maybe he had forgotten what it was like to be in charge. The thought made her strangely sad.

"He's to meet me at Bill Hoolihan's house by the River Tar tomorrow at noon. It's only a few minutes' ride, due northeast. Then I was to continue on to Araglin to meet with the executive." He grimaced and looked at the floor. "It would have been a historic meeting."

"It still can be," Nora urged. "Just a small delay, that's all." Lynch narrowed his eyes. She pressed her lips together. Had she said too much?

He turned back to Fionn. "Find Cosgrave and tell him to meet me at Mahon Bridge instead. We'll have to delay the council meeting, but if your information is right, it will be worth it."

"I'll go straight away, sir," Fionn said. "Let's go, Nora."

"The lady stays here."

Fionn whipped around to face Lynch. "The lady comes with me."

"She won't be harmed. Once the message has been delivered, she'll be free to go."

"It's grand," Nora said, stepping between them. "What matters is that you get away from here now," she said to Lynch. "I don't know the exact timeline—they could be combing the hills by now, looking for you."

"She's delivered her warning, hasn't she?" Fionn said, his hands balled into fists. "She came here freely, and she can leave freely. I'm not leaving her behind."

"Fi—Thomas, leave off. Can I speak with you for a moment?" She grabbed his arm and dragged him to the other side of the room. "What are you doing?" she whispered. "It doesn't matter if I stay here. I can take care of myself. You need to get to Cosgrave. This is your chance. If we make sure that meeting goes off without a hitch, we can change history. You'll have *done it*—you'll have saved Ireland, and you'll finally be free."

His eyes were clouded by a deep-brewing storm. For the first time, she realized what an ancient being he was—how much he had seen, how much he had experienced. A thrill of awe swept through her. She was in the presence of the sacred.

She took his hand. "Don't be afraid," she whispered. "This is what you've always wanted."

He held her gaze for a long moment, then bent and gently kissed her. A jolt of surprise—and pleasure—ran through her. She closed her eyes and savored the feel of his lips on hers. Was this just part of the act?

Fionn pulled away as suddenly as he had kissed her, then stalked over to Lynch. The men conferred quietly before Fionn cast one last glance at Nora and left the room. She fought the urge to run after him. There was too much at stake to let her feelings—whatever they were—get in the way.

"Right, then," Lynch said. "Time to pack up."

They returned to the main room, where the men were engaged in a heated debate. They fell silent when they caught sight of Lynch. He scanned the table. "Change of plans."

"What's going on, Lynch?" O'Casey said. "Where is Heaney off to?"

"You'll find out soon enough. It's all for the Republic, lads."

"You can't be making decisions without consulting the executive."

Lynch stared them down. "I have been chosen to lead this army. I'll make the decisions I deem best for this country. We can't have a three-day meeting every time a choice needs to be made."

"Where is Heaney going, then?"

"I said you'll find out soon enough. But right now we have to pack up and leave."

"Why? You're not for believing this woman, are you? Our scouts have said nothing about Stater activity in this area. How d'you know she's not the one leading you into a trap?"

"Miss O'Reilly is my guest. Take care how you speak about her. Be ready to leave in an hour. We head toward Mahon Bridge."

"And what of the executive meeting in Araglin?"

"Send a dispatch rider to tell them I'll be delayed. By at least a day."

O'Casey pushed his chair back. "What are you playing at, Lynch? We've had enough delays already."

"I know this is a personal matter for you, Richard, but we cannot rush to a—"

"My son is going to be executed!" O'Casey shouted. "We're not going to win! You need to end this war *now*."

Lynch held up his hands in a conciliatory gesture. The other men looked back and forth between O'Casey and the Chief. Some appeared worried. Others emboldened. "I'm trying to negotiate—" Lynch began.

"No more negotiations!" O'Casey pulled a revolver from inside his jacket. Three other weapons were instantly drawn and pointed at O'Casey. Two of the men at the table sat still, not moving. "The longer we wait, the more of our sons die," O'Casey growled. "It's over, Lynch. Admit it."

A sickening horror descended on Nora, a cold, swooping sensation deep in her gut. This wasn't happening. Not now, not after everything. She stepped in front of Lynch and withdrew her own gun out of her purse. She pointed it at O'Casey.

"Get out of the way," O'Casey growled.

"Put it down!" Her voice was shrill now, desperate. "You don't know what you're doing."

"I know exactly what I'm doing. Now move before I put a bullet through you."

"Richard, for the love of God, put that down and we'll talk about it," one of the other men urged, pointing his own gun at O'Casey, then at Nora.

"I'm done talking. That's all he ever does—talk. He talks while our sons die. You all agree with me! It's over. He's the only one who doesn't see it."

Nora moved closer to Lynch. He stepped out from behind her, but she moved with him, blocking his way. "Put it down, or I will shoot you!" she said, her finger tightening on the trigger.

"For my son!" O'Casey bellowed.

Nora fired.

There was an explosion of thunder. Then another. And another. And a crippling, searing pain. Her head hit the floor, and a swarm of stars attacked her vision. When she could finally see, she wished she couldn't. Lynch's eyes were level with hers, glassy, unblinking.

"No." She could barely hear her own voice. There was shouting, someone crying. A dog barking. She crawled to Lynch, pushed aside the hands that were already on him, and took his face in her hands.

"Wake up!" she yelled, incoherent in her pain. It wasn't supposed to happen like this; it was a skirmish on the mountainside on April 10. Not this, not murdered by one of his own men in a cottage on April 9. She grabbed him by the lapels and shook him. "Get up! Get up!"

Someone pulled her off him. She struggled to get back, to try to wake him, but a pair of strong hands dragged her across the room and into the small office she had just been in with Lynch. The door locked. She tried to stand, but her leg buckled beneath her.

"Let me out!" she yelled, pounding the door with the palm of her hand. Over and over again she pounded and screamed, but she was of little consequence to them now. She could hear more shouting but couldn't make out any details. Finally, she slumped against the door and watched the blood pool around her leg. *I should fix that. A tourniquet . . . or something.* But her mind was still focused on Lynch, lying dead in the next room. He could have changed everything . . . and now he was just another casualty in the centuries-old conflict.

There was a crash and a gush of wind, and she was pulled to her feet. The searing pain in her leg brought her to her senses. Fionn's arm was around her, lifting her, dragging her. The other held a revolver pointed in the direction of the room where Lynch had been murdered. Then they were outside, and the cottage was growing smaller behind them.

"Stop! Put me down; we have to go back." She tried to wrench away, but his grip was too tight, and she was in too much pain. "Fionn, we can't just leave."

He shoved the gun into his waistband and picked her up with both arms. Bran came running beside them. "We can't go back. He's dead, and we need to get out of there. They'll think you're a traitor, or a spy, or a witness. If you go back, they'll kill you."

"There's still time; we can tell them about the deal. They can still make the deal—"

"There was no deal."

"What?" Her leg blazed with every step, and she felt like throwing up. She kept her eyes trained on Fionn's face. *Focus.*

"I went to find Cosgrave—and found the Free State Army instead. It was a setup, Nora."

"Are you sure?" Lynch had been so certain, so determined to keep this meeting.

Fionn nodded grimly. "They were waiting for Lynch, just as you said. But not in Araglin. At Bill Hoolihan's, where he was to meet Cosgrave."

Nora closed her eyes. "It was all a trap."

"Yes. Cosgrave wanted him dead."

"Well, he is."

"Yes."

They reached the motorcycle, and Fionn laid her down beside it. Bran paced around them, whining. Fionn took off his shirt and tore it in strips, then wrapped it around the wound in her leg, saying something about a hospital nearby. But she wasn't listening. It didn't matter, any of it. She'd lost her chance.

The North would be cut off from the rest of Ireland, the IRA wouldn't stop fighting, the English would strangle them all in a choke hold, and her father would fight back, and die. And her brother wouldn't want to fight, but he would, and die. And her mother would find relief at the bottom of a bottle, and die. And Nora would be left alone to keep fighting.

Fionn hoisted Nora into his arms and climbed onto the bike. "You'll have to hold on to me," he said. She wrapped her arms around his neck and screamed silently into his shoulder as the bike jostled back to the main road.

"What happened in there?" he asked after several silent minutes.

Haltingly, she told him the whole story. His jaw clenched as she spoke.

"I shouldn't have left you," he said.

"I'm glad you did. They probably would have killed you."

"Not possible, remember? Especially since, well, nothing's changed. But they could have killed *you*."

She shifted position and winced. "Where are we going?"

"Hospital."

"No. I'll be fine. Just . . . take me to Kildare."

"Nora, you were shot in the leg. The bullet is still in there. I'm a decent field medic, but I've nothing for the pain. I'm taking you to hospital. The one in Newcastle doesn't ask a lot of questions."

She didn't have strength to argue.

When she woke, a nun was standing at the foot of her bed, writing on a clipboard.

"Hello?" Nora croaked. Her throat felt stuffed with cotton.

"Ah, you're awake," the nun said. "How do you feel?"

"Like I've been shot."

The nurse smiled. "You'll be fine. Didn't hit anything major, just muscle tissue. Would you like to see Eamon?"

"E . . . Eamon?" Had it worked, after all? Was she back in 2005? Was her brother somehow alive?

"You've been asking for him since we gave you something for the pain. I assume he's the gentleman waiting outside? Tall, gray hair?"

Nora stared up at the ceiling. Of course. "No. Eamon is—was—my brother. He's . . . not here."

The nurse flushed. "Ah. I'm sorry. Well, your friend outside has been very attentive. Would you like me to bring him in?"

"Aye."

She stared at a long crack in the ceiling, dividing the room in two. What now? She could go to Kildare, find the Brigidine Sisters, explain to them what had happened. She'd tried to help Thomas—Fionn. She'd done everything she could, but it hadn't worked. She could ask them to send her back—if they could. Or . . .

Fionn entered the room, cap in his hands, blood still staining his clothes. "How are you feeling?"

"I'll live."

He sat on the metal chair next to the bed and scraped it forward. "They tell me it's not serious. Your wound."

She nodded, still looking at the ceiling.

"Thought you might like to know they brought Lynch here as well."

Now she looked at him. "He's not . . . ?"

"He's dead. So's the man who shot him—O'Casey. They're saying it was a Free State ambush. At least, that's the story they're putting out to the public."

She huffed and sank farther back into her pillows. "O'course."

He pulled out a cigarette but didn't light it. Instead he twirled it through his fingers, his eyes unfocused. "You know, I honestly thought it would work this time." He shook his head and lit the cigarette. "How stupid of me."

"You can't smoke that in here."

He looked honestly perplexed. "Why not?"

"Never mind. Give me a drag."

He passed it over to her, and she inhaled slowly. That was better.

"You don't think . . . I mean, he's dead, but it happened a day early," he said. "You don't think that will change anything?"

She could tell he was trying to be nonchalant, but the hope in his voice was audible. She wished she had a different answer for him. "I'm no expert, but I don't think so. The date isn't what's important. The deal with Cosgrave is dead; that's all that matters. Not that it was ever a real possibility, from what you said. They'll still carve up the country. Everything will happen as it did."

He nodded, his face tightening. "I heard something else. That guard who helped me escape. He was an O'Reilly."

"I know."

"Any relation?"

"My great-uncle."

"Did he know—"

"Who I was? No. But the date of his death was written on the back of a picture at my aunt's house. I warned him, and he stayed home that day, so he lived. I thought it would work the same with Lynch, but . . ."

Fionn looked at the floor, avoiding her eyes.

"What is it?"

"He was arrested. Apparently I wasn't the only prisoner he tried to free. They caught him smuggling bolt cutters to a couple of the others. He was executed this morning."

No. Roger . . . Nora could only stare at the ceiling while tears pressed out of the corners of her eyes. *What have I done?* She lifted a hand and crossed herself.

Fionn grabbed her hand and held it. "Don't beat yourself up. I can't say I understand this whole coming-back-in-time thing, but . . . the way I look at it, he would have died anyway. It's not your fault."

"Don't say that. It *is* my fault. I gave him the idea; I goaded him into helping me. And it was all for nothing. *Nothing* has changed."

"You don't know that for certain." But his voice betrayed him. He knew they had lost. She had failed in every way possible.

"That's the thing, I do. I *know* what happens next. The government will take the easy way out. Hand over Northern Ireland. They'll say it's only temporary, but it's not."

They sat in silence for a long time. Her leg was starting to throb. She closed her eyes, wishing she could fall asleep and wake up on her cot in Sudan in 2005. Wishing this exercise in futility hadn't happened.

"You say—you said the war ends, soon after Lynch's death?"

"Aye. I can't remember who it was, but the man who took over from Lynch gave the order to stand down and dump arms. It'll happen soon. They'll say Lynch's death ended the war."

He dropped her hand. "Nora . . . you really want to keep this war going?"

She squinted at him. "Only for as long as it takes us to win it."

"But you said we do get a republic, eventually. So, we do win, in the end."

"Twenty-six counties do, aye."

"A partial victory is better than none, don't you think?"

"Not if you're the part that loses."

He stood up and looked out the window. "I understand, I do. But you haven't lived through the last several centuries of war. Your people—our people—have suffered so much. *So* much. I'm not glad Lynch is dead. I wish we could have changed things. Believe me, I want it more than anyone." He turned back to her, a rueful smile on his face. "Maybe I'm just used to losing by now. But I'm glad the war's going to be over soon. For the people's sake."

"Some of the people," she corrected. "The war isn't over for everyone."

She turned over and closed her eyes.

"There will be another chance," he said. "There's still hope."

"I thought you didn't believe in hope."

"Maybe I've changed my mind."

She didn't respond. She could imagine him standing behind her, silhouetted by the window, contemplating her with his ancient gaze. What had started out as a lark, a few foolish dreams, had turned into so much more. But for what? Lynch was dead. Roger was dead. Maybe the past couldn't be changed, after all.

"I'll let you rest," he said, but made no move to leave the room.

Chapter Twenty-Two

Nora left the hospital two days later, leaning heavily on a wooden cane. The nuns had laundered her dress for her. She felt ridiculous, dressed in cream and lace and hobbling along, wincing at every step.

Fionn and Bran were waiting for her outside.

"Hello, Bran," she murmured before Fionn helped her into his carriage.

"I thought the carriage might be more comfortable," Fionn said. "I had the motorcycle returned yesterday. Do you still want to see Mrs. Gillies?"

"Aye. I need to do what I can to make amends." *And I need to say good-bye.*

"I brought you this," Fionn said, handing her the handgun she thought she'd lost in the chaos at Lynch's hideout. "You seem to have a knack for getting yourself into situations where you need one." Nora smiled and tucked the gun into her beaded handbag, beside her rosary.

Bran ran behind the carriage as they bumped along the road. Nora braced her leg with her hands, trying to minimize the pain. After they'd traveled for a few silent minutes, she said, "I have a plan."

"Why am I not surprised to hear that?" Fionn said, a smile playing on the corner of his lips.

She didn't return his smile. Her last plan hadn't worked out for anyone. There was no guarantee this one would, either. But she wasn't ready to give up. Not yet. "I need to see Brigid."

The light faded from his face. "One does not summon Brigid. Believe me, I've tried."

Nora scowled. "Then how do you speak with her?"

"She shows herself. At her own leisure."

"But what if you need her help?"

"I've needed—or wanted—her help many times in my life. Turns out I can handle most problems myself. Of course, I'd like to think she's keeping an eye on me." He smirked. "But that's probably wishful thinking on my part."

"I think she cares about you more than you realize," Nora said, remembering the tenderness in Brigid's voice when she spoke of "Thomas."

"Perhaps," he said wistfully. "She has been my only constant these many years. She and Bran."

"Which is why she sent me to help you lift your curse."

He turned so that he was facing her directly. "I've been thinking about that. How exactly did she intend for you to do that? I mean, why you in particular?"

Nora stared at the road ahead. She'd been asking herself that same question. "I don't know. I think it means I need to help you save Ireland. That's what I thought I was doing with Lynch. Only . . ."

"It didn't work out that way."

"But that doesn't mean it can't." She held his gaze fast. "You said it yourself: there will be another chance. Just because we messed this one up doesn't mean it's the end. For either of us."

"So that's your plan? To try again? Using your knowledge of the future?"

"In a sense, yes."

"Then why do you need Brigid?"

Nora didn't answer. She didn't want to get his expectations up. She was saved by their arrival at the McQuarrys.

"Wait here while I inquire," Fionn said. "No sense in you moving if there's no one here."

Mrs. McQuarry met him at the front door. They had a hurried chat; then Fionn returned. "She's gone back home."

"Back? To what?"

"You'll see."

A few minutes later he pulled up in their yard. Half a dozen men and women were hard at work, re-thatching the roof and repairing the furniture.

"Nora!" Mrs. Gillies came running across the yard as Fionn helped her down from the carriage. Mrs. Gillies gasped. "Whatever has happened to you?"

"I was shot," Nora said grimly. "It's a long story."

"God between us and all harm, will it not end?" Mrs. Gillies exclaimed. "Are you all right, Thomas?"

"I am, Mrs. Gillies, thank you. And you?"

"Well, so much better now that Pidge is home."

"Wait, what?" Nora said, spinning around and then wincing as pain shot through her leg. "Pidge is home?"

"They released her yesterday," Mrs. Gillies said happily. "Along with the rest of the hunger strikers."

"And . . . how is she?" Nora held her breath.

"She's weak, to be sure, but they didn't let it go on too long, thankfully."

"Can I see her?"

"Of course. She's been asking about you. Come along, now."

Fionn went to join the men re-thatching the roof, and Nora followed Mrs. Gillies inside. An elderly woman was sweeping black dust out through the front door. She gave Nora a toothless smile as they squeezed past her.

"I've had so much help," Mrs. Gillies said. "All the neighbors have come round. They all have their own share of troubles but have spared me no kindness."

The inside of the house was taking shape again. A couple of chairs had survived, and one of the beds. The unbroken crockery and pots had been cleaned and were stacked next to a huge basket of peat bricks near the fire. Something savory was cooking in the pot hanging over the flames.

"She's in there," Mrs. Gillies said, pointing toward Pidge's old room. "I'll leave you to say hello, now."

Nora crept toward the doorway, then peered inside. Pidge was lying on a straw mattress on the floor, covered in thick blankets. An empty bowl and spoon were on the floor beside her.

"Ah, Nora, God bless you," Pidge said as soon as Nora stepped into the room. "Ma said you'd gone off and done something reckless."

"I did, I suppose. How are you feeling?" Pidge's cheeks were sunken and pale, but her eyes sparkled.

"I'll be all right. Told you the bastards would let me out."

"Aye. I'm glad. Pidge . . . I'm so sorry—"

"Don't apologize. I'm the one who's sorry. We all have to make our own decisions. I was wrong to fault you for yours."

Nora eased herself down onto the floor next to Pidge's bed.

"Jesus, Nora! What's happened to you?" Pidge exclaimed.

"It's nothing," Nora answered. "I'll be fine. It's you I'm worried about."

"Me? I'll be back to normal after a week of Ma's cooking. But what's wrong with your leg?"

Haltingly, Nora told her the tale—or part of it, anyway. She refused to say how she knew Lynch was going to be killed, and after a while Pidge let it drop.

"So that's why you needed to leave Kilmainham," Pidge said.

"Aye. I'm sorry I couldn't tell you."

"But he was killed anyway."

Nora nodded grimly.

Pidge stared up at the ceiling. "They're saying it's near the end. That we're going to lose."

"Maybe. But there's still hope. I set out to change the course of history for Ireland. And I'm not giving up. I'm going to change things for all of us."

"How?"

Nora shook her head. "I can't say. I'm sorry."

Pidge took her hand. Amazed at how thin and frail it seemed, Nora held it gently. "They say Da and Stephen might be executed. Whatever you're going to do . . . will it save them?"

Nora's heart constricted. "I don't know—not for sure. But . . . I have hope." Pidge's eyelids fluttered, and her grip on Nora's hand weakened. "I'll leave you to get some rest," Nora said. "You know, I didn't expect to find you here. But I'm very glad I did." She leaned over and kissed Pidge on the forehead.

"Good luck, Nora. Ireland needs more women like you."

Nora hobbled out of the room, fighting the lump in her throat. How was it possible that she'd grown to love these people so deeply in so little time? She tore herself away from Pidge, from Mrs. Gillies, from this family that had taken her in and treated her as one of their own. Her lips moved in a silent prayer for their safety. In the yard she found Fionn hoisting timber up to another man on the roof.

"Can you take me into Kildare?" she asked him. "It's as good a place as any to look for Brigid."

"She's not going to be just hanging out in Kildare, you know," he said with an arched eyebrow. "The whole world is her playground."

"The Brigidine Sisters might have a way of contacting her," she said stubbornly.

Fionn sighed and wiped his hands on his trousers.

"Fine. And if we can't find her, then what? What's your plan? To return to your own time? Is that even possible?" He glared at the ground as he said this.

"I don't know," she said honestly. First she had to find Brigid. Then she could start thinking about plan B.

Fionn seemed sullen as they drove toward Kildare. *He's disappointed it didn't work with Lynch.* How many times had he tried to save Ireland—and failed? Had he really been there during the Norman invasion, during all the failed uprisings in the centuries that followed? She didn't think this was the time to ask him.

He hitched the horse outside Saint Brigid's Cathedral while Nora limped inside. "Hello? Bernadette?" she called. The Brigidine Sister had been waiting for her last time—would she still be around? Did she even live in Kildare? "Hello?" she called again. "Is anyone here?"

There she was. The same woman, the same shawl, sitting in the same pew as last time. Nora edged toward her, then hesitated. Was this woman always at the church? The coincidence seemed . . . odd.

"Bernadette?" She walked slowly up the aisle toward her. Bernadette turned.

"Hello, Nora."

"Did Brigid tell you I was coming?"

"Yes."

"I need to speak with her."

"She knows."

"Where is she?"

Bernadette waved her hand at the pew beside her. "Don't be so hasty, child. Have a seat—that looks painful."

"It's fine." Nora stayed standing. She could hear Fionn enter the church, but he didn't approach.

"Did you find your young man?" Bernadette said with a wink. Nora frowned.

"Yes, but—"

"And tell me"—the woman leaned forward—"what did you think of him?"

"What?"

"He's handsome, is he not?"

What was going on here? Nora looked around them. Fionn was hovering at the back, pretending to look at one of the sarcophagi. "He's grand. But I really need to speak with Brigid."

Bernadette's bottom lip stuck out in what was unmistakably a pout. "'He's grand,' you say. Well, there's still time, I suppose. Yes, I can help you. What do you want with our blessed saint?"

"It's . . . personal."

"Personal! There's a good start."

Nora stared at her. Then she heard Fionn come up behind her.

"Hello, Brigid," he said.

Nora spun around to face him. "*Brigid?*"

A wry smile flickered across his face. "Can't you tell?"

When she turned back to Bernadette, the woman's auburn hair and wrinkled skin were gone. Brigid's wide mouth was stretched in a grin, and her peat-black hair hung loose around her shoulders.

"I can never fool you," she said to Fionn with an affectionate wink. "Now sit, both of you, and tell me your tale."

"How did you—" Nora whispered to Fionn as he helped her into the pew, but he simply shook his head. "When you've known Brigid for hundreds of years, you'll be able to recognize her no matter what the disguise. She has a certain . . . irrepressible spirit, you might say."

"You flatter me," Brigid said, beaming.

Nora felt strangely small, sitting between two such legendary figures. For the umpteenth time, the thought *What am I doing here?* stabbed at her mind, but she dismissed it. It didn't matter why she was here. What mattered was what she could do with it.

"How much do you already know?" Nora said.

"Let's pretend I don't know anything," Brigid said, adjusting the shawl around her shoulders.

Fionn and Nora told her about his escape from prison, their flight from the Free State soldiers, and the unsuccessful attempt to save Liam Lynch's life. As she spoke, Nora gained confidence.

"Obviously, it didn't work," she said, learning forward. "Because of that arse O'Casey. But it could have. If we could have gotten him away safely, things would be different. So I have a new plan. But I need your help."

"Mmm?" Brigid hummed.

"I need you to send us further back."

Fionn gaped at her. "What?"

"Don't you see? You need to save Ireland to lift your curse. I need to prevent the Troubles—the war in Northern Ireland—to save my brother. We're too far down the path here—too many things have already been set in motion. Maybe that's why it didn't happen the way we'd hoped. But if we can go further back, think of how many lives we can change."

Fionn was frowning. Why wasn't he excited about this?

"Nora, it won't work. I can't travel through time."

"Why not? If I can, surely you can." She turned to Brigid. "Right? You can send both of us."

Brigid regarded her carefully, not looking at Fionn. Then she spoke slowly. "I believe I can."

"See?" Nora said, grinning.

"Why have you never mentioned this before?" he asked Brigid. "We've known each other all these years, and you never told me you had the power to send people through time."

She reached across Nora and patted his leg. "Because, dear, you were very good at moving forward. At enduring."

"So you'll do it?" Nora asked.

"Do you have a particular time in mind?"

"I've been thinking about that. But I really don't know what would work the best. You've both lived through the far past. When would we have the most impact? The War of Independence? The Easter Rising?"

"I was thinking a little farther back than that, actually," Brigid said, the tips of her fingers pressed together. "I think you should pay a visit to a friend of mine."

"And who's that?" Fionn asked. Nora grew suddenly nervous. What kinds of friends was a goddess likely to make?

"Gráinne Ní Mháille," Brigid said.

"Gráinne Ní Mháille?" Fionn repeated. "You mean Granuaile? The pirate queen of Connaught?"

"The very one." Brigid beamed. "Are you familiar with her, Nora?"

Nora was still digesting this. She had been thinking of going back a dozen years, maybe fifty at the most. But the notorious pirate Grace O'Malley, more commonly known as Granuaile, had lived in the sixteenth century . . . over four hundred years ago.

"Aye, a bit," she answered. "My brother used to tell me stories, and I've read stories about her. Did you really know her?"

"I know everyone worth knowing, dear. I think the two of you will get along quite well."

Nora swiveled to face Fionn. "Did *you* know her?"

"I didn't have the pleasure, no," he said. His face seemed flushed. "I've heard the stories, of course."

"How can she help us?" Nora asked Brigid, but the goddess was already getting to her feet.

"I'll leave that for the three of you to figure out," she said with a wink.

"You're going to send us back in time without telling us what we're supposed to change?" Nora protested, also standing, cringing again at the pain.

"I daresay you'll discover it soon enough. But you won't get far on that leg. Allow me." Brigid placed her smooth white hand over the gunshot wound in Nora's leg, and immediately the pain disappeared.

"Jesus Christ," Nora breathed, running her own hand over the spot Brigid had touched.

"He's not the only one who knows a thing or two about healing," Brigid said.

Fionn stood beside her and gripped her hand, as though what had just happened was no big deal. "Are you sure about this, Nora? Going farther back?"

She squeezed his fingers and gave him a lopsided smile, bolstered by Brigid's display of power. "It's the sixteenth century. How hard can it be?"

His expression was serious. "It was a very different time. You have no idea—"

"That's why I'll have you. You *are* coming, aren't you?"

He looked from her to Brigid. "What do you think?"

She gazed at him from under heavy lidded eyes. "My dear, this is *your* curse we're talking about. I, for one, have always been rather fond of second chances."

"Don't you want to be free, Fionn?" Nora whispered.

He looked at her with his stormy blue eyes, and something smoldered deep in her chest. "Of course I'll go with you."

"Well, that's settled, then!" Brigid clapped her hands and stood up, ushering them out of the pew.

"Do we need . . . the relic?" Nora asked. "I don't know where it is."

"I have it, of course," Brigid said. She handed Nora the tiny red box holding the finger bone. "Now come, keep holding hands. Concentrate very hard. Think about Granuaile. Fifteen ninety-two should do it, I think."

Nora tightened her grip on Fionn's hand. "Bran!" he called, and the wolfhound came bounding down the aisle. Fionn buried his free hand in Bran's fur. Brigid put her arms around them all, and Nora clutched the relic in her palm. She caught a faint whiff of smoke and roses before the goddess whispered, "*Ádh mór ort*, my children. May luck follow you."

The last thing Nora knew was the sensation of falling.

Historical Note

Writing historical fantasy requires a fine balance between the factual and the fantastical. I strove for historical accuracy regarding the Troubles and the Irish Civil War. As for the possibility of time travel . . . I'll leave that for you to decide.

Some of the characters in this novel actually existed or are based on real people. Likewise, I've tried to stay as close as possible to the historical record when describing the events and the timeline of the Civil War. A few items of note: The method of Thomas's escape from Kilmainham Gaol was inspired by the 1921 escape of Ernie O'Malley, who described it in his memoir *On Another Man's Wound*. Likewise, Frankie Halpin's ordeal is based on the Ballyseedy massacre, in which Stephen Fuller was the sole survivor.

As far as I am aware, there was never a secret deal between Liam Lynch and W. T. Cosgrave to keep Northern Ireland part of the Free State. And the forcible removal of the women from Kilmainham Gaol actually occurred three weeks after the death of Liam Lynch.

The notes that Jo, Lena, and Pidge write in Nora's autograph book in Kilmainham are taken from the autograph books of Republican prisoners in the Civil War. Jo's note was written by Hanna O'Connor, Lena's by Annie Fox, and Pidge's by Bridie Halpin.

And as for Fionn mac Cumhaill? Legend has it that he is not dead, but only sleeping—waiting to return to save Ireland at the hour of her greatest need.

Acknowledgments

I am deeply indebted to both friends and strangers who have given hours of their time to the betterment of this book.

I am very grateful to Liz Gillis of Kilmainham Gaol, Niall Cummins of Trinity College Dublin, Tom McCutcheon of the Kildare Town Heritage Centre, and Mario Corrigan of Kildare Library and Arts Services for their invaluable assistance as I strove for historical accuracy. Any faux pas that remain are mine alone.

Michael Perkins, Lucy Cox, Lesley-Elaine Caldwell, Gemma Gallagher, Melissa Giles, Shawn Plummer, Karmen McNamara, and Ewa Gillies shared from their deep wells of knowledge on everything from Catholicism to the Darfur crisis to Belfast curse words.

Thank you to my marvelous first readers, who gave extremely helpful feedback: Erika Holt, Jessica Corra, Mike Martens, Kari Petzold, Janice Hillmer, Janelle de Jager, and Adam Cole.

As always, I'm so thankful for my editor, Angela Polidoro, and the wonderful team at 47North, in particular Adrienne Lombardo, Jason Kirk, and Britt Rogers. Your enthusiasm surrounding this book is both encouraging and inspiring.

About the Author

Photo © 2015 F8 Photography

Jodi McIsaac is the author of several novels, including *A Cure for Madness* and the Thin Veil series. She grew up in New Brunswick, on Canada's east coast. After abandoning her Olympic speed skating dream, she wrote speeches for a politician, volunteered in a refugee camp, waited tables in Belfast, earned a couple of university degrees, and started a boutique copywriting agency. She loves running, geek culture, and whiskey.